Turn of the Tide

Margaret Skea was born in Ulster, and now lives with her husband in the Scottish Borders. Her degree in Linguistics at St Andrews University was followed by a Ph.D on the Ulster-Scots vernacular, which led, in turn, to an interest in 16th century Scottish history. An Hawthornden Fellow and award winning writer: Beryl Bainbridge Best First Time Novelist 2014, Historical Fiction Winner in 2011 Harper Collins and Alan Titchmarsh People's Novelist Competition, Neil Gunn 2011, Chrysalis Prize 2010, and Winchester 2009. A finalist in the 2012 Historical Novel Society Short Story Competition and short-listed for Mslexia Short Story 2012, she has been long-listed in the Fish Short Story and Fish One Page Prize, and published in a range of magazines and anthologies in Britain and the USA.

The sequel, *A House Divided*, has been long-listed for the Historical Novel Society New Novel Award 2016.

D0877349

sanderling

Also by Margaret Skea

A House Divided (sequel to *Turn of the Tide*)

Dust Blowing (short story collection)

Turn of the Tide

Margaret Skea

[signature: Margaret Skea]

sanderling

First published by Capercaillie Books Limited in 2012

This edition published by Sanderling Books in 2017

© Margaret Skea. The moral rights of the author have been asserted.

Printed by Antony Rowe, Chippenham

A catalogue record of this book is available from the British Library.

ISBN 978-0-9933331-1-8

Acknowledgements

To the many family, friends, and fellow authors on Authonomy and elsewhere, who encouraged me while I was writing this novel – thank you. Particular thanks to James Long and Sam Llewellyn who, by suggesting I focus on Munro, led me, one sunny afternoon, to revisit my manuscript, and thus to begin *Turn of the Tide*.

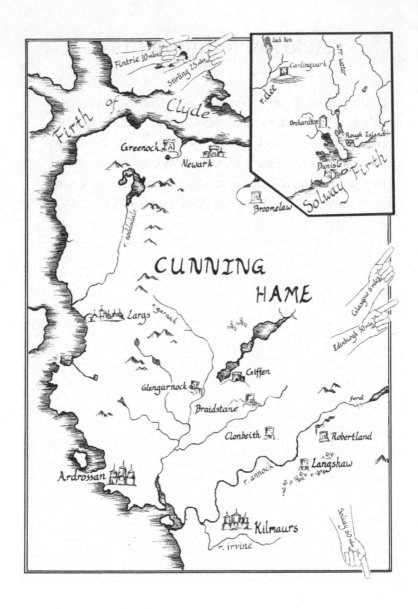

CUNNING
HAME

Firth of Clyde

Fintrie 10 mles
Stirling 25 mles

Greenock
Newark

r. nedsdale

Largs
r. garnock

Glengarnock
Giffen
Braidstane
ford

Clonbeith
Robertland

r. annock
Langshaw

Ardrossan

Kilmaurs
r. irvine

Glasgow 6 mles
Edinburgh 50 mles

Solway 60 mles

loch Ken

Carlingwark
urr water

r. dee

Orchardton
Rough Island

Dunisle
Solway Firth

Broomelaw

Contents

Main Characters

All the main characters are real unless specified otherwise. By convention Earls were often referred to by their title rather than family name and lesser nobles by their place of residence. This avoided confusion among the many branches of one clan.

The Cunninghame Faction

Earl of Glencairn:	The head of the Cunninghame clan, ranked 11th in the order of precedence among the Scottish earls. These rankings were often a matter of dispute, with earls petitioning the King to raise their ranking. His primary residence is Kilmaurs in the bailliewick of Cunninghame in Ayrshire.
Lady Glencairn:	his wife.
John:	his brother.
William, his eldest son and heir	Master of Glencairn.
Clonbeith, Robertland, and Waterstone:	other prominent members of the Cunninghame clan in Ayrshire, owing allegiance to the Earl of Glencairn.
Patrick Maxwell of Newark:	a cousin of the Cunninghames.
Lady Margaret Langshaw:	a Cunninghame by birth, but married into the Montgomerie clan.

The Montgomerie Faction

Earl of Eglintoun: The head of the Montgomerie clan, ranked 12th in the order of precedence among the Scottish earls. His primary residence is now Ardrossan, Eglinton castle having been razed to the ground by the Cunninghames.

Robert Montgomerie: brother to the earl and Master of Eglinton.

Jean Montgomerie: Robert's wife.

Adam Montgomerie of Braidstane: a Montgomerie laird, close kin to Eglinton.

Hugh, his eldest son: Master of Braidstane.

George, Adam's second son: a cleric at the court of Elizabeth Ist.

Patrick: a cavalry officer in a French regiment, Adam's third son.

John: a physician in Padua, Adam's fourth son.

Grizel, Braidstane's daughter. (Fictional) Though evidence exists of Adam having (un-named) daughters, few records remain.

Alexander Montgomerie: a poet and favoured courtier to King James VI, who is later accorded the title of 'Master Poet'.

The Munro Family

(All members of this family are fictional.)

Munro: a minor laird who's family have had close connection to the Cunninghame clan since the 14th century. They live at Broomelaw, a tower house near Renfrew, gifted to Munro's father by the Cunninghames.

Kate: his wife.

Robbie and Anna: his 3-year-old twins.

Archie: Munro's younger brother.

Mary Munro: his mother.

Sybilla Boyd: a family friend.

The Shaw Family

James Shaw: a merchant with many connections to Europe, and laird of Greenock; his tower house is prominently situated above the port of Greenock.

Jean, his wife: a Cunninghame by birth.

John, his eldest son: Master of Greenock.

Elizabeth (marries Hugh, Master of Braidstane), Christian and Gillis: his daughters.

Sigurd Ivarsen, (Fictional): a Norwegian merchant regularly trading into Edinburgh, charged with transporting Queen Anne's carriage from Norway, following her marriage to James VI.

Foreword

In 1567 Mary Queen of Scots was forced to abdicate in favour of her one-year-old son James and fled to England. A magnet for Catholic plots, including the infamous Babington conspiracy, which threatened both Elizabeth I's throne and her life, Mary was imprisoned in England and finally executed at Fotheringhay on 8th February 1587. The years of James' minority were characterised by lawlessness, brutality and the escalation of many of the centuries old feuds between clans and families. Nobles jostled for control over the young king and over precedence in the official ranking of the earls. When James became king in his own right every aspect of Scottish life, political, social, religious and economic was in turmoil. He set out to subdue the earls, to encourage a professional aristocracy from among the lairds, to regulate the new Protestant religion and to establish a more settled and stable society.

The Cunninghame and Montgomerie feud was the most notorious in Ayrshire's history, beginning in 1448 and not finally resolved until the early years of the 17th century.

Part One

April – May 1586

*In all of Ayrshire there was no feudal hatred so long
and so engrained as that between the rival Lords of
Eglintoun and Glencairn.*

Ayrshire, Its History by William Robertson

Chapter One

The dying sun held no heat and little colour, nevertheless it dazzled both mare and rider as they crested the rise.

'Easy, lass, easy.' Munro slid his hand from the reins to gentle Sweet Briar, his palm, as he stroked her neck, dragging against the salt sweat. Stifling his disquiet, he pressed again with his heels and, his thoughts focused on the task ahead, allowed the mare to pull away, trusting her instinct to carry them safe over the uneven ground. They flowed swift and smooth across the grassy, heather-studded hillside, flushing a scattering of partridge as they went. Had anyone watched their passing, they would have found it hard to distinguish where man finished and mare began, for both were dun coloured – from the top of Munro's soft bonnet, devoid of decoration, to the mare's fetlocks – the only flashes of contrast the dark hooves and the pale oblong of Munro's face in the fading light.

Another mile, another crest, and Langshaw's towers ahead of them, drowsing, half in, half out of the shadows. The mare faltered again, her ears flattening.

'Come on lass,' Munro's hand strayed to the letter tucked into his jerkin, 'I haven't a choice, and the sooner it's done the sooner food and rest for us both.' He leaned forward to flick at her ear and she snorted back at him, accepting his pressing.

As they came through the arched gateway, a stable lad tumbled from the hayloft, his legs spindle-thin.

Munro slipped from the saddle. 'I'll not be long. Walk her, and find a blanket and some hay, but no oats mind.'

The lad took the reins without enthusiasm or any mark of respect and Munro felt a flash of irritation. He flicked a glance at his clothes, then back to the lad – it wasn't always politic to draw attention. He thought it an unmanly thing to take much stock of looks and so, despite his wife's best efforts, wore his clothing almost to extinction: his leather jerkin polished to a shine around the buttons and his boots heavily scarred along their length. He injected an extra edge of impatience into his voice, 'Look sharp. We have travelled a distance and have a way to go yet, and I don't wish for her to be chilled nor to stiffen.' Behind him the sun slid below the west tower, the last rays, fractured by the battlements, casting a gap-toothed grimace on the cobbles. Munro shivered, turned towards the tower entrance, and pausing at the top of the wooden steps, caught the smell of baking bread, which settled on his stomach like an ache.

As he entered the solar Lady Margaret Langshaw rose from her seat by the inglenook, one cheek flushed, the draught from the door rippling the tapestry on the wall behind her. She came towards him: a figure come to life. He bent over her hand, her skin, buttermilk-white, unblemished, drifting with the scent of almonds as they touched.

'A request, Lady – from Glencairn.'

'My husband is from home. Can this wait?'

Munro proffered the letter. 'It's for you. Glencairn expects a reply tonight.'

Frowning, she slid her forefinger under the wax seal, her grip on the parchment tightening as she read. She looked up at Munro. 'To betray a guest . . . a kinsman . . . and to such an end . . . Glencairn presumes much.'

Slate eyes met blue. Munro made his voice flat. 'The Montgomeries are kin in marriage only. You are a Cunninghame.'

She bent to pick up the small shift, fallen to the floor as she rose to greet him, her fingers teasing at the edge of the unfinished smocking. 'And for that I must risk my peace and that of my children?'

He dragged his eyes away, focused on the fire flaring in the hearth, on the basket of split logs calloused with moss, stifled the unbidden thought – her bairn is likely ages with my own. Blocking the anguish in her voice and hating his own tone, he said, 'We are none of us at peace. Our cousin Waterstone's lady lies cold in bed at night and his bairns they say still cry out in their sleep.'

'And am I to bring trouble to my lord too?'

'No trouble. Glencairn asks a signal only – the real work is elsewhere.'

'And if it goes awry? The sound of the rout will rebound to my door.'

'Am I to take your refusal to Glencairn?'

She spoke so softly he had to bend his head to hear her. 'I am a Cunninghame, God help me.' A hesitation . . . 'I expect the Montgomeries tomorrow, some ten or twelve only. Braidstane is bid meet Eglintoun to sup here, and make for court thereafter. You may tell Glencairn to look to the battlement, on the west side. If they arrive as arranged, there will be a white napkin hanging.' She was looking past him to the square of window framing the darkening sky. 'Beyond that I cannot do more.'

He bowed over her hand. 'Glencairn is grateful, lady.'

She dismissed him with the smallest of nods. 'Good-day Munro.'

He bowed again and escaped, clattering down the stair. Outside, glad of the sting of the air on his face, he wheeled through the gateway, closing his ears to the sound of children's laughter floating over the barmkin wall.

William Cunninghame, Master of Glencairn, turned from the gable window, his dark eyes sparking. He made no offer of his hand to Munro, nor any concession to ordinary courtesy, his voice echoing under the high-raftered ceiling of Kilmaur's long hall.

'What kept you? The job is done?'

There was only one suitable answer. 'She will provide the signal.'

'As she should. And willingly I hope.'

Silence.

'She can be trusted?'

'Oh yes . . .' Munro thought of the look with which Lady Margaret had dismissed him. 'Your father is a dangerous man to cross. She understands that.'

'As do we all.' William's laugh was a bark, resounding over the clusters of men grouped in each deep window reveal, muting their conversations. Munro inclined his head to each group in turn. They numbered about thirty and all were known to him, albeit slightly, for all hailed from North Ayrshire or thereabouts and all shared allegiance to the Earl of Glencairn and the Cunninghame name. What they did not all share – clear, even from his cursory glance – was an equal inclination to answer this summons. Prominent among them was Clonbeith, noted both for intemperance and, more importantly for the current purpose, his skill with a hackbut. And with him, Robertland, another close kinsman, who no doubt thought to make capital from the venture. In contrast, Glencairn's brother, John, stared at the Cunninghame arms carved into the lintel above the hearth and shifted his weight back and forward from one foot to the other, as if he suffered from a stone in his boot.

Munro studied the floor – dear God . . . there is not a house within twenty miles that will not feel the weight of what we do.

'You took your time.' The Earl of Glencairn filled the doorway. 'I had not thought to have to wait supper beyond our normal hour.'

'His horse. . .' William, with a sideways glance at Munro, lied fluently, 'a lameness delayed his return, but the news is good.'

Glencairn shot another look, a little warmer this time, at Munro, who forced himself to smile in return. Glencairn was, like his son, tall, but without William's languid manner, though both took great stock of their dress. He wore the latest cartwheel ruff over burgundy trunk hose and a cream, brocaded doublet, lined with the same blood red. Stationing himself at the head of the table, he grasped the carved horn of the Cunninghame unicorn which crowned the back of the heavy chair, the gold ring on his forefinger catching the light.

Munro met his gaze. 'The Montgomeries are expected at Langshaw tomorrow. Eglintoun and Braidstane both.'

'And Lady Margaret? She will do her duty?'

'She hangs a white table napkin from the battlement. It will be easy seen.'

'And numbers?'

'A small company only, some ten or twelve men.' The candle in front of Munro flared and he looked down, lest in the momentary brightness any trace of reluctance showed on his face. Clearly not fast enough.

William, picking his nail with a cheese-knife, glanced at Munro. 'Have you not the stomach for this fight? I hadn't placed you for a coward.'

A muscle twitched at the side of Munro's eye. 'I too know my duty.'

'See that you do.' Glencairn sat down, William on one side, Clonbeith and Robertland on the other. They attacked the supper with relish, as if the gathering was no more than a social occasion; their conversation spiced with the latest gossip: the rumour of the return of the pestilence to Perth; how the young minister Andrew Melville, with a taste for presbyterianism, was well set in St Andrews as a thorn in the flesh to Bishop Adamson; the plummetting value of the pound Scots against the English currency. Munro settled near the foot of the table, toying with a cutlet, and noted that John Cunninghame, folded into a space half-way down the long bench, shredded his slab of beef as if he prepared it for a grand-dame with no teeth.

Clonbeith helped himself to a handful of pickled chestnuts. 'This talk of a school at Stewarton. Word is the minister at Ayr subscribes to the notion that everybody should have their letters – lads and lassies both.'

'I have no problem with education for those who can make good use of it.' William looked around, as if daring challenge. 'We have a minister in every parish and I daresay derive some benefit . . .' he acknowledged the ripple of laughter, '. . . but to educate folk beyond their station, that I can't see the sense of. There may be reason in a bonnet laird with a grounding in French, if only to avoid being cheated when he buys his wine, but if we can all spout Cicero, who will clear the middens? Tell me that.'

'When you spout Cicero,' slivers of chestnut sprayed from Clonbeith's mouth, 'I'll clear your midden myself.'

A louder burst of laughter, reaching the length of the table, so that William flushed, half-rose, his right fist clenched.

Glencairn was on his feet, thrusting back his chair, grasping William's arm. 'Save your spleen for the Montgomeries. We ride at dawn. I wish no thick heads riding with me.'

There was a hasty scraping back of benches as most of those present followed Glencairn and William from the hall. Munro slumped back into his chair; knowledge of the proposed ambush acting as a band tightening around his chest. He reached for the ale – thick head or not, it was as well to dull tomorrow's business.

He was up and rousing himself under the pump in the corner of the yard while the sky was still black, the only sign of approaching dawn a grey edge to the heavy clouds that bunched overhead. He had a good head for ale, but had taken more than enough, even for him. It had been gone two in the morning, before he had finally drunk himself to a stupor, though no one would have guessed at it as he joined Glencairn. His boots were laced up to his knees, his doublet tightly buttoned against the rain moving in a sweep across the valley. William was already mounted, his black velvet doublet slashed with silver, a peacock feather in his hat, indicating that he had made no concession to the job

21

in hand. Glencairn too was dressed with care, but the others were, like Munro, soberly attired and could have passed for gentlemen of any ilk.

'Easy to see who does the work,' Munro said in an undertone to John Cunninghame, who circled on the cobbles beside him.

The clatter of hooves covered John's reply. 'Have a care you don't share your thoughts too widely. There are those who would gladly take the favour that your displacement might provide.'

Munro changed tack. 'What do we wait for? Are we not all here?'

'That we are, but Lady Glencairn is bid bring the younger children to give us farewell.'

'So . . . Glencairn's not as confident as he seems . . .' Munro broke off as the family appeared at the main door.

Glencairn didn't dismount, only leaned down, to rest his hand on the youngest child's head. Shy of her father, she pulled back and buried her face in her mother's skirts.

'It isn't the child's blame.' Lady Glencairn spoke quietly. 'She scarce knows her father . . .'

'See to it that you teach her then, madam.' Glencairn's voice was also quiet, but far from gentle.

She inclined her head and stepped back as he turned his horse, spurring it towards the gateway. Munro thought of his own farewell: of Kate, white-faced and taut, the twins round-eyed, uncertain. Of his forced cheerfulness. 'This call – it may not signify. I could be gone a day or two only.' Of his equal failure to draw a satisfactory response.

Once through the gateway, they rode in a pack, tight at the front, straggling at the rear, according to the quality of the horse, or, more like, the fitness of the rider. Munro sat easily, his grip light, and moved forward without effort until he rode again at John's side, but made no attempt at conversation, unable to think on anything other than the present affair. They had climbed beyond the cleared ground where cattle grazed, last season's bracken crackling under-hoof: autumn-gold shot through with curled fronds of fresh green.

William paused on the brow of the hill, turned. 'More eager now, Munro? Last evening I thought you less than comfortable with your duties.' His horse pranced backwards, nudging Munro's, as if to emphasize the thinly veiled threat. 'Do you wish it, we could relieve you of your place.'

Munro bent his head, re-gathered the reins and gave himself time to frame a reply. 'I have no such wish. I thought only of the King. The talk is . . .'

William scowled. 'Ah, James.' There was a contemptuous twist to his voice. 'And we are to pass on our obligations while others hold to theirs? We have lost much to the Montgomeries, and do well to remember it. This call to court – it is an opportunity to strike at their heart, that we cannot pass.'

'Revenge may not be so sweet if the King gets wind of it.'

'Who's to tell?'

Munro stroked his thumb along the edge of the reins but refrained from answer, as William talked on.

'The Ford of Annock is a goodly choice. We should have no trouble in accomplishing our present end.'

'And the timing is right.'

'You think it isn't?' William glared at the rider who dunted him from the rear.

Munro hesitated. 'At this pace I fear we make Annock

too soon. With the need to keep the horses quiet, it may be that we should walk a distance.'

With a tightening of his face William slewed sideways, skirting round the riders in front of him until he reached Glencairn. Munro saw the heads bend together. Saw the sharp glance cast backwards towards him.

John Cunninghame's voice at his shoulder. 'Careful laddie. It is a thin line you tread. William may not be eager to face a musket, but he fancies himself with a rapier and is aye keen to show his prowess, though not in a game such as this.'

Munro turned. 'I know, but there are times when he makes me fair sick with his dress and his airs. No doubt when it comes to the bit he will find a task for himself that hasn't danger in it.'

He saw the slight settlement of John's shoulders. 'For all that you arrived a mite late last night, you have a handle on the way we are to play it. Glencairn and William make straight for court and hope by that to keep the Cunninghame name clear.' There was scepticism in his voice, 'We are charged with making as neat a job as we can, then those who are bid, to join them at Stirling, looking as clean as if they came straight from home.'

'Neat is it?' Munro clenched the reins, so that Sweet Briar startled. 'One hundred and thirty years of tit for tat and none the winner isn't what I would judge 'neat'. And for what? The Bailieship? Precedence? Eleventh or twelfth earl? Does any of it signify?'

John waved Munro's voice down, glanced about, kept his own voice low. 'Glencairn doesn't see the office of King's Bailie of Cunninghame as a small matter. Nor did our father or grandfather before him. And in truth, to give the charge of the Bailiewick over to a Montgomerie hardly seems a master stroke, for all that they were close cousins, indeed the kinship likely increased the affront. . . . But you have the right of it – death breeds death – look in any direction you please and there is a ruin to testify that we are all the losers. It would be a fine thing if it was only the English we had to fear and not the sow who roots in our own byre.' His voice dropped further. 'If I had a choice I would rather be anywhere but here, but we are bid and we have come and may pray we succeed. Else . . .'

Ahead of them, Glencairn had stopped. Below, the ground fell away sharply, the valley spread out like a plaid. The slopes swathed in the brown of last year's heather were streaked with grey cuts where water ran in thin rivulets down the steep hillsides. In the valley bottom there was evidence of strip farming: turned earth for the growing of hay marching side by side with grazing land. A river snaked through the strips, the banking sharp.

He gestured downwards raising his voice to combat the wind. 'We make good time and need not haste. Nevertheless, follow me close, till we make safe ground. If the Montgomeries see us now, then we must link like the best of friends, or our opportunity is lost.' He turned his horse, heading for the cover of the woods. Beyond them, in the far distance, the topmost turrets of Langshaw reared. A rider broke from the trees as they approached and galloped towards them, slithering to a halt.

'Well?' Glencairn was abrupt.

'A clear signal. The Montgomeries are there. I didn't have to go close.'

'You took your time then.' Glencairn was turning his horse as he spoke, wasting no effort on thanks.

They cut diagonally across the hillside towards another clump of woodland, and once among the trees spread out, each choosing their own route, but always keeping others in sight. It was a difficult ride: the horses easily spooked, the riders, although most would not have admitted it, also wary. Each time a woodpigeon was raised or a squirrel disturbed in the undergrowth, all looked about, seeing in the shadows the possibility of danger. It was a relief when they emerged at last through the treeline and saw above and beyond them the heather-covered hillside. Glencairn broke into a trot, leading the fan of riders towards the higher ground.

Without warning the rain came, heavy and straight, visibility reduced to almost nothing. The horses, wary of the soft ground, became nervous and difficult to handle and of necessity all slowed. As they crossed the skyline towards the hill that overlooked Annock, Munro steadied Sweet Briar, disappointment rising that there was little fear of being sighted.

Glencairn's plan was clear: to come up below the ford taking advantage of the natural cover the lie of the land provided. It would likely be a miserable wait. As the rain slid down his neck and trickled inside his jerkin, Munro felt for his gun and bag – hopefully drier than his clothes. Another thought, neccessarily stifled – or perhaps better the pan or match be damp and the plan foiled without loss of face for anyone. He urged Sweet Briar onwards, the slick on her coat seeping through his hose where his knees gripped. As if they crossed an invisible line, the rain stopped. Munro stood in his stirrups and looked back to where rain still fell, merging the valley into the sky, and off to the right a second edge, where the landscape returned, blurred and sodden. Silhouetted against it, another group of riders, moving, slowly it seemed, along the ridge.

The Montgomeries would come this way then – dear God, this is a price to pay for old ties.

In front of him, Glencairn had halted, motioning the riders to come up close. He swung his horse to face them, William also. Their twin expressions were evidence, if any was needed, that each was eager for this prey, yet each determined that hands other than their own be soiled. As the last straggler brought his horse to a halt, Glencairn raised a hand. In the silence, broken only by the soft snorting of horses, he said,

'Do you wait here for Eglintoun and his men, and when you are done, make for home. But separate quickly, that you do not draw undue attention.' He turned towards John Cunninghame. 'A small company only is bid to court. You brother, and you . . .' his eyes swept the riders and fixed on Munro, '. . . you, Munro, make for Stirling. We will put it about that we look for you by nightfall.' He jerked his horse round. 'See to it that we do not hear of today's business from any other source.'

Munro urged Sweet Briar towards the ground that dipped steeply away from the ford, – no doubting the wisdom of Glencairn making an early appearance at court, but as for William, his was the cowardly choice.

Glencairn and William were no more than an hour away when the first of the Montgomeries appeared on the brow of the hill. From his vantage point Munro watched their coming, focusing fiercely on the horses, on the shrinking

distance between them, his gun cocked and resting on his knee. He wasn't one to spend much time thinking on God, but as he waited, timing the moment, the thought came to him – if God is watching, I trust He sees the principals in this.

Behind Munro the rest of the Cunninghames slipped into position at his signal. His first shot took the leading rider in the belly. He saw him falling, blood spouting through the splayed fingers etched into his side. A second rider urged his horse forward, but before he could reach the water's edge, Clonbeith took him from the left, shooting him in the head at close range. The third rider turned his horse and drew his sword, shouting to the others to pull back. He was rushed by three Cunninghames at once; who carved him up as he toppled, blinded from the rush of blood in his eyes, spearing his own foot as he fell.

A lad, knocked sideways by the force of the shot that took him in the shoulder, was screaming as he was hauled from the saddle. Munro heard the sharp snap of his wrist as he landed, saw him kick upwards, the man who had pulled him from his horse doubling away, clutching his groin. The lad, his face drained of colour, was dragging himself onto his knees, his left hand dangling, a jagged edge of bone protruding like a dagger point from his cuff. Munro, his gun re-primed, took aim, but before he could fire Clonbeith plunged into the water, blocking Munro's line of sight, and smashed the pommel of his sword into the lad's face, stamping on his damaged wrist. Another scream: high-pitched and animal, as the lad made one last effort to twist away, Clonbeith's sword-slash taking him on his left side, ripping him open from armpit to thigh.

Out of the corner of his eye Munro saw the last of the Montgomeries, still mounted, turn, his sword raised.

Munro swung and fired in one motion, but the shot, higher than intended, took the man in the mouth. The impact tipped him from the saddle, his jaw exploding in a mess of cartilage and bone. He fell backwards onto a jumble of rocks and was scrabbling up again on one leg when from behind a second and third shot pitched him face first into the peat-muddied waters that swirled upwards to greet him.

Munro lowered his gun.

Clonbeith came up beside him, his voice betraying no distaste for the job just done.

'Do you remain and finish the business. The rest will ride home.' He paused and with barely concealed reluctance added, 'And take my horse. You have further to go. He's fresher and will ensure that you make good time to Stirling.'

And so it was left to Munro and to John Cunninghame to pick their way among the scattered bodies, searching for any life. There was a sour taste in Munro's mouth as he splashed through the water and reached down to turn over the first body – Eglintoun the Montgomerie earl – to judge by the device stamped on his doublet buttons. He sprawled, one foot still trailing from the stirrup, the horse moving restlessly, trampling the sodden ground. Releasing the foot, Munro led the horse to solid ground. The Laird of Braidstane, likewise identified by the initials woven into his saddlecloth, was trapped, his leg caught between two rocks as he swung slowly in the current, which sucked at him, but failed to carry him away. The youth that Munro should have dispatched cleanly had not Clonbeith intervened, lay, his sightless eyes open, one hand tangled in the mess of entrails that spewed from his side. Munro wheeled around, emptying his stomach onto the fast flowing stream.

They worked quickly, stripping the bodies of anything that could identify them, the horses likewise, before slapping each one firmly on the rump and watching as they galloped away. The job done, it were as well that neither the victims nor those responsible would be easily identified. Fine chance that any part of the day's work would remain a secret for long: about as likely as snow falling in midsummer, but it was lack of ready proof that Glencairn sought.

As he followed John, already urging his horse up the slope towards the higher ground, Munro welcomed the return of the rain, thought of his wife – pray God Kate doesn't hear anything of my part in this.

Pausing at the top of the rise, John echoed his feeling, 'We may be thankful. A downpour will destroy all trace.'

Even dry it would have been a silent journey, for neither had a heart for conversation. John gave his horse no guidance and Munro, noting the uncharacteristic careless-ness, understood that he too was less than comfortable with what had been done. A few miles past Annock, the weather, though not their spirits, cleared, and they quickened their pace; so that it was still light as they entered Stirling and presented themselves at Glencairn's lodgings. Thanks were not forthcoming.

The earl looked up as they entered, but did not trouble to rise, 'I trust you can wait. Dinner will be a little delayed. I had not thought to see you quite so soon.' It was a question of sorts.

Munro sensed John searching for appropriate words. 'It was a speedy journey, and nothing to hinder us. We came through heavy rain, but left it behind shortly past Annock, though there it seemed as if on for the day.'

'Well, well. I have a room prepared.' Glencairn turned to

Munro. 'You I trust will find lodgings nearby, but do not lag for we have a guest or two contracted to join us for dinner.'

Munro acknowledged the dismissal and with it Glencairn's adroitness, not only in placing himself in Stirling timeously, but also in ensuring that they had independent witnesses to prove it.

Chapter Two

Word came to Braidstane.

Grizel Montgomerie was in the solar, the castle accounts spread on the table before her. She had taken the ordering of the estate upon herself some three months since, when, following on her mother's sudden death, her father had shrunk in on himself, seeming unable to face even the most mundane of tasks. At first a duty, it had become an interest and a pleasure. Her absent brothers she knew had thought it but a temporary ploy, that would serve to distract her somewhat from her own troubles.

And with little time to grieve, she had indeed found the memory of her husband fading, so that the brief, if happy, interlude at Annan, their family home, had become like a mist, that lay on her when she awoke, but evaporated so soon as the day was properly begun, her first, sharp grief of widowhood replaced by an understanding that fulfilment could come in more than one guise. Though debts remained aplenty, a situation difficult to remedy without ready cash, she took satisfaction in the knowledge that, college education or not, she had as fine a head for figures and as good a manner with the tenants as any man. Her father restored, she had been guiltily pleased when he was summoned to accompany the Earl of Eglintoun to court, leaving her once again in charge.

She rubbed at the ink-stained indent on her index finger

as she rose to greet the messenger who appeared in the doorway, blocking out the light. Since her mother's death the lad had shuttled backwards and forwards between Ardrossan Castle, the Eglintoun stronghold, and Braidstane, his increasing awkwardness keeping pace with his height. The corners of Grizel's mouth began to lift – *he grows like a nettle*; then froze, as she took in the hair hanging in damp shanks over his collar, the doublet and hose heavily splattered with mud.

'Mistress Montgomerie.' He held his hat in his hands, twisted like rope. 'I'm sent from Ardrossan . . .'

She felt a tightness grip her chest.

He tried again, raising his head and fixing his gaze somewhere above and beyond her left ear. 'Your father and my lord and those who attended on them . . .'

She grasped the edge of the table to counteract the weakness in her legs.

'. . . Are murdered. Ambushed at Annock ford. We wouldn't have known of it save that the king . . .'

She forced herself to look at him. 'All of them?'

He was able only to nod, his mouth half-open as if he gagged on his tongue.

Subsiding onto the settle by the fire she gestured to the opposite chair, all thought of normal hospitality forgotten. 'How?'

He stared into the flames, spoke low. 'We know little, mistress, save that they left Langshaw Castle early, and expected to make Stirling for supper. The king they say, wasn't best pleased when he found Eglintoun hadn't come as he was bid and remarked on it with some sharpness. But it wasn't till yesterday, when the messenger came from court seeking a reason for Eglintoun's tardiness and demanding his immediate attendance, that we knew of anything amiss. Word was sent to Lady Margaret of Langshaw and others of us to follow the route . . .' He swallowed hard, his Adam's apple moving in his throat. 'The horse was near home when we spied her . . .' he swallowed again. 'It was my father's, his trip to court a reward for fine service and his horse safe and steady, so that we knew. . .'

Grizel focused on the scars in the leather of his boots, their age and comfort apparent in the way they moulded to the shape of his feet, the heel worn down at one side. Water had run off and lay in a puddle around his feet, steaming gently with the heat from the fire. The mud was beginning to dry on his hose, and she watched without her usual irritation as he picked at the drying flakes, his nails chipped and filled with grime. She looked up again, and, as if there had not been a long pause, asked,

'You found them?'

'When we came to the hill above Annock . . .' He balled his hand into a fist, the knuckles white, his words coming in spurts and strings, as if through a mincer. '. . . the bodies were jumbled . . . some face down in the stream . . . others half-in, half-out of the water . . . there was a lad . . . his side open to the sky . . .'

Grizel held her hands tight in her lap. 'Were they . . .' she thought of wolves, '. . . ravaged?'

He shook his head.

'They were all there?'

'Aye.'

Grizel in her turn stared into the fire, seeing, in the dancing flames, the Montgomeries as they had gathered in the barmkin: her father newly upright on his horse, the youngest lad who betrayed his excitement at his first foray to court by circling impatiently as he waited for the others to mount. It was a moment before she realised that he was speaking again.

'The bodies . . .' he was biting at his lip, '. . . they are to be dressed, and sent by cart . . .' a deep breath, '. . . and those of the horses that are found . . .'

Grizel felt a surge of anger. 'Horses?' She forced herself to breathe more slowly, to think of this lad, riding hard to bring the news, all the while battling griefs of his own and rising, placed a hand on his shoulder. 'Come, Ishbel will show you to a chamber.'

He looked down, as if seeing his clothes for the first time: the mud-streaked hose, the jerkin heavy with rain. Gesturing awkwardly at his legs, said, 'I have nothing . . . I didn't think . . .'

It was what he did not say that Grizel understood: that he had been dispatched, in haste and without preparation, to distance him from the sight of the bodies face down in the stream-bed. To bar him from that other journey, no doubt already underway: the rhythm of hoofbeats hammering across the moors: crops to be torched, doors to be splintered to kindling, steel to be drawn without mercy. A vision that fleetingly found an answering leap in her, the accompanying shame of it sharp. Vengeance, she thought, isn't God's. Not here. Not now.

Morning dragged in with a wind that rattled the case-ments and chased smoke down the chimney, funnelling it out into the solar. Grizel's response: to pile up the fire so that it blazed constantly, keeping the smoke at bay; trying and failing to ward off the images that had invaded her dreams and now crowded her waking mind also. All night she had been a child again: bug-eyed, huddled between her brothers on the turret stair, her knees pulled up to her chin, her nightgown tucked under her feet against the rising chill; listening outside the door of the hall to the tales of other butcherings. Boyds against Stewarts; Maxwells against Johnstones; Kennedys, who, failing another family to fight, savaged amongst themselves.

Her brothers had delighted in the telling and had honoured each fresh atrocity by playing out old Montgomerie wounds: legends from their grandfather's time, but well remembered and oft rehearsed for all that. They brandished their wooden swords, hacking and slashing at each other with whoops and cries as they circled the stump of the old castle on the hill behind Braidstane. Her part: the lady to be rescued, her bonds loosed just in time to save her from the flames, smoke from the makeshift fire of twigs curling around the barrel she perched on. Or the one surviving child hidden among the gorse, emerging to their calls, hair tangled, arms scratched. Or, least comfortable of all, the grieving widow who swooned at the news of her family all gone and required to be revived by a liberal dousing with bog water. For Grizel the child, the stories had been a delicious shiver that rickled the length of her spine.

Grizel the adult had shivered in a very different way when, periodically, news of that sort came, and each time had thanked God that their own family enmities seemed, if not dead, at least to slumber. This new awakening so brutal, so unexpected, so impossible to thole. And yet . . . staring into the flames, her eyes rubbed red, the tears, which had eluded her on the previous evening washing her cheeks raw, she thought perhaps she should have expected some ill thing to follow hard on her mother's death, her own widowhood: for troubles aye came in threes. And by what right should her family be immune from the sickness that had plagued Scotland for more generations than anyone would care to remember, and our own county no healthier than the rest? She stamped on a shower of sparks that arced onto the floor from an exploding log. And thought of Hugh. Eldest he might be and with a temper to match his flaming hair, but pray God she could convince him to halt the madness.

She didn't know how, or in what fashion, to communicate their father's murder to her brothers and in the end sent word to George in London, as the nearest, charging him with the task of informing the others in Europe. Then there was nothing to do but wait, first for the bodies, then for her brothers, her father's funeral delayed till their return. For the rest, they would bury them together: a single stone to tell the horror.

Chapter Three

Munro was in an alehouse half way up Stirling's High Street, rehearsing his frustration at the enforced stay at court to a pair of lurchers sprawling by the turf fire. Their coats were dull and matted, their eyes oozing, though whether from the smoke or infection it was impossible to tell. One scratched sporadically at a bald patch behind his ear, likely the result of a tick. The Cunninghames had been five days at court, and had, as far as Munro could gauge, accomplished little, barring Glencairn's small satisfaction as James cried Eglintoun for his tardiness, a satisfaction quickly dissipated as news of the murder came from Ardrossan, forcing him to busy himself professing outrage at the deaths.

Munro was not drunk, nor even nearly so, but boredom and forced inactivity weighed heavy on him and drove him to a moment of carelessness. He shook his head at the dogs. '. . . Who believes him?'

One, the younger by a good margin, thumped his tale in response.

'You're right.' Munro glanced round – dangerous talk. Fortunate that all attention was focused on a dwarf of a man with wild hair that sprouted in random tufts of brown and white, who was perched on a table-top near to the door, gabbling. Interested in anything that might relieve the tedium, Munro swung on his stool, prepared to be amused; but catching the name 'Montgomerie', buried his head again in his tankard, an empty feeling in the pit of his stomach. He forced himself to call for another drink and downed it as if he had the whole day to waste, watching and listening to the man's tale with every appearance of appreciation. The kernel of it, that someone had been careless and word was everywhere about that blame for the Montgomerie murders lay at Glencairn's door.

Afterwards, he headed straight for the Cunninghame lodgings. And found John. 'Where's Glencairn? Have you heard the news?'

John was matter of fact. 'Gone to James to make claim that some distant connection has over-reached themselves.'

'I know now how Peter must have felt at the High Priest's fire. It was all I could do not to react when I heard the clack. I was waiting for the challenge: 'Aren't you with the Cunninghames?' Then, as John's words penetrated, 'How distant?'

'Far enough to pass you by.' John injected a note of reassurance into his voice. 'Besides, you were here with us. We may both have reason to be grateful for the care that was taken to ensure our timely arrival was noted.'

'I was thinking of asking leave to go home.'

'I wouldn't advise it.' John poked his toe at the fire that sputtered in the hearth. 'If, that is, you want to reach it in one piece. Worse news will come and when it does, I for one will be glad to linger. There is nowhere safer than close to the King.'

He was right. By the end of the fortnight, word of other atrocities came almost by the hour, until the number of Cunninghames, fallen or fled, surpassed that of Montgomeries killed at the ford. Munro, directed by

Glencairn, dipped in and out of the alehouses and taverns that clustered below the castle precincts, reporting daily the grim tally. Few of those gathered at Kilmaurs before the ambush had escaped.

He brought word of Robertland, one of Glencairn's closest kin. 'He is put to the horn.'

Glencairn, staring out the window onto the cobbles below, spoke without turning. 'Banishment? That I knew.'

'And has gone to Denmark.'

'A chill choice.'

William, lolling on a bench, looked up, swung his legs to the floor, headed for the ale. 'France is gey crowded with Scottish exiles the now. No doubt he thinks to find a better billet.'

Shame stabbed Munro. 'It is said that many, having the misfortune to carry the Cunninghame name are, though innocent, likewise forced to flee their homes.'

William raised his tankard. 'You are fortunate then, on two counts. You aren't at home, and your name isn't Cunninghame.'

John saw Munro out.

At the top of the steps they halted. 'When will it end?'

'Soon, I hope. . . . The worst is likely over.' John spoke with apparent confidence, but Munro, reading his eyes, knew it to be a lie.

And so it proved.

The fate of Clonbeith was whispered everywhere, and received variously in shock or horror or gleeful malice. Munro refused the offered dinner and stayed with the Cunninghames long enough only to convey the message, revulsion clear in every syllable, his preface stark. 'I think it probably correct in essentials, if not in each particular, though it may have gained something in the telling. Credited with leading the massacre . . .'

At his side, John shifted.

'. . . Eglintoun's brother and others with him carried the pursuit to Hamilton. A little money spent, they found Clonbeith out in a chimney . . .' Munro swallowed, continued, '. . . Pollock, he that is son-in-law to the Montgomeries of Langshaw, hauled him down and, it is said, hacked him to pieces on the spot.'

William took a seat at the table, lifted a knife and began to carve a side of ham. 'A clever, if bloody way to distance himself from the Montgomerie murders.'

As if to himself Munro said, 'I still have Clonbeith's horse.'

'That I imagine,' said Glencairn, 'is the least of his troubles.'

John, his glance flicking towards his brother turned Munro away from the table. 'If you cannot eat, at least have a drink before you go.'

The last rumour Munro brought to them was of Lady Margaret Langshaw. 'Gone to Ireland it seems, and not expected to return. I think now that we are all accounted for. Perhaps we can go home.'

Glencairn nodded. 'Can't say I'm sorry. A respite from James will be welcome. You talked of your brother. Send him to Kilmaurs: we will make a position for him there.'

It was at once a recognition of obligation and a dismissal. In the narrow wynd that dropped towards the lower town, Munro stumbled over a pile of rubbish lying in the drain, scattering chicken bones across the cobbles. Half-decomposed cabbage leaves and assorted peelings stuck to his boot and he carried the sour whiff to his lodging, like a guilt impossible to quell.

He returned home, wearied and with a conscience and stomach alike uneasy; even the sight of the sheep pens prepared for lambing and the fresh thatch on the stable roof failing to raise his spirits. To be met with stony silence and a chill in the atmosphere, indicating that a whisper of some sort had beaten him. The presence of the twins clamouring for attention protected him from immediate censure, but alone in their chamber Kate rounded on him.

'A day or two only? It may not signify?'

He reached out, but she twisted away as if his touch would soil her.

'The Cunninghames have lost much.' It was an unconscious echo of William.

'The half of Ayrshire has lost much, and over many years.' She sucked in air, as if to fan a flame. 'Indeed all of Scotland is salted with old rivalries that erupt, in season and out of it, like boils, which, doctored or not, leave scars aplenty to mar our lives. Must we have part in it?' She took a handful of twigs from the basket by the hearth, snapped them into kindling. 'It is a dirty business, and no-one the winner, save perhaps the coffin-makers and clothiers who aye make good money of men's folly. Cunninghame or Montgomerie, it makes no odds. . . . Dear God to think more of obligation than our children.'

He wanted to protest that it had been their children he thought of, and her . . . and her . . . for to refuse Glencairn . . . but risked only, 'I did but as I was bid; as I was bound to do.'

'No-one is bound – save by the laws of God.' Turning her back, she unpinned her hair, snuffed the candle, spoke into the darkness. 'There is always a choice. If this is yours, do not look to me to share it.'

He lay, the centre of the bed a chasm beyond which Kate stretched, rigid, unwelcoming – small consolation that women did not fully understand such matters; that it was not so easy to slough off inherited ties; that there were unpalatable duties in this life. And, sleep eluding him, he found it impossible to banish entirely the sight of the bodies at the ford. Clearest in his mind the mutilated youth close to the laird of Braidstane. Though likely younger than his own brother, Archie, the build and colouring was sufficiently similar to provide a constant reminder of what had been done in the name of loyalty. He thought on Glencairn's pledge; decided to let Archie go. For didn't the lad itch to get to court and had plagued long since for permission to take himself to Kilmaurs?

Perhaps Braidstane had been equally pressed.

He rode to town to call on his mother, leaving his horse in the care of an ostler and picking his way through the clutter of buildings that jostled the Mercat Cross. He had never understood her need, following the death of his father, to replace the fresher air and relative quiet of Broomelaw with the bustle of a townhouse, but so she had chosen, and there she had stayed. He presented her with a piece of Flemish lace. 'It is quite the fashion and I thought to bring a little of court home to you.'

Mary fingered the lace.

He noted her stillness – she also has heard something. I might have saved the effort, and my silver.

After a moment, she looked up. 'There is something I thought to say to you.'

A knot tightened in the pit of his stomach – what was done was done and it did no good whatever to waste time in regrets.

'Glencairn's retinue is growing?'

He was unsure of where she was headed. 'There are always those who seek to rise.'

She held his gaze, her pupils dark and distended, the irises reduced to a blue smudge around the edge. 'There is talk . . . though I haven't heard it direct . . .'

Waiting, Munro thought – she plays me like a fisherman, letting out and reeling in, reducing my resistance little by little, before she comes to the landing.

'A rumour only . . .' she continued, '. . . but likely enough; of Archie, and a girl, and perhaps a wedding. I had thought you wouldn't welcome the drain on your purse.' She bit her lip, as if she spoke reluctantly and he was filled with a grudging admiration. 'If Glencairn seeks other followers . . . you might look to your brother, else he will be always hanging on your cloak-tail.'

Relieved that her thoughts had not been running on his own activities and glad that he could claim prior thought on the matter he said, 'Already done. Glencairn has promised him a place. Indeed, Archie agitates to go and I would have sent him already, were it not for the lambing.'

'You've managed without him before and can again.' She smiled and touched the lace on her lap. 'This is a fine piece, and well made, I am grateful for it.'

Understanding that her gratitude extended beyond the lace he escaped before she could question him further.

With a welcome spell of fine weather carpeting the woods in aconites: a splash of yellow that should have cheered anyone, Munro sought to smother the memory of the massacre. And without his brother's face constantly before him might have succeeded, but for Kate. He caught the shadow of it in her eyes each time she looked at him, her instinctive recoil from even accidental touch stretching the distance between them. What speech was neccessary: for the running of the household, the sake of the children, was edged with ice. The easy camaraderie that had been the touchstone of their marriage and that he had not thought to truly value until it seemed lost became a silence beyond bearing. And the likelihood that it wouldn't be the end of the matter, at home or abroad, lay in the back of his mind, like an awkwardly placed slub in the weave of a bedsheet: impossible to ignore however you turned.

Chapter Four

May came in soft and mild. And to Braidstane, all four brothers come together. Meeting at the entrance of the hall, Grizel flung herself at Hugh and he crushed her against him. She searched his face. Anger she saw, and a weariness that was little to do with his journey from Holland. She could see he felt this death more keenly than their mother's. And not without cause. For his last parting from father was not well done. Dear God, she thought, meaning it as a prayer, let him bide awhile and find some other focus. Her voice was muffled, 'I am sore in need of you all.' She hadn't meant to cry, but the pressure of Hugh's arms enfolding her, the imprint of his jerkin buttons stamped across her breast, the sharp stab of his nails biting into her arms, all combined to force her pain, dammed these weeks past, to well up, threatening to engulf her.

He held her and rocked her and eventually, when the flow subsided, spoke over the top of her head, as if a prepared speech, learnt by rote. 'I am come home,' he said, 'and when the estate is sorted, I will have to look to other pusuits, for my commission is sold.'

'There are debts . . .' she began doubtfully, '. . . and not a few calls on us that weren't looked for.'

He waved her words away. 'Tomorrow is soon enough for that, the now . . .'

She felt his deliberate lightening.

'Know you your duty, sister? We are fair starved and like to ransack the kitchens.'

Watching as they attacked the capons and the fruit pies and the ale brought from the stillroom, she thought with a spark of envy how men could aye be distracted by their belly. Though, given the formalities that must be faced, she doubted that the mood would last long.

She had misjudged Hugh. He pored over the estate finances, questioning her closely for the explanatory details that gave life to the bald figures, seeming to find a satisfaction in seeing the books in order and in discussing which accounts were immediate and which could wait the transference of other funds. It was an unlikely answer to her prayer, but an answer none the less.

Whether, or for how long it would have lasted, they were not to know, for fast on her brothers' heels came a new summons from court. It little pleased the King to have his nobles fighting like stags at the rut, and he commanded Hugh, as the new laird of Braidstane, along with Robert Montgomerie, Eglintoun's heir, to meet with Glencairn to swear that all enmity between them was at an end.

Grizel, as soon as she saw the messenger and understood from whence he came, feared for Hugh. Her fear well founded. He raged: against the King, against Glencairn, against the whole Cunninghame connection.

'Friendship. Hah! Whatever others feel, I'm not for dancing to James' pleasure in this. Not even . . .' as she turned to him, her face taut, '. . . for your comfort. It is too much to ask. Do you wish that I swear and smile and be a laughing stock of all?'

Though she spoke quietly, there was steel in her voice.

'We have lost our father, is that not enough? And had you been here, I would no doubt have lost you too. If this is truly a chance to halt the killing I would wish for that.'

A letter had come from John Shaw, Hugh's close friend, counselling caution, but despite Grizel's hopes it seemed but fuel to the fire. 'Blood will out,' Hugh said. 'The Cunninghame taint aye stretches far.'

Knowing the injustice of the remark and suspecting also that it bore the stamp of a private pain, she left him to his rant, warning the others, 'Leave be for now; sense will prevail, if left to stew a little.'

That her sentiment owed less to past experience and more to a dogged hope she would not have cared to admit. Yet so, to her great relief, it proved. Two days later as John left to return to his studies at Padua and George to his duties in London, Hugh and Patrick, with a small following, set out to travel in their father's footsteps to court, and to the meeting with Glencairn.

At the last, knowing that it made him sick to think of it, she grasped his bridle. 'Compliance with James' command is as necessary to our well-being as breathing, you know that. Promise me, whatever the provocation, you won't rise.'

He covered her hand with his and repeated, 'I won't rise.' Then, as if he feared to promise too much, 'But will make enough of a play of it to pass.'

And with that she had to be content.

Chapter Five

Munro was in the lambing field, halfway through the skinning of a dead lamb when the messenger arrived from Kilmaurs, sweated and muddied from the ride. A ewe butted against the makeshift gate of the sheepfold, bleating. Munro raised his head at the rider's approach, but continued with his task. The setting on of an orphan lamb was a delicate job at the best of times and one that must needs be done quickly, else the loss was double. He finished the skinning, then tied the lambskin, still warm, over the back of another, smaller lamb, who wobbled under the extra weight. She made a few experimental wiggles of her rump in an attempt to cast the unfamiliar burden, then stood quivering, head down. He picked her up and placed her in the fold, allowing the ewe to nuzzle at the skin he had applied, guiding the lamb to the teats that hung, pendulous and oozing. He held the lamb against the ewe, and worked the teat, squirting milk into the lamb's mouth until it latched on and sucked greedily, tail flicking. Satisfied, he wiped his hands on a rag and turned to the man who waited by his horse. 'Well?'

The man looked at the ewes dotted about, a few with lambs, but most still heavy with pregnancy. 'Glencairn is summoned again to court, and wishes for you to attend him.'

Munro likewise surveyed the flock. 'Today?'

'Yesterday.' The messenger stretched his lips into a mockery of a smile.

'More trouble?'

'If you call the public mending of a quarrel trouble . . . though neither Glencairn nor William seem overly keen.'

Munro shot a glance at the man's face, but didn't reply. Instead, he tossed the rag to the lad who was busying himself with a second ewe recently birthed. 'Stay with them.'

He turned to lead the way up the track to the house. It was a simple rectangular tower, three storeys and a garret, surrounded by a small barmkin. Below the wall that bounded it a few cattle grazed. Munro was proud of his livestock: the small flock of sheep, begun with two ewes, which now provided wool enough for all their needs, the cattle and pigs which kept them in milk and meat most of the winter. And due, in large part, to the Cunninghame connection.

Kate looked up as they entered the solar. 'Are we to have no peace?'

Munro examined his hands. 'I am bid return to court.' Then before she could reply, 'It is to be an end to the enmity.'

'And they are to beat their swords into ploughshares?'

He sought to diffuse the scorn in her voice. 'It may be that they'll keep to it.'

'It may be.' She was picking at a rag-nail, pulling at the skin, and he saw a bead of blood begin to well. 'But forgive me if I'm not over confident.' She turned to the messenger. 'Have you time for a bite?'

Thank you, aye.

'I'll see to it then.'

The messenger, his gaze on her retreating back, forestalled Munro. 'Don't say anything. I had the same myself. I hope to God it is an end of it, else there might be little point in going home.'

Munro found Kate in the kitchen, standing in the

window alcove, her forehead resting against the glass. He came close, but didn't attempt to touch her; strove to inject a note of reason into his voice. 'It's best I go. Glencairn thinks me safer in sight than skulking at home. For his own sake no doubt. But it will serve us to watch his steps also.' It was out before he thought: the nearest he had come to an open admission of guilt. And instantly regretted.

Her eyes were fixed on some point far out on the horizon, a suggestion of dampness tingeing her cheeks. Without turning she said, 'Go then, if you must. We will do very well without you and be safer withal.'

They were fed and away in under an hour. As he mounted the bay, Kate appeared in the doorway, the twins clutching at her skirts. He swung himself down again, and scooped them up, one on each arm, hugging them tight so that they squealed. Above their tow-heads, his eyes met Kate's.

She accepted his kiss, but did not return it. 'Take care . . . if not for yourself, at least for your children. I have no wish that they be orphaned yet awhile.'

'I neither . . .' He delayed the moment, hoping for something more, while the twins, Anna and Robbie began to wriggle. Setting them down, he reached for Kate, but she retreated beyond arm's length.

As they picked their way down the rough track that led through the grassy slopes to the valley floor, and forgetting for a moment that it wasn't Sweet Briar he rode, that she no doubt fretted in Clonbeith's stable waiting to be reclaimed, Munro leant forward to mutter into the mare's neck. 'It's an ill-leaving, lass.' That his wife despised the business at Annock was clear. How long she would nurse her disdain of him, less so. But the sight of her, turning away as he left, remained as a pain in his chest that no physic could shift.

On his arrival in Stirling, Munro lost no time in presenting himself at Glencairn's lodgings. His original intention had been to seek his brother first, but he was out and not expected back before supper. Glencairn, it seemed was also elsewhere, so William it had to be. There was perhaps some capital to be gained from a timely arrival, though he doubted that it would make much difference. Still.

William was standing at a narrow window giving onto Stirling's High Street watching a pedlar, as first, he displayed to the small crowd who gathered around him the very latest cure for warts, then turned to calling them for the foolishness of refusing to buy. All the while a child, probably no more than six or seven, moved around the outer fringes neatly slitting a purse or two as he went. Munro, peering past William, judged that they worked together. Guessed also from William's broad smile that it amused him to see the gullibility of lesser folk, confident that he himself would not be prey to such a ruse.

William glanced sideways. 'You made good time.'

Below them, the pedlar redoubled his efforts, his hands flashing, voice strident.

'Little point in arriving too late for the show.' It was an unhappy choice of words.

Dark colour suffused William's neck. 'Is it that you relish this business?'

'I can pretend to relish, if required.'

'And a pretty pretence it will be.'

Munro focused on the scene on the street below, his lack of reply itself a challenge.

'Have no fear, Munro, I shall not pick a quarrel, not here, and not now. I have need of father's favour at present, and he of James'.'

'No doubt'

'We can make a play of swearing anything to Robert Montgomerie, if so be it will satisfy the King, but as for Braidstane . . .' William struck his hand against the window-sill. 'We shouldn't have to waste our breath on such as he.'

There was a downdraught in the chimney and a dusting of ash sifted into the room, peppering their shoulders, so that William beat at it scowling.

'In truth, William,' Munro's tone was deliberately light. 'You hate him.'

'In truth, I do not. One doesn't hate a cur for his bad breeding, but one may kick him for it.' William turned back to the window. The pedlar was packing up, the folk melting away, one or two clutching a 'cure' that would no doubt turn out to be worthless, while the child skulked in a doorway, out of sight. 'Wait on us at six.'

An angry flush spread across Munro's cheeks.

'And close the door when you leave. The draughts are something cruel.'

Outside, Munro kicked his way through the muck and stour of the streets that straggled below the castle complex, imagining William on the end of his boot.

The urchin sitting on the doorstep looked up as Munro's shadow fell across him. 'You have a visitor. I showed him to your room.' He fixed Munro with black, button eyes, holding out a grubby palm, his other hand straying to his jerkin.

Munro, guessing correctly, made his voice stern. 'You needn't be asking twice.' He took the stairs two at a time, and pushed the door. Archie, who had been stretched out on the narrow cot dozing, shot to his feet and then seeing Munro relaxed again onto the bed, pulling his legs up and leaning back against the wall. Munro grinned, 'Well, well, too many late nights, I fear.'

'Early mornings, more like. I have seen more dawns in the last month. . .'

'There is some gain then in your new employ. That'll commend Glencairn to our mother.' Munro kicked off his boots, and flung himself down on another bed, as yet untenanted. 'What of the court? Is it as you fancied?'

'Well there are plenty lassies . . .'

'And at what cost?'

'A ribbon or two, and the learning of a ween of poetry . . .'

'That I don't believe.' Munro broke off, remembering his mother, 'Serious though, have you not an understanding at home? '

'Oh, that.' It was Archie's turn to grin. 'A means to an end,' and, holding up his hands, 'Don't worry, Sybilla Boyd isn't broken-hearted.'

Laughter bubbled in Munro's throat. 'Sybilla was it? She'll not be broken-hearted, not over you, but what's in it for her?'

'I'm not the only one who wishes to rise. I'm to send her word of the court and speak for her in the right quarters.'

Munro's laughter died. 'I'm not sure if we are in the right quarters. The Cunninghames are a gey quarrelsome lot. James has this notion for a nobility at peace, and I'm thinking that it shouldn't be discounted. It would be better for all of us if we didn't have to walk down the street with a ready eye to our backs. And, as for rising, better not to carry such a weight of family. Aye and safer too.' He saw that Archie's grin had slipped. 'Don't fret, however much I may wish it, I can't distance myself from the Cunninghames yet awhile. It isn't easy to change sides, and to abdicate altogether from old obligations is a chancy business, especially at present. Any whiff of disloyalty and the responsibility for Annock would likely be laid to my charge. Besides . . .' he summoned a grin, 'I wouldn't like to have to answer to mother, if I spiked your chances.'

Chapter Six

For Hugh Montgomerie, the journey to Stirling was an uncomfortable reminder of that undertaken by his father not five weeks since. Though they didn't make by Langshaw, yet much of the route was the same and he tormented himself: this rain-washed scree, that outcrop newly scarred, this line of trees, freshly greening; thus and thus it must have looked to father also. The others followed his pace, stopping at his choosing, rising again at his beck. He didn't lag, knowing that he would likely be less rather than more ready to comply with the King's wishes the longer he delayed. When they breasted a hill and came upon Greenock spread out beneath them, he halted, his hands gripping the reins as if he struggled to hold a runaway horse. Looking west, he indicated the castle perched high above the town.

'We wait the night here.'

As they rode through the gateway, he straightened, mindful of eyes that might be watching their arrival. Of John Shaw's welcome he was assured, their friendship of such a standing that long absences did not detract, but as for his sister Elizabeth, though if John was to be believed then she also thought fondly of him.

At the rear of their small party one of the men queried, 'He has forgot the Cunninghame connection then? Or is it that he can forgive a woman anything?' He was swiftly silenced by Patrick's glare.

As they swung down from their horses, the door opened and John Shaw himself appeared, with two of his sisters. They lined up, a formal greeting belied by the laughter which accompanied it. Six-year-old Gillis was the first to break rank, running to Hugh's horse and stretching a finger to scoop a gob of the white lather that streaked its flanks, popping it into her mouth.

'Oh Gillis!' Christian, by Hugh's reckoning now seventeen and comely, gathered up the child, shaking her gently, pulling her finger from her mouth.

'Salty,' Gillis said, wrinkling her nose.

John tousled Gillis' hair. 'It won't kill her.'

Christian's frown slid into a smile and Hugh was reminded of that other arrival, more than six years ago, when he had stopped by on his way home from college in Glasgow. Then it had been she who had swung on John's arm and plagued him for the presents that were promised. Noting the pallor of her cheeks and belatedly remembering the reference in John's letter to an illness that had taken them all in turn, he said, 'I heard you were not well, I trust you are much recovered.'

'Yes, thank you, I'm bravely now. But Elizabeth . . .'

John cut in quickly, 'Elizabeth was the last to succumb. She nursed us all and seemed hearty enough till a few days ago, when a fever took her. Slight,' he said, as he saw Hugh's face. 'She is abed, but a precaution only. In fact she didn't wish it, but Christian insisted, and, as you will remember, it is not politic to disoblige any of my sisters.'

'She will come down?' Hugh tried and failed to sound casual, afraid that this visit might be, if not altogether a wasted effort, somewhat of a disappointment.

'I'm sure she will once she knows you are here. But

come, I mustn't fail in our hospitality, or I'll be soundly bated for it.'

There was no need to change from their travelling clothes, for the weather had been favourable: a pale spring sunshine, with enough air about to make the journey comfortable; the ground under-foot firm and dry so that they had no tell-tale mud-spattering to show the distance they had travelled. Nevertheless, Hugh spent some little time in the chamber that had been allotted to him, damping down his hair and brushing his doublet and hose with his hands to remove any trace of dust that might cling to them.

John lounged in the doorway. 'I hadn't thought to find you quite so changed.' His tone was mocking, but mild. 'You used to scoff at such care.' He drew Hugh towards the door. 'It's an offence easily forgiven, by the ladies at least. Mind, I don't think Elizabeth would care if you arrived covered in glaur, so long as you are come at all.' He sobered, 'We had a fear, my mother especially, that her name would play against us. Cunninghame she may have been once, but she has long been a Shaw, and we none of us desert our friends.'

Hugh stiffened.

As if unaware of any awkwardness, John continued, 'But I counted, if not on your good sense, at least on your need for a good dinner.' He parried the playful cuff that Hugh directed at his head, and ducked through the low doorway onto the stairwell. 'Come on, do you wish all the world to know that Hugh Montgomerie has at last taken thought to his appearance?'

John's sisters were waiting in the hall, the meal set, when John and Hugh entered. They were clustered by the fire, and for a moment Hugh thought that Elizabeth had not, after all, been well enough to come down. Then

Christian turned and he saw through the gap that opened behind her Elizabeth seated on the bench, her hands outstretched to the flickering flames.

She made to stand up, but he hunkered down in front of her. 'No need to rise.'

Her eyes were inches from his and shining, her voice a little lower than he remembered, husky, perhaps from the fever. 'I would wish that you were come in better circumstance, but am happy for it none the less.'

He floundered, aware of a flush in his face and heat in his palms and cross that he stammered like an idiot boy. 'I have been away over long and you have . . .'

'Changed? I find you much changed also, and more than your name; six years ago you had plenty to say for yourself. Indeed . . . rather too much.'

'I believe I owe you a gown.'

'I shall expect it then, and before another Yuletide, else you may claim the year of Jubilee and the debt cancelled.'

'You shall have it and soon.' He was beginning to find himself. 'I am home now and to sort the estate. But the debts cleared, there will be a wee pickle left to settle with my personal creditors.'

'Do you have many gowns to buy?'

Despite that he knew she teased, the colour crept in his face.

Gillis was swinging on Christian's arm. 'Are we never to eat?'

Christian patted her head, 'Hush, child. It isn't polite to hurry the greeting of our guests.'

Gillis pulled her eyebrows into a frown, 'But I'm hungry.'

Hugh turned. 'And so am I, and so I'm sure is everyone.' He proferred his arm to Elizabeth and through the fine cambric of his shirt felt the touch of her fingers as a flame. John sat at the head of the table, his manner easy saying the grace and ordering the seating and the serving of the ale. At twenty-five, his face had broadened and carried a shadow of stubble. His jaw, sharp at nineteen, had begun to merge into his neck, indicating the thicker figure he would likely become.

Belatedly noting the absence of the elder Shaws, Hugh said, 'Your parents are from home?'

'My father thinks to set up a permanent trading base at Veere in the Low Countries and mother has accompanied him in case, I think, that he will find too much distraction among the continental ladies for her comfort.'

'Tush, John,' there was disapproval in Elizabeth's voice. 'You know the truth of it: that she wishes for once to have the choosing of silks and velvets rather than be forced to depend on father's erratic taste.'

John rolled his eyes, began to protest that it was a joke only, as Christian cut in,

'And I for one will be happy for it.'

There was a general ripple of laughter at the intervention, for all knew the store she set by fashion, so that she blushed and smiled and the awkward moment was past. The evening spun on, Hugh at Elizabeth's side and attentive. She plied him with questions: about France and The Hague and Prince Maurice of Nassau, and how it was that he was not called 'Orange' despite the death of his brother. From the way in which she followed up each of his answers with another, often more pertinent, question, Hugh realised with pleasure that she had an interest in, and a not inconsiderable grasp of the politics of Europe. But some of her questions were more personal.

'Tell me of life in the barracks.' Her pause seemed just a fraction too long to be for breath. 'And out of it. Is it exciting?'

Afraid that his laugh was too loud to be altogether convincing, Hugh was dismissive. 'Exciting enough in its way, I suppose.' Misdemeanours there had been, but minor, and relatively infrequent, and of no importance at all. 'It's not all roistering. There is much of routine and court life can become very tedious.'

'And court ladies?'

He held her gaze, 'They also.'

The dimple came and went in her cheek. 'But how will you find life at Braidstane now? There will be little to distract you bar the sheep, and they are not noted as the liveliest of creatures.'

'To tell the truth, I don't know how I shall do but,' he smiled, 'there shall at least be time to keep up with old friends. That I am determined on.' Remembering his last leaving of Greenock, he said, 'If your father will make me welcome.'

Elizabeth's expression was thoughtful. 'Six years – I don't think it was of sufficient importance for father to recollect.'

He took a swallow of ale, felt it on his stomach like meltwater. He had come to Greenock, ignoring their Cunninghame connection; on the back of a memory that had surfaced often and unbidden during his years abroad. Triggered by a glance of hazel eyes, or a discussion over-heated, or the smell of mulled wine mingled with roast pig: the memory of this table and of his own youthful voice: '. . . I have little wish to settle to the rearing of cattle . . . or children come to that, or to grow a paunch to match my station'; of the steadily darkening countenance of

61

James Shaw, and fifteen-year-old Elizabeth, lifting her glass and tipping it, so that wine the colour of juniper berries flowed across the table, slipping over the edge and splashing the front of her gown. Of how she jumped up, dabbing at the damp stain that spread across her embroidered plackard, biting her lips in good imitation of vexation and apology. And, over the memory, Jean Shaw's superscription, 'You are fortunate, it seems. Elizabeth is not noted to be careless'. An implication that he allowed to lie in his mind as an anchor that shifted a little from time to time with the moving tide, but always held: that Elizabeth had perhaps more than a passing interest in her brother's friend. Now, afraid that the memory was his only, he said, 'It was of importance to me.'

She met his eyes. 'To me also.'

He put himself out then to entertain the whole company, mimicking some of the more memorable of his fellow soldiers. John watched, a wistful expression on his face, so that Hugh knew he thought of the experiences he might have had, should he too have been able to sell himself as a mercenary. When Hugh caught Christian in a yawn, so that she blushed a rosy red, he turned to talking of the courts of France and Holland, the masques, the games, the plays, the meals that went on long beyond sufferance. But when the girls fired questions on the width of a farthingale, the height of a bonnet, or the pattern of a lace, he flung up his hands, 'I didn't pay such close attention, but am sorry for it now.'

And in the midst of this company, was able to forget for a time the journey he must resume on the morrow.

Chapter Seven

The Montgomeries' arrival in Stirling went unnoticed, and they took the chance to find lodgings before making their way to the court. Hugh chose to slip in quietly, finding a space towards the rear of the great hall, despite that he could see Alexander Montgomerie, a close kinsman, near to James. It was a connection that Hugh was minded to foster, for what use an uncle close to the King, if gain was not made of it? For the now though, he preferred to watch from the background and, with a soldier's eye, gauge the mood of the moment. Mindful of his own quick temper and of James' command, it were as well to note those that he should take particular care not to insult.

Later that evening, making a show of wasting no time, he presented himself at the entrance to the King's apartments. The Presence Chamber was full as he elbowed his way through, for there were many who, mindful that the King had not yet reached his majority, sought to make capital of his youth. The bedchamber was more private. Alexander Montgomerie was there, and a few others, including John Stewart of Baldyneis, who had the additional privilege of near kinship to the King to add to his membership of the poetry circle. His name Hugh remembered because his father had made a jest of it once on his return from court. Some verses were spread out before the King, a lively discussion in progress.

James gestured towards the parchments strewn across the coverlet. 'Ah, Braidstane, you are not a poet, like your good uncle here?'

Hugh bowed low, gave himself time to compose his features. 'I have not that gift, sire.'

'No matter,' Both James' voice and expression suggested that a verse or two would have greased the wheels a little. 'I trust that you are come in a mood of reconciliation. Anything less will not please us.'

'Sire.'

'It is our wish that all should swear to end this folly.'

'We Montgomeries aren't so many that we can afford to be picked off over precedence . . .' Hugh was struggling to keep the anger out of his voice.

James narrowed his eyes. 'As to precedence, we will make a judgement on it . . .' He rubbed at an imaginary roughness on his right hand, '. . . when the moment is opportune.'

Hugh wanted to take the opportune moment and stuff it into James' prissy mouth, but, mindful of his promise to Grizel, and aware of Alexander's careful expression, said instead, 'I am grateful sire.'

The King's expression didn't soften. 'Wait on us then – in the morning, and early.'

Hugh bowed and escaped through the Guard Hall into the fresher air of the passage where Patrick paced.

'I have pledged myself, despite the likely ill to my stomach. The sooner it's over and we can turn to more pleasing matters the better.' As they left the royal quarters, Hugh tried to sound casual. 'I mustn't forget I have the makings of a gown to buy.'

'This I want to see,' Patrick paused by a window over-looking the courtyard, the sound of female voices carrying through the open casement. 'You have trouble enough buying clothes for yourself.' And when Hugh didn't respond, 'Serious then? And not just about the gown?'

'With your experience to aid me . . .' Hugh glanced out the window, '. . . I heard tell of a young lady in Leyden, whose dress is particularly fine.'

Patrick refused to rise. 'Our cousins at Giffen speak well of a clothier in Glasgow. Maybe that would meet your need?'

Hugh matched his neutral tone. 'More than likely, but come, we don't want to find our lodging taken. Flea-ridden no doubt, it is at least a bed.'

They turned towards the gap between the Royal apartments and the Great Hall, picking their way across the cobbles in the failing light. And flea-ridden their lodging turned out to be. But this they did not discover until the morning, woken at first light by the snarling of a pair of dogs in the street below, as they fought over scraps that had been flung into the gutter. A volley of oaths issued from an adjacent window and the well-aimed contents of a chamber pot caught the larger of the two dogs square in the jowls, so that he sprang away to slink off down a nearby alley. Amused, Hugh watched the smaller of the dogs enjoying the fruits of a victory won for him. It was only as he saw the dog lift his back paw to scratch vigorously at his ear, that he realised he himself was scratching at a line of lumps which stretched round his waist like a belt. The skin around them was red and swollen, each lump standing out white, with a tell-tale pinhead centre. If he hadn't already been keen to get the business over as quickly as possible and seek immediate permission to leave the court, the beasties who shared his lodgings would have convinced him. The dog, having worried away at the scraps until there was nothing left worth eating, was nosing his way down the street, halting at every doorway to lift his leg. Hugh turned towards Patrick, who still lay on the narrow pallet the rough blanket pulled up to his chin, and could see from the movement that Patrick too was scratching.

'I wouldn't lie too long. There may be a whole colony of fleas waking up for their breakfast at any moment.'

Patrick stretched and swung his legs over the edge of the bed examining the clusters of bites that speckled his thighs. Downstairs, they met the bold stare of the landlady and the enquiry as to how long they would be staying, with withering looks. Hugh threw a handful of coins onto the deal table that filled the centre of the taproom and called over his shoulder as they left, 'If you wish to have company of merit, you must needs look to expelling the smaller creatures that claim space in your beds. We won't stay to be eaten alive: not if yours is the only lodging in Stirling.'

A volley of curses, which would have done justice to the roughest of soldiers under Hugh's command, followed them half way down the street. They weren't clear of her complaints until they reached the end of the lane and turned onto the wider thoroughfare curving up the steep hill towards the castle. Despite the early hour, it thronged with people, jostling and pushing, so that they kept a close hand to their purses. The gutters steamed with the contents of night-pails and they took care to watch both their feet and the windows above them. James, though not the most fastidious of men himself, was not above sniffing at others if they presented themselves with muck on their clothes. He was capable of making it a personal affront that, in the present circumstance, would hardly be designed to serve them well. Glencairn likely would have taken particular trouble with his appearance, and Robert would expect Hugh to have made an equal effort, with no allowance for any disparity in their lodgings. In the business of precedence, appearance was no small factor, so that Hugh couldn't afford to turn up smelling as if he came straight from a tumble in the mire.

At the entrance to the castle, Patrick looked Hugh up and down. 'It were as well,' he said, without a trace of humour, 'that we find our uncle, and take advantage of his chamber to improve our appearance before we present ourselves to the King.'

A potboy sought to squeeze past and Hugh grabbed hold of him, demanding that he direct them to Alexander Montgomerie's rooms. The lad shook his head, protesting unconvincingly that he knew not of any such Montgomerie, but Hugh kept a firm hold, propelling him back through the gate. He hopped up and down on one foot, clearly needing to be off on some other errand.

Hugh said, 'Take us, and quick – we'll make it worth your while.'

They followed him across the inner close to a low doorway set in the corner, where he clattered up a flight of stairs and along a narrow passageway, Hugh and Patrick hard on his heels, and slid to a stop outside a small, iron-studded door. It was obvious from the way that he grabbed the coin offered, stuffing it into his jerkin without troubling to test it with his teeth, that if he didn't hurry, he was like to get into trouble from some other source. He had disappeared around a corner in the corridor before Hugh had lifted his arm to knock on Alexander's door.

He was seated in an alcove, light spilling into the room from the window in front of him and Hugh, looking out through the narrow embrasure, noted the inconvenience, should one wish to make a speedy escape from the castle. Forbye the bars set firm into the stone, the wall and the cliff below it plunged, he guessed, at least a hundred feet into the valley below.

'I have no need of any route other than the stairs Hugh. It is . . .' Alexander placed a slight but deliberate stress on the word, '. . . but *one* advantage of my trade.'

'There are others?' The retort was out before Hugh thought, but Alexander didn't rise to it.

'Oh yes,' and then, with a smile that failed to reach his eyes, 'There are more ways than one to catch a fox, nephew, and you would do well to remember it.'

'My apologies, uncle. I didn't come to disparage, only that. . .'

'Nor have I a wish to quarrel with you, Hugh, but do not think I feel the pain of your parents' deaths the less, because I do not broadcast it.' There was an odd note in Alexander's voice. 'Your mother . . . we were fond . . . but she didn't fancy a life at court . . . and perhaps she was right. She went to bide awhile at Giffen and Adam found her there. And she came to love him and he her. And there is much to be said for that, however short their time was cut. If you are as fortunate. . .'

Hugh studied a mark on his doublet, but aware of the light pressure on his arm felt obliged to look up.

'. . . You will be fortunate, indeed.' There was a slight involuntary tremor under Alexander's eye. 'There are worse ways to die . . . and living a widow one of them.'

Heat coursed through Hugh. Despite that he had begun to make his own plans, or perhaps because of them, all the while since his mother's death it had been as if he had lain under a fallen tree, his movements constricted by the weight of the trunk. Now, with this new perspective that Alexander provided, he found the weight lifting, the anger that had been smouldering in him dying away. In its place a more kindly understanding of his parents; and with it, respect and fondness for this uncle who, laying aside his own pain, would put himself out to further Hugh's cause. For the first time in the whole exchange, he looked Alexander full in the eye.

'I am grateful, uncle – perhaps it is the soldier in me that doesn't see what a poet may discern.' He struggled to find words that would express what he felt without sounding maudlin and was relieved when Alexander interrupted.

'Let's not dwell on what is past. You have your sword, I have verse.' His smile extended a little, 'And for what it's worth, I am at your disposal. I imagine you have some little favour to ask?' A chill crept back into his voice. 'A word in your ear – favours come easier salted with respect.'

Hugh dipped his head, acknowledging the rebuke. 'I see you were at work. We didn't mean to disturb – only that we would wish to appear presentable to the King, and thought to take advantage of your lodging, our own proving less than adequate.' He was scratching at his leg.

Alexander's face now showed genuine amusement. 'You came to Stirling without a potion for flea bites? Surely you left Braidstane in a hurry. It's not like Grizel to let you away unprepared. Here . . .' He moved to a chest at the other side of the room and rummaged through it, emerging with a small bottle that he lobbed at Hugh, before gesturing towards a table with a basin and ewer, ready filled. 'Be my guests, though I'm afraid the water is cold. It is rather too pricey to expect service of real quality two storeys up. And supposing I did pay for hot water, it would likely be cold by the time it arrived. It's easier, and better, to save the silver.'

He produced a towel and tossed it to Patrick, who held it while Hugh splashed water over his face and neck, and ran his damp fingers through his hair.

Patrick said, 'At the risk of being cried for a lassie, there's a comb in my baggage that might serve you well.'

'There is nothing amiss with my hair that a few minutes in the air won't sort.' Hugh turned for support to Alexander, who said, with a twitch of his lips that might be construed as a smile,

'A wee pickle of a straighten wouldn't go amiss. You aren't in the barracks now and do not go before James as a soldier. You may despise the Cunninghame's presentation, but believe me, a little effort in that direction may serve you well.'

Hugh found the comb and attacked his hair, so that he looked, for once, more the laird than the mercenary. Alexander was leaning over the table, scribbling a last few words, scoring out here, adjusting there. Hugh paced up and down the small chamber, and unconsciously undid any good that he had done to his hair by running his fingers through it again. Patrick, having smoothed his natural curls into submission with a practised hand, tossed the comb back towards him, and in a reflex action, Hugh caught it, but looked at it in surprise.

Patrick forestalled him. 'Do it again and this time put your hat on before you wreak havoc. Thank God for a windless day – there is a chance you may pass muster, supposing we do not wait long on the King.'

Alexander turned from the table, his arms full of

papers. Hugh expected another lecture: on the value of swallowing pride, of taking a little care to his position as the new laird of Braidstane, of the responsibilities which made conforming to expectations no longer an option, but an obligation. He was steeling himself to respond and so was caught off guard by Alexander's question,

'How do you for horses?'

'Fair enough, I suppose.'

'Have they stamina, and a fair turn of speed?'

'In an ordinary way, yes, though not in the hunting league.'

'It isn't yet arranged but, if you were to invite the King to take the chase. . . .'

Hugh shook his head. 'That isn't an expense I thought to make, especially as we are not on home territory and it wouldn't just be James but half the court that followed.'

Alexander waved his sheaf of papers and said, 'There are those who would wish to join our poetry circle. I do not think it impossible that I could arrange some accommodation. Do you take care of the swearing of friendship with Glencairn, and issue an invitation to all to join with you on Thursday: as our guests. Do not say where exactly. James enjoys a mystery.'

'There isn't a fear that you can't make good the invitation?'

Alexander's voice was cheerful. 'A gamble maybe.'

Patrick made as if to speak.

'Rest easy. It is but a small risk. And the better the chase, the higher your stock will rise. Glencairn will be fair scunnered for not thinking of it.'

From the relish in Alexander's voice, Hugh accepted fully, for the first time, that his uncle matched his own dislike of the Cunninghames. 'My thanks, uncle and . . .' he tapped the page in Alexander's hand, '. . . with luck we may catch more than a fox or two, if things fall out well.'

There was the sound of running footsteps in the passageway outside.

Alexander turned, 'I'd better be away. The King set us a task yesterday, and I mustn't be behind with my response. Don't wait long to follow, but don't be over hasty either. James will wish to hear our verses first before he turns to your cause.' From the doorway, he finished, 'We need but half an hour for our mutual congratulations and if you are to hand then, my softenings may have made James disposed to look kindly on you. I trust,' Hugh heard the hint of steel in his voice, 'you won't disappoint me, or we shall all suffer for it.'

Hugh acknowledged both the advice and the warning. 'I shall play the game, uncle, have no fear. You shall find me almost a poet in my swearing. God knows I have practised enough, that I might not retch at the sound of my own voice.'

The Great Hall at Stirling, where James had chosen that the Montgomeries and Cunninghames should publicly swear to end their family quarrels, was full to bursting. Hugh followed Patrick in, squeezing through to join Robert Montgomerie, positioned near the front of the hall. The King sat on the dais surrounded by his poetry circle. Others hovered close, betraying by the stiffness of their posture a mixture of nerves and expectation, their desire to catch a glance, an invitation to join the favoured

72

few. Members of the council clustered in the large bay window area, among them Secretary of Scotland, Maitland, clutching a roll of parchment that he tap-tapped against his leg, perhaps indicating a suppressed frustration that James put poetry before the affairs of state. The man who currently was entertaining James with a poem that praised the King's prowess on the hunting field, Hugh recognized as 'Old Scott' – who in Mary's day had written 'Welcome illustrat Lady and our Queen'. – How easy it is for a poet, Hugh thought – change a word here, alter another there, and old allegiances as easily replaced. That he would shortly be up there with them, posturing and pretending a friendship that he intended to keep only for so long as was necessary, did not make him any more sympathetic to the ploys of others. As he despised what he was about to do, so he despised the manner in which others also prostituted themselves before James.

Patrick leant sideways and spoke softly in his ear. 'Have a care, Hugh. Your thoughts are as plain as the red in your hair: a child could read them, and the King, for all he hasn't reached his full majority, is no child. Nor Glencairn either, and as for William, he may play the fop, but it won't have addled his brain. . . . And if you don't let go of my arm, I shall bear the mark for months to come.'

Unclenching his hand, Hugh released Patrick, who bent his arm sideways until the elbow joint cracked, flexing his fingers. 'Better mine than Cunninghame's, I do suppose. I shan't need a fighting arm for the present – or not I trust, till I am back in France.'

There was a stir around James. Hugh saw that Old Scott had finished his piece and was moving back to let another of the group take his place.

Patrick whistled under his breath. 'Perhaps there is something in this poetry game. I hadn't thought to see a lady among the company, and pretty at that. I must ask Alexander . . .'

'We aren't here to play, Patrick. Nor will we stay long.'

'Oh I don't need long,' Patrick grinned, showing even, white teeth, 'I never need long – indeed I tire easily, and must perforce rest between bouts.'

'This lady keeps dangerous company; little use my taking care of appearance, if you will cause an affront to one of James' inner circle.' Aware that his grip was again over hard, Hugh relaxed and made a conscious effort to sound casual, 'A poet might have higher expectations than even you can meet. This is not Leyden. Nor do we wish to close doors that may be to our advantage. Offence here would be inconvenient, at the very least.'

Patrick half-turned, so that the tall, thin man nearest to them, who showed his restiveness in the way he alternately swivelled the cairngorm ring on his left hand and picked at imaginary specks of fluff on his clothes, might not pick up his words. 'I have no intention of causing offence, but a little pleasant conversation in the right direction may open doors to us, not close them. Have you ever known me to sail so close to the wind that I am over-turned?' Despite himself, Hugh grinned at him. It was true that he hadn't yet met a lady who remembered an encounter with Patrick with anything other than pleasure, though there were many who wished that they might have held onto him a little longer.

At the other side of the hall Glencairn moved through the throng, William on his tail, halting, at just such a distance to indicate availability, yet deference to the moment of the King's choosing. Robert Montgomerie also stepped forward, bringing himself into James' sightline, but not close enough to Glencairn for discomfort. Hugh and Patrick edged towards him. Hugh saw William glance in their direction and then turn to make some comment to the man who stood behind him. If he had any doubt that it was in disparagement, the way in which the other man looked around as if to see if the remark had been overheard, would have confirmed it. He noted the man's bearing – light build, about his own age, plainly dressed – and thought him an altogether unlikely companion to William, who wore for the occasion a wide ruff and a tall-crowned hat of striped green velvet, which sat on his head like a stalk of butterbur. It was trimmed by a large brooch, aglitter with pearls, ostentatious, even by William's standards.

Patrick murmured, 'We are very much the country cousins here. Take care to make capital of the invitation to hunt, for we won't impress else.'

'I have no wish,' Hugh was equally quiet, 'to make the kind of impression that William aims for, supposing I had the money to waste.' He nodded in the direction of the man behind William: 'Who's that, d'you know? I shouldn't have thought him William's type.'

'No idea, but I agree, he doesn't look altogether comfortable in the company he keeps.'

Hugh said casually, 'I think that I begin to like him. If you wish to open a door or two on my behalf, make some discreet enquiries as to his identity and the reason he finds himself in Cunninghame's company.'

Chapter Eight

At Broomelaw, the weather turned. Kate didn't normally mind the rain, if so be it was the soft westerly rain that carried the salt tang of seaweed along with the flocks of gulls blown inward like a tide. Munro thought the gulls a curse, with their raucous cries, their scavenging, and the mess that followed them everywhere. Kate preferred to think of their grace as they wheeled and circled and lit on the barmkin wall as lightly as if they weighed but a few ounces rather than the pound and three-quarters of a full-grown bird. There was something oddly attractive to her in the way they fought fiercely over the scraps she scattered for them. Though she had to admit, to herself, if not to anyone else, that their skitters didn't improve the quality of the patch of grass surrounding the tower, but rather, the opposite.

Coarse though it was, it struggled to survive the tramping of boots and of the horses that, however much she remonstrated, seemed to find their way onto it, whenever there was an arrival or a leaving. She had tried once roping off an area to preserve as a garden – on the west side where it would catch the evening sun – but had given up in disgust when Munro leapt the rope to head for the outside cludgie, refusing to take the longer route by the path, succeeding in making, instead of a general scrubbiness, a defined track. If she couldn't get her husband to comply, then small chance servants or anyone else paying attention to her wishes. But lately, the Cunninghame calls increasingly taking Munro away, she had replaced her ropes and had watched with pleasure the fresh green shoots that spring brought. And so, although the present rain was not a soft mizzle, but pelted down, pooling in every dip and hollow around the base of the tower, Kate sat in the solar and thought of the benefit to her grass that, once the fierceness of its onslaught had diminished, it would afford.

The wind was another matter altogether. When she took herself out to check on the suckling cows, their calves but a few days old, she found that she could hardly stand against the gusts that came, not from the friendly west, but whipping over the hills to the north. They tore down the valley; bending the tall pines before them, so that fresh growth that should have tipped the bough ends bright green, fell instead amidst the dusty tan of last year's needle fall.

It made her think of Munro and of the distance between them. Anger remained, the smouldering remnants of a fire, tamped down by the uncomfortable recognition that it had been his desire to protect her and the bairns that had driven him to his part in the business at Annock. And the equally uncomfortable thought, that she had not been so tested.

She spent an uneasy week, largely confined to the house, while the shutters rattled continually and draughts funnelled under the doors. The wind blew down the chimneys, so that the fires burned fitfully and her eyes stung with the smoke that billowed in bursts from the hearth. It was difficult to wait, with no word, no idea if he could manage to avoid trouble, no knowledge of how long he would remain at the court. What made the wait all the harder was the knowledge that attendance on the King was fraught with hidden dangers as well as potential rewards. Munro had the benefit of James in some five years, and though capable of trading quotations in Latin if he chose, he placed little value on book learning, considering education best kept for bairns, or for the latter years when physique was failing. And fine for him.

The old envy stirred in Kate: that boys, aye grumbling, were shipped off to college as a matter of course, while she, though taught her letters, remained at home to gain other, more practical, accomplishments. Devouring the few books and pamphlets that had come her way, she had rolled around her head the names of authors that her brother had groaned over, the shape and sound of them: Horace and Bude, Froissart, Ascham, Ronsard, sharp with elicit pleasure, like the bite of early brambles on her tongue. She had imagined losing herself in a maze of books, the air heady with poetry, thick with prose. The King, they said, had a library of some six hundred volumes; classic and modern, in a host of languages and on every imaginable theme. She thought on them now, envy became an ache. Some she knew would fascinate: herbals and the like, the text and illustrations both. Others she likely wouldn't care for: on war or sport or the responsibilities and privileges of kingship. Yet all these and more fed James' mind and framed his thinking and set him as far apart from Munro and his ilk as sun from moon. And therein lay the danger. Her husband was no player. If James' attention should light on him. . .

Anna burst into the solar, Robbie chasing her, grasping for the ribbon that flew loose at her waist.

'Whoa.' Kate spread her arms and the twins skidded to a halt. She gathered them against her and breathing in their warm scent, the hard knot that had lain beneath her breastbone since Annock, began at last to dissolve. A minor laird Munro had been born and a minor laird she prayed he might remain. And she his wife.

Chapter Nine

Sunlight from the tall alcove windows spread across the dais of Stirling's Great Hall and spilled onto the floor below, raising the temperature in the already airless chamber well beyond comfort. Munro, watching as William stepped into the pool of light, was glad on two counts not to follow. There was a shift in the group around the King, the poets moving back, others surging forwards, jockeying for position, hoping to catch James' eye. Maitland, clearly losing patience, stepped in, blocking other hopefuls.

James took the proffered parchment and laid it on the table in front of him. He beckoned to Robert Montgomerie and Glencairn. Robert stepped sideways and ushering forward the men directly behind him, presented them to James.

'Braidstane, sire, and his younger brother Patrick, recently come from France . . .' he cast a glance towards Glencairn, '. . . to sort their father's affairs.'

Munro ran a hand round the back of his neck.

James acknowledged Braidstane. 'Indeed, it is no doubt a comfort to have kin about you.' He switched his attention back to Glencairn. 'There have been over many funerals of late, and it isn't to our pleasing.' He scratched at his leg, so that Munro, speculating on the beasties that likely shared the King's chambers, much like his own, found his mind drifting to the cleaner accommodation to be had at home. James' raised voice brought him back with a jolt.

'It isn't altogether regarding the past that we have bidden your attendance, but rather that you and those with whom you have had differences . . .' he was focusing on Glencairn, '. . . may comport yourselves to our pleasing in the future.'

Glencairn's back was stiff, clearly steeling himself to play the charade out.

'It is our wish that you shall solemnly affirm, before God and this company as witnesses, to abjure any violence between you, your families or followers from this time forth.' James gestured to the parchment that Maitland had unrolled, his voice round and full-bellied as the best French brandy. 'Yet words are easy spoken and as easily forgot. I have had Maitland prepare Letters of Affirmation. A signature can hardly be denied.'

Glencairn dipped the quill in the inkpot and signed with a flourish, Robert Montgomerie following with a touch more deliberation. James waved them back and gestured to William and to Hugh to take their place, his eyes widening as William bowed over the table, the brooch and the pearls that shone in it close to his hand. The man in front of Munro shifted, craning his neck to get a better view and Munro was forced to move likewise. From his new vantage point, it was clear that Glencairn too was eyeing the brooch, his expression grim. William stepped to the side allowing Hugh to take his place, then all waited as James signed, the scratch of the quill magnified in the long hall. He raised his eyes, a small smile hovering round his mouth, reached out to William and beckoned again to Glencairn.

'We have thought on the business at Annock and . . .' The candle sconce behind James' head hung with congealed wax, putting Munro in mind of long, grasping fingers. '. . . some small token, as an earnest of your serious intention . . .' James was looking pointedly at the brooch.

Glencairn, sweeping the hat off William's head, said smoothly, 'Perhaps this, though only a trifle . . .' unclasping the brooch.

James' tongue darted over his lips. 'We will accept it.'

'Sire,' Glencairn bowed and retreated, jerking William with him.

John Cunninghame, his eyes fixed on Glencairn, beckoned Munro, indicating that they should retire also.

'Wait. The game isn't over yet and Glencairn will hardly be so good company that we should rush to join him.' Munro gestured towards the Montgomeries who held their position in front of James, Hugh still to the fore, Robert Montgomerie a fraction behind, a hint of anticipation in his gaze.

Hugh's voice was confident and clear. 'I have nothing about me, sire, fit to offer, nevertheless I too would like to give an earnest.' He paused for just long enough for James to take his attention from the brooch. 'If it please you, my uncle and I,' he nodded towards Alexander, 'plan some sport for Thursday – a small thing, but I'm told the chase will excite. We would be honoured by your presence.'

James passed the brooch to Maitland, who, examining the quality of the pearls was, if one could judge by the glint in his eyes, pleased at the latest acquisition. There was renewed animation in the King's voice as he called Alexander to his side.

'We will accompany you, but where?'

'The greater the surprise, the greater the sport, sire.' Alexander Montgomerie's reply was smooth. 'Shall we meet below the castle at first light and ride on together?'

James rolled up the Letters of Affirmation and rose from his chair, encompassing the whole Montgomerie party in his smile. 'It pleases us, and . . . ' with a glance at Glencairn that seemed to dare him to think otherwise, ' . . . it is not such a trifle.' He tapped Robert Montgomerie on the shoulder with the roll of parchment. 'You have a fine family, Montgomerie, gey fine. But now I must turn to other, more tedious matters.' With a moue that suggested both apology and reluctance, he began to move down the hall; the company parting before him like the Red Sea before Moses, Maitland and others of the council in his wake.

Munro, stepping aside with the rest, continued to watch the Montgomeries as Robert placed his arm about Hugh's shoulder, nodding satisfaction. Glencairn, turning abruptly, swept past William and what was said to him in the passing, though spoken in a hiss that made it impossible for others to hear, was, to judge by the set of William's lips, not complimentary. Again, Munro felt a tug on his arm.

John said, 'Our presence may be missed.'

'What harm curiousity?'

'That isn't a quality Glencairn prizes.'

'You go on then,' A pause. 'I'll not be long behind you.'

John shrugged, turned away.

The knot of Montgomeries were making for the door. Munro dipped his head and trusting to the press to save him from notice, slipped in behind them, straining to hear their conversation.

'Neatly done, Hugh.' Robert Montgomerie's tone was warm, 'We will have you a courtier yet. Though I wouldn't have put statemanship as your strongest suit.'

'Nor is it, but I have a good tutor in our uncle. And as

it was he who thought of the ploy, he, I trust, can carry it through.'

'I thought it already arranged.' Robert's voice rose a fraction. 'It is a dangerous thing, Alexander, to trifle with the King.'

'Have no fear, nephew, it will be done and well.' Alexander spoke with confidence. 'There are many who would wish to please the King and I have not a few of them in my pocket. It isn't yet arranged only because I didn't think of it until this morning. The details will be sorted, and in a timely fashion. Look you to your choice of horse, the rest is my concern.'

Munro risked a glance and saw it was the poet who spoke. He saw the crease of worry clear from Robert's brow as Alexander continued.

'I find it convenient on occasions to accept payment in kind and this is just such a one. Enjoy your dinner as I suspect Glencairn, and more particularly, William, will not.'

Indeed, it was an uneasy meal that Glencairn and William took, though as they kept to their lodgings, none bar Munro was able to enjoy the ill feeling between them. Glencairn was furious: with William for the stupidity of flaunting the brooch before the king, and with himself for failing to notice the wearing of it and thus avoid its loss. So that the ale was flat, the bread stale, the cheese lacking in flavour, the cuts of beef, set on a side table that they might serve themselves, tough and stringy; the whole twice as expensive as it should be, and not worth the half. Relations between them did not improve when a messenger arrived to say that they were bid to remain at the court, and to accompany James and the Montgomerie party on the proposed hunt.

Glencairn growled at Munro, 'I trust you have a change of clothes that you could oblige William with, for I doubt he is capable of being inconspicuous else. It's likely we will be spared the sight of James wearing the brooch. Maitland will not wish to risk its loss. Though that is little consolation for so substantial and unnecessary a loss.'

William's knuckles were white, and Munro watched, almost with relish, to see if the anger between them would flare into an all out brawl. The idea that they might be forced to appear before James sporting a black eye or two between them amused him, but he was careful not to betray his thoughts lest he fell foul of their aggression. And besides, his fortunes rose and fell with theirs, and he had no wish to be the bearer of their apologies to James, should they so injure each other as to render them incapable of joining the hunt. So he said, 'I can arrange for the hire of fresh horses, more suited to the chase than those we travelled on,' and before Glencairn could raise an objection, 'The sooner undertaken, the more likely that the Montgomeries will be disappointed.'

Glencairn rounded on William again. 'The likely cost, another drain on our purse that we could meet the better had it not been for this day's proceedings.' He turned back to Munro, oozing sarcasm, 'Do you make sure there is no mistake with our mounts. At least if they are hired we cannot be expected to gift them to the King.'

Munro bowed his way from the chamber, William on his tail.

'I need a drink,' he said, taking hold of Munro's arm, 'and someone to drink it with me.'

'The horses . . .'

'Cannot be got at this time of night.' William held on. 'Don't pretend to a Presbyterianism, Munro. I know you too well – it will not be the first time you have drunk yourself into oblivion. This time be grateful that you don't pay.' His eyes glittered dangerously, and Munro relaxed into his grip. 'If I don't go now, I shall run father through, and then we shall all be roasted. So if you value your freedom, you will accompany me. And we'll drink ourselves to the devil. But you, my dear Munro,' William laughed without humour, 'take care that you retain just enough of your faculties to bring me safe home.'

There was an alehouse hard by their lodgings, but William passed it by, as too close to his father for comfort, and made his way through the narrow wynds to the meaner fringes of the town. They came on a tavern, the door swinging on one hinge. 'This will serve.'

Munro peered in, noted the rough deal tables, pitted with old scars; the battered plate; the rushes on the floor matted with stale vomit. In the corner, a pot-bellied effigy of a man, fustian cheeks stained crimson, perched drunkenly on the edge of a broken stool, a rope looped into a noose snaking around its neck: clear warning to those who might have any thoughts of partaking without paying. Amusing as it might be to see William reduced to the level of this company, it was a pleasure likely short-lived and the responsibility all his own should Glencairn get word of it, so he said, 'At least let me look to your purse. You wouldn't wish to be relieved of your silver too soon.'

William flung himself down at the end of a bench and drew out a leather pouch that he tossed to Munro. It drew the attention of a serving maid, who elbowed her way towards the newcomers.

Munro breathed shallowly against the reek – we'll be lucky to get out of here with our clothes, never mind our silver. William's doublet alone would buy and sell most here three times over. If he must drink himself blind, let it be into a stupor and not the gutter. He thrust the purse deep inside his jerkin, and gestured to the girl. 'Ale and be quick about it.'

She sprawled across William, her own drink brought with theirs, while Munro kept a weather eye on the surrounding company. His eyes slid back to William and the girl. Her face was a travesty of paint and powder that failed to disguise the child beneath. The wee slip was likely not above twelve. Kate had a cousin, just such an age. This girl had learnt her trade well, but the fact that it was she and not William in control gave Munro little comfort. As he listened to her high-pitched giggle, and caught glimpses of her child's long legs and immature breasts, part-exposed as William's hands tugged at the ribbons of her bodice, Munro saw his cousin-in-law's face on the thin shoulders and felt revulsion, despite that he knew it to be disproportionate.

William gestured for another drink; his bloodshot glance passing over Munro, a slur in his voice. 'Become a prude, have you?

Munro didn't reply, but was careful to match William drink for drink, but contrived each time, when William's attention was elsewhere to tip some of his own into William's glass. Even so it was taking a long time to get William drunk, the ale clearly watered. Munro kept one hand inside his doublet, his fingers touching the handle of his dirk and although he slumped over the table with every appearance of increasing inebriation, he scanned the room from under his spread arm.

Despite his watchfulness he was taken by surprise, both by the force and the source of the trap when it was sprung. Any softer feelings he harboured for the girl who tangled with William fled in an instant. One moment, she dandled on his knee, her bodice loosened, her hair falling like a curtain across William's face, one hand resting behind his head as with his lips he scoured the pale flesh at the base of her neck. The next she drew up her leg, as if in response to the hand travelling down her back, then a flash of steel as she whipped a dirk from under her skirt. She brought it up, pulling William's head back by his hair and held the tip, unwavering, at his throat.

Munro lunged for her, but was stopped by the warning pinpricks of blood she drew as the blade stroked William's neck. A sound behind him. He tried to turn, but found his own arms pinioned. Forced across the table, he could see from William's pallor that, part-drunk or not, the danger of their situation had reached him. The girl was enjoying herself now, running the blade of the dirk back and forwards across William's neck, scoring it lightly as if she sliced the skin of a pig for roasting. He watched, part fascinated, part revolted, as blood beaded from the cuts, a ruby necklace around William's throat. With her other hand she pulled loose the padding that had enhanced her breasts, stuffing it into William's mouth so that he gagged.

'Was this your fancy my lord?'

There was a sharp pain in Munro's side, where the handle of his dirk dug into his flesh, but he was unable to shift his weight to reach it. The man holding him down reached inside Munro's doublet and grabbed the purse, weighing it in his hand before tossing it to his companion. He increased the pressure on Munro and, his gaze and voice directed at the girl, said, 'Next time move mair quickly. There is near half gone.' He leered, 'If it's pleasure ye seek, no doubt Tam or I . . . or both, can service ye.'

She swung round, her knee lifting from William's chest, the knife in her hand flashing past Munro's cheek, 'I would as soon ride a pig, and it covered in glaur.'

The other man, in the process of stowing the purse, snarled at them both. 'Spark at each other as ye please, but elsewhere.' He cast a glance around, 'We draw mair attention than we need.'

Both subsided instantly, indicating that he was the leader of the group. In a practised move, the man holding Munro twisted his arm further, raising Munro's head only to smash it onto the table with a crack.

The girl, the dirk again at William's throat said, 'The pleasure was all mine, pretty lord, but I have taken my payment nonetheless. And dinna think to follow else . . .' She again stroked his neck with the edge of the blade.

Then they were gone; neither William nor Munro in any immediate state to follow. The silence that had fallen around them lasted only as long as it took Munro to lift his head and rub at his wrists; those that had enjoyed the spectacle turned their backs and resumed their drinking and whoring as if nothing of moment had happened at all. Munro dragged William to his feet, and half-supporting, half-hauling him, made his way to the door. Outside, the cool air finished the job of sobering him, so that he made a passable job of holding William nearly upright. 'There's more than a step to your lodging, and I have no wish to attract any other scavengers, so you will do well to make an effort.'

William pulled himself a little straighter, so that they showed some semblance of control as they wove their way back to the comparative safety of the High Street, and up the winding stair to the Cunninghame's door. Munro left him propped against the lintel and, his own head and arms throbbing, made his way to his lodging hard by.

Chapter Ten

Hugh waited on Robert Montgomerie with the news that the hunt was arranged, and the assurance from Alexander that both it and the hospitality to follow, would be to everyone's satisfaction.

'Not, I think, to everyone's.' Robert's pleasure was clear. 'James has commanded Glencairn and his followers to present themselves also. It will add a little spice to the proceedings. Let's drink to good sport and to the discomfiture of the Cunninghames. And to precedence, which a fine chase with a hind or two at the heels of it, may restore to us.'

Hugh raised his glass, 'To Thursday, and to all that we may gain and others lose.' He emptied it in one draught as Robert said, 'You will stay awhile? And tell us of your home at Braidstane and Grizel and the plans that you no doubt have for the estate. There are calls on it, I daresay?'

'That there are. I didn't think these many months past to be grateful for the failure of my paymasters in Holland; indeed, I did my fair share of complaining. But now, the arrears being promised, I stand to clear the estate and perhaps a little more.'

'There is talk of opportunities in Ireland for those whose grip on Scotland may not be as firm, nor as profitable, as they might desire.'

'I had some thought of looking to Ireland it's true, but that must needs wait till James gains the English Crown and who knows how long that will be.' Hugh noted the narrowing of Robert's eyes and wondered if he would, after all, have been wiser to keep his own counsel. Perhaps this young cousin of his had designs of his own in Ireland. If so, it mightn't be politic to set himself up in his way.

Robert rubbed his hands up and down his legs, as if it helped his concentration. 'There are perhaps things that could be done beforehand, to sweeten your position. When the time comes, all will be round James like bees at a honeypot. Much may be gained by establishing advantage now, if it be done in the right way.'

The tone was so sage, the words so perfectly contrived, that Hugh almost laughed.

'My brother George has offered to send intelligences from Elizabeth's court. And he is well placed to hear much gossip.'

'George is now . . . ?'

'Vicar of Cheddar. Though I don't think that Cheddar sees much of him. Nor will it while there is something to be gained by remaining at court. Not of course that he neglects his spiritual duties.'

There was a glint of humour in Robert's eye, but when he spoke, his tone remained formal. 'A word of advice then. See to it that the intelligences are useful to James, and take care to remind him from whence they come. Let your face be seen around court. However little you enjoy the company you find here.'

Patrick said, 'See, I'm not the only person to watch your face.'

'Indeed, Patrick, there are plenty who watch and would make capital of another man's falling.' Robert turned back to Hugh. 'We are not so far off kin, that I lack an interest in your affairs, but there are few who can afford to cause offence in the wrong quarters, and I'm not one of them. I will give you all the help I can to rise, but if you fall, you fall alone.'

There was a silence, a measure of the serious turn of the conversation, and, as is so often the way, all of them tried at the same moment to break it, then stopped: Hugh and Robert deferring to each other, Patrick to them both.

Another awkward pause, then Hugh, throwing away all attempt at formality said, 'We are become a pair of old men, cousin, and wear our positions like new clothes, so stiff that we can't yet be comfortable. We are in private now. Can we not discuss things like the old friends we are?'

A third pause, a relationship hanging in the balance, then, 'You know I had no thought of this. I liked fine to be a second son, and though 'Master of Eglintoun' can hardly be considered a trial and likely temporary, . . .' there was no doubting the mischief in his eyes, '. . . this new weight of responsibility will be the easier to bear knowing that I am not the only one whose wings are clipped.' He moved across to the table and poured another round of drinks, raised his glass, adroitly changing the subject. 'But what of Grizel?'

Hugh raised his glass in return. 'She's bravely. And has proved herself these past months an able steward. We none of us imagined, with a husband of five months' standing, that she would have our affairs to look to. But our mother's death coming hard on her unexpected widowhood, and our father . . . he didn't recover his spirits as one might have hoped. Grizel took it upon herself and rightly, for there was no one else to hand, to see to the estate and troubled him as little as she could. I'm grateful for it and, although she hasn't said so, were I to take charge of matters entirely, I think in some ways she would wish me gone again. For the meantime, she has found herself a place in the world and it would be a pity to take it away from her.'

'You will have opportunity then to further your interests here, resting easy that you need not fear what happens at home.'

'Aye, though there are also visits about the country that I would make, friends that I would wish to see, acquaintances that I would wish to turn into friends.'

'These friends are of a sort that will lead you away from trouble rather than into it?'

'Indeed.'

'And any more than friends?'

Patrick laughed. 'The rumour is out and must either be admitted to or scotched.'

'Admitted to, then.' Hugh put down his glass. 'I have thoughts of taking on responsibilities of the family kind.'

'And the lady is willing?'

'And the lady is willing. At least,' he corrected himself, 'I trust so, though it isn't quite settled.'

'He means he hasn't asked,' Patrick had stretched out on the settle, resting his boots on the arm. 'The lady or her father.'

'And who is the unlucky lady?'

'Elizabeth Shaw. Of Greenock.'

'Her mother is a Cunninghame, is she not?'

Hugh coloured, but Robert put up his hand.

'That wasn't a criticism, just a thought . . . it's an aspect you might do well to emphasize to James. It will likely add to his approval, and who knows, might earn you a wedding gift . . . maybe even that bauble of William's.'

'Hugh, in pearls?' Patrick raised an eyebrow.

'They would sell. The acquaintances, I trust they are worth the trouble of investing in their friendship?'

Robert's reversion took Hugh by surprise. 'So I've been advised.' Beginning to feel hot and dearly wishing to rub his hands on his hose, but fearing to do so lest it raised doubts of his truthfulness, he contemplated making mention of the man in the Cunninghame camp, but decided not. And so was much relieved when Robert said,

'Well, if I can be of assistance . . . but now, will you stay to dine?'

Hugh shook his head. 'We're bid to supper with Alexander.'

'A last drink then.' Robert filled the glasses for the third time. 'To good sport, and to advancement and . . .' as if to show that he had not forgot the kernel of their conversation, '. . . to circumspection in friendship.'

Hugh and Patrick walked back to their lodgings towards dusk, after a handsome meal. They had talked at length over supper, Alexander placing great store on the potential value of a successful chase and pleasing hospitality to follow. He stressed, to Hugh especially, the importance of ensuring that not only was the chase fast and furious, as befitted James' taste, but that James took rather more than his fair share of the kill without any obvious holding back of others. It was clear that the scheme had not been thought of on the spur of the moment, but rather simmered for some time. Hugh wondered, but didn't enquire, for what purpose Alexander had first conceived the plan, preferring not to know what private gains had been put aside to serve his needs.

As they came down Castle Wynd, Patrick said, 'This scheme of Alexander's. It's gey . . .'

'Well planned. I know.'

'Are you not curious?'

'If it was me, I don't think I'd welcome curiosity.' Hugh was scanning the sky. Out to the west, the sun dipped towards the horizon, and he watched the few clouds, strung out like strands of bog cotton, flood with colour. 'I think I begin to look forward to this hunt. It's long enough since we had the thrill of the chase.'

'Aye . . . well . . .' Patrick was more wary. 'Just remember whose is to be the major pleasure in this.'

'Is it not enough to endure Alexander's lecture? I don't need the kill to enjoy the thrill.'

'It may not all be thrills, and it isn't only James' temper you need look to.'

'William won't keep the pace, he will be that feart for his clothes and, for the rest, between us we can surely best them.'

'On our horses? Don't be so sure. The word is that Glencairn has hired the best that could be found – and intends to keep close to James, that he doesn't lose all benefit of the day.'

As they reached their lodging Hugh said, 'What of the man with William? Did you find him out?'

'Yes. He bides but a step from us and will be easy watched. With luck, I can contrive a meeting. Though from what I've learnt, forbye his discomfort this morning, he is a Cunninghame man, as his father and grandfather and more before him.'

'A Cunninghame man is one thing, William's is another, and maybe harder to thole.' Hugh opened the door of the taproom that gave onto the stair. 'If you can meet, casual-like, it wouldn't be a bad thing to have acquaintance in the other camp.

Chapter Eleven

Wednesday broke cool and clear, with scarcely a breeze.

Munro woke at first light, and feeling it politic not to present himself to Glencairn or William too early, chose instead to ride out to the crag east of the town. Despite his attempts to restrict the amount he had drunk, or perhaps as a result of the blow he had taken, he felt as if a farrier had set up shop in his head – his right temple the anvil – and hoped that the fresher air to be had away from the town might sort it. Concentrating on minimizing the jolting as he rode over the cobbles, he paid scant attention to the rider who trailed him out of the town and who, once the buildings dropped away, struck across the valley towards Cambuskenneth Abbey.

Reaching the foot of the crag, where the tail of the hill met the marsh, Munro tethered his horse to a tree and set out to climb to the top. Used as he was to tramping the hills around his own home, looking for stock that wandered, he found himself gasping as he cleared the trees and scrambled to the summit. He bent, his hands resting on his knees, while the pounding in his head slowed and the stitch in his side subsided. Across the valley the castle reared against the skyline, the town tumbling down the slope below, wisps of smoke beginning to unfurl, first one, then another, then too many to count, as Stirling awoke.

The countryside was spread out before him like a map;

the distant hills to the south-west purple thumbprints smudged against the watery sky; the river a dark ribbon snaking through the marshland below, cradling Cambuskenneth in a giant u-shaped loop. He noted the scattered areas of woodland and wondered idly where the hunt would take them. Which brought him to thoughts of the Montgomeries. He knew little of Braidstane, save what rumour made of him, and that not always reliable, though he could hardly be worse than William. He found himself hoping that the jaunt would provide the opportunity to make his own judgement.

Behind him, a muffled oath. He swung round to an explosion of feathers as a black grouse burst upwards, gliding in a wide arc before finding new cover. The man coming towards him was a little younger than himself, perhaps mid-twenties, with a mop of dark hair and a wide mouth that looked more suited to smiling than frowning. Munro narrowed his eyes, trying to place him – he had accompanied Robert Montgomerie in yesterday's charade. *Odd that he should come on me now, just as I thought on them.*

His own breath fully recovered, Munro was glad to see that the newcomer also peched, and was therefore disposed to be generous. 'It's a step. I was a mite out of breath myself.'

The other man laughed. 'Wings are better than legs for such a hill as this.' He looked back towards the valley floor, 'I fancied the fresher air, and it didn't look such a climb.' He massaged the backs of his calves; 'I near broke my neck over that bird.'

'It were well flushed, and would have made a fine breakfast, had I expected it.' Munro held out his hand. 'We haven't met, though I believe I saw you yesterday. Are you with the Montgomeries?'

'You could say that.' A flash of even, white teeth. 'Patrick Montgomerie, brother to Hugh of Braidstane and therefore part of that pretty play of James'. And you?'

'Munro.' He hesitated, 'Of the Cunninghame connection.'

Patrick scraped at a patch of lichen with his boot, 'We can't always choose our families.'

A momentary silence, Munro's smothered thought – if he knew the whole of it. . . .

Patrick said, 'Do you join us for the chase?'

'Aye, though I'm not sure my horse will stay the pace.'

'We have something in common then.' Again the flash of teeth. 'I would wish that I could have brought a horse from my regiment. They're aye well bred and handle fine.'

'A cavalry officer?' Munro felt a stab of envy.

'And would wish myself back where I belong, though . . .' Patrick's gaze switched to the opposite hill and the castle that topped it. '. . . With horses and with women I am most at home . . . and there are one or two women of the court I wouldn't mind handling.'

Munro laughed and they made down the hill together, parting companionably enough at the bottom where Munro's horse waited, cropping at the damp grass.

'You needn't wait for me,' Patrick waved vaguely southwards. 'I came from the Cambuskenneth side. I have a wee step yet to retrieve my horse. We may each be cosy with others the morrow, but it doesn't mean we can't think on friendship thereafter.'

Chapter Twelve

On Thursday Hugh woke again to the sound of dogs fighting in the street below and to the calling of a pedlar, the accent so thick that he couldn't make out what was sold. He moved to the window and tried with his sleeve to clear the glass, but succeeded only in smearing it further. Putting his shoulder to the frame and ignoring the splintering, he thrust his head out. The overhang of the upper storey impeded his view of the street, and whoever was making the racket was clearly tucked well in towards the wall, but as he breathed in he caught the yeasty tang of fresh bread. The light filtering into the room around his head roused Patrick, who stretched and yawned and swung his legs onto the floor.

Hugh said, 'There's a right good nip to the air, but little wind. We shall have a good run today, if so be that the quarry prove easy to flush.'

Behind him, Patrick relieved himself into the pot in the corner then turned his attention to the basin and ewer.

'Our good landlady is generous with water, I doubt a sparrow could make much of a job in this.'

'Have it all and welcome. I've no wish to wait around till the bread that has just been delivered be spoken for. I hold no great hopes of our host taking account of our needs if we don't present ourselves promptly.'

Patrick lifted his face from the basin and shook his head like a terrier, droplets flying. The sun, filtering through the open window, made a nimbus of the water that shone on his hair.

'St Paul himself wouldn't recognize you this morning, angel that you appear.' Hugh sidestepped the snap of the towel and headed for the stair, Patrick scrabbling for his doublet and tucking in his shirt-tails as he followed. The bread was surprisingly good, even without butter and Hugh bought a second farl to carry with him. After a brief stop at Alexander's lodgings, they collected their horses and reached the meeting point well before the time appointed with the King. Groups of riders in ones and twos were heading towards the open ground in front of the castle. Glencairn was among the first to arrive, his greeting to Alexander curt, almost to the point of rudeness. Hugh, he didn't acknowledge at all, pointedly turning his mount to face back towards the town, scanning the approaching courtiers.

Alexander's smile broadened with Glencairn's increasing unease. 'It isn't done to keep James waiting. Little wonder that Glencairn is champing. We are timely, and can only benefit further if William is not.'

Almost as he spoke, two riders emerged from the cover of the huddled dwellings of the lower town and began to make their way up the hill. Hugh felt a stab of disappointment as the ring of horseshoes on the cobbles warned of the approach of the King's party. William would make it, though by a whisker.

There was a general jostling as James reached the Esplanade. Alexander, who had established himself at the prime point to meet the King and who had indicated to Hugh to stay close, held back at the last, so that it was Hugh who made the first greeting. Tutored by Alexander, he did not dismount, but made a low bow.

'Your Grace, our party is complete. We need only your lead and we shall follow, though . . .' his brown eyes, wide and guileless, met James' '. . . we may not be able for your speed or skill.'

James accepted the compliment as his due. 'If I am to lead, our mystery destination must needs be revealed.'

'We are for Fintrie, sire, and have been promised the woods won't disappoint us.'

Pleasure flared in James' face. 'Then I trust they do not.' He touched his heels to the horse's flanks and leapt away, horse and rider alike straining.

At the foot of the hill, where the dwellings began to thin, he broke into a canter, the others streaming out behind. A flash of white caught the corner of Hugh's eye as a scrawny kitten shot straight from an alleyway towards the flurry of horses. Behind it a child; no more than three or four years old. William glanced sideways, looked towards James, spurred his horse on. One hoof caught the kitten under the belly, sending it spiralling onto a jumble of rocks, its piercing wail cut short. A louder wail as the child darted towards it. Munro tugged his horse round but Hugh was there first, reaching down and snatching the child, who kicked and bit and scratched at him. He turned out of the melee, and slid from the saddle, releasing the child, and returning, rescued the kitten. Its small head was tilted to the side, a trickle of blood at the corner of its mouth. Hugh hunkered down beside the child, passed over the limp body. She cradled it against her chest, rocking back and forwards. Hugh touched his hand to the kitten's neck, felt the faint pulse, and ran his fingers lightly over the shattered ribcage. He stroked the kitten's head, at the same time easing his thumb downwards until it rested on the windpipe. His eyes fixed on the child's bent head he pressed firmly until the pulse stopped. She was sobbing in earnest now, her small shoulders shaking. Hugh turned her towards the town. 'It's best you go home.' He rested his finger against the kitten's cheek, the warmth already draining out of her. 'She had no chance. It isn't your blame.' He gave the child a push towards the cluster of houses and swung back into the saddle. The tail end of the hunt party had passed them and Munro, who had held back, along with Patrick, merged into the stragglers. Although it had been a matter of minutes only, James and the leading riders were well ahead, William and Glencairn moving up fast. Hugh had reason to be sorry that his father's hunter was at home in the stable at Braidstane, no doubt becoming fat and lazy, while he pummelled away at the sorry nag that was the best to be had at short notice.

Reaching Alexander, Hugh saw that William had caught up with James. He urged the horse again, but was held back by Alexander.

'Bide your time, laddie. Don't press the beast too hard, the terrain we cover today will tax the best of mounts – something in reserve will, I think, serve us well.'

Alexander, although making every appearance of pushing his horse, was, in reality, holding him in check.

'Not much chance of pressing this one,' Hugh saw James favour William with a smile and some pleasantry that brought an answering smile in return. 'William makes capital at our expense. This was not, I take it, in the plan?'

'Of course not,' Alexander was brusque. 'We have a day ahead of us. The end will be better than the beginning, have no fear. Let William burn himself out in the preliminaries and do you make sure you are in at the finish.'

'And how,' Hugh, gave his horse, who showed signs of slowing further, another jab, 'do you suggest I achieve that on this beast?'

'I don't. Your poor beast will serve me well enough later and mine you. There is not the expectation on me to keep up with James – my talents are otherwise. We can exchange mounts once the real work starts. I suspect William will be less than pleased when he finds yours is the fresher horse. And though I cannot swear to it, it's likely Glencairn will give him blame if his horse fades before the finish. But still, I have no wish to end the day in walking, so content yourself with second place for now.'

Chapter Thirteen

At Greenock, it was a different sort of sport that concerned Elizabeth. The steward stood at the door of the solar, rabbits in one hand, his other firmly clasping the back of the urchin's ragged tunic.

'Janet cried me to the warren to choose a fine pair of bucks and there was this rogue bagging them as if they were his own.'

'Rogue, Hamish, hardly, he's only a child and not above five or six.'

The steward did not relinquish his grip of the lad. 'Old enough to know right from wrong.'

'There are different sorts of right and wrong.'

'Stealing's stealing whatever your age and he will do well to learn his lesson now, before he grows up to swing for it.'

The lad looked up at the mention of hanging and wriggled uneasily, hopping from foot to foot, so that she saw that his feet were not only dirty, but also criss-crossed with old scars. It was likely he came from one of the clutter of cottages that huddled on the fringes of the town, though she couldn't tell if she had ever seen him before.

'What matter a rabbit or two, and that probably the only meat the boy's family are likely to see this side of the fair. With half the household away, we have plenty and to spare. Leave the child to me. I'll reprimand him and send him on his way. And take the rabbits to the kitchen.' She

106

looked down. 'I don't wish to have them drip blood on my floor, more than I have already suffered.'

He turned and she saw by the set of his back that he didn't trust her to deal with the boy, but that his sense of loyalty, if not to her, at least to her position as temporary mistress of the house, meant that he would not openly question her authority. No doubt in the kitchens it would be a different matter. As he pressed down on the latch, she said, 'And would you take a look at Star. I thought this morning he was perhaps a little lame. Your opinion wouldn't go amiss.'

He clumped away, clearly not mollified, and pulled the door behind him so hard that it bounced open again. The child shivered in the draught and Elizaeth put out a hand towards him, but he shrank back, a flash of desperation in his eyes.

Her thoughts were not easy, for it was aye fine for a laird's daughter when food was scarce and prices were high; though they might tighten their belts a little, they didn't fear to starve. But for the cottars it was a different story. Through the child's thin clothes she could see his shoulder blades and hips protruding sharp and angular, his legs stick-thin. She thought of her brother John as a bairn and how he had fought them all for crying him 'Roly-poly'. This child was so skinny that he had scarce any flesh on him at all. Under his nose she saw the telltale trail indicating a constant discharge, and the whites of his eyes were stained the colour of pale urine. Her initial pity hardened into anger: against the steward for finding the lad; against society that made of eating a crime; and, most of all, against herself, that she upheld a system which she knew to be unjust.

'Don't fret, child, I have no mind to beat you.'

He looked up, still wary, wiped his nose on his sleeve. She avoided looking at the green gob, 'Come. There'll be a scrap or two in the kitchen you may eat and then you must be off. And remember,' she made her voice stern, 'it isn't well done to poach in other folk's warrens and foolish besides.'

In the kitchen, Janet, who had already heard from the steward of the child's capture, turned from stirring the contents of a heavy black pot. 'Save us,' she exclaimed, as she looked him up and down. 'It's feeding him we should be at, not taking food away from him.'

'We must be quick about it then, before Hamish is back to lecture us.'

Janet humphed, 'It's a sin the way he went on, and not long since he was poaching himself. Aye, and not just rabbits neither. Rising in the world has surely improved his conscience.'

She bustled in and out of the pantry, the child's eyes growing bigger as she clapped a loaf down on the table, cutting thick slices and spreading them with butter. Elizabeth saw his tongue slip from between small pointed teeth and skite quickly over his lips and caught a glimpse of gums that were unhealthily pale.

'Here.' She steered him over to the table and tried to press him onto the bench as Janet topped the bread with a slab of ewe's cheese. He remained standing, staring at the food, as if he thought that if he once blinked it would disappear.

'Eat, child,'

He shook his head, balling his fists at his side, as if he was afraid that they would grab the bread, whether he would or no.

'What ails you? You're surely hungry? Else why take the risk of raiding the warren?' She dropped down to his eye level, 'Would you rather we gave it you to take home?'

He uncurled his fists.

Elizabeth sliced and Janet buttered, and the child's eyes grew rounder and rounder. The loaf done, Janet disappeared, returning with a pail, newly sluiced, and wiped it dry. Elizabeth reshaped the loaf, wrapping it in a clean piece of muslin and, placing it in the pail, topped it with the remainder of the cheese. She rolled the child's fingers around the handle.

'There. Home, and don't dawdle, else someone may think you've stolen pail and food both.'

She waited only until he shot out through the gateway before calling for the stable lad, himself not much older than the child, but healthy and strong and bright withal. 'See to it that both child and pail are safely arrived. Note if you can, which of the cottages he comes from and don't hurry back: a little dilly-dallying may teach us something of his family circumstance.'

He nodded and grinned, betraying by the skip in his step that the errand was a welcome one and she determined that if news came back of a family in more than usual distress, she would conspire with Janet to ensure that some of their wastage went to fattening them, rather than the household stock. A mite less around a pig's middle would scarce be noticed in the butchering, but the waif had been nearer to a skeleton than a child.

It was unfortunate that he had strayed rather farther from home than she had anticipated, so was not the Shaws' direct responsibility, but that of a neighbour, Elliot, whom they hadn't seen since the previous Yuletide and only then because her father had looked to some trade advantage from his company. The rest of the family had groaned when told they were to entertain him overnight and she had found it hard to stifle her laughter when Christian, catching his tone perfectly, stood at the entrance to the solar and declaimed,

'My dear James, I trust we have not incommoded you by our little visit.'

Nevertheless, she intended to attempt to move him into improving the lot of his cottagers. It was a small step from that thought to consideration of wider responsibilities. With John in Glasgow on some business or other and unlikely to return before the week was out, she spent three days in wind and rain systematically covering the low-lying land along the Clyde shore. Each time she came upon an isolated cottage or a huddle of huts she stopped, on the pretext of a few moments' respite from the elements, and saw for herself the conditions the folk lived in. It was not a few days that she wished to repeat and each day, as she came home and warmed herself by the solar fire and had placed in front of her a good hot meal, her sense of guilt grew.

Her concern now firmly focussed on the whole area, she spent the next two days visiting each neighbour in turn. And although the weather had changed, so that she rode with the sun warming her back, the exercise in itself justifying the jaunts, at most of the tower-houses her visits were a surprise. Her parents still away from home, the majority of her neighbours, closer to their generation than her own, could hardly have anticipated her social call. In several cases she caught them so unawares that there was an obvious fluster to provide some refreshment.

As to the purpose of her visit: that became an increasing

frustration. In the face of polite disinterest, she paraded her ideas like penny pamphlets and with as little effect. There were no outright refusals, for there was no doubting that a general scheme of poor relief would likely result in less thieving and poaching, to the benefit of all. There was, however, a skilful side stepping of the issue, cloaked in pleasantries; and much talk of the need for the poor to merit the support they received from those of a better class. Mention everywhere was made of the wastrels who plagued the community, and the lack of control that produced families far in excess of what was reasonable. At house after house she was soothed and petted and in the politest of tones sent away empty. Some pledged to consult with her father on his return from the Low Countries, a ploy that she suspicioned was based on the premise that he would have less of the crusader about him. In which, of course, they were right.

In only one house did she approach achievement of her end, though at the first she had thought him as hopeless as the rest. Patrick Maxwell, a Cunninghame cousin and there-fore kin of a sort to her mother, received her in the great hall at Newark and she knew that the high ceiling, the fine French tapestries, the polished limestone chimney piece, all clear evidences of his standing, were not intended to be wasted on her. His hand when he greeted her was hot and moist and inwardly she recoiled from his touch. Mindful of her aim in coming however, she didn't pull away, rather glanced downwards as if shy. God forgive me she thought, but he is a fool, and may perhaps be tempted into a promise that he can't later avoid. She swept a low curtsey, lifting her eyes and opening them wide, accepting the chair that he set by a window looking across the Clyde. It was impossible not to admire the view: the broad expanse of dimpled water, the deeper green of the woods that strayed onto the opposite shore, the purple sweep of the mountains beyond. Equally impossible to refrain from comment. Yet a compliment would be but the truth and could pay dividends. 'You are well-set. It would be hard to be miserable faced with such a view.'

'And would happily share my good fortune.' He leant across her to name the hills, the highest Ben Lomond.

She took care not to shudder as his arm brushed her breast.

Initially, he blustered at the notion of the establishment of a warren on common land, pouncing on the problem of management.

'Why not the parish? It would be but a slight extension of their customary role.'

'Indeed. Though I hardly think the additional effort would prove popular.'

The soft mockery in his voice strengthened her determination. 'My other purpose is to canvas subscriptions for a fund to be plundered in times of scarcity.'

He edged closer to her. 'Fine ambitions, Elizabeth, but who has either the time or inclination to be Joseph?'

Inwardly, irritation flared. Outwardly, she kept her tone light. 'I thought the task could perhaps be shared. . .' A new expression in his eyes caused her to rise. 'But I see I have troubled you long enough.'

His tongue slid over his lips. 'On the contrary, the topic is most interesting and I am half-way to a convert. And may be convinced altogether by dinner time.'

She summoned a regretful smile. 'With my parents and John from home, I can't leave my sisters over long. The youngest is but a bairn.'

'You have servants – let them look to the bairn.'

This time her smile was genuine. 'It isn't the child's well-being that concerns me, but rather the mischief she might make.'

'Well, then, I am only sorry that I cannot oblige the now, but . . .' his tongue flicked out again, '. . . if you will favour me with another visit, I will be better placed to swell your purse.'

The capitulation took her by surprise and she had the uncomfortable thought that it had little to do with any feeling of prodigality towards the poor. Handing her up onto her horse, she felt the dampness of his palm and a small shiver took her. He pounced on it at once,

'It looks gey like rain. Bide a while, till you see what the weather may do.'

The courtesy lie stuck in her throat. 'Would that I could, but they look for me at home.' She passed through the arched pend of the gatehouse and raised her hand in farewell, her skin rising in goosebumps at the vigour of his answering wave. And in her head made an attempt at justification that the money was necessary and whatever he thought, she hadn't given him any real grounds to suppose she looked on him with favour. Yet fully aware that neither her brother nor her father would react well that she made herself beholden to Newark, however finely set he might be, she resolved to conclude the job before John's return from Glasgow. And as for Hugh, she had no wish to give him any grounds to become embroiled in another argument. That Patrick Maxwell was thick with William Cunninghame made caution the more necessary.

Two days later, she presented herself at Newark for the second time. As she was shown into the solar, she saw the disappointment in Maxwell's eyes and was glad that she had taken the precaution of bringing Christian. He rose to greet them, taking first Christian's hand and then, holding it longer than courtesy demanded, her own.

'No doubt you've come to call in my promise?'

'Indeed. You have promised to be most generous. I shan't forget that you were the first to see the need for some relief.'

He bowed. 'I hadn't expected the pleasure of your return quite so soon. The weather . . .'

She jumped in, eager to take charge of the conversation. 'We took advantage of the break in the rain that last night's sky promised. There are others,' she allowed her smile to deepen, 'not so willing as you, who have promised to consider the matter on my father's return from Holland. I would wish to present him with the tangible proof of your generosity, that he may be the more able to exert pressure in other quarters.'

'I applaud your forethought, Elizabeth.' He was pawing her arm and she took a half step back. 'Fortunately, I am in a position to make good my promise. But I must trouble you to wait a little.' His breath blew hot across her cheek. 'My steward returns this afternoon from Glasgow, and I will have monies then. In the meantime . . .' Forced to look upwards, she noted the hairs that curled inside his nostrils and took another half step backwards, coming up against a freestanding candle sconce by the side of the fire. He passed his hand around her to steady the sconce.

Christian, feigning a coughing fit, sank onto the bench

by the hearth, so that he was forced to drop his arm and call for water. He turned back to Elizabeth and waved his hand at the lad, 'Tell cook we are ready to eat. Our guests . . .' his teeth were small and sharp, like a weasel, 'are, I'm sure, hungry.'

. Though the hunger was all on one side and likely not for food, there was no room for protest. Elizabeth bore, with as much grace as she could muster, the intermittent warmth of his leg against hers each time he leaned to reach for a sweetmeat or a refill of ale. They had been seated for barely an hour when the door opened and the steward appeared.

'Ah, Hector, your return is timely. Mistress Shaw is come to plunder our purse to help the poor. I trust you had no problems carrying out our business?'

'None at all. I have the monies, though I hadn't thought to disperse them quite so soon.'

Maxwell frowned. 'That isn't your affair.'

Elizabeth pushed back her chair, made to rise.

He laid a hand on her arm, and she could fault neither his light touch, nor his voice, as he said, 'We'll do the business presently. You ladies haven't finished. I wouldn't wish to rush you away.'

Later, as they turned their horses out through the castle gateway Christian let out a long breath. 'It's a hard-earned five merks.'

'Well . . . it's done now . . . and will not be so again. A name or two on the list and no-one will think to ask how they got there.'

It was an uneasy ride. On any other day Elizabeth would have relished the freedom from noise and unwelcome attentions that skirting around Greenock would have ensured. But, less than comfortable with her own thoughts on the visit to Newark, she had no desire to hear Christian's on the matter, and so preferred the inconvenience and extra caution that picking their way through the narrow streets crowding the river required. Sun and moon both hung pale and almost indistinguishable in the darkening sky as their horses slithered their way across the quayside cobbles. The fish market was long since closed and they sought to avoid the litter of rotting fish-heads, the stench of them spilling into the back alleys that twisted upwards towards the terraced slopes to the west of the town. Empty creels were stacked at intervals along the harbour wall and the few fishermen still working at their boats, swilling down the decks or tidying sails, raised their heads only briefly as they passed. Most were already drinking the proceeds of the day's catch in one or other of the alehouses that lined the water's edge. The sound of them, scarcely less raucous than the gulls, rolled out through half-open casements: tuneless singing, raised voices, the splintering wood of an over-turned stool.

Elizabeth pulled sharply sideways as a door burst open and two men sprawled in front of her. They rolled over and over, until one raised his fist and knocked his opponent's head against the cobbles with a crack. Christian hesitated but Elizabeth reached out and tugged at her bridle. 'This isn't the time to look to someone else's trouble. There's danger enough in our own journey, and I have a mind to be home before it's full dark.'

They didn't look back.

Intermittent rain came in short flurries, blowing horizontally into their faces so that they bent their heads against it, trusting to the horses to find steady footing. Their father, however else he economised, did not spare silver when it came to finding a good mount, so though the horses also ducked their heads against the spiking rain, they made good time.

Settling down to a quiet meal in the solar, Elizabeth parried Gillis' questions. 'We have been making our collection for the poor relief.'

'You should have taken me. Father said that we should have fresh air.'

Elizabeth brushed a loose strand of Gillis' hair behind her ear. 'It wasn't an exciting day, nor a particularly pleasant one but,' as Gillis opened her mouth to protest further, 'if you wish to spend an hour or two sitting quiet, listening to adults wiggle their way out of making a contribution and then be made cold and wet by the ride home, I promise you shall accompany us next time.'

Gillis had listened only to the promise and jigged on her chair, her eyes dancing. And that was the sight that greeted John as he entered, holding his finger to his mouth, so that he was able to come up behind Elizabeth and place his hands over her eyes. She gave a start and felt the colour in her face, thinking for a moment it might be Hugh. Her prick of disappointment when she swivelled, immediately displaced by relief that she hadn't dallied on the road home.

'John, this is so good – we hadn't thought to see you tonight, for business aye takes longer than is supposed. Have you supped? Gillis, run down to the kitchens and tell Janet . . .'

John headed for the hearth. 'Clear as it is here, it was dreich in Glasgow.

'I know. We were near so . . .' She broke off, thankful that, concentrating on poking a blaze into the fire, he failed to notice her slip.

Christian, under the pretext of moving dishes aside to make room, whispered, 'It's as well you come clean, for I suspicion that Gillis won't be distracted from re-telling your promise for long.'

'I know. I will . . . only . . .'

John, admiring the flames now flaring on the hearth, cast a quick look towards them. 'What are you two whispering about? Have I missed something – a suitor for Christian perhaps?'

Christian flushed and looked away.

'Elizabeth?'

She was saved from answering by Janet's appearance with a tray, Gillis skipping behind her, a tankard, fortunately empty, tilted in one hand.

John sniffed at the bowl of rabbit stew, the steam forming beads of water on his nose. 'And I feared it might be scrapings only.'

Several times as he ate Elizabeth caught him watching her, but she steered the conversation along safe paths: the latest word from Holland; the new lambs that frisked in the temporary pens below the castle; the progress of the kittens that the tabby had dropped, not in the box that had been made ready for her, but in the linen chest, left open when Janet had been called away by an insistent knocking at the castle door.

'Which turned out to be a pedlar and one that she thought little of, so she sent him away with a flea in his ear, but not so quickly that she remembered the job half-done upstairs.' Christian set down her spoon. 'I found them, while taking Gillis to bed. We heard squeaking coming from the chest, and when we peeped in and saw the kittens, I dropped the candle and we were left in the dark, Gillis shrieking like a banshee.'

'And I flew up, thinking a leg broken at the least,' Elizabeth took up the tale. 'I came upon Christian kneeling on the floor, a bundle of soft fur in her lap, which, on closer inspection, proved to be four bundles, with eyes tight shut and tiny mouths that sucked on her skirts, mewling for lack of their mother's teats.'

Gillis cut in, 'They're in a box in the stable, though the tabby has three times tried to carry them back into the warmth of the kitchen.'

Elizabeth stroked Gillis' hair. 'And this lady has been at Janet all day to let them bide.'

'But she won't!' Outrage in Gillis' voice made them laugh.

John wiped the last remnants of stew from his plate with the heel of a loaf, while Gillis hovered at his elbow, desperate to accompany him to the stable to show off the latest additions to their household. Elizabeth shooing them downstairs before John could resume his questioning. He was like a dog with a bone when something caught his attention, and she wished to give herself a little time to prepare a suitable answer.

'You have your story ready?' Christian's voice betrayed a nervousness that pricked at Elizabeth's conscience. 'I'm not the best at hiding things, especially,' she looked into the fire, 'when I'm not sure that what was done was wise.'

'Say nothing then, and leave it to me. You know I have never yet landed myself in something I couldn't handle, and I won't fall at such a ganch as Patrick Maxwell.'

Chapter Fourteen

As the hunt party approached the woods that stretched out to the south and east of Fintrie, the King reined in his horse. Behind him William, with Munro at his side and a little to their rear, the Montgomeries.

'Is it beast or rider, I wonder, that falls so readily behind?' William's comment, directed at Munro, was just loud enough that it was unclear whether or not he meant the Montgomeries to hear.

Munro saw Patrick shoot a warning look at Hugh, who addressed himself to adjusting his stirrup.

Again, the low drawl, 'A pity that our host cannot make the pace. But hardly surprising seeing that his mount is poor and he had, I believe, little in the way of silver to bargain with and no contacts of note.'

Hugh, clearly aware of William's comments, but managing to ignore them, allowed his horse to slip sideways, bringing him up on James' left.

Seeing the smile that James bestowed on him, Munro said, 'I wouldn't bait Braidstane in James' hearing.'

William's lip curled. 'I dare say you wouldn't. But I think I'm qualified to judge for myself.'

'See that your judgement doesn't fail then.' Glencairn had reined in on William's other side.

Munro switched his attention back to James.

'Your Grace,' Alexander's voice carried. 'We have been bid to take a cup before the chase. The lady of the house,

Mistress Graham is prepared for our arrival, and will send us on our way warmed, that we may make a good day of it thereafter.' He indicated a track that skirted the wood. 'If I may suggest . . .'

James was impatient. 'Yes, yes, out with it, man.'

'It will be better sport if we don't disturb the woods too soon. And though this track is a little longer, it will give the horses some respite. Not that your mount requires such consideration, but . . .' he indicated his own horse, which, in truth, he held very firmly in check lest it betray more vigour than he wished, '. . . others of us are not so fortunate.'

An expression of irritation passed across James' face so that Munro thought for a moment that Alexander had played it wrong. Then the King laughed and the danger was past.

'Lead on then. We shall allow you to set the pace for now, but don't expect us to wait when the work begins.'

Alexander inclined his head and swung his horse round.

James looked first at Hugh and then towards William. His voice was satin-smooth. 'Do you two ride by my side. We shall see how you sit your new friendship.'

They moved off, James riding squarely in the centre of the track so that both William and Hugh had the disadvantage of uneven ground.

Munro kept his distance, almost missing the sidestepping of William's horse and his hasty apology as the King reacted swiftly.

'Maybe Cunninghame, you need to draw back, lest my horse is harmed and the day not started.' A pause, a hint of malice, 'Braidstane and I will rub along rightly for the now.'

Munro settled far enough from the front to distance himself from either faction, but close enough to keep a clear view of the foremost riders. Although he couldn't hear what was said, he prepared to enjoy the rivalry between William and Hugh. Behind him he could hear Patrick Montgomerie conversing with the Master of Gray, who had the dangerous privilege of being a rising favourite. He trotted along and allowed his thoughts to drift: to the likely length of the day and the stamina of his horse, without a doubt the least promising of those he had hired, and therefore the probability of missing out on at least some of the chase. To William and Hugh. To home, the bairns and Kate. To William and Hugh – would serving one be any different from the other? Perhaps: if the ragged child with the injured kitten was anything to go by. Patrick Montgomerie seemed likeable enough. But then so was John Cunninghame. And none of his affability evident in William. Automatically he pressed his horse, and although she snorted and tossed her head in surprise, she responded. Surprised in turn, he found himself coming up on William's left.

'Still with us?' William glanced at Munro's horse. 'By her looks, maybe not for long.' They were rounding the edge of the wood and Fintrie Castle was in view, her towers topping the rise, the sun catching on the newly glazed casements.

'I've ridden better but . . .' Munro looked ahead to James and Hugh, '. . . I'm not in competition.'

The hunt party gathered themselves in the courtyard, horses and riders alike refreshed by their halt. Munro saw that Hugh waited a little to the side, his horse more restive than had appeared earlier. Patrick was working his way round towards him and under the pretence of settling his own horse Munro too circled the group, to finish within earshot of the Montgomeries if he strained.

Hugh's good humour was evident. 'The woods, I trust, will serve as well as the hospitality. I hadn't guessed a poet could be so useful an ally.'

'Nor I, but,' Munro saw Patrick glance around as if to check that none who mattered were listening and so bent his head as Patrick continued, 'I wouldn't grin so widely, Hugh. You look as if the day is already yours and the hunt not yet begun.'

Hugh looked down at the dust his horse scuffed up.

Patrick continued, 'William isn't so stupid as his interest in clothes might indicate and if I were you I wouldn't wish to risk the end game. Our cousin has played James well, and you are set fair to reel him in, so be it you don't jerk the line.'

James spurred his horse, gesturing for all to follow and they funnelled through the gateway and down towards the beckoning woods. Munro in the rear saw that William, caught unawares by the speed of James' departure, was seeking to move up through the pack, but was blocked by Patrick, seemingly oblivious to the rider behind him. Munro was surprised to see that Hugh didn't press forward, but allowed himself to jog along halfway back. It was an interesting, if unexpected, ploy – he doesn't wish to push his horse, fearing that it won't last the course? Perhaps, though it looks eager enough. Munro flicked his gaze to Alexander and back again. – So that was the game. How long till William realises? I won't be the one to tell him, tempting though it is.

Out of the corner of his eye, he saw Patrick fan out to

the left, William surging forwards to take his place. Others blocked his passage now and Munro saw him jab with his boot at a grey with white fetlocks. It started sideways and William raised his hand in apology to its rider as he kicked his horse past. The pace in front was quickening, the hounds along with the foremost riders already swallowed by the trees. Hugh's horse sprang forward, a loud blast of the horn alerting them to the flushing of fresh quarry. Alexander, checking his mount, allowed Hugh to slip through the gap, so that he came up on James' left in time to match the King's surge.

James acknowledged Hugh's presence with a sharp glance, somewhat moderated by his warm tone, 'Ha! Braidstane.'

Munro admired Hugh's timing, but seeing William's ill-disguised scowl, kept his face blank and dropped back. All around was the baying of hounds and the sound of horses crashing through the undergrowth. He listened to the crack of fallen branches, the squelch of hooves sucked into boggy ground, the soft whinnying as they wove in and out of the trees. The pack was now together, now apart, each rider straining to follow as closely as possible the trail led by the hounds. He caught glimpses of Hugh: near enough to James to give the appearance of competition, yet without passing him. Now a little behind, now level, occasionally moving either to the right or the left, but always when they came together contriving to be just a fraction in James' wake. The first run was fast, taking little over ten minutes for the hounds to bring their quarry to ground. It was a young roe deer, which stood quivering in a small clearing, surrounded by dogs held in check by the master. When Munro broke from the cover of the trees he was in time to see James drawing a bow and despatching it with an arrow through the heart, before dropping from his horse to rest his boot on the deer's flank and pull the arrow free. Blood spurted and James turned towards Hugh, grasping his bridle with a bloodied hand, 'Well, well, Braidstane, a goodly start to the day.'

The hounds had barely begun to nose in the dense undergrowth before they were away again, flooding out of the clearing in the direction they had come, the sound of the horn re-echoing through the woods. James flung himself back into the saddle and wheeled round, so that the riders who had bunched up behind him had to pull their horses aside to let him through. In the ruck one unfortunate courtier pressed too close and was rewarded with a glower and an oath that his apology did nothing to deflect. Hugh was boxed in and unable to take up his previous position, but Munro saw by his smirk that he took some small comfort from the fact that it was a Cunninghame who had so annoyed James. A smirk that quickly changed to a frown as William cut in as James passed, daring others to intervene. He matched James' pace as they flowed across the open ground following a four-year-old buck. And so it was William who, when the buck suddenly turned back on himself and shot off sharply to the left, was best placed to head him off, running him towards James, presenting the opportunity for a clean kill.

Thus it was throughout the early part of the afternoon: now Hugh, now William, who shadowed the King, each taking opportunity when it came to make a kill, but contriving to leave the choicest prey for James to bring down.

Munro found Patrick beside him.

'Honours even, I'd say.'

Munro ran the reins down his horse's neck, skiting off streaks of white lather. 'Fortunate that Braidstane has a fresh mount, else William would have it.'

'You must admit it was neat.'

'Indeed. And you, I see, have recovered sight and hearing, both of which seemed lacking earlier.'

'Oh, my ears aye block in certain kinds of company. It's a shocking inconvenience, I know.'

'One that sits easy on you.'

They had fallen back, the main pack now some distance ahead.

Patrick sobered. 'We should rejoin the pack. There are those who wouldn't appreciate us keeping company.'

'Aye, though I don't know if I can make up the ground.' Munro patted the horse's head, as if to show him he bore him no ill will. 'Speed doesn't seem to be his strongest suit.'

Late in the afternoon the wind, until then scarcely a breeze, picked up and veered to the north, clouds boiling on the horizon. As most of the earlier runs had been flushed on the northern side of the woods, the master pulled the hounds around to work from the southern edge, so that they remained downwind of any quarry. Munro, his horse clearly flagging, found himself equally envious of Hugh and William, both matching the pace easily. Seeing Alexander also trailing made him wish that he could have found so convenient a change of mount and set him thinking on the character of a man whose family so readily put themselves out to serve his interests. Watching James become more and more animated as the tally of kills increased, Munro suspicioned that despite William's efforts, the day would be the Montgomeries'.

The party was thinning. Some of the riders, finding their horses grown sluggish, were forced to head back to Fintrie. Munro, aware that his mount hadn't much more to give, weighed up the danger of remaining and perhaps ending the day on foot, against his desire to watch the contest between William and Hugh played out to the end. And chose to stay. Ahead of him, the horn sounded again, and he saw James swing away to the right. Hugh was neck and neck with him, William caught unawares by the sudden turn. They disappeared into the trees and Munro turned to follow, contenting himself with a gentle canter. It was the longest run of the day, ending in the bringing down of a fine stag with grey-streaked fur and eight-pointed antlers.

Munro made the clearing just as the sky directly above began to darken. He halted at the edge of the trees and steadied his horse against the sudden flash of light that speared into the ground ahead of him. Automatically, he counted the seconds before the rumble of thunder – three miles: time to get back to the safety of Fintrie before the brunt of the storm and likely enough leeway to ensure that the kill was also safely transported.

Hugh glanced upwards as the first heavy spots of rain splashed onto the ground and gestured Patrick forward. 'Stay with the stag until it be prepared.' Then to James, 'If it please you, sire, we should perhaps make for the castle and shelter. We have done justice to these woods. And though, no doubt, there is more to be had,' he waved his arm at the pewter sky, 'It would be a pity to catch a fever in the taking.'

James was standing over the stag admiring the antlers,

no doubt imagining them mounted on the wall of his bedchamber, or fashioned into a fine set of cutlery. Just as he seemed about to over-rule Hugh, the rain came down in earnest, a curtain blotting out the surrounding woods.

James scratched at his groin, a smile creeping over his face, 'It hasn't been a bad day at all. And yon fellow,' indicating the stag, now being trussed ready to be dragged away, 'is a fitting end to it.'

The hall at Fintrie, though roomy enough in normal circumstances, was strained to bursting with the hunt party. Munro squeezed onto a bench beside William, who shifted along a fraction commenting, 'Your horse wasn't up to much. Did you see any of the kills?'

Munro ignored the mockery. 'I didn't have the advantage of your mount.' Then thoughtlessly, 'Though Braidstane's seemed to match.' And remembered, too late, both the boast he had made to Glencairn about the hiring of the horses and that William was likely still unaware of Alexander's ruse.

'And whose blame is that? If I recollect aright, our horses were to be the best . . .' William's gaze shifted to the top of the table, his eyes darting between Alexander and Hugh.

Munro kicked at the rushes under his foot – why could I not keep my mouth shut? The trick may have been Braidstane's but the fault'll be mine.

William smashed his fist on the table, sending a tankard spinning.

John Cunninghame glared at him 'It would be ill done, nephew, to raise a rumpus in this company, and foolish besides.'

'Well seen the Montgomeries had to resort to a cheap trick. We would have bested them else.'

It was so close an echo of what Munro had said to Patrick, though not the sentiment intended, that he flushed, but William was oblivious to all feelings but his own.

'See to it they do not beat us that way again.'

Oh, aye, Munro thought, it's that easy.

John's lips barely moved, his words coming out as a hiss, 'Keep your voice down, William. We don't wish to draw attention.'

Servants began to place steaming platters on the tables and James, his eyes glistening, broke a momentary hush in the general hubbub. 'We are grateful for your hospitality Mistress Graham. Montgomerie is fortunate in his friends.'

William dug the point of his dirk into the table, so that John, his eyes fixed on James, reached across and gripped his wrist. Munro saw the colour bleed out of William's hand until he was forced to release the dirk, John sliding it into his own doublet, saying,

'I take it you can be trusted with a spoon?'

Munro was not best suited to long, formal meals, preferring the more relaxed atmosphere that home provided, and William's ill-humour did little to aid the situation. An ill-humour that became increasingly evident as they listened to James rehearse again and again the thrills of the chase, expressing his pleasure in it and his regret that he couldn't extend the outing. Glencairn was seated on Robert Montgomerie's left and what little entertainment Munro found in the proceedings came from observing the forced civility that their close proximity to James required. It was clear that James enjoyed toying with them, like a cat having cornered two mice at once. Patrick, on the far side of the table near the top, caught Munro's eye, as if he too found the spectacle amusing. There was a burst of laughter from Hugh and an answering bellow from James.

William stiffened. 'Look at them, laughing with James as if they were all that took the honours of the day, my share in it forgotten.'

Much as Munro would have enjoyed to see William fall foul of James, it carried risk for them all, so he said, 'James is in a mood to play. It is enough that he baits your father. The Montgomeries ride high today; tomorrow they may fall.'

'If we have anything to do with it.'

'Take care that we do not,' John spoke up. 'Whatever you feel, William, it behoves us to play it canny. This friendship wasn't lightly sworn and mustn't falter, neither in appearance, nor in fact. If you can't at least look as if you hold to it, then maybe it's best you find some excuse to go home.'

'I don't need any excuse.' William swung his leg over the bench, but was once again restrained by John.

'For pity's sake, not the now. James isn't finished, so neither are we.'

The skeletal remains of quail and partridge were replaced by crowns of beef and lamb cutlets each drowned in rich gravy; accompanied by side dishes piled high with roast vegetables. Conversation faded to an intermittent rumble, punctuated by the occasional complementary belch. The serious business of supper had begun. The table, laid waste for the second time, was cleared again, to make way for clear jellies and candied fruits and hot cinnamon pastries dotted with almonds, served with jugs of thick cream.

Replete, Munro saw Alexander lean towards Hugh and speak into his ear. Hugh stood, causing a lull in the conversation that passed up and down the table, and in the ensuing hush, broached his matrimonial plans. Munro was aware of renewed tension in William and was impressed afresh at the Montgomeries manipulation of the situation, though he was careful that nothing of what he thought showed in his face.

James, as well fed, as he was satisfied with the day's sport, boomed his blessing. 'Make it soon, man, and we shall be pleased to attend. We will be glad to see this sore with the Cunninghames plastered over in so pleasant a fashion.'

Hugh bowed, keeping his head down a fraction longer than necessary so that Munro wondered if he sought to conceal dismay at the prospect of the King as part of his wedding celebrations. And who would blame him? For it would likely make of it an expensive business.

James turned back to Glencairn. 'A wedding gift wouldn't go amiss. No doubt you . . .' his glance travelled the length of the table, '. . . or William, will have a bawbee and to spare.'

There was a moment of silence before Glencairn dipped his head in acknowledgement. Munro swallowed a grin. James raised his tankard, everyone else hastily following suit. 'To Braidstane and his bride . . . and to the chase. It is a fine gift you gave, Montgomerie, gey fine. . .' and, with a pointed glance towards William, '. . . baubles are very well, but I won't forget, when the occasion arises, who it is that can procure such sport.'

Chapter Fifteen

There were a few sore heads on the following morning as the hunt party assembled for the return to Stirling. Munro was not one of them. He had risen from supper as soon as James had retired, leaving William, by this time more maudlin than angry, wheedling from a servant 'another wee mouthfu to see him right'. He had sought, and been given permission from Glencairn to return home: the lambing not finished and the calving already begun. Now, milling in the courtyard waiting for the King to appear, he thought on his poor showing in the hunt and his lack of Sweet Briar and he determined he would not go home without reclaiming her however inconvenient and time consuming a detour to Clonbeith might be. He noted the Montgomeries gathered by the gateway and drifted to within earshot. Hugh was airing a worry to Alexander regarding his proposed marriage.

'My stock with James Shaw isn't so high that I wish the risk of adding to the expense of the thing.'

Alexander seemed untroubled. 'Have no fear, it will be a small matter to choose a wedding date that you may proceed in a simpler fashion than the King's presence would dictate. Leave the choosing to me and I'll make sure it doesn't turn him sour.'

'You prove your use again, uncle. My debt mounts.'

'Keep the ground gained, and I shall be satisfied.'

James appeared in the doorway. Alexander dropped his voice so that Munro strained to hear him.

'Go home and prepare for your wedding and I shall write a poem for your lady that will stand against any in the country. But don't delay your arrangements long, for I may not be able to give you much notice of the most propitious date.'

Mounted, the King beckoned Hugh and Alexander, 'Do you two ride with me.' I shall not press the horses too hard.' This to Alexander. To Hugh, he said, 'It was a fine day, and won't spoil in the retelling. I have a mind to go over it again.'

Munro noted that the Montgomeries also had a change of horses and so presumably had made similar arrangements for the return of the hired mounts.

'If it please you,' Alexander was conspiratorial. 'Hugh has wedding plans to further, and is expected daily at Greenock.'

A ghost of a frown flitted across James' face, then cleared. 'Aye, you're excused. The lady I daresay will enjoy hearing tell of yesterday's sport. But mind,' he was smiling now, 'mind in the telling whose was the best kill.'

As the last of the courtiers exited the gateway, Patrick crossed to Munro. 'I believe you make for Clonbeith. We travel the same road, for a while at least. Shall we ride together?'

Munro indicated Hugh. 'If I don't intrude?'

'No intrusion for a friend of Patrick's. But if we are to ride together, we mustn't stay strangers. Hugh Montgomerie, Mas. . .'

Patrick chipped in, 'It's 'Braidstane' just, though you wouldn't think it to look on him. And this is Munro. He took the same foolish notion as myself the day before yesterday and we met on the Abbey Crag. Though I don't think I was as peched as he.'

Hugh snorted, 'That'll be right.'

With Patrick by his side Munro looked down towards the woods that swallowed the last of the party headed for the court. 'I think,' he said, 'the air in the west may be cleaner than in Stirling.'

Ahead of them, Hugh had broken into a canter.

For a moment the lack of reply made Munro regret the hint.

Patrick touched his heels to his horse, 'Air is always fresher among friends.'

The stop at the clothiers in Glasgow was brief. Patrick rifled through bales of fabric with a practised ease, recommending in the end an emerald brocade, which Hugh bought and paid for without questioning the cost; Munro, guessing that it was a present for the intended bride. Hugh led them through narrow wynds, twisting and turning, so that Munro lost all sense of direction. There was the sound of running footsteps and a series of shots in an alleyway to their left. Patrick was nearest, his horse rearing. Gripping firmly with his knees, he leaned forward and laid his head against the horse's neck, directing a stream of soothing murmurs towards her ear, until she steadied, flanks heaving. He kept up the soft flow without pause, drawing long, slow strokes from her mane to her withers until her quivering stopped.

Munro grinned a compliment. 'You have a way with you right enough. With horses and women, you said . . .'

Patrick grinned back. 'D'you want a lesson? In either?'

'I can handle my horse, and as for women, I have a wife.'

'And has she eyes? Well then, a wee bit spoil will bring the sparkle back.'

Munro thought of the chill that had sprung between Kate and himself in the aftermath of Annock.

'Long married?'

'Four years.'

'And bairns?'

'Twins. A boy and a girl. Of nearly three.'

'And have you presents for them all?'

'I didn't think. I was that keen to get home.'

Patrick shook his head, but his eyes twinkled.

'I make for Braidstane, but Hugh is for Greenock to his bride-to-be and will bide there the night. It has a ween of shops where you could find a wee pickle that would pass.'

'The Shaws. They won't object to an extra guest?'

'If you arrive with Hugh, I think you could be a Mohammedan and they wouldn't care.'

Gillis was playing with a hoop in the barmkin when Munro and Hugh broke from the trees onto the grassy knoll surrounding Greenock castle. Their first sight a bright head appearing over the curtain wall, short blond pigtails sticking out on either side like handles. She disappeared briefly to reappear in the gateway, shouting for John, Christian, Elizabeth . . . anyone, to come. She stood very straight, the long stick that belonged by rights with the hoop, now brandished as a makeshift weapon, and barred the gate, demanding they declare themselves before she could allow them to enter. Munro, amused, held back, allowing Hugh to reach her first. Feisty as she appeared, she was but a wee bit thing and might take fright at a stranger. Hugh dismounted and bowed, sweeping off his hat and allowing it to trail on the ground at her feet.

'Mistress Shaw: Hugh, of Braidstane, at your service.'

She stood her ground.

Seeing the careful gravity of Hugh's expression, Munro bent his own head to conceal the twitch of his lips.

Hugh dipped his head again. 'We wish you no ill, lady.'

She leapt at him and he birled her round so fast that her slippers flew off and landed at the feet of a slim lass, who Munro judged to be twenty or thereabouts, hovering at the castle door.

'This is a surprise.' Her voice was husky, as if she recovered from a chill.

Hugh made to put the child down, slipperless or not, but she clung around his neck, and a smile passed between Hugh and the lass over the child's head. Munro noted the hazel flecks in her brown eyes and her auburn hair, shining like a well-groomed roan – this then was the girl for whom Hugh sweated in the clothiers over the choice of a brocade. Patrick is right, green will suit well. He held back, unsure of his welcome, despite what Patrick had said. That there was something between Hugh and the girl, whether formally acknowledged or not, was evident, and he was amused to see the tinge of pink that crept into Hugh's cheeks. It seemed to Munro that she struggled not to laugh.

'There is something wrong surely and it barely a week gone since we saw you last. I hadn't expected you for a year at least.'

'Debts weigh heavy on me, Mistress, though . . .' Hugh

shifted the child from one shoulder to the other, '. . . not half as heavy as some.'

Munro looked away, for watching them felt uncomfortably like intrusion. He was still studying the state of his boots when Hugh pulled him forward.

'I should have introduced you. Elizabeth Shaw, to whom I owe a gown, and Gillis, the youngest and . . .' Hugh tweaked one of Gillis' braids, '. . . pawkiest of her sisters. This is Munro – we rode together from Stirling. He makes for Renfrew the morn, but has an errand that takes him to Clonbeith, so I offered him a bed on your behalf.'

A trickle of sweat ran down Munro's spine – if she was to enquire . . . Elizabeth held out her hand, 'My apologies, you must think me rude, chiding an old friend before welcoming a guest.'

He bent over her slender fingers and for a moment was back at Langshaw, greeting Lady Margaret, the message from Glencairn burning in his throat. But when he felt the roughness of her palm, indicating that laird's daughter or not, she didn't spend her days in leisure just, the moment passed. 'I trust I don't intrude?'

She directed her smile at him, but he had a feeling that she chose her words for Hugh. 'Any friend of Hugh's is a friend of ours also.' She slid Gillis' slippers onto her feet, and set her down. The lad began to lead the horses towards the stable as Hugh, pivoting on his heel, pulled at the cord that held the plump package strapped to the saddle.

'Now that one weight is removed, I wish to discharge another, that I may sleep undisturbed at night.'

'Indeed. Well then, I trust it will serve that purpose, even if no other.'

'I trust it will serve at least one other function.'

She took the package and Munro again felt a sense of intrusion as their fingers touched. He turned away to study a pair of gulls on the barmkin wall who squabbled over a crust – she reminds me of Kate: not short on spirit.

She retraced her steps to gather Munro up, the parcel stowed under her arm. 'We have dallied long enough. Christian will be crying me all sorts for keeping you out here in the cold. I'm sure you're ready for a bite.'

He answered her, smile for smile, 'That I am – the breakfast at Fintrie was adequate, I can't say else, but it was a while ago and the journey extended somewhat by our stop in Glasgow. The clothier clearly didn't have much regard for Hugh's knowledge of fabrics. It's a blessing that Patrick was there to aid in the choice.'

'That isn't quite the experience I look for in Hugh, or not yet awhile.'

In the lull between their arrival and the serving of supper, Munro sat by the fire playing cats-paw with Gillis. Opposite him Christian blushed each time he caught her eye. Gillis, tiring of the game, disappeared onto the stair and Munro heard the slip-slap of her slippers on the stone steps and the muffled creak of a door. It was a matter of moments only before she burst back into the hall.

'Hugh and Elizabeth are by the caphouse, and Hugh has lent her his jerkin.'

Christian turned from the laying of the table. 'Well? It's a mite chilly. Earlier I felt the need of some air, and was likewise unprepared.' She took Gillis by the hand. 'You can help with the bringing of the dishes. It will all be ready I'm sure.' And ignoring the child's scowl, marched her towards the door.

Munro stared into the fire – how these sisters look to

each other. As it should be, of course. But not always so. Hugh reappeared and Munro searched his face for telltale signs of a job well done, chiding himself as he did so – why should I care? I scarcely know them. Though I can't help liking them both. Elizabeth reappeared, but as she carried nothing, Munro knew that it wasn't from the kitchens she came. She gestured him to the table.

'I trust you aren't famished with the wait.'

'You had other, more pressing affairs to see to?' He drew the suspicion of a smile, and thought of Kate, who had that same ability to convey much in the twitch of a lip. It would be easy to see them friends.

Gillis sidled in, tongue protruding between her teeth, carefully balancing a jug of ale in both hands, John hard on her heels. Elizabeth moved swiftly to take it from her, but Gillis jerked back so that ale splashed on the stone flags.

Her face puckered into a frown and she stamped her foot. 'See what you made me do – Janet said I could carry it myself and I was careful.'

Munro stifled his laugh, for there was some justice in the complaint, and though it didn't do to countenance rudeness in a bairn, he could tell by Elizabeth's tremor that she likewise struggled.

'Put it down else there will be more spilt than saved. And run and wash your hands.'

Gillis put them behind her back. 'They don't need.'

Elizabeth scrubbed at an imaginary mark on the palm of her hand, 'Well, mine do. We'll do them together.'

For Munro the evening that followed was a blur of good food laced with laughter, so that he had a wish that Kate was there to share in it. Not a feeling he'd ever had at Kilmaurs.

Hugh chose the moment as Elizabeth was gathering Gillis for bed, to stand up and rap on the table. John jumped up.

'I see she has landed you at last. Though whether my father will look with favour on such a troublesome addition to the family . . .'

Hugh made a show of protest.

'You needn't fear. I'm not keen to cross Elizabeth if she's a mind, and I doubt father has a stouter heart. Or you for that matter – are you sure you know what you're taking on?'

It was Elizabeth's turn for mock anger. 'I don't need an enemy to speak ill of me, for my own brother does it well enough.'

Munro, laughing with the rest, turned his head sideways in time to see Gillis, who had been pulling on Elizabeth's arm and demanding to know what John was talking about, finally lose patience. She screwed up her face, opening her mouth as wide as she could and screeched at the top of her voice. The effect was instant.

With everyone's attention on her, she stared hard at John, 'No-one has asked me if I want another brother.'

'Nor Hugh if he wants a corncrake for a sister'

Hugh bowed to Gillis, 'And do you wish it, lady? And will I serve?'

She cocked her head to one side like a sparrow, her expression severe. 'I dare say there could be worse . . .' then stamped her foot when everyone around her dissolved again into laughter. She prepared to repeat her earlier performance but Elizabeth tugged her plait, 'Before I am to have a husband, I must needs have a maid. Do you think you can do that?'

The conversation broke then, words flying like shuttles,

humorous and atrocious in equal measure, with Hugh, and Elizabeth, when she slipped back to her place, in the midst of it all and perfectly at ease. Afterwards Munro lay on the pallet in the small chamber above the solar, listening to Hugh snoring rhythmically beside him, thoughts of the past few days killing sleep – how easy they are. How easy I am with them. He thought of Broomelaw. And of Kate who had been first his friend, before his wife and lover. Who he had thought, wrongly, all softness and dimples, with hair lustrous as a raven's wing. Who was totally without malice, yet had a core of steel. Who wasted no words, but armed with a quiet intelligence that under-pinned everything she did or said, could slice into his soul with all the precision and efficiency of a well-judged sword thrust. Who had made a home of their modest tower-house, warm and secure. And who would see danger in his current ease. He thought on the bairns; perhaps Kate's greatest weapon: Robbie, fine-boned and dark, his mother incarnate; Anna, small and sturdy and feisty yet. Falling into an uneasy sleep, his dreams disjointed and irrational, he woke to the memory of his own words to William on his return from Langshaw. 'Your father is a dangerous man to cross . . .' And as he took his leave and rode for home, regret at what couldn't be dragged at him, like an anchor snagged on weed.

Chapter Sixteen

Elizabeth was leaning on the barmkin wall, shading her eyes against the late afternoon sun.

Behind her, John's footfall. 'It is a goodly thing you do. Hugh has long had need of a wife, and one that he can trust withal.'

She thought of the visits lately made to Newark, and of how she had not yet explained that circumstance and how it were as well she did before she was forced to tell their father. She picked at the lichen on the capstone, now was as good a time as any. 'I meant to tell you, Christian and I made some visits while you were away, and have contracted that father will make others, so soon as he returns.' John, his thoughts still on Hugh and the wedding and therefore not entirely listening, queried,

'Visits?'

Encouraged, she continued before his concentration improved sufficiently to protest. 'There was a child . . . he was taken stealing from the warren . . . we fed him and sent him away, but . . . it's a shameful thing that there are folk half-starved, and we wasting more than many families have to eat altogether. I set about raising a collection.'

Something of her words seemed to penetrate. 'What?'

'A collection: from those of our own class, to provide aid for the unfortunates who, through no fault of their own, find themselves with less than enough food. To tide them through to harvest just, and ensure that they don't start the winter half-starved.'

She had his full attention now. 'So that was your secret. Do you think that father will look kindly on you begging from our neighbours, even if it isn't for ourselves?'

'I couldn't just ignore him.' Then, as a softening, 'And neither could you if you'd been here. The child was just a rickle of bones and gey feart. At least we thought at first he was too feart to eat when offered, but then I said he could take the food away and he was that pleased.' She pictured the waif running off down the valley, the pail of bread hugged to his chest. 'I haven't asked for much, and in truth have got less, though some have promised to think on it, and to speak to father on his return. Maxwell has been generous.'

Under her fingers his muscle hardened. 'Maxwell? For why was he so ready to loose his money? He is no philantrop.'

This was difficult water. 'I think that the moment I picked was right. His steward was but lately returned from some trading deal: sufficiently successful that he was disposed to be helpful. I didn't stay long.' She found herself flushing at the remembrance of his hand on her arm and his breath hot on her cheek. 'Indeed, I won't look to go a-begging there again, for to find him so kindly disposed another time would be to expect too much.'

'And how many of our near neighbours have you seen fit to hector on their responsibilities to the poor?'

'Not hector, John. It was all done in the best of spirits.' She fought to keep her temper. 'I have a list of those who have promised at least to think on it and perhaps . . . if you could look to it before father's return, then I needn't trouble him at all.' She was smoothing the nap of his doublet sleeve, but he tossed her hand away.

'As far as father goes, you may do as you please. But don't expect me to go cap in hand to anyone.'

She stared out across the valley, tried again. 'If you don't want to be involved in the collection . . .'

He snorted.

'. . . I had another idea . . .'

'Which was?' His tone was hardly encouraging, but she ploughed on.

'A common warren.'

'You're crazy. Who'd have control?'

'Why not the parish?'

'The parish couldn't agree the day of the week, far less a scheme such as that.' He thumped the capstone beside her. 'And I suppose you have a list of those who will support you in this also?' When she didn't reply he continued, 'The sooner Hugh takes you to Braidstane the better, so that your meddling will be his problem and not ours.'

Her eyes sparked. 'It's fine for those who have enough lard about them to keep them warm all winter.' And in case he missed the point, 'You were aye roly-poly and set fair to be so again. If my own family won't support me in this, I swear to God I'll be proud to meddle. Our warren released onto the moor and it won't be long before the countryside is overrun with meat, for all and to spare. And not before time.'

Chapter Seventeen

Munro stopped briefly at Clonbeith to retrieve Sweet Briar and in Greenock to buy gifts: a tiny carved wooden horse for Anna and a miniature brightly painted top for Robbie. Kate was harder. He didn't know how she would receive him and wished to choose carefully: something generous enough to please, but not immoderate, lest she thought he sought to buy her renewed favour. He settled on an embroidered cushion filled with lavender, the scent of it enveloping him like a cloak with every jolt.

Dusk stalked him as he reached Broomelaw and he halted in the gateway, slipping from the saddle to look up at the tower windows. 'No light, lass,' he said, fondling Sweet Briar. 'I trust they aren't from home, else we must look to ourselves.' He had paused his hand as he spoke and the horse lifted her head and nudged his palm, so that he petted her again. 'You shall be first.' A square of light spilled across the courtyard as the lad opened the top half of the stable door, then, with a rattle of the bolt, swung wide the bottom section also. Munro relinquished the reins, 'It seems you will be well cared for, but as for me . . .' He nodded towards the still dark house. 'Is your mistress at home?'

'Aye sir, they are but lately returned from a visit to your mother at Renfrew.'

A light flickered on the stairway as Munro reached the door. He watched its progress through each of the three small windows that lit the turnpike. For a moment again there was darkness. Under his breath he counted: six steps to the top of the stair, two to the door of the solar – now.

Light flared.

Kate's face was in shadow, so that he couldn't tell whether she smiled or not.

'We hadn't expected you so soon. No matter . . .' her voice was half way between uncertain and warm, her body stiff.

'Kate? What use courtesies if things aren't straight between us? It isn't right to waste what we have in regrets. God knows I'm not proud of what was done, but however much I may wish it, I can't go back.' When she still avoided his eyes he stretched out one finger and ran it lightly down her cheek and across her mouth, resting the fingertip against her lips. 'Kate?' She leaned towards him.

Anna burst onto the stairwell, short plaits flying, Robbie behind her. 'Dada,' they chanted in unison, tugging at the saddlebag slung over his shoulder.

He hunkered on the floor and delved in his bag – bairns aye appear when they aren't wanted. The carpenter from whom he had bought the toys had, at Munro's request, wrapped them individually in scraps of hessian, so that he had a parcel for each of them.

Robbie didn't open his immediately, probing at the shape, his eyes narrowed, the tip of his tongue wiggling between his lips. He looked at the knot intently, then worried gently at it till it loosened and the string fell away, the coarse cloth springing back. Rocking on his heels he said, 'What is it Dada?

'Watch!' Munro set the top on the floor and flicked the knob between his forefinger and thumb.

Robbie clapped his hands as the colours spiralled outwards. When it stopped and fell over, he dived to pick it up. 'Again Dada, again.'

Munro set it spinning twice more, then, taking the small hand in his, placed Robbie's fingers against the knob. 'You try.'

Three times he held Robbie's finger and thumb and tried to help him to start the top, but each time it wobbled and fell over. Munro saw in the tightening of his lips determination building. He tousled Robbie's hair. 'We can try again later.'

'Now,' Robbie said. 'I shall try now.'

Munro caught Kate's eye and risked a smile. Anna was tugging at her string, pulling at the knot, first with her fingers, then with her teeth, succeeding only in making it tighter. As she threw the parcel away Kate slipped onto the floor beside her.

'Careful, you don't want to break it, else Robbie will have his top and you will have nothing. Let me help.'

'Stupid string,' Anna said.

Kate freed the knot and laid the bundle in the child's lap. Anna kept her small fists tightly clenched, scowling, but when neither Kate nor Munro intervened, she slid one hand to the hessian and pulled it aside, staring down at the tiny horse. For a moment Munro thought he had chosen badly, but when she looked up, her eyes sparkled. She rubbed her finger down the ripple of mane and over the smooth swell of belly, contoured from the grain of the wood, then cantered the horse across her knees, up her chest, across her throat and all the way down again. Uncurling her legs, she ran to the window that overlooked the courtyard and climbed onto the sill to gallop the horse backwards and forwards, 'clip-clopping' vigorously.

He rummaged again and produced the parcel for Kate.

'It's but a wee bit thing. Nice enough in its way, at least, I trust so.'

She fingered the parcel, 'I trust so too. Else I may be forced to steal Anna's horse and that . . .' there was a hint of a thaw in her voice, '. . . would likely cause a riot.' She bent her head and in her turn worried at the string, which had somehow worked itself into a knot.

She too poked her tongue between her lips and bent her dark head close to the parcel, illustrating the origin of Robbie's patience. There was a flash of colour at Munro's feet and a crow of satisfaction as the top spun briefly before tilting to a stop. Satisfied, Robbie set it carefully on the table and clambered up onto the sill beside Anna. She shifted sideways, leaning her back against the angle of the wall and trotted the horse onto Robbie's lap. Munro touched Kate's wrist and pointed. Her face softened as she looked at the twins, cross-legged, like a pair of happy brownies, the horse between them. Kate's hand was small and fine and warm, and, without conscious thought, Munro traced a line from her wrist to the tip of her fingers.

Her breathing shallowed. She turned her hand over and he nudged her fingers apart to slip his own into the gaps. Her skin was dry, the scar at the base of her thumb, where she had torn it on hawthorn as she helped him clear ground for the lambing pens, rough under his touch. He tightened his grip and was rewarded by the first full smile since Annock. 'Can you not manage?' he said, looking at the parcel on her lap.

'Not one-handed, I can't.'

'Well then, I shall have to help.'

Again the smile. She pulled the parcel against her stomach

and caught at the string with her free hand while he took the other end and pulled, but too hard, so that it skidded off her lap and dangled, the knot remaining stubbornly tight.

'It isn't going to damage?'

'It'll take no harm. There. I'll hold and you pull. A lighter touch may do it.'

Light or not, it took several more attempts before the string was released and the hessian put aside. With all the tugging and pulling the scent was strong, even before the cushion was revealed. She held it against her face, breathing in deeply, then traced the pattern of lavender stems appliquéd onto the smooth silk. Her mouth trembled between a sob and a smile and he tried to think of something comic to say, but couldn't find words.

'Nice enough,' she pressed her palm against his, the smile winning, 'in its way . . .'

With his free hand he ran one finger into the hollow of her throat then downward towards the swell of her breasts. He felt the flutter of her pulse and bent his head and kissed her. She didn't pull away. It was a mood that lasted the evening through, past the children's bedtime into their own, so that they lay together for the first time since Annock.

Afterwards she said, her head tucked into his neck, a strand of hair lying across his face, the scent of it wholesome, 'I feared for us.'

His voice was hoarse. 'I think that I feared more.'

She settled firmly against him. 'It wasn't the house, nor the land, nor even the safety of the bairns that plagued me. It was this. Us. The thought that whether here or not, you might have gone somewhere I couldn't follow.'

He knew that he should tell her of his detour to Greenock, his meeting with the Montgomeries, for if they were to start again, there should be no secrets between them, and was searching his mind for appropriate words when she continued and the moment was gone.

'Now maybe isn't the time to talk of obligations, but there is nothing . . .' he heard the steel in her voice, '. . . nothing we owe, to the Cunninghames or anyone else, is worth that loss.'

He lay, inarticulate, able only to press his chin onto her head, to hold her more tightly for fear that he might rock the fragile peace. Finally, when he felt her draw back, he said, 'Without your anchor these months past, I have been adrift and like to founder. I don't know yet how things will turn, but . . .' he pulled her close again and spoke into her hair, '. . . if it's a promise you want Kate, I won't risk losing you again.'

Part Two

October – November 1589

Whatsoever a man soweth, that shall he also reap.

King James Bible, Galations 6:7

Chapter One

Munro heard it first. On the quayside, as he stood in the small crowd waiting for the line of fishing boats nosing into the harbour. A rumour only, insubstantial, fragmented, like the mist that drifted in curls on the Clyde and eddied among the masts of the few trading vessels moored against the sea wall.

He thought it hardly credible, yet it amused him to imagine James slipping away, the court abed, to rescue his Danish bride, as if it was ardour that drove him. As indeed it might be if he were not the King; for the bride was not yet fifteen, and winsome, so it was said. Who wouldn't have chosen as he had, and the choice a lass eight years older or one eight years younger than himself? Still, for all his love of poetry, it was a match that owed more to politics and the need for an heir, than any sonnet he might write. And if the King was indeed on his way to Norway, it was a foolishness that wouldn't be appreciated by most of his council. The truth would be known soon enough, and, in the meantime, it was a fine piece of gossip to take home.

He had been sent to the harbour for salt herrings, more to get him out of the way than anything else. He watched the fishing fleet emerging and disappearing again into the mist, a wee pickle larger each time he spied it, and the notion took him to wait for a fresh catch to salt at home.

'It'll give me something to do, lass,' he murmured to

Sweet Briar, 'And save Agnes the trouble of imagining another unnecessary errand.' It irked him that each time there was a birthing, the womenfolk shut him out, so that he was forced to pace up and down in the hall or the courtyard and nothing to do but wait.

'Anywhere you please,' Agnes had said, 'so long as it isn't under our feet.' She had been Kate's nurse and was now both midwife and nurse to Kate's children; and so thought nothing of speaking her mind to Kate's husband when the need arose.

An hour later, when the sounds from upstairs had temporarily stilled, she had appeared in the doorway of the hall. 'Kate's resting the now and like to be so for a while. If you can't find anything to do other than pace, you might away and get some salt herrings. That will at least not waste your time altogether.'

'I don't wish . . .'

She brushed aside his protest, as she would swipe a fly that buzzed about her kitchen. 'We can't be doing with you ranging up and down, the tramp of your boots on the flags like the beat of a drum pounding at Kate's head till she is fit to burst.'

And so he had saddled Sweet Briar and set out, in one way glad of the excuse for the ride, yet guilty also for the gladness. This was her third confinement, and the first two straightforward as the dropping of lambs, though not so fast. Yet however hard he tried, he couldn't help but fear that something would go awry. No amount of telling, from Agnes or the apothecary, would settle him until it was over and the bairn safely delivered. The other children: the twins, now six, and Maggie, a placid, roly-poly two-year-old, who you couldn't so much as glance at without smiling, had been sent to his mother at the first twinge and no doubt romped to their hearts' content with no-one to check them.

He had kept tight to Broomelaw these three years past and was glad of it, glad too that events abroad had turned greater folks' thoughts aside from their own squabbles to other dangers. News had filtered to Broomelaw in snippets: arriving with pedlars; confirmed in the market; thundered from the pulpit. And if hard at times to guage the accuracy of the reports, the kernel was no doubt true and enough for their needs: Babington's execution, sufficiently horrific that Munro spared Kate the detail. Queen Mary, beheaded at Fotheringhay: protesting her innocence and her adherence to the old faith to the end. A seemly death, if you discounted the talk that it had taken more than one cut. Eclipsing all else, and producing a ripple of fear that bought temporary peace between the warring Scottish Lords: the talk of a Spanish fleet, bound for England, yet threatening the peace of Protestants everywhere. When word came that the vast ships, nipped and harried by the English, had been defeated, thanks to the fervent prayers of the faithful and to the weather, relief returned, along with reawakened interest in personal affairs. There was scarce a seaboard parish without their own tale of the tattered Spanish fleet. And the Clyde shore no exception. The immediate danger past, the Munros, like many others, had spared a thought for the poor sailors who found themselves washed up on a foreign shore, the sorry remnant of a vast endeavour.

On the quay a cluster of women, their sleeves rolled past their elbows, headed for the tables set out at the head of the steps where the catch would come in. One, young and fair, smiled shyly at him in passing, a bairn strapped to her back, perhaps three months old, his skin dark as a gypsy. Munro smiled back, thought – shipwreak isn't aye a disaster, or not for the young at least.

On the ride home his thoughts returned to James and his Danish princess and the storms that had delayed her arrival. And politics aside, he wished them joy. Though it was hard no doubt for a King to find the easy companionship of lesser folk, yet it was not unknown.

'If he is half as happy as I am this day, or will be when the bairn is safely come, then fine for him.'

Sweet Briar tossed her head.

'Aye, lass, fine for us all if the King is taken with his bride.' He was paying little attention to the journey, and so was surprised when Sweet Briar stretched her neck, breaking into a canter, and he found himself nearly home.

All was quiet as they entered through the gateway and although dusk was falling he saw no flicker of candles. For a moment he remembered that other home coming, three years earlier, when he had feared that the love between them was gone, snuffed out by his part in the business at Annock. It hadn't been easy to repair the damage, and though Maggie was likely the fruit of that first night's loving, the real work had stretched through the months of the long, hot summer that followed and into the winter beyond. The spectre of the Cunninghames and the demands that they might yet make upon them an intermittent fear, never spoken of, but no less real for that.

With the birth of Maggie just short of nine months after his return, a shadow had lifted and, Glencairn making no further calls on them, they had begun to live as if their lives were truly their own. From the start, Maggie had been a placid child, plump and well favoured, her engaging smiles bestowed generously on all who looked at her. Whether it was due to her presence or not, and Munro was sure that at least in part it was, Broomelaw had begun to prosper and the relationship between himself and Kate to bloom afresh. And so to today and the new fruit of their love pushing its way into the world.

Now and then he thought on Hugh and Elizabeth and wondered if their marriage was equally blessed, but was forced to keep the thoughts to himself, for he had never found the right opportunity to confess the Greenock visit to Kate.

He crossed the courtyard to the stable, not knowing whether to be uneasy at the lack of lights. The door creaked as he entered, startling the lad curled on a heap of straw, half-asleep.

'You're surely tired to be asleep the now. Were you not sleeping last night?' It was an innocent enough question, for Munro had no thought but to chafe the lad, and so was startled by the flush that crept across his face. At another time he might have probed further, for though it was fine for a lad to set his eyes on a sonsy lass and she was willing, Munro had a certain responsibility to see that those in his employ didn't over-step the mark, or if they did that they were ready to make amends. 'No harm done.' He passed the reins over and released the bag with the herrings. 'She needs a good grooming. The smell of the harbour is on her, and I don't think she's overly keen on the stench of fish.'

The lad led Sweet Briar away, the colour fading in his face and Munro headed for the castle doorway – I can't be hard on him and the evidence of my own pleasure clear for all to see. I wonder which it will be . . . no matter, so long as they both are hale.

Agnes was in the kitchen, refilling a pail from the kettle

157

on the fire. She turned at the slap as he dropped the bag of fish onto the table. 'Save us all,' she said, 'You nearly made me drop the pail.' And then, in response to his questioning look, shook her head. 'Nothing yet, though I suspicion it won't be long.'

'I'll carry the pail,' he said, moving to take it from her.

'You'll do no such thing.' She smiled at him, so that he saw that however slow this child was in the coming, she didn't fear for the outcome. 'Content yourself. I'll call you, just as soon as it's over.' She turned at the door, 'And leave the herrings on the slab in the larder. They may be wanted later – a tasty morsel is aye welcome when the job is done.'

He started to say that he hadn't brought salt herrings, but she was already part way up the stair, so he took himself out to draw cold water and begin the job of gutting the fish. He heard her up and down the stair twice more before he had finished layering them into a barrel. He wasn't altogether sure of the amount of salt that was required, the setting down of fish being woman's work, but he was liberal and hoped for the best. Restless, he climbed to the hall and saw that the fire was not yet lit, yesterday's ashes un-raked on the hearth. Dropping onto his knees he spread them into a bed, ready for the kindling, and because of the rustling of the sticks, missed the faint wail from above.

Agnes' voice behind him. 'Praying is it? Well, you've been answered. You have another daughter, and well-made she is too.'

Kate lay back on the bed, her face pale, her eyes, soft and luminous, fixed on the wee scrap snooked into the hollow between her arm and her breast. He hunkered down at the side of the bed and put out a tentative finger to touch the child's cheek.

Kate looked up and though she smiled, he saw doubt in her face. 'You aren't disappointed?'

He shook his head, smoothing back the hair from her forehead. 'I can't have too many ladies to look to me.'

Agnes, busy with the spreading of fresh rushes, humphed, 'True enough. You're over much trouble for one.'

His finger stilled against the child's cheek, and she moved her face against it, much as a kitten would if you paused in the petting of her. Her eyelids flickered and he found himself staring into a pair of periwinkle-blue eyes below the smooth cap of auburn hair. He knew that she couldn't focus, that she turned rather to the sound than the sight of him. Knew also that her eyes mightn't aye be blue, nor her hair bronze, but found himself hoping for it.

'She's a bonny lass.' He bent, meaning to kiss Kate's forehead, but she stretched upwards so that instead their lips met. He held the kiss, gentle and long, and then, as the child began to mewl, rocked back onto his heels.

Agnes said, 'Away with you. They're tired both and the bairn needing fed. If you want to be useful, you can help with the fetching and carrying, for Kate too is in need of a bite. A salt herring or two mightn't go amiss.'

'Ah,' he felt like a child caught in some sin of omission. 'The boats were just newly home, so I thought to buy fresh.'

Agnes shot him a look, as if to say, 'Could you not just have done as you were told?' but said only, 'Well then, I dare say fresh will have to do.'

'I've set them down already.'

From the depths of the bed, Kate choked.

Agnes raised her eyes to the ceiling. 'There are some who, if they have other than straw between their ears, don't give much indication of it.'

Kate choked again, the sound mingled with the rhythmic suckling of the babe. 'Bread and cheese will do fine, and will be less trouble.'

'Aye well, it'll have to do and you want fed the night.' Agnes headed for the kitchen, still muttering.

Munro dropped down again beside Kate. 'I didn't think. It was something to do, though . . .' he thought of the ladling of the salt, '. . . I'm not sure if they'll be fit for the eating, for I didn't know how much salt to use.'

Kate waited until the sound of Agnes' slippers had faded. 'Someone will eat them, even if it is only a passing pedlar that we wish to discourage.' She settled the babe more comfortably against her then, perfectly mimicking Agnes, nudged him with her elbow. 'Away with you. I amn't that tired, but a bite to eat wouldn't go amiss and company as I eat wouldn't go amiss either. If Agnes will allow it.'

It was as they finished their supper, Kate lying back against the pillows, Munro stretched out alongside her, that he remembered the talk of the harbour. He chewed on the last lump of cheese and ran his tongue around his mouth, cleaning the fragments from between his teeth. After a final swallow of ale he said, 'Oh, I forgot. The gossip is all of the King. It seems he has taken it into his head to go to Norway to collect his bride. He and a fleet of five ships slipped out of Leith without the knowledge of the rest of the court, a letter left behind, taking responsibility for the jaunt, and naming those to look to affairs in his absence. And I imagine the council won't be best pleased. That is . . . if the rumour be true.'

'It would be a mighty big rumour that sent five ships into the North Channel in October if it wasn't true.' Kate wriggled closer to Munro. 'It's as well you didn't volunteer to accompany him. Else you would have missed Ellie's arrival.'

'Ellie, is it? Do I have a say in the naming?'

'No.' She spoke in a 'whatever made you think that' voice.

'Ellie it is then, though I know one member of our household who may take umbrage that she wasn't consulted.'

'It's properly Eleanor Catharine,' Kate continued, 'Though she seems over wee to bear the weight of her whole name yet. But speaking of Anna – when are you fetching the bairns home?'

'Tomorrow, in the forenoon. They'll be fair spoiled already, Mother is aye easy on them; which is not quite how I remember it when I was wee.'

'They're easy to spoil when you don't have to live with the effects of it. My grand-dame was the same. Was yours not?'

He had a mental image of his paternal grandmother, holding him at arm's length lest he soil her clothes. 'No.' It came out like a sigh. 'She didn't have much time for bairns.'

Kate's tone was soft. 'Be glad then that your own children are more fortunate.'

Chapter Two

Archie came home, full of his life at Kilmaurs and the possibilities for advancement. He had changed in the three years that he'd been away and not for the better. There was a hardness in him and a 'devil take it' attitude that Munro and Kate both found distasteful. Nevertheless they strove to make him welcome and to listen with every appearance of interest as he talked. William, it seemed, hadn't changed, or if he had, it was to become more arrogant and self-centred than ever, and Archie seemed to wish to follow him.

'I can't stay above three days.' There was scarcely disguised relief in his voice and Munro found he matched it in thought, if not in word.

'Mother will be sorry for it.'

Archie waved his hand as if he swept away anyone's thoughts but his own and continued, 'Buried here, you'll not have heard the latest from court.' He was leaning against the chimneybreast, one arm stretched along the lintel as if it was his own hearth he stood at and not his older brother's.

'If it's the jaunt of James you're referring to, we had the news two weeks since.' Munro was pleased to see Archie's chagrin, 'Maitland's doing they say and his the ships that carry them. Was Glencairn not invited?'

Kate shot him a look of caution and censure in equal measure, and he looked away, for he had, as she clearly divined, meant the barb.

'No, and though he wouldn't have relished the journey for he isn't the best of sailors, it didn't please him to be forgot.'

'He's in good company, I hear the half of the court knew nothing of it till the scheme was fully cooked.'

'That doesn't lessen the affront. Not to Glencairn, nor to William, especially as word has it that Montgomerie was bid.'

'The poet?'

'Him also, though it was Braidstane that irked William. From all I've heard, he is a jumped-up bit of little quality and less silver, who trades on his uncle's favour with James.'

Munro felt Kate's restraining hand on his sleeve, her tone conciliatory, 'You must be hungry, Archie, I'll call for supper. Then we can talk as we eat. We are quiet here and don't hear more than the bare bones of gossip. Forbye that we knew that the King was away to bring his bride home, we haven't heard much else and indeed weren't sure of the truth of the rumour. No doubt the meat of it will entertain.'

The meal set, she picked up the thread of conversation, 'And was it all Maitland's doing? I wouldn't have expected him to encourage James in such a risky endeavour.'

'No,' Archie paused, a chicken drumstick part way to his mouth, 'Though Maitland pays: James is aye canny. The story is . . .' he took a bite, as if, Kate thought, to give himself time to choose his words, as if he were not at home, but rather in dangerous company, whose discretion could not be guaranteed. She suppressed her irritation, encouraged him to continue.

'Go on . . .'

'When James had word of the damage to the Danish ship that carried his new bride and that she was forced for the second time to make for shelter, he ordered Bothwell, as Lord Admiral, to take a fleet to Norway to fetch her here.'

'But it was not Bothwell who went.'

'No.' Again the slight hesitation, countered by an enquiring look from Kate and a nod from Munro. 'When Bothwell presented the King with the cost of the venture, he wasn't slow to change his mind. And that no great surprise.' Archie was finding his stride now, his previous reluctance seemingly forgotten. 'That's when Maitland, no doubt thinking of future gain, stepped in. It wasn't Maitland's intention to take the King, but that James himself, now that the cost wasn't his to bear, took the notion of a grand gesture.' He reached for another drumstick. 'If you believe the proclamation that James left . . .' He raised his voice, '. . . I take this resolution only of myself as I am a true Prince . . .' then returned to his normal tone, 'Whatever the origin of it, others of the council had no idea until the scheme leaked too late to stop him.' He was scouring his platter with a chunk of bread, mopping the remains of the gravy. 'It was the size of the retinue that angered Glencairn, nigh on three hundred strong and he not among them.'

'Forbye the Montgomeries.' Again a hint of amusement from Munro.

Kate pressed hard on his foot, and turned back to Archie. 'You haven't said much of yourself. You've been at Kilmaurs long enough to know if it suits you to stay.'

'Well enough. At least we aren't buried in the back of beyond. And visitors there are aplenty and there isn't much that passes but that we hear of it.'

Again Kate forestalled Munro. 'And what of the lassies? Your mother's first thought will be that you have come to cry her to a wedding.'

'Well, I've not. Though there's plenty willing.' He seemed to dare them to contradict. 'But I'm not just going to fall for the first sonsy lass who lifts her lashes at me. I intend to see myself set fair before I am saddled with a wife and bairns.'

'Ambition,' Kate said, Munro recognizing her undertone of anger, 'is all very well, but take care that you don't gain a fine place and have no-one to warm it with you.'

It was Munro's turn to seek to diffuse the tension. 'I have much to be grateful for in my wife and not just the bairns she has blessed me with. Quiet we may be here, but if you are half so lucky, you will be fortunate indeed.'

Archie's gaze was defiant, though there seemed a forced quality to his words. 'I have my mind set to rise and when it's done, will look about me. I've not missed the boat yet.'

'No, indeed.' Kate closed the conversation.

Munro sought safer ground. 'Will you ride to our mother tonight?'

Archie looked towards the west window, where the sun still cast a shaft of light across the flags. 'I thought to wait until the morrow, but perhaps . . .'

'I'll ride with you. It's a day or two since I was there. We have a new horse, bought cheaply for that she seemed sluggish. I took a gamble on her that good food and exercise would see her right. You can try her and tell me if you think she was worth the buying.' He had struck the right note: Kate was smiling and Archie willing to be persuaded. 'We can be there and back in time for supper, though mother might have other ideas. But if we tell her you haven't yet seen the bairns, nor the babe, she won't hold you back.'

'Is she hale? I had the impression from your last letter,

165

though I couldn't put my finger on it, that she wasn't as hearty as you'd like.'

'She tires easy, though won't admit it, but there is nothing actually amiss, or not that we can tell. She insisted on keeping the bairns for the birth and has, I think, suffered since, but the twins have energy enough for ten and would tire anyone. As you'll see, for they'll run you ragged before they're done.'

'Where are they the now?'

'Down by the loch – Robbie has taken to the fishing, though we haven't yet had our supper from his efforts, but it keeps them out of mischief and gives Kate a bit of peace.'

She cocked her head, listening, 'If you're going, you should go, before the bairns return. I have a babe to feed, else the wailing will bring the others home.

There was a freshness in the air as they took the slope to the east of the tower and Munro gave Sweet Briar her head. She pulled away easily and he relaxed into the rhythm of the ride, the breeze welcome on his face. When the distance between them stretched beyond good manners, he reined back, turning to watch Archie's progress. It was easier to tell from a distance how the horse moved and he was pleased to see that the gait was steady, and as Archie encouraged him from a trot into a canter, that the action was fluid.

Archie pulled up beside him. 'He'll not be carrying you far in the chase at present, but with good treatment and plenty of opportunity to run, I wager you'll not recognize him in three months' time.'

'Worth the gamble then?'

'Depends what you paid, but if he was cheap enough, I think I'd have chanced on him.'

Munro nodded, satisfied, then, as an afterthought, 'How sweet is he? I thought to give him to Kate.'

'She'll handle him. She manages you well enough, and horse or man, it isn't much different.'

The words were fine enough, but the intonation, the curl of Archie's lip, was William's.

Munro covered the momentary awkwardness, 'Has mother any idea of your coming?'

'I hadn't any idea myself until yesterday, when William proposed the visit.'

'William? For why?'

'I'm not sure . . . he mentioned that there was need of another maid, and if I had a mind to bring one back with me, she would be welcome.'

'And?'

'I thought on my promise to Sybilla Boyd, but rumour has it that Lady Glencairn's maid whose place it is, has been sent home with more than she came, and the blame lying at William's door.'

'That I can believe.'

Archie leant forward to slap at a clegg that had landed on the horse's neck. 'It isn't the first time, and I wouldn't like to be the means of sending Sybilla down that road.'

Kate would have known how to foster the finer feelings that Archie's words betrayed, Munro, though recognizing them, did not.

'There are other maids?'

'Plenty.'

'And are they all alike troubled?'

'No.'

'Well then. She has a head on her shoulders and I imagine can take care of herself.'

Archie was chewing at his lip.

'You owe it to her at least to pass on the offer.'

'I daresay. It's just . . .' he circled his shoulders as if to relieve stiffness, '. . . I'll go and see her tomorrow.'

Munro held Sweet Briar to a walk. 'Are you about much, or do you keep to Kilmaurs.'

'Lately we have been most at home, though William chafes at it. And I with him. Visitors there are, but it isn't the same as being abroad. Glencairn makes for the court, three or four times a year, but doesn't often take many with him. He hasn't forgiven William the loss of the pearls and doesn't fail to remind him of his folly every time he thinks to suggest he represent the Cunninghame name. There are times . . .' Archie was looking past Munro, '. . . when I fear Glencairn may push William too far. And who knows what would be the end of that?'

'And if it comes to it, whose man are you?'

'I trust it won't come to it.'

'But if it does?'

'Glencairn is ageing. I haven't a choice.'

And nor, thought Munro, have I.

When Archie continued the hard note was back in his voice. 'I mean to rise, else my time at Kilmaurs is wasted.'

Mary Munro was resting when they arrived, but came to greet them readily enough, though there was an unhealthy pallor to her cheeks.

'Archie!' She reached up. 'It's good to see you and after such a time. I had thought you become a Cunninghame altogether.'

'It's not so easy to get away. Indeed, it was only that William had his own ends to serve that brings me now.'

'And can you bide?'

'A day or two only.'

Munro cut in, 'Kate expects us back for supper-time. Archie is promised to the bairns and hasn't yet seen the babe.'

'You'll not bide here then?'

Despite the disappointment in her voice, Munro had the feeling that she wasn't altogether put out.

'I'll ride over in the morning, and if you can spare me a bite, I'll take it then and gladly.' Archie was deliberately casual. 'Have you heard anything of the Boyds? I have a message for Sybilla.'

Mary looked up, a new light in her eyes, but Archie shook his head.

'Don't get excited. I'm not looking to wed. It's a position she's offered at Kilmaurs, if she's a mind to take it.'

'I haven't heard that she has aught else, and if you're there, I imagine she'll be keen enough.'

'Mother!' For a moment, Archie sounded as he might have done at sixteen and she crying him to take care and ride easy as if he were but a bairn. 'It's only friendship between us, but I promised to help her to a good position if I could and Lady Glencairn's not difficult to please.'

'What then? You don't seem entirely comfortable with the notion.'

Munro thought – she hasn't lost her sharpness, whatever else ails her.

Mary rose, as if in dismissal. 'If she goes with you I trust you know your duty to someone who has been long your friend and fond forbye.'

Munro had his back to the light and looked down at his

mother, troubled afresh at the way she squinted up at him. On impulse he said, 'Come back with Archie the morn and bide a day or two with us. You haven't been properly introduced to the latest Munro. Kate thinks she favours you, though how anyone can tell and the child not two weeks old, I don't know.' He saw willingness and hesitation fighting in her face and kept his voice light. 'Come and judge for yourself, and besides, Kate has some strange notion for the re-painting of the ceiling in our bed-chamber. An unnecessary expense that you could maybe discourage.'

An impish glint lit her eyes. 'I'll be ready the morn then, but shouldn't you rather fear it'll be encouragement I offer?'

The ride home didn't take long, for Archie pressed the new horse as much as he could, and more than Munro thought reasonable, giving no chance for conversation. He would have welcomed the opportunity to test Archie's reaction to their mother's state of health, for the small changes that he saw, or thought he saw, each time he visited, worried him; though he found it hard to judge if his concern was justified. The proposed visit would give Kate the chance to have a good look at Mary. She'd know.

Archie set out early the next morning.

'You're surely desperate for a sight of Sybilla?'

'How many times . . .' Archie broke off as Kate appeared in the doorway, but his scowl remained.

Munro thought – this fear for Sybilla is more than a passing concern. Please God it isn't justified as I encouraged him to give the lass the chance.

'I merely mean to give her time to make whatever preparations she needs if she's a mind to accompany me.'

'Of course.' Munro tried to sound matter of fact, but, judging by Archie's flush, failed – it would be a fine thing not to have to walk on eggshells with his own brother. The twins erupted into the room with Maggie trailing placidly in their wake.

Anna flung herself at Archie, 'We've been waiting and waiting and you didn't come. And you promised to go fishing with us.'

'I will. But later.' I have a message or two to do first. There is the whole day ahead of us.'

His tone was patronizing, and Munro had the feeling that he paid attention to the bairns as much to avoid closer contact with himself and Kate as anything else.

Anna was not giving up. 'Agnes says it will be sunny later.'

'Well then, that'll be fine for a jaunt to the loch.'

She looked at him, pity etched on her face. 'You're not much of a fisherman. They don't bite in the sunshine. It's much better when it's mizzling.'

Archie glanced towards the window, 'The sky is still gey grey. I doubt there'll not be much sunshine the day.'

They were already at table when he returned with Mary. Munro noted that although there was colour in his mother's cheeks from the ride, there was a looseness to her skin that the flush couldn't hide and a weariness in her that belied the shortness of the journey. It was pleasing to see that she hadn't lost her appetite, though he would have been a mite more concerned had he known that this was occasioned by her deliberately eating nothing since the previous afternoon. Robbie ate steadily, Maggie following his example, but Anna, periodically checking the gable window, picked at her food. A shaft of sunlight broke the dullness of the day, spilling the length of the table. When it reached her she squirmed like a fly trapped in a web.

Munro saw the warning signs. 'Run away and play till we are done.' He lifted Maggie from her place, turning her towards the door, commanding the twins, 'Do you two look to your sister.'

Anna's small face was mutinous, 'Archie promised to take us fishing and now the sun is out and it won't be any good and it isn't fair.'

'It will be even less fair if I don't let you go at all.'

Archie scraped at his plate. 'By the time you've made ready, I'll be there. Do you have a pole long enough for me?'

'You'll fish?'

'Why not?'

Talk veered to the court and to the King's jaunt: those who went with him, those who had been left at home.

Munro couldn't resist bringing it back to the Montgomeries. 'Did you say Alexander Montgomerie and Braidstane both were bid accompany the King?'

'Aye. And a ween of others equally undeserving.'

'How many are away?'

'Five ships and Maitland, as the provider, with a hand in the filling of them.'

'Is Braidstane thick with Maitland then?' Munro didn't think it a likely partnership, but it had been three years since his own last appearance at court and Braidstane, though but a newcomer then, might have bedded himself in since.

'Alexander is James' 'Master Poet' now and Braidstane aye

hangs on his tail. William is fair scunnered that we don't have anyone so close to the King to keep our name high.'

'There are no poets among the Cunninghames?'

Despite himself, Archie laughed. 'Poet? I don't think it's in the Cunninghame temperament, though William can spin a prosy tale or two when he's a mind.'

'To wriggle out of trouble?'

'What else?' Archie toyed with the cheese in front of him, turning the point of the knife round and round. 'What is it with Braidstane? No-one dare mention the name in front of William unless it is in disparagement.'

Munro shifted in his seat. 'The Cunninghames and the Montgomeries have aye been at each other's throats as you know, but with William and Braidstane it's a mite personal. Hugh, for all he is but a laird and therefore, in William's book, not in the same league, has the advantage in having already gained his place and answers to himself. It doesn't help that it was our doing that gave him his inheritance, small though it may be. Nor, I imagine, that he has found favour with James. Alexander was aye a good friend to him in that regard.'

'I didn't think you had dealings with the Montgomeries.'

'Nor do I,' Munro avoided Kate's eye. 'Except that I took the same road from Stirling, fresh from that charade of James, when you first came to court. I bided a night in Greenock with the Shaws – Elizabeth, that is now married on Hugh, the hostess and to tell the truth, I liked them fine.'

'A liking you took care to hide.' Kate's voice was deceptively quiet. 'For fear I wouldn't share it?'

'No! No. Had you been with me, Kate, you would have liked them too. But Hugh is all that William despises and I know the feeling is mutual. I admit I wouldn't wish to be caught in the middle of them.'

'Perhaps you should temper your liking with good sense then.' Kate was warming to her theme, Munro regretting the turn of the conversation. Bickering voices floated up from the kitchen and switched Kate's attention to Archie.

'The bairns will be tired of waiting. It would be an idea to keep your promise, else we will all suffer Anna's grumping the rest of the day.' As his footsteps died away, she rounded on Munro. 'I thought you'd have more sense than to rake over old quarrels. It's not healthy to dwell on past troubles, unless it is to learn from them. And it won't do Archie any good to fill his head with such notions.'

'I can't help taking some pleasure from William's discomfiture. Besides, you aren't any more enamoured of the Cunninghames than I.'

'I'm not enamoured of anyone who brings ill to our door. Cunninghame or Montgomerie it makes no odds to me.'

To distract her, he cocked his head to one side. 'Is that Ellie?'

She was on her feet in an instant and sticking her head into the stairwell, picking up the faint hiccuping cry.

As she disappeared Mary said, 'You don't deserve the luck. You should know fine that women aren't quite them-selves after a birth. And not the most sensible time to raise difficult memories. Besides, you are at peace the now. Why go looking to disturb it?'

'It was talk among family only. What harm in that?'

Mary brushed at some crumbs that clung to her bodice. 'You can't depend on Archie to know what to speak and what to keep silent.' She ran her fingers over her lips in an unconscious, nervous gesture. 'Family we may be, but it's William he serves at Kilmaurs and you would do well to remember it.'

Munro hesitated. 'There are times I wish he didn't. Indeed . . .'

She was ahead of him. 'You wish you hadn't introduced him in the first place.'

'Aye.'

'So I have thought times.' Her eyes were troubled. 'But what's done is done.'

Silence stretched between them, broken by a shower of sparks that burst like a scattering of shot from the grate.

He sought to reassure her, 'Archie is here only a day or two. I won't give him anything worth repeating.'

'See that you don't. I have no wish to see my family tear itself apart; there are plenty others would do it for us.'

'I neither.' Kate reappeared in the doorway, bouncing the baby on her hip. She brought Ellie to her mother-in-law and held her out. 'It's a good time to dandle her when she's newly fed, except . . .'

'I'm not a stranger to a babe's dribbles. Besides . . .' Mary smiled down at the child, 'one of the consolations of a grand-dame is that I can aye hand her back.'

Ellie had been fed and slept and fed again before the other children returned with Archie. They burst into the solar where Kate and Mary sat by the fire, Ellie asleep in the crib beside them. Mary was startled awake by the gleeful shouting as they ran to show Kate the five small trout that were the reward of their labours.

Though they wouldn't go far, Kate, after admiring them, shooed Robbie to the kitchen. 'Take them to Agnes, we can have them at supper if they're gutted in time.'

Archie said, 'They should have gone back by rights, but I didn't have the heart.'

Robbie, part way to the door, turned.

Archie forestalled him. 'They are a fine catch and I'm a dab hand at the gutting. Would you like to see how it's done?'

'I know already.'

'Well you can show me then.'

Kate flashed a smile at Archie. 'It will be helpful if you can try to see that there is some flesh left, so that the bairns at least will get a taste.'

Anna was hanging over the edge of the crib, poking Ellie.

'Let be. She's only just away.' Kate touched Anna's hair.

'I want her to wake up.'

'She will, soon enough.'

'Me too.' Maggie, who was scarce tall enough to see over the edge of the crib, was hanging on the side, tilting it, sliding Ellie towards her.

Mary picked Maggie up and she nestled in, her thumb slipping into her mouth. Kate thought on her children and on her husband, who had gone out shortly after Archie, to see to the bedding-in of the cattle. And hoped he would come back in different fettle. She shared his discomfort at their Cunninghame connection, but as Glencairn hadn't troubled them in a while, it was her policy to concentrate on what they had, rather than fret after what they hadn't. His discussion with Archie indicated a dangerous interest in the Montgomeries and their doings; perhaps a result of more recent, un-admitted contact with them. An unwelcome thought that wouldn't be dislodged.

'Why can he not just settle at home?'

Mary shook her head. 'Men aye have a different view of things. It's as well to put up with it, or pretend to. If you don't argue, it doesn't give them any chance to try to persuade you to their way of thinking.'

'I'm not afraid of his persuading me, but rather of what he may do, persuasion or not. We have four healthy bairns and a fine house and food and to spare. It should be enough.'

'And so he told Archie. And so I'm sure he feels. I believe it is a fear that his brother may be too comfortable with Kilmaurs and their way of going that has brought him to wish the old bonds broken.'

'And new ones forged in their stead,' Kate's voice was bitter. 'Pray God we could be free of them all.'

'As to that, it is a foolish thing to fight what cannot be altered. We have a place in life that puts us under obligation. Pray rather that it doesn't weigh too hard and perhaps you may live as if free.'

Chapter Three

Archie stayed two more days at Broomelaw. Whether it was the presence of the children, who plagued him constantly, or the unseasonably mild weather, he gradually thawed, revealing in unguarded moments glimpses of the boy he once had been. Munro, mindful of his promise to his mother, avoided any chancy talk. Robbie became Archie in miniature: his hands clasped behind his back, his mop of curls subdued by saliva-slicked fingers into a semblance of Archie's smoother head. It seemed the visit would, after all, be more a pleasure than the trial Munro had first feared.

He encouraged Kate and Mary to spend an hour in the middle of each afternoon on the south-facing bench in the barmkin. 'It is only sense to shorten the winter where you can and it will be good for the bairn to have some air.' From the hillside below the tower the girls' squeals and Robbie's high, piping version of Archie's lower rumble made a happy counterpoint to the squabbling of the rooks who were their nearest and noisiest of neighbours.

Munro appeared as Mary leant into the basket to touch Ellie's fine wisps of hair. 'It's a red-head she'll be and maybe brighter than Anna.'

'So I have thought and I don't mind, except . . .' Kate grimaced, '. . . two bairns with a temper to match their colour may be gey hard work.'

'Bairns are aye hard work and can aye have a temper,

178

red-haired or not.' Mary smiled. 'You'll manage fine for you have a way with you that I'd have welcomed when my bairns were wee.'

It was an unexpected compliment that seemed to embarrass Kate and when Agnes emerged into the sunshine to ask about supper, she made an excuse to accompany her to the kitchen. Ellie began to make small noises, turning her head back and forwards as if she sought the breast. Mary lifted Ellie, walking her up and down, the small head cuddled into her neck, her crooked finger held against Ellie's lips. She fastened on greedily, but after a moment of concentrated effort began to wail. Though Mary had carried her for but a few moments and the bairn a wee bit thing, Munro saw that she felt the weight as if the babe were half-grown, so he said,

'We should go in. Fine and all as it has been, when the sun fails there is a bite to the air.'

In the solar he saw to the fire and so was only half-listening as Kate said,

'What is it about a baby's smell?' Is it only me or do women aye find it soothes?'

'I did. Do yet. Indeed to nurse a bairn still gives me a broody feeling, for all that I'm an auld hen and far past laying.'

'Who's past laying?' Munro swivelled, 'I trust our hens won't fail us now. We have the winter to wait and we can add to our flock.' He rose and touched his finger against Ellie's palm so that she closed her fist around it. 'And with another mouth to feed, I don't know if we can stand the expense.'

Mary laughed. 'You needn't worry. It was I we spoke of.'

'It's well you said it then, for I wouldn't dare. True or not.'

She laughed again. 'Is Archie still out with the bairns? He has lasted longer than I supposed.'

'They have gone coney-chasing. Though there are more effective ways of catching a rabbit or two than letting those three loose in the warren, and Robbie so puffed-up I don't know how we will squash him once Archie is gone. Anna no less so. Maggie aye tags along, but will, I think, quickly settle to her old pastimes.'

Kate slid one finger against Ellie's mouth to break her sucking. 'Archie has seemed easier these last days and will, I hope, carry that feeling away with him.'

'The influence of the children may stretch past the barmkin wall, but I doubt it'll last in William's company.'

Mary frowned at Munro. 'Archie used to be gey easy going. And may be so again.'

'Maybe.'

As if on cue, Archie appeared, the three children in tow. Robbie was immediately behind him, struggling to keep his step in time, forbye his shorter stride. Telltale traces of blood seeped through the corner of the canvas bag he carried.

'You were sucessful then?'

'How did you know?' Robbie sounded disappointed.

Kate nodded at the sack. 'How many have you?'

'Only the one. We should've had more but,' he cast a disgusted look towards Maggie, 'she squealed and gave warning of our coming and set them all running. Archie said I did very well to get this one.'

'Indeed I did. He has the makings of a fine stalker.'

'That'll be one less job for me then.' Munro ruffled Robbie's hair. 'It's a fine thing to have a son with his wits about him.'

Robbie tugged at the strings on the bag and thrust it under Kate's nose.

She peered in. 'A goodly size and a welcome addition to our supper. Maybe Archie could help with the skinning.'

'Come on then.' Archie hefted the sack, 'If it's rabbit stew we're after, we need to get on.'

'Me too.' Anna was right on Robbie's tail.

In the kitchen, Agnes looked up. 'What have you then?' Robbie held out the open sack.

'Well now. It's a fine buck and will make a tasty stew.' She pulled on Anna's plait. 'If we leave the men to the easy job, d'you think you could take a hand in the vegetables with me?' She ignored Anna's scowl. 'Rabbit is all fine, but without well-prepared vegetables, it isn't much of a stew. And it takes a woman to make a good job of them.'

Mary returned to their earlier conversation. 'I wish that Archie could bide a while.' She kneaded her palm with her thumb. 'Whether it is the bairns doing or not, he's neither so tense nor so hard as when he came.'

Kate said, 'They can't all favour William at Kilmaurs?'

It was a new thought to Munro, but one that raised difficult memories. He thought on the Cunninghame party present at the meal after the hunt at Fintrie, and further back, the evening at Kilmaurs before the business at Annock, though most of those who had gathered then were dead. As he was fortunate not to be. Of those that remained, though they might not all favour William, would any openly withstand him? It was a question that came uncomfortably close to home. Kate was waiting for an answer.

I don't know. I had a suspicion that John Cunninghame doesn't sit easy with William and would wish himself elsewhere.'

'Wishing is one thing . . .' Mary tailed off.

Kate, as if determined to be cheerful, said, 'Don't forget Sybilla Boyd. Looking to her may keep Archie on the right track.'

Munro crossed to the window. The sun, bleached of colour, was slipping behind the hill. The half-shadows emphasized the unevenness of the ground, the hillside a crumpled plaid of brown and purple; bracken and late-flowering heather criss-crossed with narrow tracks where sheep wandered. He spoke his thoughts aloud.

'Is there a right track in the Cunninghame household?'

Kate came to stand behind him, her breathing not quite even. 'Let be. We're peaceable the now. Why trouble over what may never happen.'

'Sufficient unto the day?' The mockery was unintentional, but so it came out and so she clearly took it.

She spoke to Mary. 'It's time Maggie was away, else she'll be gey grumpy in the morning and we don't want to present Archie with a sour face as he leaves.'

With the distant click of the latch on the bedchamber door Mary turned on Munro.

'Have you no wit at all? Did I not say yesterday that now wasn't the time to pick a quarrel with Kate?'

'I didn't intend . . .'

'Men never do. You have a fine wife and bairns to be proud of and a fitty house with a well-stocked storeroom. Is that not enough for you?'

'I know, I know . . .' He stared into the gathering dusk. Sheep on the slope below the tower moved like pinpricks of light, while across the courtyard answering candles flickered as the horses were bedded down in the stable. From above, he heard Maggie's protests as Kate undressed her, and from below, the twins laughter mingled with Agnes' gruffness – it was enough. Of course it was . . .

'Go after her. It isn't that she doesn't know what frets you, but every wife wants to feel important to her husband and especially so the now.'

'She knows she is.'

Mary sighed. 'Try telling her again. A soft word or two never goes amiss.'

Supper was a quiet affair. The twins, allowed to stay up for Archie's last night, were unusually subdued; Kate and Munro still somewhat at odds, despite that he had taken his mother's advice and gone to her. She had taken his apology, but tension remained, indication that she saw the Montgomeries as a new cloud on the horizon, the size of a man's hand maybe, but a cause for concern for all that. To begin with Archie made a good show of heartiness, but became more morose as the meal progressed, snapping at Anna as she rehearsed for the third time yesterday's tale of his fall into the loch trying to save Robbie's rod, pulled out of his hand by an unexpected bite. Mary put an end to the ordeal, pleading tiredness and declaring her intention to retire. Kate, equally glad of an excuse, also rose, taking the children with her, leaving Munro and Archie to finish or not as they pleased.

Munro broke the silence. 'I'll ride a way with you to-morrow. It will give Sweet Briar some much-needed exercise: with the birth we haven't been any distance for above three weeks.' It was clear that the suggestion wasn't altogether welcome and he searched for some way of extending the conversation. 'Do you go by Sybilla's?'

'No. She's to meet me here. It seemed more sensible than that I add to the journey.' Archie was toying with the chunks of rabbit on his platter, his normally hearty appetite seeming to have deserted him, a sign perhaps that despite his selfish-sounding words, he was thinking more of Sybilla and of what he took her to, than of himself. And likely not comfortable in his thoughts. Alone with him, in the quiet that the bairns' absence brought, Munro thought to take the opportunity to broach the subject of their mother's health, but watching Archie's face judged it wasn't the right moment for discussing anything of consequence. He sought neutral territory. 'The bairns will miss you. It's been a fine few days for them. I don't know how they will take to having to entertain themselves again. If you could have bided longer . . .'

'They would have tired of me.'

'Or you of them perhaps.' It was a joke, but Archie echoed, 'Or I of them.'

Munro rose. 'Or I of you.' An instinctive response, instantly regretted.

Archie shoved his food away. 'Don't let me hold you back.'

'I have my peace to make with Kate and better now than later. She isn't quite herself yet and women are gey odd creatures as you'll find out soon enough when you have a wife and bairns of your own.'

'I told you – I'm not for marrying soon.'

Munro still sought a light note. 'Ill-favoured as you are, some body will have you. And taken in the round, there's more to be gained than lost.'

'So you say, though I've yet to see the proof of it.'

It was a defensive retort, born of Archie's unwillingness to admit to his growing appreciation that the atmosphere at Broomelaw was an altogether happier thing than it ever could be at Kilmaurs. A lie spoken without thought to what it implied of Kate; Munro's reaction instant.

'Brother you may be and guest, but if you cannot at least try to be civil, then it's best you go, and don't hasten your return. Kilmaurs is welcome to you.'

They were both on their feet, a pair of dogs spoiling for a fight.

'Fine by me. Three days is more than enough time to bury myself in a wee bit tower, a clutch of bairns the only distraction.' Archie turned back to the table, lifted his tankard. 'And you needn't trouble. I can see myself off in the morning, that is . . .' his lip curled, '. . . if you aren't turning me out tonight.'

The gesture was William's. Munro, thinking of his mother in the chamber above, held his fists pressed against his side, forced himself to respond in word only. 'All that any man could want is here, Archie, if you only had the sense to see it. You have been too long in William's company. Take care that he does not blind you altogether. And extinguish the candles when you're done and rake the ashes. We have no wish to be burnt in our beds.'

The stairs did nothing to calm him as he climbed to his chamber, so that Kate, who lay back against the pillows, her hair loose about her shoulders, caught his scowl full face as he entered.

Munro saw the instinctive narrowing of her lips. 'It isn't you that deeves me. Archie is determined to give offence and I . . .'

'And you to take it. If it is distance from William you

wish, I share it, but bickering at home will not save us from fighting abroad, only make us less able to withstand it.'

'I'm sorry.' He leant towards her. 'Kate?'

'Promise me you will at least try to talk to him in the morning. To let him go in this frame, it would not be well done.'

He turned her face towards him, sensed a softening. 'I promise. I had no wish to. . .'

'There's more than one way to apologize and some . . .' she grasped the tangle of hair at the nape of his neck, pulled his head down, '. . . some are more fitty than others.'

Sybilla arrived early the following morning, to be met in the barmkin by all bar Archie. Munro helped her dismount, sought for an excuse to explain Archie's tardiness. And found none, only a return of the slow-burning anger that had taken him the previous night, so that he had to make a conscious effort to hide it.

The reins looped over her wrist she looked directly at him. 'What ails him?'

'I don't rightly know.'

'He isn't over keen to be back at Kilmaurs? Or too keen perhaps? I could see for myself that Kilmaurs has changed him and not for the better.'

Munro tried to sound reassuring. 'The problem lies with William. But you are to see to Lady Glencairn. She is, I think, more kindly.'

'You know her?'

'Only slightly. But what I don't know, I have by reputation, and that good.'

Above them a kestrel hung suspended against the growing light, the movement of his wings invisible. They watched him arc like an arrow and disappear.

'Archie didn't say . . .' Sybilla stopped, started again. 'Do you know what went awry with the maid I am to replace?'

'Lasses marry, have bairns . . .' It was true in its way. 'And not always at their Lady's convenience: she went, I think, to Largs.'

'Oh. No matter. It's no concern of mine, though I daresay I'll find out soon enough.'

Robbie and Anna were playing 'follow my leader' Maggie trudging valiantly in their wake. Mary shivered at the doorway. When Archie did appear he had all the markings of a bad night: his face flushed, the skin puffy around his eyes. The twins rushed to hang onto his elbows, Maggie bouncing up and down behind them. Mary stepped forward, but was arrested by his stiff bow.

'Mother . . . Kate.' He cast off Robbie and Anna and swung himself into the saddle, jerked the reins. 'Sybilla?'

Robbie dropped back but Anna clung on to his stirrup, her face crumpling as he detached her again. When he turned towards the gateway he wore again the closed, wary look of his arrival. Munro kept his voice low. 'You could at least look civil, for our mother's sake.'

Archie's only response to spur his horse. Munro handed Sybilla into her saddle, swung into his own. Making the promise to Kate had been easy; keeping it would not.

Sybilla turned, 'It's as well you're here, else it could be a gey lonely ride.'

'I don't go far with you, indeed, for all the good it does me, I mightn't be here at all.' Belatedly, Munro realised the rudeness. 'I didn't mean . . .'

'We are old friends and I'm not easy offended: what did you mean?'

'Last night . . . we parted ill. Kate hoped that this morning would mend matters. Besides, I had intended to seek his opinion of our mother. When you see someone almost daily it isn't easy to know . . .'

'Whether she fails or if it is only imagination?'

'Aye.'

'I haven't seen her for a while but she seems wearied. It isn't my place to advise but if she doesn't wish to draw attention to how she feels, I wouldn't pry. My mother wished to pretend it wasn't happening and we gave her this wish for as long as we could. And for that, I think she was grateful. . . . What does it serve to fret over what can't be changed?'

She sounded so like Mary that he laughed. 'Mother said the very same to me yesterday, though with other than health in mind. So thank you. Place or not, it is welcome advice.'

She reached across, touched his arm. 'As for Archie . . . I will do what I can. He is changed, but,' faint colour tinged her cheeks, 'I do not think him all lost.'

'Thank you again.' He clicked his tongue at Sweet Briar and she sprang away, Sybilla's horse following. 'We mustn't let him get too far ahead, else it will indeed be a gey lonely ride for you and not so safe either.'

Chapter Four

Hugh Montgomerie stood on the quayside at Flekkefjord watching the *Svanen* slip its berth, his thoughts on Elizabeth and on the tall Norwegian he had accosted at the dock. He had seemed reliable and willing enough to take a message and the silver to pay for its carrying, and so Hugh spared a quick prayer for the *Svanen's* safe passage.

It was a notion that had come to him as they nudged towards the shore. Docked, Hugh had seen from the bustle on the ship alongside, that she prepared to take the tide. Fortunate for him that despite James' desire for haste, the delay in their horses' arrival meant that their party waited on the quay, stamping their feet to stave off the nipping cold, their breath eddying against the sharp brightness of the sky. Fortunate too that the master of the *Svanen* had come to pass common courtesies with their captain, and to hear what weather awaited him. It was a lucky strike that the *Svanen* made for Leith. Unfortunate that there wouldn't be a way of knowing if his message arrived, for the royal party would likely be in Oslo when the *Svanen* returned, but at least he would have tried.

'It's a sop to your conscience surely,' Alexander came up behind Hugh. 'You were keen enough for the venture before, so little use in guilt now. The horses are here and all mounted save us. James is tolerant enough and will respect your concern for your wife and bairn, but only so long as it doesn't hold up his own plans. Remember that you are here and others are not, and make what capital of it you can.'

Hugh turned. 'I shan't forget who I have to thank.'

'There are those I would choose to winter with and those I wouldn't, and family is aye better than strangers.'

Hugh saw that James was leaving. 'You have the right of it. The King is gey impatient.'

'And to so little effect. It's a long road to Oslo and won't be easy on either men or horses, forbye what the weather may throw at us.' Alexander, seeing Hugh's expression as he took the reins of the sturdy pony that was all that was left for him, laughed outright. 'It has four legs and I dare say will carry you. Though catching up with the James may be a different matter.'

Hugh's legs were bent almost in half as he kicked encouragingly at the pony's flanks. Whether it was his firmness or that she disliked the smell of the dock, the pony sprang away, and they made the tail of the party quicker than either of them expected. They skirted round until they found Maitland.

'You took your time. James wasn't for waiting.'

'Aye, well. Hugh had a mind to send word home.'

'Oh?'

'There is a bairn expected . . . they have lost two, so it is to be hoped . . .'

'It'll be a long winter then, for we can't expect much word.'

Hugh dug his heels into the pony, which, having caught up with the rest, now seemed to have lost all impetus.

Maitland couldn't hide his amusement. 'Is it the man over hefty or the beast over small?' Then, 'You needn't fret. The journey would be a mite much for that beast, but I dare say you can improve on it. This is but a short hop to where we lie for the night and then we sail the first leg to Langesund. After that it won't be just days to Oslo, but likely a week, and plenty hard ground in it.'

'It's hard enough already.' Hugh shifted in the saddle, 'and I feel every jar.' The wind was picking up, blowing across them from the west. Hugh felt the chill of it like toothache. 'And nippy with it.'

'This is nothing.' Maitland indicated the clouds scudding across the horizon. 'When the wind turns to the north, then we'll know. We're lucky there isn't snow the now, but we can't expect our luck to hold much longer.'

A clutter of buildings reared ahead of them: homely looking, with angles and jut-outs and crow-stepped, cream-washed gables topped by red pantiled roofs.

'I shan't be sorry to stop.' Hugh flexed his ankle to relieve the stiffness and, paradoxically, the pony found a burst of speed, perhaps sensing the warmth of the stable and the feed and water to come.

'He's surely as keen to be shot of you as you are of him.'

James was already dismounting. 'Montgomerie, I thought we'd lost you. We press on in the morning. I have waited long enough to meet my Queen.'

Alexander bowed, 'And she you.'

Maitland spoke into Hugh's ear. 'Be grateful for your uncle, Braidstane. There are those who would envy his place by the King and the credit you gain by it. In a long winter much may be achieved.'

It was so like Alexander's sentiment that Hugh wondered how much he had been talked of. Something of his thoughts must have shown in his face, for Maitland lowered his voice further.

'Glencairn isn't here, nor William: an opportunity not to be missed. And mark you, most will be despatched home so soon as the wedding feast is past. Play it right and you may be among the few who stay. In your shoes, bairn or not, I'd wish for that.'

The journey overland began well enough, the air crisp and clear, with little wind; the sound of horse-shoes ringing on hard ground, magnified in the stillness. But on the third day the snow came, the first flakes settling on their caps and shoulders like flakes of wood ash; clinging to their clothes and the horses' rough winter coats. Then the sky was full of it, a whirling mass that turned the whole procession into a long line of white knights, surrounding the white King. With the snow came silence, in which every jangle of harness rang out like a bell. Hugh, who had shed the first pony, was now mounted more appropriately on a piebald of sixteen hands, with a gratifyingly soft mouth and the will to run. He turned his face upwards thinking on the oddity of the rise in temperature that snow always seemed to bring and glad of it, for cold as Scotland was, Norway had it beat.

It continued to fall throughout the day, gradually slowing their progress and Hugh, coming on one of their guides that led the column, noted the straight set to his mouth.

'Have we far to go before we halt?'

'A fair way.'

Tired of the same company and thinking on the weeks ahead, Hugh persevered. 'Now that the snow has come how long will it last?'

'Till Spring.'

'You'll be used to travelling in the worst of weathers?'

'When need be.' The Norwegian, who had turned his face to scan the pewter clouds as if to gauge how much, if any, daylight was left to them, muttered as if to himself, 'Not that travelling half way across the country because a fool of a King hasn't the sense to wait fair weather is the kind of need I look for.'

Hugh risked, 'We can all be fools over women, King or not.'

Unexpectedly, the man smiled and Hugh was struck by a resemblance that he couldn't place. He ducked his head in formal introduction, 'Hugh Montgomerie, Laird of Braidstane.'

'Ivar Ivarsen, Flekkefjord, pressed into service as a guide, a way of passing the winter that I hadn't looked for.'

'You have a brother? A captain?'

'Sigurd?' Ivar's smile spread. 'You know him?'

'Met him,' Hugh corrected. 'Briefly. When we first docked. I looked to find someone to carry a message of our safe arrival to home. I couldn't believe my luck that he made for Leith.'

Ivar laughed. 'He always makes for Leith – it is our best market, though why you should want paving stone from here rather than from England is hard to understand.'

'Many Scots would rather buy anything from anywhere but England, even if, and this you may believe or not as you please, it means paying a mite more for it.'

'Our gain then.' Ivar was still smiling, but the combination of poor light and the steadily thickening snow that swirled around them clearly concerned him.

'Is there a danger that we might not make our destination by dark?'

'A danger that we miss it altogether. If you'll excuse me.' Ivar turned his horse and ploughed backwards, encouraging the file of riders to quicken their pace.

By morning the snow had stopped. To be replaced by a wind that whipped up drifts the height of a man and made any chance of progress impossible. Even the King accepted the inevitable and settled to enjoy the hospitality provided. For six days they waited, until the winds abated and the snow gradually packed down, the skies turning a clear, rinsed blue. As they left, in the twilight that precedes the dawn, Hugh thought on the food and drink that had been consumed during their prolonged halt and pitied the family on whom the burden had fallen, speculating that their generosity might stretch them thereafter.

At Borre, James' frustration increased in pace with the storm that put paid to his plans to cross the fjord, so that they turned inland again, reaching Vaale by nightfall. Intermittent flurries of hail and snow left them chilled and damp, but nothing worse, so that they halted but briefly to eat and rest the horses and grab a few hours' sleep before tumbling again into the half-darkness. The local guides watched the sky with an unease that increased as the temperature dropped, and even without a wind, the air bit at their cheeks and made their jaws ache. They covered the remaining distance, not in the four days that both sound sense and consideration for men and horses should have dictated, but in two: no one, either of the Scots or their Norwegian hosts daring to question the madness of the pace. And so, aching and sweated, their faces grey with tiredness and grime, they came to Oslo three weeks after leaving Flekkefjord.

Akerhus reared above them, the cream and red of the buildings complementing the Danish flag flying proudly from the water tower sitting astride the sea wall. Despite the length of the journey, and that a messenger had preceded him to give warning, James, obeying his notion of seeming haste, waited only long enough for a groom to take his horse before bursting in upon the court, still booted and spurred, his followers behind him, the sweat and stour of the journey carried with them.

The company parted, and the young princess, her ladies around her, swept a deep curtsey. When James raised her up, Hugh saw that her face, initially pale, like skimmed milk, had flushed a sweet, apple red under the King's scrutiny. To her obvious embarrassment, James made to plant a kiss on her cheek and for a moment she demurred, then submitted to the embrace.

Alexander had dropped back to Hugh's side, 'We aren't the most savoury to be greeting our new Queen.'

'Nor does she look altogether comfortable.'

'Do you blame her? Warning she may have had, but she might be forgiven for expecting a more formal greeting. Customs differ, but James is aye one for the grand gesture and doesn't stop to think how others will view it.'

'Ha, Montgomerie,' James beckoned Alexander forward. 'The verse man, the verse.'

Alexander pulled a roll of parchment, slightly crumpled, from inside his doublet. It was a pretty piece and well received, not so much, Hugh thought, for its quality, but because of the chance it gave the court to recover somewhat from their rough arrival. Afterwards, James and Anne conversed in French, his dark head bent close to her fair. Hugh was half-listening to the stilted conversation, glad that he did not have to pick the words to say to a bride, chosen for her marriage portion and her portrait, now met for the first time. She was prettier than her picture, no doubt a bonus for James. He admired her demeanour: though clearly nervous, she knew what was expected of her and made the effort to fulfil it. Does she think James handsome? Perhaps. She was holding her head up, her smile fixed. Impossible to tell what she thinks, good or ill. His admiration increased.

Alexander had retreated from James' side, his palms damp, the parchment darkened by the imprint of his thumb. 'A canny lass and game. She has the makings of a queen. Slim she may be, but not, I think, delicate. And young. Strong blood will be no bad thing.'

Hugh was looking about him, wondering how many of the Norwegian court would make their way to Denmark for the winter and if, among them, he would find congenial company. He had had little opportunity to speak with Ivar again, but hoped that he at least would accompany them. In dress there were plenty who appeared to match his preferences: for the plain and serviceable rather than the showy, which perhaps augured well. Thought of dress took his mind to the Cunninghames. And the opportunity to stay close to the King without the inconvenience of passing pleasantries with those that he couldn't but despise.

The King was speaking in Latin. 'That we might be truly joined to our earthly Juno and our gracious Queen.'

Alexander half turned so that only Hugh had a clear view of his face. Not that anyone watched them, but nevertheless. . . 'For Anne to be driven by adverse weather to shelter in Norway is one thing, for Oslo so unexpectedly to have to host her wedding ceremony quite another.'

'Lucky then that James is impatient – they can't be expected to provide much spectacle.'

'Did you not know? Granted they weren't on our ship. James has brought his own entertainment: a troup of four dancers, dark as the devil himself. His intention is that they dance in the snow and thus be the more striking.'

The main door to the hall opened and a blast of air lifted the hair that curled on Hugh's collar. 'Striking maybe, but it's to be hoped that they don't dance for long, else we all may perish with the cold.'

Chapter Five

Elizabeth and Grizel sat either side of a small table in the solar at Braidstane; between them a jumble of embroidery threads, the colours a splash of cheer in an otherwise grey afternoon. Making sense of the tangle was a job that Grizel had been meaning to tackle for some time. But an autumn blessed with fine dry weather had kept her in the garden that now thrived on the west side of the castle. When she did finally look to inside work, there were plenty more pressing jobs than the sorting of a mess of thread. For three weeks Elizabeth had blown through the castle like a gale, brushing and scrubbing with a will that gave Grizel fright for the bairn she carried, and so, with a thought to keep her to a more sedate task, she had brought the box from her chamber and tipped it out onto the table.

'It's fine time I made some sense of this,' she said, and, casting a glance to the rain that slanted against the window, '. . . it may brighten up the day.'

They sorted the strands into their separate colours, curling them into neat twists, Elizabeth's half-smile evidence that she took some pleasure in the mundane task and in the sense of order conveyed by the rows of thread lined up like multi-coloured soldiers. It was a new found pleasure in domesticity that Grizel supposed sprang from the pregnancy, a thought which sharpened the accustomed pang in her own chest. As much to distract herself as anything she made a careless reference to the weather and the likely rough seas that the King's fleet might encounter. A remark she wished back so soon as it was made. In the three years since Hugh and Elizabeth's marriage, they had grown used to his irregular excursions to court, carrying the gossip that came from England by their brother George's hand, accepting the wisdom of them, despite that there was little to show for it. But this gallivant was different. Hugh and Alexander had stressed the honour in his being bid to accompany James to Norway, but Hugh had gone with an alacrity that, however hard he tried to hide it, showed how much he chafed at home. Since his departure, they had avoided the subject, a tacit agreement not to air the issue. Elizabeth's pregnancy was now in its seventh month and, though likely safe, it was an unnecessary foolishness to fret her.

Elizabeth twisted a thread more tightly than she had the others. 'It isn't the season for travel. If the King didn't know that, Hugh at least should.'

'He is a soldier and has a soldier's need for excitement.' Grizel tried to make it sound reasonable.

'He is a husband and should have a husband's feeling for a wife near her time.' There was an uncharacteristically petulant note in Elizabeth's voice, her guilt immediate. 'I'm sorry, Grizel. It isn't fair that you should bear the brunt of it.'

'I have a broad back. Besides that you have an excuse to be vexed . . .' Grizel broke off, flushing.

'I won't lose this one, whether Hugh is here or not, but I would have liked him by me.'

'We'll do fine on our own. Menfolk are more often in the way at a birth than anything else.'

'It isn't so much the birth that vexes, but the thought that the bairn may be half-grown before he sees his father.'

Grizel pounced on the 'he'. 'Have you been dangling a ring over your belly? And it swung for you?'

'He or she then. I haven't tried any of Ishbel's tricks, though I wouldn't like to swear that she hasn't done it herself and me asleep.'

The idea of plump Ishbel creeping about in the night to test the superstition made them both smile and when, moments later, the door opened to admit Ishbel herself, to burst out laughing.

She said tartly, 'It's well you've time to sit and laugh. There's some of us have more than enough work to do and little help to do it.'

'I felt the need of a wee bit rest. Grizel but kept me company and sought to drive away my doldrums over Hugh's absence with the thought that he'd likely be troublesome at the birth if he was here.'

'Men are aye troublesome.' A spinster who had no wish to be anything else, Ishbel didn't think much of men's abilities in any sphere, far less one clearly women's work. She moved to the hearth and was clicking her teeth as she swept back the ashes that had spilled out onto the stone flags, and poked vigorously at the smouldering logs, daring them to refuse to blaze. Her reward a few small flickers of flame which she fed from the box of kindling.

'Well seen I came when I did, else the fire would have been far gone and the pair of you half-starved. But I didn't trail up here to sort the fire, which you could have dealt with yourselves,' she creaked to her feet. 'Rather, to cry you a visitor.'

Grizel rose. 'Where is he then?'

200

'I saw him into the hall.'

It was clear from Ishbel's voice that it wasn't someone she welcomed.

'Who is it?'

'A wee foreign mannie, who can barely talk, or not so I can understand. From Norway, he says.'

'Word from Hugh. And it barely a month since he went away.' Heedless of the thread still twisted around her finger, Elizabeth flew for the stair.

'Though why Braidstane would send a queer foreign body I don't know.'

'Because those who are with him are to swell the King's company. We mustn't show ourselves ungrateful, nor our hospitality poor.'

'Hospitality is all fine,' Ishbel grumbled at Grizel's retreating back, 'but I don't trust foreigners and that's the truth.'

'Wee' was hardly the word Grizel would have used to describe the man they found waiting for them in the hall. He was standing by the north window, his hands resting on the sill, his fingers drumming in time to the rain, his back bent like a bow because of the height of him. At the sound of their footsteps, he turned and crossed to meet them, water dripping from his hair.

'Mistress Montgomerie.' His voice, despite Ishbel's claim, was accented just enough for the sound of it to be a pleasant novelty. He smiled, showing even, white teeth that suggested a younger man than the rest of his face, lined and comfortable like old leather, implied.

Elizabeth curtsied awkwardly, one hand on her stomach.

'I trust I do not intrude. Braidstane mentioned your condition, but not that you were so near your time.'

'News is aye welcome – doubly so the nearer my time comes.'

She stepped back and he turned to Grizel, his grip on her hand firm. She felt a constriction in her throat and said the first thing that came into her head.

'Have you ridden from Leith? And in this weather?'

'As to the weather, there is nothing that Scotland can throw at me that Norway cannot better.' Again the smile, wider this time, 'and skin doesn't hold the rain.'

She coloured under his scrutiny, but irritated at her own weakness, refused to drop her gaze. 'We can't keep you standing here and no fire lit. You'll be hungered, I'm sure.' And to Ishbel, who hovered in the background, 'Set supper in the solar.' She had a suspicion he laughed at her, 'I'll cry you to a chamber.'

'A towel is all I need. Lest I drip on you further.'

Her suspicion hardened to a certainty.

Ishbel was still hovering. 'It's a mite early for supper and nothing cooked besides.'

Grizel spoke sharply. 'There's broth and cold beef and cheese – it will be fine, I'm sure.'

Elizabeth said, 'You have the advantage of us. We don't wish to keep you a stranger.'

He bowed again. 'I am remiss. Sigurd Ivarson, master of the *Svanen*, lately blown from Norway.'

Hovering on the edge of unaccountable irritation, Grizel said, 'We don't always live by the clock. Nor does Ishbel rule us, however she may like to think.'

The rain, which had diminished as they stood, came on again, pelting the windows. Elizabeth shivered and Grizel, her irritation melting into concern, said, 'It's freezing here and no wonder. You away to the solar and see to the fire, else we'll suffer another of Ishbel's lectures. I'll fetch a towel for our guest.' She moved towards the door and gestured to Sigurd to accompany her, yet kept her distance as if she feared contamination.

Elizabeth had the table cleared and platters set before Grizel returned to the solar, her face slightly flushed, her breathing shallow as if she had been running. When Ishbel appeared, puffing from the stairs, with a tray well laden, Grizel moved to relieve her of it, smiling. 'You've enough here for a ween of visitors.'

'I don't want any foreigner thinking we can't keep a good table, forbye he looks as though he can put away plenty.' It was clear she was part way to a thaw. 'He's a well-made man and seeming friendly.'

Grizel was arranging and re-arranging the table.

Elizabeth set three chairs. 'I trust he isn't so famished that he can't answer questions while he eats. I am fair desperate to hear how Hugh does.'

'And I to tell,' Sigurd filled the doorway, his tousled head bent, his now dry hair curling light blonde. He spoke to Elizabeth, but his eyes rested on Grizel. 'It is a commission that has brought an unexpected pleasure.' She found herself flushing again and to cover the confusion he awoke in her, busied herself with the food.

'Well, then.' Elizabeth waved him to the head of the table, the chair creaking as he sat down.

Grizel, who had regained some of her usual composure, responded to the expression on his face. 'You needn't fret. It has held heavier, though . . .' her natural mischief returned, '. . . maybe not by much. We needn't be formal.' She indicated the food. 'Easier and best if you help yourself, and don't be afraid to eat plenty, for we aren't used with those who pick.'

'I see you have the measure of me. And I had thought to maintain a polite pretence.' The look of comic regret on his face made them both laugh.

'The broth will be cold if we don't start, and we daren't ask Ishbel to heat it again.' Grizel slid the platter of bread towards him and he sniffed at it appreciatively.

'I haven't had fresh bread since we left Oslo and, though we made a swift crossing, it is the homely things you miss.'

With the reference to Oslo, Grizel took pity on Elizabeth.

'What news of the King's fleet? Did they all make it safe?'

'Indeed, for the winds were favourable, and I believe the crossing took but six days, though winter or summer the North Channel is rough and I daresay there were some who felt the worse for it. Not Braidstane though. I suspect he relished the journey. He came onto land looking as fresh as if he had just left home, apart from the tang of salt on him. He was on the ship berthed next to mine.'

Elizabeth made a fair job of concealing her impatience as he worried at a gap between his back teeth with his tongue.

'I intended to sail on the evening tide and took the opportunity to extend the normal courtesies of one master to another, and thus gain first hand knowledge of sea conditions. But your King wasn't for wasting time in courtesies. They were no sooner tied up than he was off the ship, his entourage scrabbling behind him. It caused a flurry at the dock, for there were no horses to hand and he wasn't best pleased at the lack. It was as they waited that I met with your husband.' He reached forward and cut a wedge from the block of cheese and another slice of bread. 'Scots bread is always good and this better than most. I have a mind to steal your baker.'

'That,' Elizabeth said, 'won't be so easy, for it's Grizel who does the baking here.'

He pulled down the corners of his mouth. 'It would have been a fine thought at sea, that I came home to such.'

Grizel bent her head to hide the treacherous colour in her cheeks, glad of Elizabeth's interruption.

'And Hugh?'

'He took the chance, seeing that the *Svanen* was fully loaded and ready to slip anchor with the tide, to ask where I was headed. Hearing it was Leith, he commissioned me to send a message of his safe arrival. He said it wouldn't be hard to find someone glad of such a job.'

'Harder than you thought then, seeing as you are come yourself?' Mindful of the distance, Grizel added, 'We are grateful.'

'It is I who is grateful.' Sigurd leaned on the chair, tilting it back onto two legs so that it groaned under the strain. 'We took a scrape on some rocks rounding the north coast of Denmark. Nothing major and it could have waited our return, but as we shipped some water, I decided it was best to have the repair done. Waiting is tedious, so I took it upon myself to bring his news in person. And am glad of the welcome I received. At least . . .'

Grizel, seeing once again the hint of laughter in his eyes, leapt to fill the pause. 'Ishbel may not be over friendly at the first, but now that she knows you are indeed come from Hugh, she won't hold back.' She rose to clear the table. 'Indeed you may wish at the end that she did, for she can be gey familiar and aye speaks her mind.'

As if on cue, Ishbel opened the door. 'And why not?' Grizel paused in the act of lifting a platter, her cuff riding up her outstretched arm, exposing her wrist, and turned, would have answered, but Ishbel gave her no chance to interrupt.

'It's no use in saying what you don't mean. A spade is a spade and shouldn't be called a shovel.' As Grizel continued to clear the table her hand brushed against Sigurd's, the momentary contact sharp as a bee sting.

'You were hungry, right enough.' Ishbel looked at the almost empty plates. 'You can't do better than good Scottish fare.'

'Indeed no.' Sigurd's reply was the essence of polite. 'And the cheese had a fine bite to it.'

'From our own sheep and matured these three months past.'

'And well worth the wait.'

It was obvious that the compliment pleased Ishbel, her acceptance of him complete as she waved away his offer of help with the tray saying instead, 'If you want to be useful, you can see to the fire. I haven't the time for everything, and it wouldn't be the first time today I found it near out.'

They settled for the evening: Grizel on the bench by the hearth, Elizabeth lying on the settle, and Sigurd stretched out on the warm flags, resting his back against the chimneybreast; raking intermittently at the logs each time the flames threatened to subside. Candles flickered in the wall-sconces casting alternate strips of light and shade, broken by the occasional bright flare. Grizel, seeing Elizabeth's eyelids begin to droop, felt a tightness in her chest. To cover it she said,

'Did Hugh say aught of the King's plans?'

'We had little time, otherwise he would no doubt have written a note to you himself. Your king isn't the most patient of men and though the light was already beginning to fail, and they were to travel but a short distance before halting for the night, he brooked no delay. Whether for sentiment or not I cannot judge, but their chosen lodging was to be the same that kept his princess on her first night. The wedding, I believe, is to take place in Oslo.' He forestalled the inevitable question, 'A journey of some two weeks or more; then some will make for the Danish court to winter there. Your husband said to tell you he would write when he could.'

Elizabeth pressed her fist into the gap between her ribs as if trying to find extra room to breathe. 'It's not the writing that will likely be the problem, but the bringing of the letter.'

'True. This will certainly be my last voyage before the spring.' Sigurd's eyes were fixed on Grizel, regret in his voice.

Sure that they must be able to hear her heart hammering, she looked towards the tapestry on the gable wall moving in the draught from the window. It was one that Elizabeth had brought from Greenock: in the foreground, a merchant ship running under full sail, waves boiling about its keel, heading for a distant estuary and calm water. In the background a storm built, ragged black clouds threatening to overtake them. For the first time she saw it as a race that the sailors mightn't have won. She cast about for a happier thought.

'The talk is that James' princess is bonny?'

'So she is. Golden-haired and lissom, but young yet and sturdy and may run to a stouter figure in good time.'

'Sturdy,' said Elizabeth, 'is a fine thing. There have been

gey too many weak bodies married into Scots royalty. Infant kings and rule by nobles the result. And factions and fighting and no-one safe, whether earl or laird.'

Sigurd's face was a question mark.

'There is a feud,' Grizel said in explanation, 'and we part of it and though small-bit players have suffered much. James has a notion to stop all such.'

'Pray God he will succeed.' Elizabeth rested her hand on her stomach. 'I wish my bairn to keep his father, whether that is in James' hands or Hugh's own.'

'Can we not talk of something cheery? Else our guest will think the Scots are aye dour.'

Sigurd smiled at Grizel. 'An unwarranted reputation in this company, I'm sure.'

Elizabeth rose. 'If you'll excuse me, I don't sleep well the now and must needs to bed early, else I'm not fit for anything in the morning.' Sigurd also rose, but she shook her head at him, avoiding Grizel's eye. 'There isn't a need for anyone else to keep my hours. Indeed they are hardly sociable. Grizel will be glad of your company for a while yet I'm sure. She has sat alone many nights of late and will have to do so again. It's a favour you do us by your visit in more ways than one.'

As he handed Elizabeth to the door, his gaze flicked to Grizel. 'My pleasure,' he said, 'for I am rescued by congenial company both from the tedium of waiting my ship's repairs and from the likely discomfort to be had in lodgings at Leith.'

Grizel tried to concentrate on the hiss and spit of the resin beading on the split logs. From the fire, the scent of pine rose, sweet and sharp, as if it was in a forest they sat, the deep velvet quiet of it enveloping them like a cloak.

Sigurd broke the silence, talking with obvious affection

of his home, his family, the business he shared; the soft cadences of his voice eroding the reserve that she struggled to maintain.

Much later, she climbed the curving stair to her chamber and, sleep deserting her, curled on the window seat, leaning her cheek against the cool stone. And to avoid other, more treacherous thoughts: the touch of his hand on her wrist, the glimmer of laughter in his eyes; she wondered how it would be to ride on a sleigh pulled by dogs, swathed in arctic fox and miniver. Or to bide in a little wooden house with overhanging eaves that could, at a stretch, be touched from the ground. Or through the long dark winters to toast her toes, not at an open fire, but at a pretty wood-burning stove set on a hearth of blue and white porcelain tiles.

Chapter Six

Munro's head was pressed against Sweet Briar's neck, one hand on the dip of her back, the other brushing at her flanks, specks of salt and dust flying with each downward sweep. He should have been occupied otherwise: seeing to the cattle lately moved into the byre for winter, mucking out, spreading fresh straw, carting clean water, hay. Instead he lingered in the stable, doing the work of the lad rather than his own, finding in the regular brushstrokes a peace that had eluded him for weeks since. The horse for her part stood quiet, but showed her pleasure in the extra attention by turning her head from time to time and snorting into his ear. He gave a final slap to her rump and took her head in both hands, pulling her face downwards, the slick of saliva as she lifted her lip moistening his cheek.

'A month now, and no word,' he said, as if in answer to an unspoken question. 'Not even a line or two for the sake of our mother.' He leant his forehead into the angle between her face and neck and felt the faint hirsel in her breathing that stemmed from a cold taken two years past, which, though it had never quite settled, seemed to trouble her not at all.

'Is this where you're hiding?' Kate was framed in the doorway.

'I thought to see to Sweet Briar myself: the lad was gey busy.'

She flashed him a 'you might try for a more convincing lie' look. 'We thought we were going to have to take our dinner without you. The bairns are fair peeved with waiting. Not to mention that Agnes isn't best pleased that the pudding she made especial blackens in the oven.' She linked her arm through his and, as if an afterthought, said, 'No news has aye been good news in the Munro family.'

He tossed the brush into a basket hanging on the wall. 'You know in what frame Archie left.'

She faced him, gripping both his arms. 'I know how he was when he came; and how he softened. And besides, there is Sybilla now and we cannot discount her influence. I don't think, for all his protests, it was pure chance he fixed on her to take back to Kilmaurs.'

'It is William's influence I fear; he has had three years of that. The softening . . . I should have encouraged it, not sent him off in bad fettle.'

'And starving yourself in the stable? Will that accomplish anything? Bar irritating Agnes and the bairns. Do not think I lack concern, but I won't destroy all that is good here for an ill not yet come. It is a matter of weeks only; last year there were months at a stretch without word.'

'Naught of himself is one thing, but naught of how Sybilla fares . . .'

She shook her head, placed one finger against his mouth. 'There may be naught to tell. Or if there is, insufficient of significance to warrant the sending. She is a lady's maid, what in her daily concerns would interest him?' She linked with him again. 'Dinner.' she said.

For the rest of the week he tried and failed to settle, despite all Kate's efforts. At mealtimes he ate swiftly, but scarce knew what he was eating. When the children demanded his attention, he responded absently, often saying 'Yes' when he would normally have said 'No' so that they took full advantage of his dwam, Robbie claiming wide-eyed, 'Dada said I could,' each time he was caught in some new mischief.

'And the trouble is,' Agnes complained, 'It's probably the truth he tells.'

Anna, who had played constantly with the wooden horse that Munro had brought from Greenock, now plagued to have a pony of her own, or failing that, to be allowed to try the latest addition to the stable, so that he began to regret both purchases. To prove herself capable, she took to sitting cross-legged, tack spread all around her, rubbing goose-fat into the leather with a rag scrunched into a pad the size of her fist. Munro, coming on her one afternoon, her legs thrust under a saddle, noted the shine she had worked and commended it, tweaking her plait, but failed to pay proper attention to the question she fired at him, unaware that he had agreed to any request.

Inside he fidgeted; outside he either snapped orders at the men or missed giving them altogether, so that no one knew whether they came or went.

Realising himself to be poor company, but with no idea how to sort it and aware that Kate watched him with increasing exasperation, he took to spending, not only the best part of the day outdoors, but the evenings as well; coming to their chamber late and rising early.

Agnes tackled Kate. 'Can you not do something with him before the entire place falls apart? I've sorted him before and I will again if needs be, for we can't have this carry on all winter.'

'I'll speak to him, though I doubt he'll settle till he can find some excuse that takes him to Kilmaurs, and perhaps it would be for the best. This quarrel with Archie is more than a scratch and may not mend without salve. Despite that Archie was more than half to blame, Munro feels the fault is his.'

'Whatever the cause, we all feel the brunt' There was a speculative glint in Agnes' eye, displaced when Maggie erupted through the door holding aloft a ribbon, Anna in pursuit. Maggie dived behind Kate's skirt screeching, 'It's mine, is, is, is,' emphasising each word with a stamp of her small foot.

'It is not.' There was real anger in Anna's voice.

Agnes whisked Maggie away, protesting still, while Kate caught hold of Anna.

'I hate her, she's aye taking things, an then she ruins them an . . .'

'No, you don't. And I'll sort it. It's only a wee bit ribbon.'

Anna dug her face into Kate's bodice. 'It's aye 'only a wee bit'.'

Kate's lips twitched, but she kept her tone stern. 'I've said I'll sort it.' She put her hand under Anna's chin and forced her to look up. Her voice softened. 'It's a fine supper that'll be ruined if we don't get a move on. Run along and find Robbie and your father.' She headed Anna towards the door, all thought of tackling Munro for his ill temper forgotten.

And so the following morning, despite the change in the weather that the sky threatened, Agnes took Munro in hand and despatched him with a list of errands that would take him half way around the county, all of them sufficiently urgent that they couldn't be left to a better day. 'Here's a piece for you,' she said briskly, 'but we'll not expect you the night for you'll doubtless bide at Kilmaurs. But mind,' she wagged her finger at him, 'Don't waste over much time in the morning for I can be doing with all the pruch. And,' she wagged her finger again, 'if there's anything you can't get, don't just decide to bring something else. I'd rather do without than have your choosing.'

Kate lifted her face to his, 'Ride safely . . . if William is at home take care, however difficult he may prove; you will not aid Archie's cause by rousing him.'

Maggie, bored with the farewells, was casting stones at the horseshoe hanging by the stable door.

'I'm away now,' he called as Robbie burst from the stable, a brush flying after him. He nipped smartly behind Munro.

'I didn't do anything.'

'So it was badness that made Anna fling the brush at you?' Kate was struggling not to laugh.

Robbie squirmed. 'It's just like a girl not to see a joke.'

'And the joke was?' Munro too was finding it hard to keep his face straight.

'Only that I'd rather have a boy for a twin.'

'Did you give her a reason?'

Robbie looked at his feet.

Kate swallowed her smile. 'You must have said something else.'

'I'd rather have a boy than a lassie who mooned over Archie as if she was wanting to marry him.'

'I remember a boy who followed Archie like a shadow.'

'And wetted his hair and poked his thumbs in his jerkin and strutted . . .' Anna was marching towards them in such perfect mimicry of her twin that Munro and Kate both laughed outright. Robbie launched himself at Anna and brought her down, so that they tumbled on the ground, fists flying.

Kate made a grab for Anna with one hand and Robbie with the other. 'You may knock lumps out of each other if you choose, only this isn't the best place, for likely your clothes will take the biggest beating.'

Maggie clip-clopped across the yard and slid to a stop, enclosing both Munro and Kate in her smile.

Munro smiled back, turned to Robbie. 'You're the man remember while I'm away.'

Anna wrested free from Kate, fixed Munro with a stare. 'Do you bide away?'

'Only a night.'

'But you said . . .'

Noting the gathering storm in her face he sought to forestall it, 'There's aye tomorrow, sweetheart, or the next day.' As she twisted away from him something tugged at his memory but failed to surface.

Kate, judging it an appropriate moment, stepped back.

He rode west, enjoying the warmth of the full sun that followed him across the moor. Far ahead, clouds bunched on the horizon. 'They may not be dark yet,' Sweet Briar pricked her ears, 'but I hope it's not a wetting we'll get before we're done.' The going was easy, the ground autumn-soft, a welcome respite between the hard-baked summer soil and the winter frosts to follow. High above his head an escort of swallows: a volley of arrowheads suspended against the sky. He didn't think he'd like to be a swallow, aye chasing the sun and not able to settle for more than a season. Below him a tower house nestled in the turn of a river, foursquare and sturdy, much like his own, a curl of smoke issuing from the chimney. Heading towards it, strung out like beads, a line of black and white cattle, driven by a speck of a boy with a stick nearly as big as himself. 'That's more like.' He patted Sweet Briar. 'You'd rather winter in your own warm byre with sweet-smelling straw and so would I.' He thought of the curtains pulled around their bed, of Kate, flushed and welcoming, the heat of her drawing him, and regretted the distance he had put between them these weeks past. And senseless with it, for they shared the same concerns, for all their method of dealing with them differed. He had a vision of Kate as she had come on him in the stable, the expression in her eyes mirroring his own. And yet, whatever her private fears, she did not give others grief in consequence, as he did. A pity to have to spend this night away, however good the cause. Perhaps if he pressed on . . . Sweet Briar moved through a smooth canter into a gallop and the ground sped away beneath them.

He had a number of calls to make before he could head for Kilmaurs; none, it seemed to him, of much consequence. No matter, he was glad of the chance to see Archie and to mend the atmosphere between them. But as he rode up the valley and Kilmaurs came into view, he felt the memory of his last visit, *en route* to Annock, as a chill wind in his face.

It was a quiet coming, the courtyard deserted as he slid from the mare's back and allowed the reins to dangle. Dismayed at the lack of life, he ran up the short flight of steps to the heavy oak door, but though he rapped loudly, it remained firmly shut. He had no better luck with the postern, nor could he find anyone in the stabling, though a couple of horses stirred restively as he entered. He led Sweet Briar into an empty stall, filled a bag with hay and a bucket with water from the pump and, taking a brush from a shelf in the tack-room, began to groom her with long sweeping strokes. A rustle behind him. He stepped quietly round Sweet Briar, his hand resting lightly on her nose. More rustling, a scuffle, giggles. Whoever dallied in the hayloft, they were at least evidence that he wouldn't starve. He went back to his rhythmic grooming but swung round as a lass of about fifteen slid down the ladder.

'We didna hear . . .' She brushed at her skirts, her gaze darting between Munro and the loft above.

'Is it only the pair of you here?'

The lad slid down the ladder and stood, his arm circling the lass. 'An if it is?'

Munro admired the sharp, upwards jut of his head, his combative tone, his protective intent. He held up his hands. 'Nothing. Only that I hoped to find the household at home.'

'Well you havena.'

The girl wriggled loose. 'Glencairn and William . . .' she began.

The lad cut her off swiftly. 'I said you havena.'

'Hamish!'

Munro saw that her colour, which had begun to return to normal, bloomed afresh.

'We have a guest and mustn't be rude to him.'

'We dinna ken if he's a guest or no.'

'And do you know Archie Munro?' He saw the look that flashed between them. Relief . . . and something else.

'If it's Archie you're after, you've just missed him. He's gone to Glengarnock to bring Lady Glencairn and the

bairns and Sybilla, she that is maid to Lady Glencairn.'
Words were tumbling from the girl, and again the lad cut
her short, but with less agression.

'We dinna expect them till tomorrow. Glencairn's wi'
the court and no likely to be home anyways soon and as
for William, I wasna tell't an I didna ask.'

Munro stifled a smile. 'And the rest, you've surely not
the whole place to look to?'

'They'll no be long,' a defensive note crept into the girl's
voice. 'It's no often that we have the chance of the whole
family away. They're at the fair. I didna go for I wasn't
feeling just the best.' She hesitated and then in a burst of
almost defiance said, 'I'm bravely now.'

'I can see that,' Munro kept his voice level. 'And what
would you advise that I do? I came to see how Archie and
Sybilla fared.' Again the disquieting flash. 'I don't wish to
delay my return beyond the morn.'

'Go to Glengarnock then. You have the time, though . . .'
the boy ran his hand over Sweet Briar's rump. 'If you've
come far . . . '

Munro, seeing that his thought was for the horse,
warmed to him.

'I didn't press her hard and though she may not be
altogether pleased at leaving a comfortable stable and will
no doubt show me so, she has plenty of run in her yet.'

'You'll take a wee sup before you go?'

He saw the pucker of worry in the girl's face and
guessed that she feared that word would come back of a
lack of hospitality. 'A wee pickle would be grand, and in
the kitchen just.'

Her smile took in them both. 'If you'll come then, I'll
no be a minute.'

Rain came and went before Munro was ready to leave, his stomach heavy with bread, its solidity masked by a liberal spreading of butter, the flavour marginally improved by the sharp tang of the ewe's cheese that topped it. He sat with the boy and forced himself to eat with a semblance of enthusiasm while the lass hovered, her nervousness diminishing with each slice. At his fourth slice the line of worry disappeared altogether from her forehead and he judged it safe to stop.

Saddling Sweet Briar, he wondered if she would notice the additional weight, then chiding himself for the thought, turned to offer his thanks and was rewarded by a shy smile. The bread was maybe not her blame, though he wouldn't be seeking to steal her for his own kitchen just in case.

Steam rose around Sweet Briar's hooves, as so often happened when heat followed a heavy shower, the air filled with the scent of moss and dying bracken. The wind behind them, it was still light when he saw the line of Glengarnock's curtain wall ahead. The tower was prominent on the skyline, gable-end onto the stream that tumbled at its base. He took them by surprise, Lady Glencairn recovering quickly, though it was clear that she thought the excuse he proffered for the visit a flimsy one.

'I trust you didn't find it inconvenient to have to ride the extra mile. It would indeed have been a pity to return home without news of your brother. Did he not write lately?'

'Not since his return and our mother . . . age has made her more anxious and as I was to be close to Kilmaurs . . .' He had the sense that she let him off the hook.

'Well, you're here now and we will have a doubly fine escort to take us home.'

Supper was an informal affair, the general atmosphere relaxed, though for both Archie and Munro the memory of their last meal together intruded: an awkwardness that needed to be set right.

Archie spoke first, 'I owe you an apology. My leaving . . . it was not well done. Indeed,' he smiled across at Sybilla, 'It was hot tongue and cold shoulder I got once you were gone.'

Munro was quick to respond. 'We shared both blame and consequence then. And have, I trust, learnt from the experience.'

'Since we came back . . . I see things differently.' Archie glanced at Sybilla again, dropped his voice, 'You asked me once where my loyalties lay. Well you may pray Glencairn is hale for many years yet, for William is increasingly hard to thole.'

The worry, which had irritated Munro like an itch since Archie's departure from Broomelaw, began to subside. 'We may all pray that.'

The cook at Glengarnock was clearly a step up from the baker at Kilmaurs, so that he could eat to his fill with an honest relish. He watched and listened and occasionally contributed as conversation washed around him. There was much talk of the new-fangled paper making, fine and handy no doubt and at a price that couldn't fail to please, though the quality was, as yet, a little lacking. Much laughter too over Roche's latest venture: his gold mining plans having come to nothing, he had convinced the King of the cleverness of a patent method of salt production, guaranteed, or so he claimed, to make all who would venture with him wealthy men.

'We shouldn't mock,' Sybilla choked on a sweetmeat. 'He should be paid for the entertainment value of his schemes and he would indeed be a wealthy man, salt or not.'

In the morning, as they made for Kilmaurs, Munro reined in at Sybilla's side. It was the first chance he'd had to speak to her in private since she left Broomelaw.

That it was in her mind also was obvious. 'How is your mother? Is there any change?'

'A little more tired perhaps and less ready to have the bairns scrambling over her. I have sometimes thought, though I haven't tried to discover the right or wrong of it, and maybe couldn't if I did try, for her servants are gey loyal; that she saves her appetite and her energies both for when we are there. . . . But what of you? Does Kilmaurs meet your expectations? And the Cunninghames?'

'I'm good. And it does, though,' a worm of disquiet, laid to rest again as she continued, 'I had forgot how good a cook could be till we went to Glengarnock.'

'It wasn't only yesterday's bread then? I had a taste on my way and was the heavier for it.'

'It's as good a way as any to watch the figure, for there isn't much inclination to over-eat.'

'It will be good for Archie then, I had a fear he might run to fat.' He was aware she hadn't said anything of the Cunninghames and so asked again. 'And the Cunninghames?'

'Lady Glencairn isn't hard to please and,' she nibbled at her lip, 'I don't have much to do with Glencairn himself, for he doesn't spend much of his time at home at present.'

'And William?'

'Nor William.'

Her voice was devoid of intonation, but he saw her stiffen. They had slowed without realising and were falling behind.

'We should keep up,' the twinkle was back in her eyes. 'I may be free, but you have a reputation to guard. I wouldn't wish to be the means of raising a rumour.' She moved ahead of him and, despite the twinkle, he had the suspicion that it was their conversation rather than other gossip that she wished to end.

When they rode in through the turn of the gateway and halted in the cobbled yard, two lads appeared immediately: one the boy from yesterday, clearly in charge, who signalled to the younger lad to look to the children's ponies but came forward himself to grasp Lady Glencairn's bridle. He glanced at Munro and as quickly away again, as if afraid that he might make reference to yesterday's arrival.

William held himself upright against the doorframe. 'Mother!'

'You're back? Business done?' Without waiting for an answer, Lady Glencairn swept past him, indicating for Sybilla to follow.

Munro was startled by her tone. William swayed in the doorway as Sybilla approached, a snake poised to strike. She didn't stop, only ducked her head and gathered her skirt more closely, turning sideways to squeeze past. Archie stiffened.

On impulse, Munro turned. 'I won't bide,' he said to Archie. 'Make my excuses to Lady Glencairn. I was well fed at breakfast. Besides that,' he tried to inject humour into his voice, 'Agnes has given me strict instructions not to dally.'

William's attention switched to him. 'You're surely not at the beck of your servants?'

'I am at no-one's beck.'

'Dangerous sentiment, Munro. It's as well I don't take you serious.' He straightened up and waved his arm towards the stair. 'Have a drink before you go.'

Archie added, 'It will set you up for the ride.' He half-turned, his back to William, spoke in an undertone, 'You may be going, but I have to stay and William annoyed isn't pretty, drunk or sober. You can spare a minute or two.'

There was no sign of Lady Glencairn, nor Sybilla, when they entered the hall. The frown on William's face deepened. 'My mother forgets the courtesies.'

'No matter,' Munro hovered near the doorway. 'No doubt she sees to the bairns.'

'We have servants to see to the bairns.' William flung himself down on the settle and snarled at Archie. 'Are you still here?'

'I thought . . .'

'I don't pay you to think. Nor to be social. Now get out and bring us a drink.'

William's breathing was ragged and fumes of ale rolled from him in waves. 'How long does it take to fetch a drink? That brother of yours isn't very satisfactory.'

'Perhaps he has been called on to provide another service.'

'That slip with my mother, he aye wishes to serve her. As I do myself.' His tone became confidential, 'And she is willing, that I'll wager. Redheads are aye hot.'

Munro dug his nails into the palms of his hands.

'You have another brat, I hear.'

A movement of air behind Munro, un-noted.

'The bairn,' he emphasized the word, 'is a fine wee lass and sonsy with it.'

'A lass,' William licked his lips. 'When she is full ripe, bring her to me: I'll tell you if she be sonsy.'

Drunk or sober it was outrageous. Munro leapt forward and smashed his fist into William's face, sending him sprawling against the angle of the window. He was hauling himself up as Munro swung at him again, and this time William's head splintered the glass behind him. He grasped the window frame, snarling, levering himself towards Munro, a cut on his head pouring blood. Glencairn was between them, thrusting William back into the window reveal, closing it off with his arm. Archie grabbed Munro from behind, held him.

'He said . . .' Munro was straining.

'I heard what he said.' Glencairn stood his ground, imprisoning William. 'Offensive indeed, but the voice of a drunkard.'

'You cannot expect me to ignore such conduct.'

'Oh but I can.' Glencairn's voice hardened. 'And I do. Go home Munro. Do not overstretch my sympathy. I will not contenance a brawl in my own house and damage to my property on account of William, whatever he may say. Archie, take your brother to the kitchens and get him a drink to set him on his way.'

The kitchen was deserted. Munro took the proffered ale, downed it in one draught. 'How can you stay? He is insufferable.'

'He is dangerous.' Archie drew a deep breath. 'For myself, I would leave tomorrow, but there is Sybilla. I brought her here, and must remain to offer some protection. You go. Look to Kate and the bairns. If anything should befall Glencairn, God help us all.'

Chapter Seven

In the end, though they were never to know it, it was a small thing. And in the months that followed, that lack of knowledge was the canker that burrowed into Munro like a worm into an apple, a surface blemish become a gaping core.

It began with Maggie and a resumption of hostilities over the disputed ribbon. Anna, resentment simmering, took herself to the stable and perched precariously on a stool, brushing to an ebony shine as much of the new horse as she could reach. Eddies of dust settled on her hair and in her nose and on the tip of tongue protruding between her teeth, each stroke containing, unchecked, all the anger that her six-year-old frame could muster: her mother had promised and failed to deliver the ribbon back to its rightful owner. Her father, off on some errand of his own, had dismissed her protest as if today and his promise mattered not at all. Outrage built in her: a kettle coming to the boil.

A particularly firm slap of the brush and the horse startled, wobbling the stool. Contrite, she leant her head into the neck, her reassuring babble a high, fluting version of Munro's. The horse quieted and Anna, determined, slid from the stool, backed around into the adjacent stall, climbed the slatted partition and, straddling the top, slid onto Midnight's back. She gathered in imaginary reins, clicked twice with her tongue and felt the willing power bunching under her.

And that was how Robbie found her, sent to cry her in

for dinner. Stomach warred with pride and won, but, greatly daring, she ignored the partition and slung her leg over to drop onto the stool, which Robbie obligingly held steady. At the door of the stable, she halted, her childish treble fierce with unshed tears.

'He promised me a lesson.'

Robbie, awkward, looked up at the sky, 'It's gey like rain, he wouldn't have let you out in the wet.'

Her look shrivelled him into silence, a reply the more cutting for its lack of words, so that he offered, 'You looked fine and easy, with a good seat.'

An older child would have laughed at the pedantry of it. Anna, taking it at face value, was mollified. She jutted out her chin. 'It won't be a Sheltie I'll be having, you'll see.'

Unfortunate that Maggie, nursing her victory over the ribbon, had wheedled Agnes into plaiting it through her hair. Doubly unfortunate that Kate, occupied with her own thoughts, on Archie and Sybilla and how they fared at Kilmaurs and what fettle Munro might be in on his return, failed to notice, so that Anna, fixing on it, boiled afresh. And, most unfortunate of all, the arrival of a knife-sharpener; so that Kate, who had intended to ride out to visit Mary and had ordered Midnight to be saddled to that effect; was occupied for a good hour or more.

Robbie, after a whispered debate with Anna, in which she stubbornly refused to give up his fishing line until he made her a promise, took himself off to the loch and settled to practising his cast. Anna waited until the stable lad disappeared towards the kitchens with some of the more blunt of the outdoor implements, then unlatched the stable door and, tugging Midnight against the partition, clambered onto his back. She would be back long before Kate was free and none the wiser. The horse needed little encouragement, walking on at Anna's command, with only the merest prick of his ears and a quick sideways shuffle to indicate his awareness of a new and less confident rider.

Once through the gate, Anna, unsure on the rough ground, turned to follow the line of gorse that stretched across the hillside, climbing crabwise towards the brow of the hill. At the top she paused, pulling too hard on Midnight's mouth, so that he began to toss against the bit. A kind of instinct led her to relax her hold, though not enough to stop his backwards lurch. Fearing to slide, she dug in her heels, and misinterpreting the signal he sprang away, moving swiftly to a trot. Unable to find the rhythm, she was jolted with every stride, up when she should have been down, down when she should have been up, the saddle bouncing firm and unyielding against her buttocks, so that she bit her lip with the pain of it. He moved from a trot into a canter and she found temporary respite in the smoother flow, but only for a moment before he lengthened his stride to a full gallop. With the increased speed, she lost her hold on the reins and lunging forward was forced to grab a fistful of mane.

She lay along Midnight's neck, pressing herself into him, bone and muscle etched along her length, so that on the following day, a mottle of bruises showed blue-black through her skin. Her breath came in gasps and sobs, the scent of horsehair laced with salt and sweat lying in her mouth and nose, half-choking her. She had no thought but to hang on, no sense of where she headed, no idea of how to stop. Her hair was plastered to her face, a pulse pounding in her head. Had she been older, or unloved, she might have recognized the sensation as fear. As it was, she knew only that she thought her head might burst.

They reached a long incline stretching towards a ring of trees and their pace decreased, the gallop become a canter, the canter a trot, the trot a walk, until, finally, Midnight stopped. For what seemed a long time Anna didn't move, pressed down by the weight of her head, powerless to unfurl her fingers from the tangle of mane, fighting the urge to be sick. When she did open her eyes, it was to see that lather striped Midnight's neck and lay in flecks along his nose, white against black.

Contrite, she whispered, 'I'm sorry. I didn't know how to stop.' She smoothed Midnight's glossy coat with her trembling hand, trying to reassure herself as much as the horse. 'You shall have all the grooming you want when we are home.' Then, raising her head a fraction, noting the unfamiliar ground, questioned, 'Do you know the way home?' Her voice wobbled to a sob, 'For I'm not sure that I do.'

For a few minutes more she lay motionless, resting her cheek against Midnight's neck, feeling the slowing of his breathing; aching for her mother. It was, though she didn't know it, the best thing she could have done in the circumstance, for herself and for the horse. Finally, cautiously, she sat up. She had no idea how far she had come, and nothing around her provided any clue to her where-abouts. She shut her eyes against a renewed impulse to be sick, allied now to a need to relieve herself and forced herself to concentrate on teasing out strands of mane with her fingers, until the twin urges subsided. A whisper in her head, told her that if she did get down she wouldn't be able to get up again. Then as she looked towards the far away ground, she realised that she couldn't even get down. She was close to tears and knew it, knew too that tears wouldn't take her home. And so she sat up straighter in the saddle and focused fiercely on thoughts of the horse that she wanted, the promise she had extracted from her father, her boast to Robbie. She chided herself – that she wouldn't get anything at all if she couldn't get Midnight back safe . . . and how Robbie would crow. Deep inside herself, she knew that to be unjust, but some instinct made her nurse the thought, while she took a second, more careful sweep of the surroundings.

Failing a second time to find any familiar landmarks, her mind turned to rehearsing what she could remember of their flight through the heather. Which was almost nothing and of no use at all. Her right hand, lying on Midnight's mane, turned warm. Surprised, she saw that the sun had sailed from behind a cloud, and again tears pricked her. But this time 'good' tears, for Anna knew the sun and where it shone at Broomelaw and hence the direction she should take.

Had she been on the ground, she would have danced a jig. As it was, she gathered the reins and careful not to tug at his mouth, turned Midnight and clicked softly to him. Under her breath she repeated the mantra, 'Sun to the right, shadow to the left' and feeling the heat on her right shoulder, began to relax. Midnight began to move more confidently, his head up and eager, but submissive to the direction of her choosing.

In the end it was a small thing.

They were within a mile of Broomelaw, on the top of the rise, the familiar sea of gorse stretching up to meet them. Anna had regained a measure of confidence and, no longer having to concentrate so hard on keeping her touch light, had begun to think instead, and with apprehension, of the reception she would receive on her return. The sun was behind her now, their joint shadow almost twice their length, so that she knew with certainty that not only had she failed to return in time for her mother's excursion but had probably missed supper as well. But reckoning that an extra half-hour was unlikely to increase her punishment, while returning with Midnight in poor shape likely would, she was careful not to push him, so that they jogged along comfortably, the gable of Broomelaw's garret firmly in her sights.

The grouse burst from the heather under Midnight's hooves and flew straight up at him, calling her protest. Munro would have known to a nicety the degree of pressure to exert with hand and knee to steady the horse; Anna, jolted out of her thoughts, reacted to the lifting of Midnight's front hooves with a sharp pull that jerked his head up and back. A small thing, but the worst possible. The horse was vertical, flipping backwards, casting her over the rump, his tail flailing her face. She landed on the flat of her back, the mass of horse above her toppling, blocking out the sun.

They had been searching for three hours when they found her, laid out on the heather, limp and crooked. And when they lifted her, her head flopped, her hair swinging behind her like a rope, her eyes wide open and staring as if caught by surprise, much like the raggedy doll that Kate had made for Maggie out of scraps. Kate, who had refused to remain indoors, was right on the heels of the lad who caught first sight of her and so it was Kate who, dropping to her knees, placed her fingers on Anna's forehead and drawing them downwards, shut her eyes for the last time.

She too, moving ahead of the small procession that wound down the path to the tower, gathered Robbie and Maggie close and, hugging them fiercely, told them that Anna wouldn't be learning to ride a pony at Broomelaw after all; that she had gone away, that they would miss her, and here she choked, but that they must try not to be too sad, for she had gone to heaven and heaven was a beautiful place. And when Maggie, tugging at the ribbon in her hair, asked,

'Will she have a pony?' Kate crushed her against her chest and kissed the top of her head and said, with a swift prayer that God would forgive the fiction, 'The best.'

Maggie, curious, said, 'What like will it be?'

And Kate, choking afresh, found an answer. 'Snow-white and fine, with a mane of silver and hooves of gold. Handsome and . . .' Her voice cracked, '. . . sweet-natured and kind.'

But afterwards, the children finally asleep and the servants dismissed, she went to the stable and savaged Midnight's saddle cloth with the newly-sharpened scissors until it was barely fit for stuffing. And when that wasn't enough, tossed it, sodden with tears, onto the midden.

It was the remnants of the saddle cloth that caught Munro's eye as he returned home, so that he slid from Sweet Briar's back and left her standing, reins trailing while he went to investigate – dear God . . . sensing something was amiss.

Kate met him at the foot of the stair and keeping him at arms length, told him, in a voice devoid of emotion, that Anna was dead. That they had found her, her neck broken, bruises blossoming along her length, Midnight cropping at the grass nearby. That if the tinker hadn't come; if Midnight hadn't been saddled; if she hadn't sent for the axe and scythe . . .

He cut through her babble in a voice that far surpassed the grimness of hers. 'If I hadn't been obsessed with William. If I hadn't gone to Kilmaurs. . .' The realization, surfacing from deep in the recesses of his memory, was sharp as a stab wound. 'If I hadn't bided away. I promised . . . dear God, Kate, . . . I promised her a riding lesson.' He plunged back down the stairwell and out onto the hill to fling himself prostrate in the Anna-shaped hollow of crushed grass; and railed in anger, at himself and at William and at the God that he was now almost sure couldn't exist, or if he did was the God of the Old Testament only and not of the New.

As dusk fell he shut himself in the tack room, his head resting on the saddle that Anna had polished so vigorously, the smell of it stripping his nostrils as if it were acid she used and not goose grease. He found the rag wad and buried it inside his doublet, so that it pressed against his rib, a constant irritation reminding him of what was lost.

In the days and weeks that followed he found he could not bear to look at the horse, whose fault it was not, nor himself, whose fault it was, nor Kate, whose every movement seemed an accusation, nor the bairns, who sought attention that he couldn't give. Nor could he go away, which was his inclination. Instead he marked out an area of ground in the valley below the tower, and refusing all offers of help, began to clear it of stones. With the stones he made a wall, and it was as if he built it as a defence, not to protect the sheep whose new lambing pen it was to be, but as a barrier around himself, that no-one could breach.

Part Three

January 1590 – April 1591

This above all: to thine own self be true . . .

Hamlet: Act 1 scene 3

Chapter One

Winter passed.

Little word came from Kilmaurs to give them either quiet or dismay, their unease over Archie and Sybilla displaced by more personal ills. Kate kept herself occupied with the children: nursing Ellie, braiding Maggie's hair and playing endless games of marbles and Nine Men's Morris with Robbie. A clear attempt to bring a forced gaiety to the long evenings; so that Munro, unable to speak of it, ached for her, for the children and most of all for the Anna-shaped chasm that yawned everywhere you looked. Robbie had lost his competitive edge and despite that it had often been a trial, Munro missed his quick flare of temper when things went awry. Maggie, though still with a ready smile, seemed also to have lost her bounce. Even Ellie, for all that she was but months old, grizzled at odd moments as if she too felt the lack.

He was taken by surprise that the usual concerns of winter: the timely servicing of the ewes and the cattle, the repairing of walls and byres, the worry that the straw wouldn't last out, that the food laid by would be insufficient to see them through to the spring, that the animals confined to the byres might ail, were just as they had been every winter for as long as he could remember. Daily, the thought weighed on him: only we have changed. And all my blame. His mother failed each time they saw her and he dreaded another funeral, the pain of Anna's still with the power to fell him like a blow.

March came in wet and wild, an unusually fierce storm lifting the foot-square roofing slabs on one side of the tower and scattering them across the rough slopes below. Although some were recoverable, most were not, and Munro was forced to plunder their small savings to pay for the new stone and the mason to replace them. There were few jobs he wouldn't tackle himself, but the roofing of the main tower one of them.

Paradoxically, the setback seemed to ignite a spark of the old Kate. She placed a hand on his arm as the mason left, two-thirds of their hard saved cash clinking in his saddle-bag. 'There is always a blessing. No-one is hurt and the job is well done and should see us right for years to come.'

'I know, only . . .' he had been about to say that he had a mind to take Kate away for a bit: abroad even, to Holland or France. But little point in speaking of what they could no longer do.

'Only what? We have a wee pickle still aside if we need it, though with spring just around the corner, I can't think for what.'

'It doesn't matter.'

It was the first normal conversation in months and both of them aware of it, both equally afraid to continue lest they strayed into dangerous territory.

At the beginning of April with lambing newly on him, Munro received a summons from his mother. She received him in her bedchamber, the first time he'd been at her bedside since a child, and though she pulled herself up against the pillows, it was clear that even that effort was much for her.

238

He touched her shoulder, the bones fine as a bird's under his fingers. 'I should have been here sooner.'

'For why? To carry worry the longer?' Her skin was parchment-thin and heavily lined, a map of veins like clogged tributaries through which her blood battled to pass. 'When it is time I will know.'

'Come back with me.'

'I wish to die at my own hearth.' She gripped his hand, but there was little power in her fingers. 'I am well looked after here. And death isn't for the young. . . .' Her eyes signalled her distress, the silence between them a weight crushing his chest. 'Let the bairns mind me as I was.' She closed her eyes and he thought that she had slipped into sleep and wondered if he should leave. But whatever else had caused her to call for him, it wasn't that he could sit by her side a while and begin to grieve, though her not dead. And so he waited, perched on the edge of the bed, her hand lying in his, almost weightless. The silence deepened and, for a moment, he thought her wish fulfilled, that she had known and so had cried him. He had time to begin to be glad of the call before he heard the fresh in-gasp of breath.

She spoke as if the conversation between them had never been interrupted. 'Wabbit I can stand, wandered I couldn't. If you wish to make a prayer on my behalf, let it be that I go before my wits desert me.' Again a silence, her gaze sliding past Munro to settle on the hanging behind him. He pictured the embroidered initials – AM and MC, the colour of the silks faded to a dull brown, and guessed, wrongly, that she minded his father.

'What of Archie? Have you word?'

He was startled back to attention. 'None since I was last here. He was aye a poor correspondent.'

'And the Boyds? Have they had anything?'

'No idea.' He turned the conversation. 'You should see Ellie now. Red-headed for sure, and already starting to curl for all it's no length.'

'And a temper to match?'

'Oh, aye. She may be but a wee mite yet, but there's nothing wrong with her lungs, and when she's cross, she clenches her fists and hammers her heels that hard that if she forgot what angered her in the first place, she'd still be howling from the pain of it.'

'Maybe it's a blessing I won't be around to see the fallings-out between her and Maggie then.'

It was his turn to look past her, to the cross-stitch that Kate had given her last Yuletide but one: of the bairns in the barmkin. Anna, riding the wooden horse across her knees, Robbie whittling at a stick and Maggie, kneeling on the cobbles, a kitten sleeping at her feet. He admired the spirit in his mother that made a joke of imminent death but found himself unable to reply in kind.

She touched his face so that he was obliged to look at her. 'I have had my share of this world and am ready for the next. Only . . .'

He waited.

'. . . I would wish to see Archie settled. The last time . . .' She began to worry again at the embroidered coverlet. 'Last time he was here he seemed over hard for his own good.'

'Yet when I went to Kilmaurs, I found him changed, less William's man.' Her hand fluttered under his fingers. 'You will say when I must cry him home? And in good time?'

'If I can.'

'Should I send the now?' He was searching her face, trying to draw out a sense of how she really felt.

240

'A week or two maybe. Tell him I won't make his wedding, but a wee sign of intent would be welcome.'

'I'm not sure . . .' he began.

'He has long had more thought on Sybilla Boyd than you might have supposed. And I don't think biding in the same house will have cooled him any.'

Munro thought of the expression on Archie's face as Sybilla squeezed past William, his admission that he stayed at Kilmaurs to protect her. 'Marriage wouldn't do him any harm, or so Kate would say.'

'You were lucky in your choice.'

He heard the real affection in her voice and so tried one last time. 'Are you sure you don't want to bide with us, even for a little while?'

She shook her head, her voice vehement, 'I've told you no.'

He raised his hands in a gesture of surrender and stood up.

'Don't go yet. I didn't call you to talk of death just, though it is likely my most pressing concern . . . I was thinking May is aye a fine month.'

He knew that her abrupt change of direction was deliberate and that the seeming inconsequential remark would have a point to it.

'Mother?'

Her eyes, though washed out, danced.

'If you don't tell me what your game is now I'll have to go.' It was a shrewd move.

'There is a box under the bed.'

He hunkered down and lifted the edge of brocade that swept the floor.

Hoisting the small oak chest onto the bed, he thought – she has heard of the roof. 'We don't need . . .'

'This isn't about need.' She was fingering the clasp.

'They say the King and his new Queen are expected shortly and May a fine month for a celebration.'

He shook his head, gave a half laugh.

'I had thought it might be a fitty thing for you to take Kate to see the Queen's entry.' She halted his withdrawal. 'To leave the bairns awhile would do no harm. Indeed, it may be what is needed.'

'I don't know if we could.'

'I have done my share of grieving and home isn't always the easiest place for it. The loss of a child . . .' A single tear formed at the corner of her eye, slid down the side of her nose. 'It will always be with you, but the pain of it will dull. She paused, as if to draw strength to continue, 'Blame is a poor bedfellow: A jaunt may help you both.' She traced the lover's knot on the lid of the box. 'I know your roof hasn't bankrupted you, but it will have made a dent that isn't so easy to fill. Open it.'

Two drawstring pouches lay in the base of the chest, the outline of coins stretching the soft kid leather.

'One will be yours soon enough. Why not now? That I might share some of Kate's pleasure in the spending of it.' A wistful note crept into her voice. 'I didn't have the chance when Queen Mary came, but that isn't a reason to keep others back.' She pulled herself further up in the bed, a spasm crossing her face. He placed one hand under her arm, lifting and tilting her so that he could raise her pillow.

'One more thing,' she gestured to the large kist under the window. 'There is a dress: burgundy and silver and scarce worn.'

'Kate isn't . . .'

'I don't mean for her to wear it. Forbye the fit, it's hardly fashionable, but there is a breadth of material in it that should provide the makings of a fine gown. Something new is aye welcome.'

She looked past him to where the last rays of sunlight slanted onto the rush floor, criss-crossed with shadows cast by the window bars, and weariness settled on her like a layer of dust that had been raised in the passing and now fell again. He stood up and caught the flash of a bird swooping past the window. As he bent to kiss her she tapped his cheek with a cold finger. 'I won't be long a prisoner and I have a notion that I shall enjoy to fly.'

Chapter Two

He arrived home bringing with him both the proposal that they make for Edinburgh for the Queen's entry, and the burgundy gown. At first, Kate was adamant. 'I have lost one bairn and can't think of leaving the rest'.

Agnes was equally firm. 'I have looked after all your bairns and you before them. If I can't be trusted to watch them for a ween of days, I don't know who can.'

'You see?' Munro, thinking of what his mother had said, risked rebuff by catching Kate around the waist and spinning her like the top he had once bought for Robbie. Strands of her hair escaped from her cap, the pomander that dangled from a ribbon at her belt swinging wildly. Dizzy, she collapsed against him and he wrapped his arms around her. Lest she took flight he said nothing more, only began to draw circles on her back with the tip of one finger, while with his other hand he stroked her hair.

It took Kate three evenings to unpick the pearls which dusted the mitred sleeves of the dress that Mary had sent, that she might re-use them on the bodice, which she pinned and tucked and corsetted and re-cut into a long, narrow point. The remainder she set aside for outlining the waist and trimming a new cap. She added a double ruff to the shoulders and a hanging oversleeve that came far past the end of her fingers. The timely arrival of a pedlar allowed her to buy a set of tiny silver buttons to match the lattice-work that trimmed the full skirt. Daringly, she altered the neckline; the décolletage softened somewhat by a lace frill. Even so, Agnes sniffed when she saw it and Kate herself, though she wouldn't have admitted it, wondered if she had perhaps cut it a little too fine. When it was done, they took it to Mary to let her see the result.

It was the first time that Kate had ridden out since Anna's death and she betrayed her nervousness in every twitch of the reins. But lifting her face to the sun and relishing the breeze that ruffled her hair, she relaxed. The horse Midnight having been sold, she rode the one that Munro had bought the previous autumn, its coat, now that it had shed the winter shagginess and had been both well fed and well groomed, gleaming copper in the sunlight. The newly fashioned dress, carefully wrapped, straddled the saddle in front of her.

Mary was complimentary, 'I knew fine you'd make a job of it,'

Kate revolved, her fingers slipping to the lace at her chest.

'And don't worry about that neckline. They have been lower before and I dare say will be so again, but you have nothing to fear from the sight of your throat. Come closer that I may see the buttons.'

It was the fourth week of April when a pedlar brought the news that the King's fleet was expected within days. Munro left immediately to ride to Edinburgh to seek accommodation, contracting to take two rooms on the third floor of a house on Merlyon's Wynd. His first thought, though a mite optimistic, had been to try the High Street, perhaps even to stretch to a balcony. But generous as his mother was, her money hadn't been any match for that of the lords and earls who flooded into Edinburgh to await the return of the King and his young bride, and who competed for lodgings to match their station.

'We are lucky to get even these,' he said as he led Kate down the narrow wynd and up the flight of stone steps to the low door. She ducked to enter, rubbing her finger against one of the iron diamonds that studded the dark oak, noting the sharpness of the point, not yet blunted from repeated painting. Inside, they climbed up a stair that clung to the wall, emerging onto an open landing with timber rails and a pitched roof. A second stair dog-legged up to an even smaller doorway set in the corner, the timber treads creaking and groaning as they climbed so that she said,

'No risk of surprise visitors then.'

The door opened straight into the main chamber, which ran the full depth of the house. A narrow window at the far side, set in a triangular alcove, spilled a shard of sunlight across the centre of the floor. Munro waited, saliva flooding his mouth, as Kate leant her elbows on the stone sill, pressing her nose against the glass. She moved to the bedchamber and swung the door back and forwards. It was made of broad planks about eight inches wide, curiously put together: on the one side the planks set vertically, on the other horizontally.

'Why d'you think . . .' she began, sliding her thumb up the edge.

'It's to avoid warping.' He wondered if she concentrated on the door to save commenting on the rooms.

And then she was beside him, linking her arms around his waist. 'We are here. That is what matters and I don't expect to spend over long inside. She moved to the bed and pressed down firmly on the centre of the mattress, then pulled back the coverlet to examine the sheets. 'Or not by day, at least. It doesn't sag and the sheets are clean. What more do we need?'

Munro woke first. Daylight slipped into their bedchamber like a wraith: grey and insubstantial, filtered through the grime and soot that coated the outside of the window-panes. He had little idea of the time and lay without moving, allowing his mind to drift. Beside him Kate stirred, then slid from the bed to go to the chamberpot, tucked into the corner behind a wooden screen. He stretched and yawned, lying back against the pillows, his hands behind his head. As she moved to the window her hair, caught in a caul, curled and sprung on her back, rich blue-black against the white of her shift. He travelled the outline of her body, past the narrowing of her waist and the spread of her hips, need rising in him. 'Kate?'

She turned and lifted her arm to push a strand of hair from her eyes, her shift tightening against her breast.

'There aren't cattle to feed, nor lambs to check, nor bairns to distract . . .' He heard her breathing quicken, 'And I'm not hungered, or not for food, the now.'

When they woke again, though the light hadn't altered, noise from the High Street surged through the close, the volume rising and falling in waves. Kate lay, her head tucked into Munro's shoulder, one arm thrown across his chest. In the background expected sounds: the rumbling of cartwheels on the cobbles, the creaking of axles, the click-clack of wooden pattens, a pedlar, calling his wares up and down the street. The scuffling and cursing as stall-holders set up for the day: flinging back shutters on the lucken-booths, dragging tables onto the street, hanging bells in doorways. A jangle of accents and languages: Scots, French, Gaelic, even the occasional burst of English. Kate sensed an extra excitement.

She shook Munro.

He muttered and turned and sat up, rubbing his eyes. 'What is it?'

'The noise. It may be nothing but . . .'

'Of course there's noise. This isn't Broomelaw.'

'There are the noises I looked for, but it doesn't sound . . . she cocked her head to one side and searched for a word to describe her feeling. 'It's the voices.'

He reached up to pull gently on a curl that had escaped from her caul. 'You didn't expect to hear only Scots?'

She refused to be distracted. 'It isn't the languages. It's . . .'

'Intuition?'

'You may lie all day if you please, but I'm for finding out what's going on.' She was out of bed, twisting her hair into a knot, stepping into the dress hanging over the screen. 'The King and Queen may have arrived.'

'They won't come without warning.' He lay back, 'James may have slipped away quiet, but he won't return without suitable fanfare.'

She was struggling with her fastenings, so that Munro, taking pity, padded across the bare floorboards to tug at the strings, nipping her waist tight.

'Forgiven?' His breath was warm against her ear.

'If you're quick. For I'm not for waiting.'

Emerging into the wynd that led to Edinburgh's High Street, Kate lifted her skirts high. Beside her, Munro lifted one eyebrow.

'I won't have my new gown ruined for the sake of a wee bit sight of my stockings. Or not at least till the Coronation is past.

'It isn't the stockings I'm looking at.' His grin was wicked. 'Rather the ankles.' He brought his brows together in pretended thought. 'Shapely still, though I suspicion there may be a slight thickening. . . .' He side-stepped, but not fast enough, as her foot flashed out and caught him neatly on the shin. He rubbed at the spot with his other foot. 'You didn't warn me I might need the protection of my boots.'

'You didn't warn me I came to be insulted.'

'Glad you came then?'

'Maybe.' She looked down at the cobbles dipping against the edge of the pavement, and with the toe of her shoe poked at the gutter, where a mess of vegetable peelings mingled with the rotting remains of fish bones and wood ash. And among them the ribcage of a crow, his wing part splayed, slivers of white bone visible through the sodden feathers. His head was twisted to the side, staring fixedly at the sky from the empty eye socket, the beak open as if for one last indignant squawk. Kate's hand flew to her mouth. Not that she wasn't used to the sight of a dead bird. On the contrary, it was common enough on the open moorland, but this bird, unlike those at home, swiftly picked clean by other scavengers, had lain over long and maggots crawled at the corner of its mouth.

'Dust and dirt I expected, but not this glaur.'

'It doesn't say much for the street cleaners, I admit.'

Her eyes widened.

'Don't look so sceptical. There is a contract for the cleaning of all the paving. It's to be kept smart till the royal entry is past. Maybe they haven't got this far yet.'

'Or maybe they've no idea what clean is.'

As they emerged into the sunlight from the dimness of the close, Kate, courtesy of Mary's thoughtfulness and her own skill with a needle felt perfectly at home amongst the crowds of well-dressed ladies that paraded between the Castle and the Canongate and dallied at the stalls that lined the broad street. Fingering the nap of the velvet she hoisted the hem a little higher.

Munro slipped his arm around her waist, his fingers counting out the pearls that circled it. 'Glad you came?' he repeated.

Her answer: to lean into him as far as the width of her skirt would allow.

They sauntered towards the Tolbooth and she spent a happy hour browsing among the riot of colour that was the cloth market: the deep plums and reds and burgundy velvets, the tawny and gold brocades, the blue and silver satins. She lingered longest at a stall piled high with bales of shot silks, irridescent at her touch. 'Perhaps you shouldn't have brought me,' she said, turning them backwards and forwards in the light.

'Should I send you home? It wouldn't please Agnes.'

She let the cloth slip, the colours rippling through her

fingers, and lifted her eyes. 'No. They're pretty to see but I won't grieve for the lack of them, or . . . only a little.'

Reaching the stalls that sold more mundane offerings, she by-passed the plain linens and white-bleached cambrics, but halted again to finger the woollens. She dismissed the coarse heavyweights, but hesitated over a fine weave, the colour of standing corn. Behind her a yawn, quickly stifled.

Taking the edge of the cloth in both hands, she pulled at the bale unravelling enough that she could rub it between her fingers. It was fine and soft, without even the hint of scratching. 'D'you think this would suit your mother?'

'Belly wool, the best. Soft enough for a babe.'

Kate smiled at the young stallholder. 'It's for a grand-dame I thought it.'

The girl changed her pitch. 'Warmer than some twice the weight.' Her voice was eager, 'And home-spun and dyed and woven. I don't sell foreign stuff.'

Kate ran the cloth through her fingers again. 'It would be a fitting thank you for the gown,' she said, as much to herself as to Munro, who stood behind her, shielding her from the jostling and pushing of the crowds. 'D'you think?' At the last, when it was paid for and roughly wrapped and they had turned away, Kate glanced back to see the girl, who had protested, mouth drooping, that she didn't make so much as a bawbee on the sale, dance a little jig on the cobbles.

'Did I pay too much?'

'You did fine and the price fair to all, I reckon, though,' he squeezed her waist, 'I'm not an expert on cloth.' He shifted the parcel more comfortably under his arm. 'Have you seen enough?'

'For the now, perhaps.' An expression of dismay, quickly masked, flitted across his face and she laughed up at him, tucking her arm through his. 'I may not be here again and wish to make the most of it. There are the jewellers and the haberdashers and . . .'

'And fleshers and brewers and bakers . . .'

As if she took him serious, she continued, 'Those too, and souters and baxters . . .'

'There are sights other than shops.' He had fallen into the trap she set for him, but tried to recover some ground. 'And we will have time for a few.'

'Four days,' she said, '. . . time for them all.'

The first cannon shot came as Kate placed the cloth for her mother in law in the chest in their bedchamber, so that she dropped the lid with a bang. Munro was lounging on the settle in the main room and she flew through to him, her eyes shining.

'They must have arrived.' She was running a brush through her hair, smoothing it into a coil, replacing her cap. 'Come on!' She pulled at him and he allowed himself to be dragged to his feet.

The sound of cannon fire was all around them now, coming from the castle as well as the port, the smoke that accompanied each bang hanging in a pall above the battlements. The High Street seethed with people, as if the whole of Scotland packed Edinburgh to welcome their new Queen. Caught in the surge, they were swept up the hill towards the castle. Munro fought to keep a grip of Kate and tried to work his way across the heave of bodies towards the

Grassmarket, intending to skirt round and tunnel their way down to the Cowgate and thence to Holyrood.

Someone dunted him sharply from behind knocking him into a fat burgess who glowered and trod heavily on Munro's foot. He had a face as round as a neep and a similar colour: purple mottling, as of an over-indulgence of claret, spreading across his cheeks and bleeding into a jawline as pale as a babe's. A scuffle and a shout and one moment Kate was clinging tight to his side, the next her arm was wrenched from his, and she was carried to the left, her capped head now sucked towards him, now away. Each movement increased the distance between them, the surge of people carrying her like a piece of flotsam tossed on the tide. He fought to follow in her wake, pushing and jostling, struggling to keep sight of her. In front of him a woman swayed, then crumpled. Instinctively, he put out his arm and caught her, the dead weight making him stagger. He was holding her up and elbowing people sideways, all the while bawling for space and air. A young lad took her other arm and between them they propelled her towards the edge of the street and stumbled against a doorway, hammering for entrance.

'You'll not get any joy there.' The voice behind him was matter of fact. 'If you had a lucken-booth and your stock your only capital, would you open your door in this rabble?'

Munro stopped pounding. Something registered in the voice, but not enough to distract him from the problem in hand.

'If you'd any wit, it would be a close you'd make for, not a shop.' The voice was still behind him, still detached, still niggling for recognition, as the woman stirred. Munro spoke without turning. 'And you could help by making a bit of a clearance.'

'I could.' The man was already herding those who pressed in on them away from the walls. 'There's an entry about ten yards to the left that will take us out of the flow.'

Once into the entry, Munro and his fellow helper paused for breath. Ahead of them, through another archway, steps led downwards. The stranger now leading the way, had all but disappeared in the shadows of the close. Munro heard the footsteps stop, the voice floating up.

'If it's air she's after, don't stop there.'

The woman stirred again, this time opening her eyes. She tried to detach herself from their grasp, but Munro held on and spoke softly to her as he would to a horse. 'Rest easy, we mean you no harm. You had a faint and we have brought you from the crush.' He and the lad, who had likewise grasped her as she fell, continued downwards, half-supporting, half carrying her and she made no further resistance. The steps led under a third archway and into a small cobbled courtyard, lines strung across it, stone troughs set around the walls, the sting of ammonia indicating that it was a bleaching yard.

'Not the most savoury of airs, I admit, but space to sit at least.' Munro helped the woman to a seat on the edge of one of the troughs.

'You'll not be needing me now,' and the lad bowed to the woman then dashed back along the close to resume in the festivities.

The man who had led them to safety lounged against the wall, grinning.

'Patrick!' Munro, peered into the shadows, 'I thought I knew the voice but believed you were still in France?'

'Clearly not.' Patrick's grin widened. 'It suited me to take some leave . . .'

Mentally colouring what Patrick had left unsaid, Munro heard nothing more until the mention of Elizabeth.

'Elizabeth? She's here?'

'She wouldn't stay away, with Hugh likely to be stuck until the coronation is past. They have a daughter and Elizabeth wished that I bring her and the babe both that she may meet her father.'

The woman was slowly rising, dusting down the apron that covered most of the front of her gown. She touched her head and finding she still had her hat, ran her fingers around the brim, in an attempt to improve its shape. 'You have my thanks, sir, but I must go. I have family but we were separated . . .'

'Dear God . . . Kate.'

The woman looked up at him questioningly.

'I also am separated . . .' He bowed, 'I trust you find your family.'

'And you.' She bobbed a curtsey and hurried away.

Patrick took hold of his arm. 'Your wife was with you in the press?'

'Yes . . . no . . . we had been separated minutes before. I was trying to make for her when the woman collapsed. God knows where she'll be now.'

'We'll find her.' All the fun had gone from Patrick's voice. 'What direction was she taken?'

'Towards the castle.' They were taking the steps two at a time, their conversation breathy and disjointed. 'We thought to make our way to the park, and were trying to cross towards the Grassmarket. Kate will be fair sore if she misses anything.'

'As to that, she needn't worry. The King and Queen

255

don't come from Leith today and I can promise her a grand spot when they do.'

'If we find her.'

Patrick gripped his shoulder, 'When we find her.'

The crowds were beginning to thin, ebbing away with the rumour that the King and Queen bided at Leith while preparations were made for a fitting entrance. The main flow was down towards the Canongate and Munro hesitated, unsure of which way to go. Though there were fewer people and therefore less chance that Kate be injured by the crush, he was aware of a new mood of truculence, borne out of the general disappointment, and his worry remained.

'Perhaps we should separate.'

'You make for the castle then and I'll plough my way to the Grassmarket. If I have no joy there, I'll head for the Tolbooth.'

'We need a meeting point. Do you know Merlyon's Wynd?'

'Above the Grassmarket?'

'Aye. We have lodgings there. On the third floor.' Munro was already turning away.

'I'll make for that then.'

Munro was dodging and ducking through the knots of people. Twice, against the tide, he made his way to the castle entrance, the first time turning immediately and tacking back down again, criss-crossing the spur, his anxiety growing as each sweep proved futile. The second time he penetrated through the long passageway under the portcullis, to wash up onto the cobbles at the foot of the Lang Stair. He looked up towards the watch-tower at the end of the Forewall Battery and though he thought it unlikely that Kate would have been swept so far, he was unwilling to discount anything and so made for the main castle courtyard. Out of breath by the time he'd climbed the seventy or so steps, he emerged through the archway into the sunlight.

No sign of Kate.

He halted, bent double, his hands on his knees, his breathing jagged, resting his backside against the outcrop of rock that thrust through the cobbles directly in front of the entrance. Then he straightened and clattered back down the steps, heading for the wall overlooking the town. Directly below him the High Street stretched, people still milling but no longer packed tight. He could see shutters being removed, doors propped open, stall canopies fluttering in the wind as poles were straightened and stallholders re-established their pitch – she can't be lying hurt and I haven't found her. Perhaps Patrick . . . or maybe she's made it back to the lodgings.

They were welcome thoughts buoying Munro as he headed down through the Landmarket for the third time. Nevertheless, he remained on the lookout and drew a few angry looks and rude gestures from those who took exception to his staring as he passed. He turned into Merlyon's Wynd, and fairly flew up the stair. The door was pulled open from the inside and Kate was there, laughing and crying all at once.

'Kate! I feared . . .'

'You feared?' Her voice rose half an octave. 'I couldn't keep my feet on the ground, and breathing wasn't exactly easy. I didn't think it altogether impossible that I might die in the crush and not see the Queen at all.'

'And me?' His hands cupped her face, his eyes dark.

'And you.' It was barely a whisper, her lips close to his, their breath mingling. 'And you.'

When Patrick knocked at the door half an hour later, he found them seated in the window reveal. Kate, her head bent, was mending a long tear on the hem of her dress, Munro doing his best to distract her.

'Safe and sound, as you see.' He rose, pulling Kate with him. 'Patrick Montgomerie, Braidstane's brother. He also was looking for you.'

Patrick bowed, 'And wouldn't have found you, not by his description: he didn't have you so pretty.'

Kate managed a stiff, 'You have my thanks.'

Munro said, 'Have you time for a bite? It would give Kate a chance to become acquaint.'

'I am sent to Leith to find Hugh and bring him back with me.' Patrick was shaking his head with every indication of regret and Kate, Munro's eyes on her, said, 'Perhaps another time then. Do you stay long in Edinburgh?'

The words were fine enough but there was little of encouragement in either her tone or her expression.

'Long enough to see that Hugh doesn't get into bother, or if he does, to pull him out of it.'

'A winter away will have cooled him surely, forbye his new responsibilities.' Munro turned to Kate. 'They have a bairn, just five months.'

Patrick re-directed his smile. 'And your namesake.'

Munro, sensing a slight relaxation in her, tried to develop the topic. 'Who does she favour?'

Patrick ran his fingers through his hair. 'Without her bonnet: a cat with the mange.'

Kate tried to suppress her laughter.

Munro pressed the advantage. 'Serious though?'

'Serious: her mother. But as to temperment . . .' He shrugged, '. . . as you know, Hugh isn't always steady.'

'Is any man?' The coolness had returned to Kate's voice.

Patrick appeared to consider. 'Some . . . and those tedious.'

'Folk don't die from tedium.'

'I've come close. But have always been brought back from the brink,' He enclosed her in his smile. 'Mostly by a pretty face and a kind word.'

'Kind words need earning.'

Munro withdrew his arm, but before he could say anything, Patrick slapped himself on the side of his head.

'I almost forgot. Failing to find you between here and the Canongate, I called at our lodgings to explain my delay, for we bide in Airlie House that Robert, Master of Eglintoun has taken and I have two womenfolk watching for me and must account for every minute. They charged me with an invite for you both for tomorrow. Around noon. It will be hard words I earn indeed if I don't bring your promise with me.'

Munro ignoring Kate's bent head, said, 'Tomorrow then.' He saw Patrick to the door. 'I'm sorry she wasn't more welcoming.'

'She sees danger in our contact and with justice.' Patrick was picking at the painted stair-rail. 'Don't fret, Elizabeth will thaw her. Women have their own ways of getting on, especially with a bairn to admire.'

Patrick gone, Munro stood by the window staring over

the roofs of the houses towards the open ground beyond, the razor-edged cliff that cut the horizon rust-red against the deep green of the hill. In the distance, near the West Port where the houses backed on to the Park, he could see squares of linen draped over the bushes. A woman emerged and began to gather in the cloths: one, lifted by the wind, evaded capture and she stretched up to grab hold of the corners and jerk it taut before folding. From nowhere, ringing in his ears, the voice of Lady Margaret Langshaw. 'There will be a white napkin hanging. Beyond that I cannot do more.' He shut his eyes against the image of her hand at her throat, the slender fingers still clutching the child's shift. And squeezing around it, other pictures. A line of riders strung out along a ridge. The ford at Annock, the banks unmarked. He pressed his head against the sharp edge of the window moulding, welcoming the pain, seeking to halt the memories that pressed on him. The horses trampling the edges of the river, spooked by the smell of blood. Water flowing red over the rough stones, dragging at the bodies. The face of the young lad. Why did Kate have to bring it all back? An unjust thought, but one he carried with him through the rest of the day and into their bed also, the mood of the morning broken.

Chapter Three

'Can you not bide at peace?' Grizel was sitting on a bench under a walnut tree in the garden of a house on Edinburgh's Canongate. 'Pacing won't bring them any quicker, forbye that it may drive me mad.'

Elizabeth perched on the edge of the bench, stood up again. 'I can't settle. Patrick has been gone for ages.'

'Give him time.' Grizel checked off her fingers as she spoke, 'One, he had half the High street to traverse to check on the Munros. Two, it isn't just a step to Leith. Three, he doesn't know what vessel Hugh comes on, and he can't just take himself onto any ship he pleases without permission. And four, we don't even know how far out the ships were when the cannons were fired or if they are berthed by now or not.'

Elizabeth halted beside a climbing rose trained against the wall, 'I know. But it's the end of a long winter.' She plucked a rose and systematically began to detach the pale pink petals, one by one.

'You at least know that Hugh comes, whereas I . . .' Aware that she betrayed more of her feelings than she intended, Grizel shifted focus. 'I wouldn't let our hostess see that you destroy her roses for they aren't so plentiful she can afford the loss.'

Elizabeth looked down at her fingers, the tips stained pollen-yellow, and at the ground where the petals curled.

'I didn't realise.' She tossed the stem onto the soil at the base of the plant and trod it in with the toe of her shoe, scuffing up the soil around it. '. . . Did Sigurd give you any reason to suppose he might accompany the King's fleet?'

'Only a hint, and even that may have been my imagination, but I sent back word, that it was our intention to meet Hugh on his return.'

'Well then.'

Grizel worried at her lip. The single evening she had spent with Sigurd, while the November rain pelted on the windows and they crept nearer and nearer the fire and each other, had blurred so that she had come to fear to depend on her own recollection.

As if she read her mind, Elizabeth said, 'I don't doubt his interest in you. If he can, he will come.'

Hugh was in the cabin he shared with Alexander, cramming the last of his possessions into his bag, when the ship's bell sounded. Easy to pack on his outward journey, it was much harder in the home strait.

Alexander had laughed each time Hugh bought some new trinket for Elizabeth or the babe to add to his growing pile. 'It'll likely be wasted effort. Lad or lass, the bairn will take precedence and you be relegated to second place.'

Hugh refused to rise to the teasing, and first in Oslo, then Elsinore and finally Copenhagen had sought for tokens to sweeten his return.

It had been gone two in the afternoon when the small fleet docked in Leith. With the cannon-fire salutes from surrounding ships ringing in his ears, the fears that had fermented in him all winter, slow and feeble like the third brewing of ale, surfaced, suddenly strong. He didn't know how Elizabeth had fared, or if indeed he was a father, and chafed at the thought that James would expect his presence in Edinburgh until the festivities surrounding their homecoming and the coronation were done. Perhaps he would be able to slip away . . . he could be home and back in three days if he pushed, and likely miss little, for despite that Maitland had been chivvying the corporation for months, the word was that the city was not yet prepared for all the victualing required, the preparations for the coronation at the Abbey likewise incomplete. He hurried to the deck.

James stood at the prow, Anne by his side, slightly pale still from the rough weather that had threatened to disrupt her journey for the third time. James' mouth was close to her ear as he gestured to the crag that dominated the Edinburgh skyline and the castle that straddled the rock beneath it. Though common knowledge that James wasn't overly keen on the castle, his favoured residence Holyrood, the castle was visible and impressive and no doubt James wished to show pride for his Queen's first sight of the capital. Hugh pushed his way to the rail.

The windows of the warehouses bounding the quay were packed tight with folk clapping and cheering and craning for a glimpse of the young Queen. A cheering which redoubled in volume as the couple disembarked through the covered way erected for the occasion. It was covered in tapestry and cloth of gold, the colours glowing in the sunlight, the cobbles beneath carpetted with Turkish rugs. Cannons from the castle joined in the salute as James and Anne walked the short distance to the King's Wark which, though the customhouse, was now to do double duty as a temporary royal lodging. Anne's corn-coloured hair and pale complexion made a pleasing contrast to James: ginger as a child, his hair had deepened to a rich auburn and his skin, unmarked by the pox, was sallow.

Alexander hadn't followed James down the gangway, instead battling his way to Hugh. He looked up at the people who hung from the warehouse windows. 'If it's looks she is judged by, then her popularity won't be in doubt.'

Hugh was watching James and Anne's progress along the quay. 'She carries herself like a queen – for all that she is little more than a child and in a foreign country.'

'A child who has been bred to royalty and to the responsibilities that entails. She was but nine when a Danish marriage was first thought on, and she might have come to it sooner had not her father made difficulties over the dowry.'

'Or not at all, had not her sister been promised else-where.'

'True. Had the Orkney issue been settled sooner, then it would have been Elizabeth we feted and not Anne.'

The ship was beginning to empty, the courtiers following James and Anne in a slow stream towards their temporary lodgings.

Alexander moved towards the dock. 'Are you coming? The word is that Elphinstone waits at the King's Wark and has the task of presenting the oration.'

'No doubt as dull and predictable as the Sermon of Thanksgiving to follow.' The King and Queen had passed beyond their view, the crowds that milled on the quayside thinning, heading for the church, hoping for another glimpse of the royal pair. Hugh was just about to broach the question of whether or not it would be possible for him to make for Braidstane and be back in time for the state entry into Edinburgh, when they were hailed from the quay. Patrick took the gangway in two strides to appear at their side.

'You didn't drown then.'

'What are you doing here? I thought you in France.'

'You may blame two ladies. One here with a need that called me home and one in Paris with a need that drove me away.'

'The need that drove you away isn't hard to guess, but who called you home?'

'Elizabeth, failing a husband . . .'

'She doesn't ail? And the bairn?'

'Both well, and here.'

'Here?'

Patrick looked at Alexander. 'Is he wandered?'

Alexander laughed. 'I hadn't noticed, but then, it wouldn't be that much different from usual.'

'Where's here?' Hugh shook Patrick.

Patrick detached himself and rubbed at his arms. 'A house that Robert Montgomerie has taken on the Canongate – she and Grizel and the bairn. And looking to three ladies, forbye the babe, makes soldiering seem easy, I can tell you. I'm fair exhausted.'

'A lass, then.' Hugh was grinning.

'And bonny with it.'

Alexander placed a hand on Hugh's shoulder. 'Away with you. You'll not be missed the night, and if you are, I'll make your peace with James. Though I don't think there'll be the need. He's likely to look kindly the now on a husband's desire to be with his wife and in this circumstance.'

Elizabeth was still in the garden when Patrick and Hugh came through the archway. She was sitting in the late afternoon sunshine, a pamphlet of Andrew Melville's, on the relative merits of bishops versus a presbtery, open on her lap. He had a way with words, whether you took to him or not, but she had read the first page three times and still couldn't have given the gist of it.

Her back was to the entrance, so that Hugh was able to slip behind her and grasp her waist.

'Hugh!' If he had any doubts of his welcome, they were gone immediately. She was on her feet and spinning in his arms.

'I didn't know whether to expect you or not. Patrick thought . . . Oh, Hugh.'

'Don't mind me!' Patrick pretended affront.

'Grizel's inside with Robert's wife Jean. I couldn't settle and she got fair peeved with my pacing. Patrick, tell her Hugh is come.'

'You see?' Patrick shook his head at Hugh. 'Your wife has become a tyrant in your absence and now you're home, will no doubt rule you also.'

Elizabeth's breathing slowed as she tugged Hugh towards the shade of the walnut tree. 'You have another lady to greet . . . I have called her Kate.'

Hugh bent over and pulled back the blanket from the child's forehead, revealing a soft down of hair that lay in damp wisps. He sounded disappointed. 'She isn't fair.'

Elizabeth laughed, a mixture of relief that it was not the babe's sex that troubled him and amusement. 'We can't tell the now. Fair or dark, they don't usually keep their first hair.' She edged the blanket down still further and turned Kate's head to the side. 'Look.'

He saw the few tufts that sprouted like mis-sown grass, the bald patches like thumbprints on her scalp.

'What hair she had is coming away fast, but I don't think she'll be bald for long.' Elizabeth took hold of his forefinger and stroked it across the baby's crown so that he felt the tiny spikes of new growth, so fine and fair that they were almost invisible. 'Here.' She lifted the babe, the blanket trailing on the ground and placed her in his outstretched arms. He stood stiff, his shoulders hunched.

'Not like that.' She rearranged him so that Kate's head lay in the crook of his elbow, his forearm stretched out underneath her, the long skirt of the cream smocked gown flowing over his finger-tips. She curved his other arm so that his hand rested against the side of the babe's face. He stood as if he feared to breathe, watching the slight flutter of the babe's eyelids and the scarcely visible rise and fall of her chest. A door closed behind them as Grizel and Patrick, arm in arm, came across the grass.

'Relax, Hugh, she isn't made of eggshells.' Grizel enclosed him and the child both in a tight hug.

Perhaps sensing the commotion, Kate stirred, rubbing her cheek against Hugh's hand and opened her mouth in a wide yawn, displaying two tiny teeth. She nuzzled his thumb, her mouth pursed, then failing to find milk, began to whimper. He hastily held her out to Elizabeth.

'There's no doubting whose daughter she is at feeding time, for she's hard to fill and with no patience at all.'

'I shall have to acknowledge her then.'

Grizel settled herself on the stone bench. 'I have so many questions but . . . I daren't ask the now else you will have it all to tell again over supper.'

'Which won't be long in the coming, I trust.' Patrick

leaned against the trunk of the walnut tree, idly pulling at a cluster of blossom than hung from a low branch.

'Not soon enough, if we are to save the chance of fruit. Between you and Elizabeth, we will be lucky if the garden isn't destroyed altogether.'

Patrick released the branch and it sprung upwards, shedding petals in all directions.

'Whatever I am blamed for can wait.' Elizabeth beckoned from the doorway. 'We are bid to an early supper. The bairn will sleep now, for an hour or two at least. And Robert is as ready as we for news.'

Hugh appeared again early the following morning, poking his head around the door. 'We have a visitor.' Grizel sat up straighter in her chair, her hand flying to her hair, tucking a stray strand under the edge of her coif. He addressed Jean. 'I didn't think you would mind if I extended your hospitality to a stranger, though,' he opened the door wide, 'He isn't a stranger to all.' He presented Sigurd to Jean and his greeting lacked nothing, either in word, or the length of time he leaned over her hand, but when he lifted his head, his eyes slid beyond her and found Grizel.

'The Ivarsens were charged with the bringing of Queen Anne's carriage.' Hugh shot a glance of apology at Elizabeth and Grizel. 'I didn't know of it until this morning for they had a wee bit problem with the *Svanen* and replaced it with another ship. It wasn't one I recognized; else I would have brought him sooner. Forbye I still owe Sigurd a personal debt,' his eyes were on Elizabeth, 'his elder brother made

268

me a firm friend this winter and I like fine to give hospitality to my friends.'

Sigurd lifted Grizel's hand to his lips, his eyes fixed on her face. 'The winter is past and I am come.'

Elizabeth stood on tiptoe to whisper in Hugh's ear.

'And would have come sooner had I not been charged with waiting the Queen's pleasure.'

'No matter. You're here now. And welcome.'

'Have you eaten?' Jean's hand was on the bell-pull by the fireplace.

'Sadly, yes. Though it wasn't the most savoury, it has served.' He patted his stomach. 'If I was to eat more now, it would be greed and not need.'

Grizel smiled at the note of regret. 'There is aye tomorrow. You haven't any other engagements?'

'None that can't be put off. Though it is my intention, while I am here at the Queen's expense, to extend my trading interests and perhaps establish a base, but there is time enough for that.'

'You plan a regular connection then?' Her face was flushed, the bloom in her cheeks becoming.

'My thought is monthly, for the summer at least, and after that, if it is found to be profitable, a more permanent presence might be required.'

A pair of magpies chittered in the branches of the walnut tree and Grizel turned her head towards the window.

Sigurd came to stand close, 'There is a Norwegian rhyme. . .'

'A Scottish one also.' She wetted her lips with her tongue.

Jean joined them. 'Pretty birds. Though aye greedy. If

you were to take some bread . . . or at least show our guest the garden. The walnut tree is particularly fine.'

Hugh eavesdropped without shame as they walked down the path towards the foot of the garden, their voices floating upwards.

Grizel said, 'Your ship's to come monthly?'

'Like clockwork, I trust. At the month's end.'

'Do you accompany it?'

'When I can. It is always sensible to keep a close eye, and I shall persuade my brother that the eye be mine.' He raised a branch of the walnut tree and they passed underneath, Hugh straining to catch the remainder of his response. 'He has not the reason to come, having already a wife and family to his credit.'

When they returned to the house, the talk was of the Queen's entry and the Coronation, the enforced delay.

'It's all about money, and a lot of money at that,' Robert was matter of fact.

'But they've had six months or more in the planning. If the Queen hadn't been driven to shelter in Norway, it would all have been to do last autumn. Surely they were prepared then?'

'Perhaps Elizabeth, but who can blame the burgh for not wishing to spend before they must. They have set aside five thousand merks for the entertainment of our visitors, but it won't stretch. James will no doubt be farming them out to all and sundry.'

Jean frowned at her husband, who raised his hand in apology to Sigurd. 'No offence meant.'

Sigurd shook his head. 'None taken.'

'It would be a fine thing to impress James with your readiness to volunteer hospitality, before it is foisted on you.' Hugh was watching Grizel out of the corner of his eye. 'Sigurd's appetite is healthy, but his company is good and may save you from worse.'

Jean tapped Sigurd's wrist. 'You are more than welcome to bide with us, and not just as the least of many evils.'

'Whatever the cause I intend to enjoy our lengthened visit.' Elizabeth leant back against the settle, 'It's little enough excuse we have to be away from Braidstane.'

'Can you bide tonight?' Grizel directed her question at Hugh, but it was Sigurd's answer she sought.

'Unlikely.' Hugh was apologetic. 'We need James' permission; and though the outcome isn't in doubt, it's getting the chance to speak to him that is the problem. The world and his uncle crowd him with issues that, were I to be uncharitable, I might term trivial. It is a high price he pays for his absence. And that aside from the Danish envoys pressing daily for the inspection of the dowry and the Coronation arrangements. Even Maitland at his most inventive can't find sufficient excuses to keep them at bay.' Hugh saw the disappointment in Grizel's eyes. 'But Alexander has promised to speak for us today.' He stretched. 'Indeed, we should make for Leith the now.'

Robert followed Hugh's lead. 'It's as well that I make an appearance also, lest James find me tardy, forbye the issue of Ivarsen's hospitality.'

'You must all go?'

Hugh bent over the cradle, 'We can't spend our days lazing in a Canongate garden Elizabeth, much as we might wish it.'

'You'll miss our other guests then.'

'Who?'

'Munro and his wife. Patrick bumped into them yesterday in the throng, and they are contracted to visit at noon.'

'See if you can keep them till supper. I'd like fine to see Munro again and make the acquaintance of his wife.' Hugh brushed Elizabeth's head with his lips. 'The sooner we go, the sooner we return.'

Chapter Four

The dawning of a new day had done nothing to dissipate the awkwardness between Munro and Kate. They rose and breakfasted in almost silence, what little conversation they had more akin to that of polite strangers than a married couple of nine years' standing. The spectre of Anna had resurfaced in Kate's every action and utterance, a shadow that, even had she tried, she would have been unable to dispel. Afterwards Munro wasted half an hour in search of their landlord, muttering something about the lock mechanism of the main door, while Kate took three attempts to mend the tear in her gown.

She was pacing up and down, her shawl in her hand when he returned.

'You're ready?'

'We are contracted to go, so go we must. There is little to be gained by delay.'

They continued in silence down the stairs, across the close and through the wynd onto the street. It was almost noon and, in a transparent attempt to regain normality, he took her arm to steer her through the crowds that pushed and haggled around the booths. Passing a pie stall they were assaulted by the smell of the gravy that dribbled in trails down the outside of the thick crusts.

Munro said, 'It fair makes me hungry.'

Silence.

'But I suppose I'd better not eat on the way.'

A fractional lift to her shoulders.

'I like them, Kate.' His hand bit into her arm.

'It's easy to like. But not always safe. They are Montgomeries.' Her head was down, her sentences the staccato of controlled anger. 'What will Glencairn think of your liking? God knows I am no Cunninghame, but I am married on one and don't look to be a widow. We have lost one child,' her voice cracked, 'and the three that remain don't deserve to be orphaned because their father takes a liking that isn't wise.'

He spoke quietly, as if what he said was reasonable. 'Give them a chance, Kate. They don't wish to be our enemies. You could see that. Patrick is. . .'

'Oh yes. Patrick is.' For the first time since leaving their lodging she looked at him. 'Patrick has a way with him. I'll grant you that. But it isn't Patrick that frights me, nor even Braidstane, steady or not. It's William.'

'Glencairn can handle William. He and Robert Montgomerie have pledged friendship and have kept to it, these four years past.'

'Archie wouldn't swear to that. You heard what he said. And four years won't wipe away a hundred.'

They had reached the Netherbow Gate and as they passed through she looked about, noting the spacing of the houses, the relative quiet of the street. High above them, a peel of girlish laughter rolled from a half-open dormer. Kate stiffened.

'Robert has only boys,' he said.

She shut her eyes, the bright oval of Anna's face as she brushed and buffed at the pony's tackle until it shone, as real as if she stood by her side. She drew in a lungful of air, one hand pressed against her breastbone. 'I will do my best to be civil. But don't expect over much.'

They found Patrick lounging in the dappled shade making clip-clopping noises for a boy of about three who galloped a hobby horse up and down the narrow path that dissected the twin squares of lawn.

He broke off as they appeared in the archway and swung his legs off the bench.

'The others are inside. I thought to wait for you here.'

It was an unexpected sensitivity. He glanced up at an open window, put two fingers in his mouth and whistled. The tousled head of one of the boys craned over the sill and above it, Elizabeth, who withdrew, to re-appear minutes later at the door, Grizel and Jean close behind. She came to them, hands outstretched.

'Munro. And you are Kate. I'm glad you came. Visitors are aye welcome, though Hugh and Robert and our other guest are not at home. Gone to an audience with the King.'

'And are enjoying themselves immensely, no doubt.'

Only Kate failed to laugh at Patrick's sarcasm and was annoyed in consequence. An annoyance that translated into resentment of his easy familiarity and the way he smiled at her, assuming a friendship that she had not granted. Yet against her will as the day wore on she began to relax. It wasn't just Patrick. Nor was it the children, for besides Hugh and Elizabeth's babe, Robert's two boys were there, and although somewhat in the background as was fitting in the presence of strangers, nevertheless contributed to the general noise and chatter. She thought of home and their own bairns and felt the pain afresh, now overlaid by a prick of regret. Another time, she thought, and perhaps we may all have a jaunt.

What threatened to complete the thaw was the fondness that the whole family, from Jean down, exhibited for each other. Their teasing amusing, even at times outrageous, yet always without offence, given or taken, and thus infectious. She had never been to Kilmaurs, but suspected that she wouldn't find there the ease that these Montgomeries exhibited.

Lunch was simple: partridge and roast vegetables, followed by a syllabub and early strawberries; the whole washed down with a Rhenish wine, that made Kate, less used to it than the others, a little light-headed. A sensation that was, she discovered, not at all unpleasant. Afterwards she was glad to sit in the garden, leaning against the warm stone of the house wall, Grizel by her side, while the children romped with Patrick and Munro, and Elizabeth dandled the baby. Bees harvesting the pollen in the walnut blossom made a constant background hum and she wondered idly if there were boxes nearby and the honey for sale, or if they were wild, making their hives high on the hill behind the town. In the warmth of the sun, her eyelids drooped, the sounds around her receeding gently.

'Late in bedding last night? Or was it that the bed wasn't conducive to sleep?' Kate woke to Patrick looking down at her, his brown eyes mischievous. And though his words were innocent enough, something in his expression made her flush, the colour seeping upwards from the lace at her breast, flooding her throat and neck. The sun, which had been full on her face when she sat down, had moved round and would soon, she saw, desert the garden altogether.

'How long did I sleep?'

'Long enough to suggest . . .' in the pause her colour deepened. 'Either lack of sleep . . . for one reason or another . . . or over-indulgence in that fine wine.'

'Patrick!' Grizel, though her tone was reproving, was smiling. 'Don't mind him, he can't resist to tease when we are among friends.'

Munro had come to stand at Kate's side and she felt the light pressure on her arm as he echoed, 'And we are among friends.'

She wanted to smile back, to surrender her last reserves. But remembrance of their Cunninghame connection held her back. She ducked her head, fingered the pearls at her waist, 'I'm not used with wine.'

Elizabeth and Grizel spoke at once, broke off and started again, still together, and collapsed laughing, so that the rest laughed with them. Talk turned to the preparations for the Queen's entrance and the best location from which to view it.

'Is it really not to be till Wednesday?' Kate asked.

'Afraid so,' Patrick turned to Munro. 'But you'll stay?'

He rubbed at his nose. 'It's stretching things. We were to leave on Monday, expecting that James wouldn't wish to bide at Leith more than a night.'

'And so it was intended, but for the small matter of the work not yet finished at Holyrood.'

'Elizabeth cut in. 'Oh but you must stay. Forbye that it will only happen the once and will be worth the wait, we are only begun to get acquaint.'

'We have the bairns to think of and as for Agnes, the four days we settled on may already feel like four weeks for her.'

Kate heard the uncertainty in Munro's voice and against her better judgement added her protest. 'Agnes isn't over soft and won't be put upon.' She bit her lip. 'It's what we came for.'

The weather held fair and despite Kate's lingering resistance, the Munros spent little time in their own lodgings, pressed into the greater comfort to be had with the Montgomeries. Hugh and Robert took themselves to Leith each morning to wait on the King, so that Patrick and Munro had four ladies to look to besides the bairns. Sigurd, his interest in Grizel clear to all, was, though he also lodged with the Montgomeries, forced to spend most of the following days by the docks, his time divided between his private business and the careful unloading of the Queen's carriage and the paraphernalia that accompanied it.

The garden, pleasant enough for sitting, was a mite small to contain the Montgomerie children and so they spent most of each of the next two afternoons in the Holyrood Park. The first day, the children clamoured to brave the breeze and walk the length of the crag. Jean, unable to relax, chivvied them away from the edge, lest it crumble under their feet and they be plunged headlong into the park below. The second day, they set out to climb to the top of Arthur's seat.

They entered the park by the Abbey church, and took a path that curved in a gradual incline towards St Margaret's Loch. There they dallied, the adults watching the sunlight dappling the water and the occasional soft plop as a fish broke the surface for air; the boys amusing themselves by guddling with sticks at the water's edge, disturbing the speckled trout parr that lurked between the pebbles. The elder Montgomerie boy lay flat on his front dabbling with both hands, his padded trunk hose ballooned against his back, his legs stretched out behind him like thin brown sticks. Though he managed to hold his hands far enough down and still so that the tiny fish flashed backwards and forwards over his palm, each time he tried to scoop them up they darted an escape through his fingers.

Kate, seeing his growing frustration, glanced at Munro, who nodded upwards.

'If we wish to reach the top today, we should perhaps move.'

They carried on through a small glen, the children's voices echoing as they chased among the trees, emerging into the sunlight at the head of the corrie. Ahead of them, the hill rose steeply.

Patrick gestured to the left. 'There is an easier route with a fine view I believe, of Dunsapie Loch on the way.'

'Can we not go straight?' The boys clung on Patrick.

He looked enquiringly at Munro. 'Why do we not give the bairns a scramble and the ladies can take the more gradual way?'

'It seems you haven't much choice.' Kate jerked her head towards the boys already clambering over the rough ground. Jean frowned as if she thought to call them back, but Patrick smiled reassurance.

'We'll see they come to no harm.'

The path that the ladies took was well trodden, the ground so dry their shoes scuffed up dust. There was only room for two to walk abreast, so Grizel moved ahead with Jean, Kate and Elizabeth dawdling behind.

Elizabeth linked Kate. 'You will stay for the entry?'

'Nothing has been said and if we were to go home as planned it would be tomorrow . . .' Kate pulled a stem of grass and stroked its bearded head across her cheek. 'I don't even know if we can keep our lodgings.'

'You needn't worry over that. We have plenty of space, and can easy accommodate you.'

The sun slid behind a cloud and Kate, thinking of the Cunninghames, shivered. 'What of Jean?'

'Ardrossan is a bleak place and over large and with no-one of her own age, a mite isolated. Hugh reported her as a mouse, but here she has come out of herself and will, I think, miss the company when she goes home. They say the dowager Lady Eglintoun has never recovered from the business after Annock.'

Kate shivered again.

'You aren't cold?'

She shook her head, threw the grass aside, looked down at her feet. 'Perhaps we should go home. . .' The moment's silence seemed to stretch far into a future that she had, against her will, begun to wish for.

'Your man isn't the only Cunninghame connection here.' Elizabeth's pressure on Kate's arm was firm.

She looked up, startled.

'My mother is a Cunninghame. We feared . . .' Kate felt the hesitation, '. . . that it might count against me with Hugh. But it didn't, or not in the end.' Jean and Grizel had disappeared round a turn in the path, the low murmur of their voices fading.

Elizabeth turned to face Kate, gripping both her wrists. 'So you see, there isn't a reason why we can't be friends.'

'Munro . . .' Kate began, and stopped, the words stuck in her throat.

'What hasn't been said is easy forgot.' Elizabeth's voice was soft, but with a strength in it that brooked no refusal. 'The past is gone. Leave it there. We are none of us fit to cast the first stone.' She linked again and pulled Kate forward. 'We don't want them to think us pauchled and not able to climb a wee bit hill. Can you run?'

Chapter Five

At Kilmaurs, Glencairn circled his horse: a chestnut stallion with a white flash on his forehead and a wicked glint in his eye. John Cunninghame was also mounted: on a bay that had a sweet mouth and the manners to match, and so stood still, snorting gently. A stable boy held the head of a third horse that moved restively on the damp cobbles.

Archie appeared at the door.

'Where's William? Tell him he's ready now or we leave without him.' Glencairn was nursing his impatience. 'The King has been two days in Leith already and there are those who will no doubt make much of our delay.'

John said, 'He may not have eyes for much other than the Queen. Rumour has it that she's prettier than her portrait and pregnant forbye.'

'James aye notes those who have obeyed his summons speedily and those who haven't and it won't be counted to our credit that we had the ill luck of a messenger whose horse took lame.' Glencairn snapped his reins, causing all three horses to start.

Archie poked his head into the kitchen. 'Anyone seen William? Glencairn is gey impatient.'

The steward, occupied in decanting ale, barely lifted his head. 'Try his bed. He hasn't eaten, that I do know and last night . . . let's just say it was gone three in the morning when he knocked me up to let him in.' He bent to replace the bung in the barrel. 'I wouldn't be the one wishing to wake him.'

'You're not between a rock and a hard place.'

William's eyes were bloodshot. 'What d'you want?'

'Your father is waiting. Already saddled. And threatening to leave without you.'

'Is that so? You can tell my father I'll be with him presently.' And when Archie didn't make a move, sneered, 'I do believe you're feart.' He gestured into the room. 'Take my stuff with you, to look as if I follow.'

Archie picked up the saddlebag.

'I have a goodbye or two to make first. My mother and . . .' there was malice in his smile, '. . . that fine lass you brought me from Renfrew.'

Archie plunged back down the stair, gripping the rope handrail so tight that it burned his palm, William's voice taunting him,

'A fine lass indeed.'

The Cunninghames departed, Archie returned to the kitchen, to find Sybilla sitting by the fireplace, her fingers curved around a bowl, blowing on the curl of steam that rose from a milk and honey posset. He dropped down beside her unsure of whether to question her or not.

'They're away then?' There was more of grey and less of blue in Sybilla's eyes than usual.

'Aye, and maybe a bit of peace for those of us who are left.'

'Your usual complaint is that you don't get to accompany them. Do you not wish it this time?'

Archie pushed his hair upwards, so that from the side he resembled a collapsing stook. 'I've had my fill of William the now. Respite will be welcome'

He saw the renewed stillness in her face.

'It would have been fine to see the new Queen.' She blew on the posset, making ripples.

'Did Lady Glencairn not plan to go?'

Sybilla ran her finger around the edge of the bowl, picking up a smear of froth. 'She did. And take the bairns, but when Glencairn insisted that William attend him . . .' She lifted the bowl to her mouth, her eyes sombre. 'The babe has a cough right enough, but I don't think it much and wouldn't have held her back if there were not other reasons for her change of mind. It is her greatest sadness that her eldest son is hard to like, but so she finds him. And I imagine the harder to bear for that there is no rhyme nor reason to his churlishness, no childhood ill to blame. Born under a black moon he may have been, but such superstitions give her no comfort, rather the reverse. Suffer him at home she must, but she does not choose to suffer him abroad.'

'And you?'

'You know I haven't the choice, one way or the other. So little use in wishing. And besides,' she was scrubbing with her thumb at the hollow at the base of her throat, 'With Glencairn and William away, we will all have some peace.'

A bell jangled above and she leapt up.

'Sybilla?'

'Don't fret, Archie. I don't regret coming, not yet, and if ever I do, I will go home again . . . sooner than be sent.'

The Cunninghames made fair time, the wind behind them and the going firm enough for ease of travel but not so hard as to trouble the horses. They came to Edinburgh's West Port at dusk. The town, with its roofs and spires and the castle crouched on the hill, was silhouetted against the skyline on their left, the long crag and Arthur's seat brooding on the right. Glencairn slowed his horse to a walk as they approached the gateway.

He turned to John, riding abreast of him. 'We have lodgings on the High Street, and should be well placed.'

'And well looked after also?' William, keen as he was to be here and in the thick of it, was interested in more than position.

'There is a cook and an ostler,' John permitted himself a smile. 'Old biddies, I believe, but fit enough for our needs.'

William scowled.

'Also a lad, for the fetching and carrying. We aren't at home and can't expect more.'

As they progressed through the Canongate, past fine houses with lights beginning to show, an occasional face peered out, drawn by the noise of the horses. Snatches of conversation, music, laughter, spilled from open windows. Raised voices, the angry bang of a casement, the rattle of loose glass.

Glencairn slowed. 'I had thought to seek lodging here, and bring some of our own household, but without wife and brood to accompany me, there seemed little point.'

A couple emerged from an arched entry to the left. They were looking back, calling their farewells, so that their faces were hidden, but something in the man's voice was familiar.

William pulled to an abrupt halt. 'Munro. We had not looked to find you here.'

Munro bowed. 'I thought to bring my wife . . .' He presented Kate, '. . . to see the Queen's entry.'

'Mistress Munro' Glencairn ducked his head, his tone neither friendly nor unfriendly, with just a hint of patronage.

'A pity you did not share your intention.' William's gaze travelled over Kate, from the tip of the feather on her bonnet to the points of her shoes. 'We could have shared accomodation also.'

John slid from his horse and bowed over Kate's hand. 'Your husband is fortunate, I see.'

'Who were you visiting?' Glencairn was looking behind them, through the archway to the garden beyond.

Munro breathed in. 'The Montgomeries.'

'We were separated,' Kate's voice was combative, 'In the press the day before yesterday. One of the Montgomeries, a cavalry officer in France I believe, helped in the search for me. We but came to give our thanks, as a matter of courtesy.' She met Glencairn's eyes, her own steady.

'Do you have far to walk?' John gestured to the darkening clouds. 'Dusk is a chancy time to be abroad, especially,' he smiled at Kate, 'for a lady.'

'Merlyon's Wynd – not far, but it's a mite later than we intended and we'd appreciate company if . . .' Munro deferred to Glencairn, '. . . you aren't pressed for time.'

They moved through the Netherbow and onto the High Street, keeping to the centre of the road, Glencairn and William still mounted, John walking by Munro and Kate's side, leading his horse. Every few yards the entrance to another close; dark and echoing. A smile played about John's mouth as William's horse skittered with each slam of a door or sneck of shutters.

A man tumbled out of a low entry and staggered across

the street in front of them. He was wearing calf-length boots well worn at the heel and a thigh-length belted tunic, a satchel hanging from his shoulder. His mud-coloured hair, straggling from beneath the flat brim of his hat, hung round his face in limp shanks, like unwashed wool. Roughly hacked tails of string dangled from the stick under his arm, as if a brace of rabbit or pheasant had hung there, though the coarse leather purse on his belt was clearly empty.

Almost running into William the man lost his footing, and swinging out an arm to keep from sprawling, thwacked William's horse with the stick. It reared, neck stretched, haunches bunched, front hooves flailing. Munro jumped forward to grasp a hold of the bridle, pulling on it firmly. He was all but swinging from the harness, one foot well clear of the ground, his repeated 'Whoa, whoa, whoa', soft as the cooing of a wood-pigeon. John had pulled Kate towards the opposite side of the street, tugging his horse round to form a protective barrier. Munro brought the horse to a trembling halt hard against a jutting forestair, the man who had caused the bother bolting, swallowed up in the shadows of a close leading downwards in the direction of the Nor' Loch.

William, his face purple, growled, 'Drunk, no doubt, on the proceeds of his catch.'

There was a hint of amusement in John's voice. 'It's as well he didn't bring you down.'

'It's as well he isn't still here.'

'You have our thanks, Munro. It is a valuable horse and one I wouldn't have wished to see injured.' Glencairn looked pointedly at William who added a grudging,

'Thank you, but I could have held him.'

Glencairn gestured towards the top of the stair, 'If

you'll just take a rap at that door, William, I believe it is our lodging.'

Munro took Kate's arm. 'We've a step further and should go before we risk being locked out.'

John shot an enquiry at Glencairn. 'I could see them safe?'

Glencairn nodded but said, his tone proprietary, 'Wait on us in the morning, at ten.'

William bowed, his words carrying an undertone of insolence that Kate struggled to ignore, 'I look forward to it.'

Munro bowed and Kate curtseyed and they escaped, John at their side.

Out of earshot, John said, 'You like to live dangerously.' His gaze passed over Munro to rest on Kate. 'I would wish to have a wife who sprang so quickly to my defence and with likely so little regard to strict veracity.'

She flushed. 'Patrick did search for me.'

'Oh, I'm sure.' Above them a window opened. John, recognizing the thin screech of wood against wood, shoved them under the overhang, just as a pail of kitchen slops, greasy and rancid, splattered into the gutter.

'I didn't realise it was so late.' Munro looked up where the first stars hung, silver pin heads against the dark velvet of the sky.

Kate looked puzzled.

John gave the explanation. 'Pails cannot be emptied before half past nine at night. When all good folks should be safely indoors.'

'As we will be shortly.' Munro's smile faded. 'It was ill-luck to run into Glencairn where we did.'

'It was ill-judged rather to be there at all.' John was no longer smiling. 'Sworn friends we may be with the Montgomeries the now, but we have over long been sworn enemies, and while Glencairn may wish to keep the peace for precedence sake, William isn't so pragmatic.'

Kate was fidgeting with the cuff of her sleeve. 'We are all here to greet the new Queen, why can it not be a joyful thing.'

'We are here . . .' John said, '. . . at least Glencairn and, I dare say Robert Montgomerie also, like all the nobility, are here to make political capital. The new Queen is but a bauble to be suitably admired, the festivities an opportunity to play for James' favour.'

They had reached the entrance to Merlyon's Wynd.

Munro hesitated, 'Will you come in? We can give you a drink if nothing else. We supped with the Montgomeries.'

John shook his head. 'Glencairn will expect me and will likely wait supper, if only because it will irritate William. I shouldn't be long.' He turned away, said, as an afterthought, 'Is Braidstane with them?'

'Yes, though he spends most of the day at Leith, in James' entourage.'

'Through the good offices of his uncle, I imagine?'

'Aye, Alexander is well-placed.'

'Too well-placed, some would say. Have a care Munro. William doesn't improve with age and any link with Braidstane, however tenuous, will stick in his craw.

Pulling at his doublet as if it were uncomfortably tight, Munro mounted the stairs in the King's Wark to where James held temporary court. He had hoped that waiting on Glencairn in the morning with Kate might have fulfilled their obligations, and so had been put out by the order to attend at Leith.

Kate, who had perversely reacted to John's warning with an increased determination to spend more time with the Montgomeries, had smiled up at Glencairn, her eyes wide and disarming, expressing herself tired and wishing to rest and so begged to be excused. A foolishness that at Broomelaw she would have recognized as such. Here, her guard lowered, whether by the atmosphere of general goodwill surrounding the festivities, or by the generosity of the welcome they had received in the Montgomerie household, she allowed her desire for this new friendship to override any fear she had of Glencairn. On the way back to their lodgings she defended herself.

'We were promised to them and I won't break a promise without cause. You may go to Leith and welcome. Besides, there is no place for me there. If Jean Montgomerie does not go without special bidding, then I should not, no matter what Glencairn may think.' Colour stole into her cheeks. 'I will rest awhile, to make it true, and then fulfil our promise.' She reached up to tug his hair. 'But two days since and you sought to convince me. They are our friends now and while we may not trumpet it, I won't discard them altogether.'

Munro however flatly refused to allow her to walk to the Canongate alone. 'I won't risk your safety to satisfy your conscience.' And so, despite her protests, he saw her safely through the archway into the sunshine of the Montgomeries' garden.

Now, he supposed, she gossiped with Elizabeth and Grizel, Patrick perhaps stretched at their feet, while he suffered in this airless chamber. He scanned the room for Glencairn, and was pleased to find him outside the tight circle that hummed around James, for he had little desire to be presented to the King. He made his way through the throng, catching snippets of conversation, logging without deliberate thought the names and faces that swam across his line of sight. He was surprised to find that he recognized many of the men who thronged here, from the hunt that the Montgomeries had provided at Fintrie; and could categorize most by their competence or otherwise on a horse.

The windows that gave onto the waterside were narrow, the breeze from outside scarcely penetrating, so that crossing to Glencairn was like wading through a stew of sweat overlaid with scent. Munro squeezed past a rotund man, whose belly strained at the buttons of his doublet, jutting out over his hose like the prow of a ship. He noted with distaste the grimed rim of the heavily frilled ruff and the gravy trails that patterned the burgundy satin below. His own clothes, though no match in quality or indeed fashion, were, in all essentials, clean; only the dust on his knee-length boots indicating the long walk down from Edinburgh.

The Cunninghame party were crushed into a corner at the rear of the room, Glencairn and John deep in conversation. For a moment he thought William missing, then found him, already a mite unsteady, propping up the wall behind Glencairn. As he neared he saw Patrick Maxwell of Newark also battling through the crush and thought – and there's another reason why I would rather not be here.

Chapter Six

Hugh saw Munro enter, but made no acknowledgement, reckoning, rightly, that now wasn't the time to broadcast their acquaintance. There was a lull in the general hum, broken by a single bark of laughter. All attention swivelled towards the Cunninghames. Maxwell, whom Hugh knew only by reputation was next to William, a match in his air of arrogance and the careless ostentation of his dress. 'More silver than sense' the talk went, 'and the need to deeve any who might listen with his grand scheme for the enlargement of Newark' as if it was a royal residence he aimed for and not just a laird's house. He turned and looked directly at Hugh, radiating, even at a distance, an antagonism more personal than the long-standing Cunninghame and Montgomerie feud warranted.

Alexander, his discussion with James at an end, retreated, taking Hugh with him. 'The word from your brother George; it may be fitting to present it to the King at supper.'

'I hadn't intended to wait on supper. Elizabeth . . .'

'Will understand you cannot always be with her. You have it?'

'Aye, though I doubt its value.'

'You forget it is due to your presence at court that James invited you to share in the jaunt to Norway. Nor would you have been at court without word to bring. Don't under-estimate the worth of what George sends, new gossip or not.'

It was an argument that Hugh had listened to so many times that his attention wandered. The Cunninghames had separated into two distinct groups: Glencairn and John working their way towards the King, William the centre of a small knot who seemed to find ample amusement in disparaging those about them. Again, he caught a glance directed at him, the malice tangible. He belatedly attended to Alexander.

'The English Queen will have to die sometime, and you do well to ensure that when she does, you will be con-veniently placed to share in the good things to come. You have not only yourself to think on, and others have spent more than the odd shilling on your behalf.'

The thought of his new daughter encouraging frankness, Hugh said, 'It's been four years since and nothing to show for it. I have a mind to try for a land grant in Ireland.'

'For that, you need currency in the English court.'

'George has influence and will spend it willingly on my account, for there would be pickings for him also. Maybe more than he can presently hope for.'

'Aye, well, don't lose the standing you have here without making gey sure of better elsewhere.'

Hugh laughed. 'George won't let me do anything over hasty. He was born with caution stamped into his soul, and has a sound grasp of politics and money beside, for all that he is a cleric.'

Alexander smiled. 'Or maybe because of it.'

They were in a tavern hard by the dock, dining on cold mutton washed down by ale, passable only in that it hadn't been much watered.

'Speaking of Ireland,' Alexander picked up the conversation, 'the word is that Hamilton is for Dublin, he and Fullerton both, to establish a college. Though no doubt they will be charged with other, less talked of tasks. It's a canny move by Lennox to keep a close eye on England's back door and one that may prove profitable.'

Hugh, who had been concentrating on the sawing of a particularly tough bit of mutton, raised his head at the mention of Hamilton. 'Teaching is it? That'll suit him well for he couldn't soldier to save himself.'

'It isn't an army that the King needs, but canny folk who look to the future and bide their time. Take care that the likes of Hamilton don't steal the advantage of you, whether by Latin or not.' Alexander was thoughtful. 'Ireland is maybe not so bad an idea, but you mustn't go ram-stam at it. Allow James to think it is in his service you go.'

Hugh slid to the end of the bench. 'How can I not heed your advice when it is dinned into me from all sides and some of them too close to home to avoid. I suppose,' he pulled out the letter, 'It's time to share this with James.'

The Cunninghames were firmly lodged next to the King, Munro in the background. Again Hugh didn't acknowledge him as he approached James in the company of his uncle Alexander.

James looked across. 'Ah, Montgomerie, and Braidstane. It is well it is not.' He gestured at William. 'It is some little time since I had both Cunninghames and Montgomeries so close.'

Hugh bowed low over the jewelled hand.

'Come, sit by me. You have a bairn I hear.'

'Sire.'

'A bonny lass?'

'I think so.'

'And your wife, she's here?'

'In Edinburgh and fair excited at the prospect of watching the procession. I have told her of the Queen's beauties . . .'

James was smiling. 'You may present her to us, and the bairn.'

Hugh bowed again. 'I have word from London also.'

James waved his hand. 'I'll hear all presently, but first, how is the hunting in Ayrshire? I couldn't make your wedding but I haven't forgot that you are as keen on the chase as I and not so poor at procuring it.'

William cut in, 'Ayrshire has but poor sport, Sire, but we have recently taken a good count at Newark, without scarce a dent in the herd that run in the woods there. My cousin,' he stepped back and nudged Maxwell forward, 'Is well placed to offer a goodly entertainment.'

Maxwell bowed in his turn, a fixed smile on his face. 'I would be honoured Sire.'

The King dangled the possibility of accepting Maxwell's hospitality like a noose. 'Aye, well, we will think on it. I haven't the leisure for a jaunt for a week or two, but I won't forget the offer.' He turned back to Hugh. 'I trust you have something of interest to pass on, for I'm fair deeved with prattle that says little and is worth less.'

Unwisely, Hugh chose to start with the common talk

of the court. 'Elizabeth they say ails, and though, when done out in her wig, with caked colour on her face and the high ruffs she favours, will pass for hale, seen undressed, she is like a plucked chicken.' Aware of Alexander's stillness he hurried on, 'Her hair is all but gone and the apothecary never far from her door.'

James grunted, ignored the impertinence. 'And for that your brother has sent word from London? He might have saved himself the bother.'

'It is talk that I wouldn't have thought to repeat only that it is backed up by the certain knowledge that Elizabeth has taken up with Foreman and has granted him certain monies. As she is her father's daughter and well known not to spend lightly, nor yet to bestow unwarranted favour, the rumours of her ill-health cannot all be false. It is my brother's opinion,' he felt the need to embroider a little, 'and he has made a study of Foreman's methods; that he is a charlatan and it is a measure of Elizabeth's fear that she is driven to treatment from such as he.'

'What does a cleric know of medicine?' James was dismissive.

Hugh was beginning to sweat. 'Not George, Sire. Another brother, who has studied these five years under the best physicians that France and Italy can provide, and is indeed,' another exaggeration, 'highly sought after.'

William muttered to Maxwell. 'Plucked chicken the English Queen may be, but her neck isn't wrung yet, and much good it does us that she cannot appear without half an hour of trowelling to her face.'

'You have something to add, Cunninghame? Some new intelligence perhaps?' James swung his attention away from Hugh.

'I but commended your own good health, Sire.'

'Indeed.'

Hugh, knowing that there was danger in dismissal if he didn't leave something for James to mull over, said, 'There is other gossip with maybe more bite to it: the English court grows restive and there are those ready to ensure that the changeover, when it comes, will come easy.'

'Do you have names? Or is it but idle chatter that cannot be substantiated?'

'I have names, but . . .' Hugh glanced at the men who eddied around James. 'It may not be wise to spread the gossip so far . . .'

A glimmer of a smile flitted across James' face. 'I'll look for you in the morning then. I trust it will be worth the wait.'

So do I, Hugh thought, taking some comfort from the annoyance on William's face.

James rose. 'Ah, Cunninghame, did you have anything else to say? No doubt it will hold.'

Hugh, now that he had won another, more private, audience, was glad of the respite and a chance to chew over with Alexander how best to present the meagre scraps of information that George had sent. Despite the number of times that he had presented himself at court since his marriage and Alexander's best efforts to tutor him, he still found his tongue no match for his sword. He needed a temper on him to cut and thrust with words, and to make any display of temper in James' presence was dangerous. He stepped back to allow the King passage and was rewarded by a brief nod. Too close to William for comfort, he turned to follow in James' wake but was jostled from behind. He stepped sideways, prepared to make allowance for the general crush, but was jostled again, clearly with intent. This time he swung round, an angry flush spreading across his face, and found himself staring into a pair of pale eyes that radiated dislike.

William, just far enough to the side to be absolved of any involvement in the jostling said, 'I believe, Braidstane, you haven't yet met Maxwell, though he is well acquainted with your wife.'

Mindful of where he was, of the quiet that had fallen around them and the number of folk watching with interest, Hugh bowed; tried to move on.

Maxwell stepped in front of him and placed a hand on his arm. 'How is dear Elizabeth?'

Hugh wrested free.

William detained him. 'Come, come, Braidstane. We are charged with friendship, are we not, and are but following the normal courtesies.'

Maxwell nodded in agreement. 'And the bairn? You have a girl, I hear.'

Hugh felt a hand at his back, Alexander's voice behind him.

'Cunninghame, Maxwell.' He gave an exaggerated bow. 'I'm afraid I must take Hugh away. Robert Montgomerie looks for him presently.' Outside, Alexander released him. 'Have a care, Hugh. You know fine that Cunninghame seeks to draw you into a fight and one that will lay all blame at your door. Much good it will do you being here, if it is but to fan the flames of an old quarrel. Don't throw away the winter's work for the sake of a dolt like William.'

'Just to look at him makes me fair sick and this Maxwell, I don't know how or in what vein he is acquainted with Elizabeth, but so he claimed.'

'And so could any one of a hundred Cunninghame cousins.' Alexander lengthened his stride. 'Claiming acquaintance is one thing, having it another. Forget them and concentrate on your own affairs. We have enough to do to put together a good speir for James and little enough time to do it, forbye the truce between Robert and Glencairn is flimsy and won't stand much shaking.'

He strode ahead. Hugh was well aware that he had need of Alexander's way with words. Nor did he underestimate the value of having an uncle as one of James' inner circle. In Norway he might have been, but so had three hundred others, all seeking to make capital of their presence.

'Are you bid to Robert? Or was that a pretty fiction to make my escape the easier?'

Alexander didn't slow his pace. 'I am bid, to a late supper, and the thought of missing out on the best of it doesn't appeal, so I'd appreciate it if you wouldn't lag.'

Robert turned at their entrance, his smile, warm for Alexander, was absent for Hugh. 'I had thought,' he said, 'that we might be spared your company tonight. The talk was all of how thick you were with Cunninghame and like to spend the evening in debate with him and others of his kin, rather than your own. Correct me if I'm wrong, but didn't James make an especial decree that feuds were to be avoided. Or is it that your idea of living peaceably is to spark with William for all to see?

Hugh was defensive. 'I didn't seek the confrontation.'

Alexander supported him, 'In all fairness, it was William's doing and though there is no doubt that the

299

intention was to bait Hugh, we escaped with little said on either side that would bear repeating.'

The edge left Robert's voice. 'Steer clear of them, Hugh. It is a chancy thing to cross swords, however lightly, with anyone, far less with William. And in the present circumstance would be folly indeed.'

Elizabeth was seated in a window reveal, jiggling the baby on her hip, and opposite her, Kate Munro, her legs curled underneath her like a bairn. She straightened as Robert spoke and her hands, which until then had lain still in her lap, began to crumple at her skirt.

Alexander came towards them. 'Elizabeth is to be presented to the King and Queen.' He touched the babe's cheek. 'And the bairn. It is an honour that many would wish for.' He turned back to Robert, drawing him away. 'The plan for the procession is set, and your place in it.'

Elizabeth placed her hand on Hugh's sleeve. 'I know that you court James for our benefit, but take care the price is not too high.'

Robert and his lady had retired to their chamber, Hugh and Elizabeth ready to follow by the time Munro arrived to collect Kate. She had nearly given up on him, and was ready to accept Patrick's offer to walk her back to Merlyon's Wynd, when he appeared in the doorway. That he hadn't had the best of days was evident from his expression, so she wasn't surprised when he refused the invitation to join the Montgomeries the following morning.

'Glencairn has prior claim. We are both bid to lunch at his lodgings, and inclination or not, we have no choice.'

Elizabeth didn't press, perhaps thinking of the rollicking that Hugh had received from Robert and the consequent coolness that had marred the atmosphere all evening. She toyed with the ribbons that trimmed her sleeve. 'And Wednesday? Can you meet with us then? Robert is to be part of the procession, but we have debated at length where to stand, and have made a goodly choice.'

There was a weariness in Munro. 'It is perhaps an over public occasion on which to flaunt new friendships, however much we might wish it.' He steered Kate towards the door. 'I trust you will excuse us. Old obligations are aye the difficult ones. We should take our leave now, for we can't bide past Thursday.'

Patrick bowed over Kate's hand. 'No need to be maudlin. If we meet in the press on Wednesday, well. If not, our friendship can stand the strain. Renfrew is not far from Ayrshire; you will all no doubt have opportunity to meet again. I am the loser here, for I make for France next week and heaven knows when I'll be back. Unless there is a wedding to attend. I might,' he tapped Grizel's shoulder, 'only might mind, be able to take leave for that.'

Chapter Seven

The lunch with the Cunninghames was all that Kate expected it to be: long and tedious. The conversation, if so it could be called, a recital of Glencairn's frustrations: his inability to get the King's ear, his concern that Maitland, newly created earl, rode high, his annoyance that in the Queen's procession his place would be twelfth to Robert Montgomerie's eleventh.

She was seated between Munro and John Cunninghame, concentrating on matching her expressions to the mood of the moment, careful to hide her increasing irritation at Glencairn's self-indulgent grumblings and William's petty complaints. In this she did better than Munro, on more than one occasion having cause to lean heavily on his foot. She suspected that John was aware of her efforts and approved them, a feeling confirmed when he handed her to a seat in a window alcove.

'Your husband is fortunate indeed: a wife who watches his well-being.' Then, as Glencairn approached, an abrupt change, 'I have contracted Mistress Munro to join us on Wednesday and have assured her that the position we have gained from which to watch the entry will be second to none.'

He had left her no room to manoeuvre, but recognizing the underlying goodwill, she expressed her pleasure and excitement at the prospect of seeing the new Queen, which was the truth; and her thanks that they be included in the Cunninghame party, which was not.

Maxwell joined them and William, who until then had confined himself to minor gripes: the weakness of the ale, the discomfort of the beds, the inadequacies of the servants; turned to an airing of greater grievances: chief among them Braidstane's standing.

'I was well placed yesterday to get the King's ear until Braidstane appeared with some message from London: trumped up and exaggerated, no doubt, yet James listens to him as if it came from Cecil himself. Who is this brother George anyway?'

'Dean of Norwich, and with higher prospects.' Glencairn descended into sarcasm. 'But no doubt your offer of a hunt will weigh more heavily with James than a few meagre rumours from the English court.'

William flushed.

'I grant you one advantage over Braidstane. You get drunk quicker and more often, a condition in courtiers that James has apparently become used to at the Danish court and may prize.'

The tension palpable, Kate studied the floor, searching for some excuse to leave.

At her shoulder, John. 'I believe you make for Broomelaw on Thursday?'

'Yes, though I wish we could stay longer . . .'

'You have gifts bought?'

'Not yet for the bairns.' With a rush of gratitude for the thought, she said, 'I planned this afternoon . . .'

'No doubt we can excuse you then.'

Glencairn half turned as John spoke. 'Indeed. I leave early on Wednesday to join the procession at Leith. But John will see to you.' Then, a final barb, 'Or William, if he is capable.'

Music came first. A cacophony of sound: lutes and tambors, pipes and drums, viols and flutes and whistles; as the good citizens of Edinburgh lined the route from Leith and played, skillfully or otherwise, but with undoubted enthusiasm. The whole, however discordant, somehow glorious. And suddenly it no longer mattered to Kate that she was sandwiched with the Cunninghames just inside the main entrance to the palace of Holyrood. That in the wait she had been forced to bear with William's intermittent gaze stripping her as efficiently as if he dissolved her clothes in vitriol. That she had endured for two hours or more the barbed comments that sparked between William and Maxwell as they dissected the reputations, the character, the appearance of those, noble or otherwise, who surrounded them. Or that she held fast to Munro's arm, not for her own safety, but so that she could exert whatever warning pressure was neccessary to keep his reactions to the conversation within bounds.

Caught up in the excitement, she forgot her disappointment that they didn't spend this day with the Montgomeries, whom she had glimpsed by the inner yett. Her senses re-tuned, she revelled in the heat and the crush and the colour; in the flapping of tapestries hanging from balconies and forestairs; the fluttering of flags and pennants; the brilliance of the liveries and coats of arms. The swell of sounds: tune piled on tune, instrument on instrument, singing and cheers that rose and fell in waves; from which she tried to unpick individual melodies. And failing, gave up the unequal struggle, abandoning herself to the growing frenzy as the procession neared.

There was a shift in atmosphere: whispers become a murmur, the murmur an anticipation that rose to a roar with the first sight of the Whifflers: bright in cloth of silver and white taffeta, strewn with gold chains. They criss-crossed the roadway, white staffs flashing, laying about them with cheerful good humour to clear any who threatened to encroach upon the path.

Behind them, the nobles: Danish and Scottish side by side. In satin and velvet, in cloth of gold, in burgundy and blue, vermillion and yellow and the deepest of blacks. Pleated and ruffed and feathered and plumed, ablaze with jewels. At the front the Danish envoys and the earls attached to them. Then others of the nobles in order of precedence. Beside her a stiffening as Robert Montgomerie appeared: young, handsome, assured. His doublet was of deep blue slashed with silver, his matching short cape fashionably slung from one shoulder, silver buttons trimming his tall-crowned hat and winking on his shoes. To his left, Glencairn, in gold and bronze, a match for his chestnut stallion, its Arab blood evident in the high stepping gait, the arrrogance of the long nose.

The cheering rose to a crescendo. And with the cheers, a collective indrawing of breath as the Queen's coach came into view, flanked on one side by James and the Duke of Lennox and on the other by the Earl of Bothwell and Lord John Hamilton. Knowing what to expect from Sigurd's description, Kate was nevertheless unprepared for the magnificance of the reality: the eight perfectly matched white horses coroneted with plumes of peacock feathers, twisted cords of purple woven into their manes and tails. The silver coach, its bodywork dazzling, so that it almost hurt to look at it. The velvet upholstery: a fitting contrast to Anne, pale as an Ice Queen in white bliant, her corn-coloured hair piled on her forehead like curls of spun gold.

'No wonder she wished to bring her own coach.' Kate's fingers tightened on Munro's arm, as the coach and out-riders approached. 'Bonny indeed and regal with it, for all she's young.'

The lines of loyal subjects bent in a sweeping wave of curtsey and bow. Kate sank in her turn, and rising had time to note the brilliance of the Queen's retinue. A brilliance that, to judge by William's quickened interest, he also noted.

The foremost riders had reached the inner yett and were dismounting, peeling off to each side to form a guard of honour. The coach drew to a halt, James reaching up to hand the Queen down. Kate, craning her neck, saw that Patrick and Hugh were stationed behind Robert Montgomerie, Elizabeth and the babe at Hugh's side. The King and Queen paused in their slow passageway through the ranks of nobles, James bending his head towards Robert. He edged sideways allowing Hugh and Elizabeth to step forward. Hugh's bow was timed to a nicety, Elizabeth's curtsey deep and fluid despite the child on her arm, so that Kate dipped her head to hide her involuntary smile.

'Practice made perfect, I'd say.' Munro's comment, intended as a whisper for Kate, fell in a lull in the surrounding chatter, so that his voice carried.

'No doubt needed.' William was acidic.

Kate, lit by a spark of irritation, said, 'Her mother is a Cunninghame, I believe?'

'Some distant connection.'

It should have been a warning, but Kate, her normal good sense stifled by William's repressed scorn, her mounting dislike fed by the two days spent in his company, directed attention back to the Montgomeries. The Queen had reached out to the babe and was stroking the soft down on her head, while James turned to Hugh. It was impossible to hear what was said, but the intention was clear. A soft flush of colour flooded Elizabeth's cheeks and she made another, deeper curtsey, while Hugh, bowing also, seemed to be expressing gratitude.

'Oh look!' Kate encompassed William and Maxwell in her gaze. 'I do believe the Montgomeries are invited into the palace. They must be high in favour.'

She was aware of Munro's tension, of Maxwell focusing on straightening his cuff; of William his colour rising, as if under the skin he fizzed like a firework about to explode. The impulse to goad him strengthened. She stood on tiptoe as if to inform her stream of commentary. 'They're moving into the close . . . the nobles following . . . and Glencairn . . . just to the rear of Robert Montgomerie . . .'

John was by her side hissing at her, 'This is madness . . .'

She threw him off, past caring, past all rational thought. The pent-up pain of the last months; the surge of frustration she felt at the Cunninghame connection; the blame for Anna's death, which, though not openly acknowledged, she laid at William's door, coalesced into a recklessness that consumed her. She kept her eyes fixed on the entrance to the pend, her voice brittle.

'Do you suppose we could pass into the courtyard? There may be more to see yet. I know *we* can't go into the palace. Braidstane is fortunate in his Lord.'

John turned to William, put out a restraining hand, 'James' favour is a dangerous and volatile commodity. I for one . . .'

'I for one . . .' William's mimicry was perfect, '. . . am

not going to stay here to watch a scrag end of a bonnet laird trail after James' favour like a mongrel wriggling on his belly hoping for a bone.' He turned the full force of his contempt on Kate. 'You, of course, may do as you please.'

There was a moment when she thought that she had provoked an all-out brawl, as Munro launched himself at William. John leapt between them, shoving Munro towards Maxwell who grasped his arms, pinioning them behind his back, his grip tightening the more Munro struggled for release. William had drawn his dirk.

John grabbed William's wrist, twisted it, 'A brawl now is madness that we none of us can afford. Fight where and when you please, but not here. Your father . . .' a space had opened, a ring of spectators forming around them and John increased the pressure on William's wrist, 'Put the dirk away, you may not approve our lodgings, but they are better than a cell.'

Maxwell released Munro, motioned to William as they both thrust their way through the crush, 'the show is over, no doubt we can find more congenial company elsewhere.'

Kate, her temper subsiding, reached out in apology to John. In his gaze she saw anger, shot through with understanding.

'Drunk as William undoubtedly will be tonight, he may not remember how you baited him. You may hope so.' He turned to Munro. 'Go home.' Then, with a brutality she thought deliberate, said, 'You had a loss. Well. In that you are not alone. Be thankful for what you have.' His glance shifted to William's retreating back. 'And for what you have not.'

Chapter Eight

Summer slipped past Broomelaw like a stream dividing around a boulder, casting scarcely a ripple. The quiet monotone of the days seemed to Kate like a plain worked border, highlighting the rich tapestry of their time in Edinburgh. The new memories: vibrant, cherished, became a counterpoint to the old: enriching them, removing their sting.

Mary had been right. Anna, locked in the grave at the foot of the slope below the sheep pens, her face lost these months past, had come back to them. And though often she came in sharp shafts of remembrance, the pain and sadness undiminished, she came also in laughter and in sudden, unexpected spurts of joy. Her name began to come naturally to their lips again, her presence, though incomplete, easier to bear than the months of absence had been.

Remembered laughter in the Canongate garden slid Kate effortlessly to Anna, mischief dancing in her, looping a cord round Agnes' boot buttons as she dozed, giggling helplessly at her efforts to stand. The Montgomerie bairns guddling for trout parr at St Margaret's loch blurred into the twins at their own loch: trapping speckled smoults in a muslin net filched from the pantry; Robbie outraged when Anna, taking pity, trudged back to release them again. The gorse in full bloom in the Holyrood Park became the gorse on the hillside above the tower, Anna gathering handfuls of petals to, as she called it, 'scatter the sun'.

As for the memory of the moment when she had crossed swords with William, though she was not particularly proud of her part in it, she knew that faced with the same situation, she would likely react the same way again. Folly it may have been, but whatever it had released, in her and in Munro, their marriage was the stronger for it. And for that she had no regrets.

They visited Mary Munro every week, each time finding her a little more failed. She lay propped in the tall bed facing the window, so that she could see the birds that wheeled and swooped in the clear summer sky. Sometimes, as they sat, she would slip into sleep, her breathing laboured, and they would tiptoe away, glad to escape from the air thick with spice. Once or twice she made an extra effort, asking after each of the children in turn. But when they suggested bringing them, she refused.

'I am an old dry stick with a skin that is three sizes too large, but that isn't how I wish to be remembered. You may look back to better days, but the bairns . . . the last picture is the one they will keep.'

Munro had been for bringing them anyway, but Kate overruled him.

'Dignity is all she has left and we mustn't take it away.'

At the beginning of August Munro sent for Archie. They took it in turns to sit with her, moistening her lips with sips of a potion made from willow bark. She took four days to die, but peacefully and without pain. Towards the end, her breathing was grumbling and irregular so that they thought she left them a hundred times, but at the very last she opened her eyes and looked past them towards the clouds that hung in white puffs against a cobalt sky. She lifted her arms, her face radiant, and said, distinct and clear, 'Ah, sweet Jesus' as her head dropped into the pillows, her breathing fading to a whisper.

Then silence.

Kate was the first to move, folding Mary's hands across her chest, her eyes pricking. 'It is a goodly passing and one that I would wish for.'

They buried her among the cluster of graves in the hollow below Broomelaw, alongside her husband and the bairns she'd lost in infancy; her grave a fresh mound to overlay the newness that had been Anna's, the mason who had worked on the roof tiles returning to place her name on the rough hewn stone.

By September they had found a new equiblibrium. With Anna gone, nothing could ever be quite as it was and the smallest and most unexpected things still produced the sharpest pain. Yet the bond of family was stronger, perhaps because it was incomplete. And Kate, who had for a time indulged in Maggie traits rigorously disciplined in Anna, regained a true perspective.

A letter came from Braidstane, with an invitation for the whole family, and Kate was of a mind to go, but Munro was reluctant. It was as if coming back to Broomelaw, the grip of the Cunninghames tightened, so that closer connection with the Montgomeries held more danger than he was prepared to chance. Not that he said they wouldn't go, but each week there was a new reason why it wasn't convenient. Repairs to the stabling, the building of new cattle pens in preparation for the winter, the draining of an area of ground to allow for the enlargement of the warren: all impossible to counter, so that she was forced to bide her time.

The weather held right through to the second cutting of hay, the whole family growing brown as gypsies. Robbie spent hours at the lochside, fishing still his passion, though, had supper been dependent on his catch, they would have gone hungry. Ellie grew plump and contented, crawling about on the grassy slopes at Kate's feet while she filled basketfuls of brambles to turn into pies and preserves. Maggie had taken a fascination to anything that moved and was never happier than when she found some new creature to cherish, usually by imprisoning it in a jar, tightly stoppered, and feeding it on grasses and odd scraps until it died.

Kate was picking her way downhill, careful that she didn't drop either Ellie or the basket which swung from her other arm, when she saw a rider outlined against the horizon. He was jogging along without any sense of haste and she judged that she would beat him to the tower and so didn't trouble to hurry. Munro, straddling the roof of the byre tying in new thatch, waved before continuing, content to leave her to greet their guest.

Maggie was crouched by the barmkin wall, poking intently into a crevice, with a bodkin from Kate's work basket, trying to prise out the slaters that hid there. She had made a little pen of twigs for her captives and had provided in it both food, in the form of a docken leaf, and the shelter of two small stones. One slater lay motionless in the centre; another scuttled under the stones. Maggie gave a triumphant whoop and rocked back, a third slater held fast between her thumb and forefinger, its legs waving.

Kate knelt down beside her. 'You haven't killed that one then?'

Maggie's face was serious. 'I didn't think to kill any.'

'Here.' Kate popped a bramble into Maggie's mouth. 'We have a visitor. Maybe you should free them the now.' She forestalled Maggie's protest. 'You wouldn't want your beasties to be trod on. You can aye catch them tomorrow.' She held out another bramble and Maggie allowed herself to be distracted. Kate was still kneeling on the cobbles when the lad ducked under the archway. She rose, brushing her skirt.

'I have a message, from Glencairn.'

She felt the accustomed chill, but summoned a smile, gesturing towards the byre. 'My husband will be up shortly. You'll stay to sup?'

'A bite only. I must be back tonight.' As if to reassure her, he said, 'Wi' Glencairn the answer is aye wanted yesterday, as ye'll ken.'

'Come in then.'

He was finishing his piece as Munro slid onto the bench beside him and reached for the ale. 'How's Archie?'

'Fine, so far as I ken. I don't see that much of him. He mostly shadows William and they havn't been around much of late. Though . . .' he grinned, 'Archie seems a mite more reluctant to be away than before. He and Sybilla Boyd . . .'

'There is an understanding?' Kate turned from looking out the window to where Robbie's small head bobbed as he cast and re-cast his line.

'Not an understanding exactly, but I ken he has an interest and the talk is that she shares it.'

'Pity mother didn't see it.'

Kate half-turned. 'She'll know.'

The lad scrabbled inside his jerkin and produced a letter. Munro, narrowing his eyes against the light, took it across to the window and leaned on the sill. Kate saw the pucker between his brows disappear, his voice unexpectedly light.

'D'you fancy accompanying me to Greenock?'

'Greenock?'

'To the Shaws. Jean Cunninghame, Elizabeth's mother, is dead.'

Kate heard the pleasure in his tone, frowned.

'Glencairn has seen fit to suggest that we represent him at the funeral.'

'Why?'

He shrugged. 'For his own convenience, no doubt. He's at court and I imagine doesn't wish to be dragged away to satisfy the courtesies.'

'But why us?'

'Our acquaintance with Elizabeth, which he thinks but scratched, yet enough to pass muster.'

She rubbed at her arms. 'What about William?'

'If you were Glencairn, would you send William into Braidstane's company? It suits him to make use of us.' He turned to the lad. 'You may say that we will go.'

Afterwards, when the boy rounded the hill and disappeared from sight, Munro resumed, 'It suits us also. I know it isn't quite the same as a visit to Braidstane, but you will have a chance to renew your acquaintance with Elizabeth.'

'And at Glencairn's behest.'

'And at Glencairn's behest. A visit will be the easier another time, our better acquaintance set at Glencairn's door. Even William couldn't fault it.'

Kate slid her arm around his waist. 'I'd like fine to go. It will be good to see Elizabeth again. Was her mother old?'

'I've no idea . . . though, as John Shaw is ages with Hugh, she can't have been young. Things are well sorted here. We don't need to rush back. The funeral past,' he touched his lips to her hair, 'there may be time to make the detour to Braidstane if you've a mind.'

314

Chapter Nine

They sat on long benches brought from the castle especially for the occasion. Munro, seated beside Kate, noted that Elizabeth curved into herself, shivering despite the blanket wrapped tight around her knees. On one side of her, James Shaw, grown small and bowed, a tremor noticeable beneath his right eye. Beside him John, on the other side Hugh. Behind them, the remainder of the congregation packed close, standing hunched against the draughts that slid through the narrow window slits and crawled across the damp stone flags, snaking around ankles and funnelling indiscriminately through torn petticoat and fine chemise alike. The weather, fair for so long, had turned as those who came to pay their respects to Jean Shaw flowed in a steady stream up the terraced slopes of the town. What had begun as a weak drizzle, gaining in intensity, so that none escaped a wetting on their way to the church.

In front of the Munros the rain marked time, plopping into a wooden pail through a hole in the roof. The rhythmic dripping was a counterpoint to the drone of the minister who mumbled his way almost by rote through a homily on the life of Jean Shaw, as if his thoughts ran less on what he said than on the dinner that was to follow. No doubt it was hard to preach a good sermon with dampness seeping upwards through robes that absorbed the moisture like a sponge. Munro could see a thin trickle of water funnelling along the wall bracket of the candle sconce behind him and landing on the back of his neck – if this looby is the best that the new religion can muster small wonder that the church leaks parishioners in equal measure with the rain. At Renfrew it had been altogether different: the preacher, in his raising of Mary heavenwards, giving a tantalising glimpse of a gate swinging wide and of Mary, welcomed by a clutch of laughing children, chief among them Anna, her hair like flame.

'In the Name of the Father . . .'

The family rose, the movement rippling through the church, the crowd pressing back against the walls as the trestles under the coffin were removed and those who had been chosen took the first lift. Elizabeth swayed towards Hugh, who supported her as the coffin passed.

The procession moved slowly towards the rear of the church. James Shaw walked steadily behind the minister, placing his feet carefully one in front of the other, as if on some invisible line, his hands purple with the cold, his eyes fixed on some far-off place. Elizabeth, with Hugh and John on either side of her followed, then the rest of the girls. Christian held tight to Gillis, though whether for her own sake or the child's, Munro wasn't sure.

They clustered round the grave, dark-cloaked, silent, while the rain dripped from sleeves and shoulders to collect in puddles around their feet. It ran in rivulets down the spade cuts and pooled in the base of the deep hole that lay, like an open mouth, waiting to swallow the coffin that rested these few last minutes on the edge of their lives. Munro stood slightly behind Kate as Hugh took his place at the grave foot, sharing in the straining against the cords, the rocking of the coffin as they fed it into the ground.

Elizabeth also took her turn in the tossing of earth, her hand steady, belying her pain. Later he would hear her say that she remembered little of those last rites, save the raindrops hanging on spikes of holly and the petals of winter jasmine washed across the coffin lid.

The hall was bursting with people. Kate was with Christian, helping with the management of the food, and Munro, happy to remain in the background, stationed himself by the window furthest from the door. This was no simple family affair though Munro, seeing Elizabeth pinned against the fireplace, enduring the conversation of a spare man with grey hair like soiled string, perceived that she was less than comfortable with a wake on this scale. Her gaze was now fixed on the man who forced her attention, now scanning the room to see how the remainder of her family fared. John was moving through the press, stopping every few minutes to clasp a hand, bending his head to catch a murmured word. Kate, who had slotted into the company at Greenock as if into an old shoe, together with Christian bustled about the long table that stretched down the centre of the room, removing empty platters, rearranging dishes and chivvying the servants, so that the supply of food flowed steadily from the kitchens below.

A strange thing, Munro thought, to measure grief by the quality of beef.

The voice of the man who had captured Elizabeth surfaced in a sudden lull. 'It was a trying time, but dear Margaret . . .'

Munro saw Elizabeth nod absently, as the high-pitched

voice faded into fragments of other voices, subdued at first, then louder, as ale flowed and tongues were loosened. It was the first brewing and plentiful and he thought it likely that there would be more than one to suffer for it on the morrow. From the far end of the hall laughter burst out and was as quickly stilled.

A log exploded behind Elizabeth: a brief glitter of ruby embers crumbling to dust. The scent of wood smoke curling out from the hearth mingled with sweetmeats and roast goose, syllabub and hot punch. Kate passed close to Elizabeth carrying a tray of spiced muffins, and Munro, seeing Elizabeth flinch as if the hot tang hit her face like a blow, thought that perhaps they too had burnt cinnamon in the bedchamber to stave off infection, but with as little effect.

He caught a glimpse of Christian, her head bent close to James Shaw, suddenly dive to get a grip of Gillis who had sidled to one end of the table and was systematically picking the fruit out of slabs of plum cake, leaving them lying full of holes, like wedges of Dutch cheese. A vision of Anna speared him, and he turned his head, searching for distraction.

There was a stir of people over by the west wall. Patrick Maxwell, whose appearance at the funeral was unexpected, despite that he was a near neighbour, was making for Hugh, who stared out through the narrow window slit into the gathering darkness. Munro, remembering the exchange at the King's Wark, noticed Elizabeth renew her efforts to escape the man who deeved her – had there been any truth in William's insinuations at Leith? He would have thought not, but why then her obvious concern? He caught Kate's eye and jerked his head in Elizabeth's direction. She glanced across, abandoned the tray she carried and headed towards the fireplace. He saw her touch Elizabeth's arm and say something, so that the man bowed and stepped back, letting her pass.

Elizabeth, battling her way through the crush towards Hugh, was stopped every few feet by those who wished to express their sympathy, her progress slow. To those unaware of any deeper concerns, the mixture of anxiety and abstraction in her face could be interpreted as a measure of the shock of her bereavement; but Munro, recognizing that it increased the closer Maxwell got to Hugh, was again reminded of the earlier confrontation at Leith. And whatever the rights and wrongs of it, determined to help it be avoided if he could.

He moved to intercept Maxwell, but was beaten to it by a tall, languid man of about Hugh's age, who Munro knew, though by name only, as the son of a minister in Ayr. His long face made longer by a neat, pointed beard, he leant backwards against the wall so that the light from the candle in the sconce above his head cast his shadow, stick-thin, across those nearest to him. A gap opened in the crowd that thronged the table and Munro, slipping into it, came close enough to make out snippets of their conversation, as the noise level dipped and flowed.

'. . . A common enough trouble and for any age. Hassilhead has buried his second wife and still no heir to show for it . . . Shaw at least has a goodly family to his credit.'

There was a malicious quality to Maxwell's reply. 'Though most are girls. Fine in their own way no doubt.' He indicated Hugh, now also within earshot, 'The pattern may be set to repeat . . .'

Hamilton also glanced towards Hugh. 'Soldier he may be, but it doesn't guarantee prowess in other directions.'

Maxwell's back was to the room and as Hugh came closer he seemed to raise his voice deliberately.

'But one bairn in four years. Maybe Braidstane isn't up to the job, or not often.'

Hamilton glanced around, clearly uneasy, and no wonder, for it made little sense to look for trouble and ill-mannered in this circumstance.

'Have a care, Maxwell, they say he carries grudges . . .'

Maxwell laughed, 'As others carry love tokens: close to his heart.'

Heads were beginning to turn, conversations to falter, so that Maxwell's voice carried as he continued, still with his back to Hugh, as if unaware of his presence, 'It won't be Elizbeth's blame . . . I know that well.'

From the side Munro could see that Maxwell was well aware that he had the attention of most of the room and chose his words with care.

'She visited whiles . . .' A pause. 'The price of her company five merks . . .' Another pause, longer this time, his words dropping like stones into the silence, 'A bargain, as I recollect.'

Hugh spun Maxwell round, his voice dangerously quiet. 'You insult my wife.'

Too late Elizabeth reached them, stretched out to touch Hugh's arm, as Maxwell, shifting his focus, said,

'You have my condolences, Elizabeth.' He looked back at Hugh. 'As from an old friend who didn't think it right to stay away.'

Her face flamed. Christian, trapped by the stairwell, also stood as if frozen, Munro catching the glance that flashed between them.

Once more Elizabeth sought to restrain Hugh, but he shook her off, gripped Maxwell's shoulder.

'You insult my wife.'

Maxwell twisted out of his grip and smiled at Elizabeth, as if he played a high trump in a game of Gleek. Glancing towards the window behind him, he bowed, 'Good-day, Elizabeth, this isn't the time to trouble you for a bed.'

As he made to leave, Hugh moved to stop him, and Munro, sensing that they had reached danger point, thrust himself between them, opening up a space for Maxwell to pass, the remaining guests peeling a path before him to the door.

There was a moment of silence before a dozen conversations broke out at once, voices forced and unnaturally loud.

Hugh thrust his way through the clusters of people, head down, oblivious to those who stretched out a hand to him in the passing, his jaw set firm. He made for the turnpike, his footsteps echoing up the narrow spiral towards the wall walk. Elizabeth followed. Munro, behind her, halted at the top of the stair. Shreds of grey light, remnants of the dull day, dissected the heavy clouds that hung black against the sky. A sliver of moon showed briefly before being swallowed again. In the semi-dusk Elizabeth slithered on the damp slabs.

Hugh swung round, 'Is there to be no peace . . . ?

She reached for him.

'Did you 'visit' Newark?' His emphasis sliced the silence.

Elizabeth's 'Yes, but . . .' was almost inaudible.

Hugh gave her no chance to continue, pushing past her and disappearing down the stair.

Elizabeth was gripping the parapet as if without it she would fall, or perhaps as if she wished to, her gaze fixed on the ground far below.

Munro took a step towards her, hesitated – I should get Kate.

In the event it was Christian who, responding to Munro's fear, left the servants to see to the company and flew with him to the battlements, to find Elizabeth picking at the lichen with her nails as if she thought to scour the wall clean. Again Munro halted at the doorway, as if on guard.

Elizabeth said, 'He asked had I been to Newark.'

'But did you not tell him I was with you?'

'I saw his face . . . I saw what he thought.'

'You must speak to him, how can he know the truth else?' There was urgency in Christian's voice. 'You didn't hear all that was said, and he doesn't know Maxwell and hasn't a reason to think him a liar.'

'He knows me.' Elizabeth stared down at the dark line of trees that marked the edge of the slope leading to the town. 'Should that not be enough?'

'It will be enough.' Christian slipped an arm around her waist. 'Maybe it is best to let be for tonight. Things aye look different when the sun is shining. When he has space to consider. . .' She steered Elizabeth towards the doorway, Munro melting into the shadows.

It was past midnight, the company long gone, when Hugh re-entered the castle by the postern gate and climbed to the hall. A single candle guttered in a sconce by the hearth, solidified wax hanging from the iron bracket in a ragged fringe. As it burnt lower, it smoked and flared, casting shadows that alternately leapt and shrivelled across the floor. He flung himself onto the oak settle and stretched out his legs to the embers that still glowed in the hearth.

Munro, folded into the window reveal, his right leg dead underneath him, resisted the impulse to move. It had been his own suggestion to wait for Hugh's return, the thought of speaking reason easier in contemplation than in fact. He watched Hugh pick at the mud on his boots, dropping flakes into the ash so that it puffed up in tiny grey clouds. Hugh struck his fist against the lintel, punctuating the blows with a reprise of Maxwell's words, '. . . she visited whiles . . . the price of her company . . . a bargain, as I recollect.'

The candle flame dipped, then sputtered and died, leaving Hugh shadowed against the hearth, his face red in the last light of the fire. He stirred the stumps of logs with the toe of his boot and they flared, sending shards of light across the remnants of the supper before subsiding again into a sullen glow. Munro swung his legs to the floor as Hugh scavenged a goose wing, peeling away the skin and with it the rim of congealed grease. His fingers, smeared with fat, slipped as he tried to lift a half-full jug of flat ale. It slid from his hand and fell to the floor with a crash, spilling most of the contents.

Munro picked up the jug, replaced it on the table. He appeared relaxed, as if he came to pass the time of day, as if it wasn't the middle of the night, as if everything was normal. 'It wasn't as he said . . .'

'No? Why then Elizabeth's admission?'

'To being there, nothing more.'

'And you would know?'

'Christian knows. Elizabeth knows.'

'Knows . . . or is known?' The cruelty of it seemed to wind Hugh even as he said it.

Munro, as if what he said was commonplace, unworthy of emotion, kept his voice calm. 'She had a reason to call . . .'

Hugh gave a sharp laugh. 'I'm sure.' Pain raw and unshuttered in his eyes, he gripped the edge of the table and thrust upwards sending everything cascading onto the floor in a jumble of bones and grease, ale and wine; the mess and the smell like a tavern after a brawl. 'It's well known Maxwell is a murderer, fornication is hardly beyond him.' He made for the door, kicking at the three-quarters stripped carcase of a chicken that caught on his foot. 'It's best I go. There is nothing for me here.'

And Munro, his own demons re-awakened, made no further move to stop him.

He woke early, sounds from the hall merging into his dreams.

Kate was already awake. 'There's more of a racket than I would have expected from the wee bit mess left last night, but we should at least help with the clearance.'

He threw back the covers and swinging his legs over the edge of the bed thrust a foot into his stocking. There was a loud scrape and a heavy thud from the hall below. 'It wasn't a wee bit mess when Hugh was done.'

'What of Elizabeth?'

'She wasn't there and I was glad of it, for I don't like to think what he might have done or said if she had been.'

'Where is he now?'

'God knows. He stormed out and I judged it best to let him go.'

Grizel and Christian were wrestling with the table when they entered the hall.

'Let me.' Munro hefted the table, swinging it round one end at a time until it rested against the wall.

Grizel began to sweep at the rushes with sharp, staccato strokes.

Munro turned to Christian. 'Where's John?'

'Looking for Hugh. With Elizabeth.'

'Should I go?'

She considered. 'No. If we can get here to rights before they come in, it will be more than helpful.'

With all of them working, it took barely ten minutes to clear the debris and for Munro to reposition the table in the centre of the room.

Gillis burst through the door, unable to conceal her excitement. 'Hugh's gone. Star isn't in the stable and Hamish says. . .'

'Wheest, Gillis.' John shook his head as he followed her in.

Elizabeth, coming in behind them said, 'It's true. Hamish heard the sound of hooves on the cobbles and saw Hugh ride out . . .'

'Perhaps he's gone to Braidstane.' Christian had moved to stand beside Elizabeth.

Munro edged towards the door and motioned to Kate to follow. Reaching the stable he said, 'Hugh won't have gone home. It's Maxwell's blame and Maxwell he will follow.

'To tackle Maxwell,' her eyes were fixed on his, 'is to tackle William. Is that wise?'

'Wise? No. For Hugh or anyone else. But I cannot stand aside.' He was saddling Sweet Briar, tightening the girth, slipping the bridle over her head. 'There is more at stake here than Elizabeth's reputation, important as that may be.

If this was to lead to another Annock . . .' Kate sagged against him, her legs buckling and he pulled her into his chest, resting his chin on her hair. 'If I can halt that . . .'

'And if you cannot?'

He gripped her more tightly, 'We have twice come close to losing all that matters . . . and this feud the root of it. I owe it to you . . . to the bairns, at least to try.' His hand slid to her face, his thumb smearing a tear across her cheek. 'Sometime there has to be an end . . . wait here for me . . . or go to Braidstane. Tell Elizabeth . . . tell her that I have gone to make them see sense.'

She dipped her head against him, her voice muffled. 'Pray God you can.'

He tilted her face upwards, sought for words of reassurance, 'Neither Glencairn nor Montgomerie would thank them for any trouble, and Hugh has worked gey hard with James to lose it all now. They must see sense.'

He skewed through the gateway at Newark and brought Sweet Briar to a quivering halt. A lad was disappearing into the stabling leading a bay that Munro, with a leap of gratitiude for Sweet Briar's speed, recognized as Hugh's.

Walking the mare across to the stable, he ran his hand down her neck. 'Well done lass, well done.' And to the lad who reappeared in the doorway, 'I don't know how long I'll be, but look to her well for she's been hard pushed and deserves of the best.'

The main door to the castle stood open, thrust back against the yett and he took the wooden stairs at a run, recognizing danger in the voices that spilled out.

'This is intolerable. You burst into my home and threaten my person. . .'

'You insulted my wife.'

'I said but the truth, unpalatable though it may be . . .'

There was a crash and splinters of glass from a window showered Munro. He leapt the last two steps and slid to a halt in the entrance of the hall. Maxwell was beside the broken window, his back against the wall, Hugh's fist, blood oozing from the knuckles, inches from his face.

'Are you mad?' Munro sprang at Hugh, grabbing his arm, but Hugh shook him off as a bull mastiff might a terrier pup, sending him careering into a wooden chest, so that he tipped backwards over the domed lid, cracking his head on the floor.

He scrambled to his feet. 'Dear God, Hugh . . .'

Maxwell had ducked under Hugh's arm and was making for the door.

Hugh dodged past him and slammed it shut, ramming the bolts home. He stood against it, snarling at Munro. 'This isn't your fight and I would throw you out, but that I don't want this weasel to have any chance of running for help.' He rubbed his hand down the side of his jerkin, leaving a sticky trail of blood. 'We have unfinished business here and I'll thank you not to interfere.' He had drawn his sword and was advancing, spinning his wrist, feinting and thrusting, slicing the air in front of Maxwell's face. 'Not so cocky now, eh, Maxwell?'

Maxwell dived sideways and grabbed an iron candle sconce, using the splayed feet as a guard.

'Or is it that you are brave with women only?' Hugh was driving Maxwell back, his eyes glittering.

There was a sound of running footsteps on the stair, and a hammering at the door.

Maxwell jerked his head towards the noise. 'You won't get away with this. And who will look to dear Elizabeth then?'

Munro edged round – Hugh's the more dangerous, if I can but disarm him . . . dear God, but they are fools both.

Hugh half-turned, and Maxwell, taking advantage of his momentary distraction slashed at him with the sconce, the blunt end of one of the feet raking across Hugh's cheekbone. Hugh pivoted with a roar, his sword swinging in earnest and as Maxwell tried to sidestep, his foot caught on the edge of the hearth and he fell heavily, the sconce skidding from his hand.

It was the opportunity Munro needed, and he leapt between them, flinging up his arm to protect his face, the tip of Hugh's sword slicing through his sleeve. Behind him Maxwell was scrambling to his feet, reaching for the sconce. Munro kicked it away, and grasping Maxwell's wrist, thrust him back against the wall and held him there. Hugh had lowered his sword and was staring, bemused at the blood running down Munro's hand. Munro glared at him.

'Kill me and Maxwell both and you may have another Annock on your hands.' Then to Maxwell, 'Did you bed Elizabeth?'

Hugh lunged.

Ignoring him, Munro continued to press. 'Did she even offer?'

The hammering on the door had been replaced by a scraping.

Maxwell tried to bluster, 'I never claimed . . .'

'No?' Munro cut him off. Then you have no grounds for your claim of knowledge of her.' The scraping had become a sawing. ' An apology would be wise.'

'An apology is nothing.' Hugh made to by-pass Munro, but was once again blocked,

'Drop your sword, Hugh! You are in Cunninghame territory. Eglinton won't thank you to open old wounds and as for James – you have spent four years courting him, what good will it do you or Elizabeth if you lose it all now?' He tightened his grip on Maxwell's wrist, drawing him forward. The sawing had been replaced by the sound of a hammer and chisel. 'You'd be advised to make your apology quick if you wish to save your door.'

Maxwell was sullen. 'Elizabeth but came to make a collection for the poor. I cannot fault her virtue.'

Munro released Maxwell. 'Hugh?'

With a roar, Hugh raised his sword and thrust, Munro too late to stop him, Maxwell pressing himself back against the wall. Hugh waited until the last possible second, then pivoted, forcing the sword tip deep into the table top, releasing the hilt as if it burned. 'Let me out of here.'

Maxwell darted to the door, pulled back the bolts, pretended normality, 'Good-day, Braidstane.'

As Hugh shoved his way through the servants clustered at the head of the stair, Maxwell stepped into the doorway behind him, blocking Munro's passage.

'I take it Glencairn knows where your friendship lies? Or is championing the Montgomeries a new pastime?' The bravado was back. 'Rest assured, Munro, William will hear of this . . .'

Munro clenched his fists, dearly wishing to feel his knuckles crunch into Maxwell's face, but thought of Kate and the bairns restrained him. Better that he catch up with Hugh and make sure that he returned to Greenock, which, if they hurried they could make by dinner-time. Wresting the sword from the table, he thrust Maxwell aside. 'Dear God, Maxwell, but you are a fool.'

Kate knew as soon as she saw Munro's face that though he had brought Hugh safe home, it wasn't the time to be sociable, and so saved him the trouble of making an excuse. She kept her voice light, as if it had been the plan all along, 'If we leave shortly, can we make Broomelaw by dinnertime?'

He shot her a glance of thanks. 'Firefly won't have a problem and half an hour of respite will, I think, be enough for Sweet Briar.'

'You'll take a bite before you go then?' Elizabeth followed their lead. 'There are plenty pickings from yesterday and they won't take long to set.'

It was an unfortunate choice of words and Kate, seeing Hugh tense, excused herself. 'I have a few things to pack.'

In the chamber above the hall, Kate fingered the burgundy gown laid out to air. She could hear voices from below, but couldn't make out anything that was said, only that it was no more than a word or two each, first Elizabeth, then Munro, then Hugh's deeper rumble. She was kneeling on the floor folding the gown when Elizabeth came in, shutting the door behind her.

Kate said, 'I'm sorry we have to go. I had thought . . .'

'Yes, so had I.' Elizabeth knelt down at her side and stroked the line of pearls ringing the waist of the dress. 'It's a pretty gown and a pity you won't have the chance to wear it.'

'There'll be other and maybe happier times. Perhaps you could all come to Broomelaw?'

'You know I'd like that fine.' Elizabeth was swivelling her wedding band back and forth.

Kate tried to be encouraging. 'This thing with Maxwell. It can't have been hard to sort. They weren't long away and are back safe.' She finished the folding of the dress.

'What Maxwell said . . .' Elizabeth sounded choked, '. . . I should never have given him the opportunity to twist things so.'

'It's over now and no heads broken.'

'It won't be the end of it. It cuts too deep, and Hugh . . . it isn't in him to hold his temper when provoked, however much anyone may counsel. And besides,' Elizabeth hugged her arms against her chest, 'Maxwell is too close kin to the Cunninghames.'

Kate stiffened at the bitterness in Elizabeth's voice.

'If it hadn't been me, it would have been something else. The Montgomeries and the Cunninghames have aye been at each other's throats, and a forced clasp of the hand or a clap on the shoulder and a few careful words of regret won't change anything. I am heartily sick of them all, with their talk of insult and injury and the need for satisfaction. Why can Hugh not find satisfaction in his family, with one child already to his credit and another on the way?' She broke off, 'I didn't mean . . . Oh, Kate, I'm so sorry . . .'

'Don't be. I have felt and said the same a hundred times.' Kate tightened her grip 'You aren't the only one to wish this nonsense over. We can't undo the past, but we need not live in it. You will come to Broomelaw?'

Elizabeth patted her stomach. 'Or you to Braidstane. You have a good man and he did well to broker this peace with Maxwell. For that, I will always be grateful, however short its effect.'

Chapter Ten

For the second time, the promised visit didn't materialize.

October slid into November and no word coming from Braidstane, Kate buried her regrets and focused her energies on the rejuvenation of the attic chamber where the children slept. Munro, recognizing the significance of what she did, made no protest, mixing bucket-load after bucket-load of limewash and trailing it up the four flights of stairs.

December came in hard, heralding a season of frosts that silvered the loch with ice a foot thick, so that he fashioned wooden skates for all but Ellie, the blacksmith fitting them with narrow blades. In January, when it was clear that the cold snap would last, frost fairs were held along the upper reaches of the Clyde and it took little persuasion for Munro to fit runners to the cart and take Kate and the two older children.

It was Maggie's first experience of a winter fair and she hopped up and down on the shore, impatient for Munro to lace her skates. Kate and Munro each took one of her hands and they struck out towards the braziers burning on the ice and bought chestnuts so hot that even with mittens, they had to toss them from hand to hand until they cooled enough to eat. A flesher had set up a spit and was roasting a pig, the fat sparking like a scattering of bawbees. Maggie wrinkled her nose at the smell of mulled wine and roast meat and burning tallow, and wheedled three pennies from Munro to have her name and the date scribed on a card with a drawing of the fair.

Robbie came flying to drag them to see a man who played a whistle and had a monkey who danced and gibbered on the end of a rope. There were tents with 'fat ladies' and fortune-tellers and stalls selling simples: aloes, camphor and ginger, punguent salves of egg-white, rose oil and turpentine. One stall-holder brandished a pamphlet hailing tobacco as the cure-all for everything from toothache and bad breath to kidney stones and carbuncles.

Kate dragged Munro away. 'Don't even think on it. I have no wish to kiss a chimney, supposing it could do all that is claimed.'

There were entertainers of all kinds: tumblers in rainbow colours, spinning and wheeling like human kaleidoscopes. Jugglers spinning plates on the ends of long poles balanced on their chins. Musicians who scraped and beat and blew, so fine and so fast that those who hadn't skates hopped and jigged on the ice around them. Best of all, a conjuror: his silver hair corkscrewed around his face, who began his act by plucking a groat from behind Maggie's ear.

She was entranced: tipped forward onto the toe of her skates, leaning into Kate that she might not lose her balance; as he spun cards into spirals of kings and queens, aces and jokers, hearts and spades and clubs. He made coins appear and disappear from his hands, under pewter tankards, into a tiny, brightly coloured wooden box with a sliding lid. A dove placed in a tall-crowned hat was gone in a puff of smoke, replaced by a multi-coloured streamer yards long. And best of all: the rabbit that hopped from his sleeve. The act was finished, the conjuror bowing and smiling, Munro fishing for a penny for Maggie to drop in the bonnet he shook.

A slow, contemptuous clapping; a voice impossible to mistake. 'Well, well. Munro . . . and family. This is an unlooked for surprise. Enjoying yourselves? I daresay this is cheap enough entertainment, even for you.' William's eyes raked over Kate, lingering on her breast and she tensed, but tilted her chin and returned his stare.

Beside her Munro smouldered, 'You're a step from Kilmaurs. Are you likewise straightened, or is it that Glencairn does not countenance the aggravation closer to home?'

'I play where I choose and tonight I chose here, and might have been the sooner had I anticipated so pleasant company.'

A gust of wind lifted Kate's hair, whipped her skirt around her legs, and against her will she shivered.

William leaned close. 'But come, Munro, you do not treat your wife well. A pretty piece deserves to be kept warm . . . I have a horse-blanket that would serve.'

She was rigid with defiance, determined not to rise to his goading. 'Thank you but no. I am not truly cold, and if I was I have a shawl in the cart I could put to use.'

'Some mulled wine then? You will not refuse to drink with me?'

'We would not, but that we have already had our fill and the bairns hope to see the conjuror's next act.'

'This fellow? He is scarcely proficient, or not to a discerning audience at least.'

Maggie, who had followed the sense of William's comment, though not all the words, shot out a foot and caught him on the shin with the blade of her skate. 'He is clever and magic and . . .'

Kate caught her round the waist, pulled her back, and

though she would have dearly liked to kick William herself, reproved her. 'Maggie! It is not well done. Apologize this instant.'

'Shan't.' Maggie escaped from Kate's grasp, her eyes fixed on William, hard and bright.

'Already feisty . . . like mother, like daughter.' William was rubbing at his leg. Have no fear Kate, I take no account of a child's pettiness, how ever ill-bred. When she is grown, I shall take an apology then, no doubt the sweeter for the wait.'

Munro thrust Maggie behind him to turn on William, but Kate had beaten him to it, her hand whipping out, the crack as it met his cheek, echoing like a pistol shot. Off-balance he staggered and then Robbie was hammering at him with his fists, Maggie, who had ducked round Munro, kicking furiously at his shins. A small crowd was gathering, the conjuror, with an eye to further profit, offering odds on the bairns. Kate dived for Maggie, Munro for Robbie.

William straightened, and then as if suddenly aware of the folk who gawked, that they made of him a laughing stock, ground out, 'Ill-mannered as well as ill-bred. You would do well Munro to train your children better, or you may live to regret it.' He spun on his heel and thrust his way through the crowd, daring any to stop him.

The silence lasted only as long as it took for the conjuror to re-start his show for the new audience that the confrontation had drawn. Maggie, no longer fighting Kate, was craning to see, but Munro, recognizing the wisdom of putting as much ground between themselves and William as possible, said, his voice brooking no resistance, 'Home.'

They found their way to the cart in silence, the children unusually subdued, Munro and Kate, though both occupied with this new danger, neither wishing to air it. On the hill they stopped and turned to take a last look. Maggie, pointing to the moon riding high and full in the sky, whispered,

'There is a man. I see his face.'

The lights of the lanterns twinkled all along the shore, the flames from the braziers flaring spasmodically, figures like dolls still skating on the ice.

Kate leant back against Munro, risked, 'If it were not for William, I could have stayed all night.'

'If it were not for William . . .' it hung between them, the thought of Anna: of what they had lost; the fear for what they still had.

Kate swivelled, put her hand over his mouth, 'It is the pleasure the bairns will remember, we should too.' Maggie was cuddled into the crook of her arm, her cheeks rosy, damp curls of hair poking out from her fur snood. Robbie began to whistle, bouncing his head from side to side.

Maggie stirred. 'That wasn't it.'

'Was so.'

'You can't remember.'

'You can't whistle.'

Kate touched Munro's arm. 'Time to go.'

It was mid-February before the temperature rose sufficiently for the ice to melt on the loch and the streams to begin to bubble and splash again on the hillsides above Broomelaw. The dreich weather that followed was more chilling than ever the frost had been and the children made brief forays onto the slopes below the castle only to come back dripping and miserable. By the beginning of March,

Kate too was desperate to escape the confines of the castle, and with the first blink of sunshine, pale and watery though it was, took herself out to attack the scum of moss and blackened weeds that stifled her herb garden, clatching muck across the cobbles each time she went to empty her pail on the midden.

'Is it a gypsy I have for a sister-in-law?'

Kate leapt up, squinting into the sun. 'Archie!' Her smile widened. 'And Sybilla. This is a welcome surprise. I didn't hear the horses.'

'I doubt if you'd have heard a regiment, you were that engrossed. It's as well we aren't reivers.'

Kate scrambled to her feet. 'I'm that glad to see you. We have been starved of visitors these four months past and are wearied of our own company.' She looked at Sybilla and then down at her hands. 'I can't give you a right greeting, but come in to the fire. The bairns . . . you'll be a fine distraction.' She stopped at the door of the kitchen, nodded towards the stair. 'You know your way, Archie, I'll not be a minute.'

'You'll have heard of Sybilla's father's passing?' Archie was standing on the hearthstone raking vigorously at the fire, to encourage it into a blaze and turned his head as Kate entered the solar.

'Had he been ill? The weather has been that bad and Munro with plenty to sort at home, hasn't had the leisure to traipse about. And with Mary gone there hasn't been the same need.' She touched Sybilla's hand. 'I'm sorry. For the death and that we didn't know. You're here for the funeral?'

Archie came to stand behind Sybilla. 'The funeral was a month ago.'

'Then . . .'

'We didn't get away . . . that's why we're here now,' Archie corrected himself. 'Sybilla is here to sort her father's things: clear the house, dispose of the animals. It's to be hoped the sale of them will cover the rent owing.' His hand rested on the back of the settle and she tilted her head against it. 'We plan to be married.'

Kate beamed. 'I did so hope when you came, and then the talk of your father. I thought perhaps I was wrong. I am that glad.' A shadow crossed her face then her smile broke out again. 'And so Mary would have been. She talked of it whiles.' She took both Sybilla's hands in hers. 'When is it to be and where?'

'Soon I hope . . . if Glencairn is agreeable. Though we haven't yet sought permission, I don't think it will be a surprise and Lady Glencairn . . .'

Sybilla completed his sentence. '. . . is good to me and will want to find me happy.'

An unaccountable shiver ran through Kate and to cover it she lifted the poker to stir the fire.

'Would you wish it here?'

'We did wonder . . .'

'Wonder what?' Munro came in, brushing moss from his hose. 'Archie! Sybilla! I saw the horses in the stable. It's good to see you both, and looking well.' He poked Archie's stomach. 'They've surely got a better cook at Kilmaurs than when I was last there, or is there a new fashion for padding that we aren't aware of?'

Sybilla said, 'See, Archie. It isn't only me that thinks you not so slender as once you were.'

Archie was tracing a circle behind her ear, twisting a strand of hair around his finger. 'Slender is for lassies. This is but to keep me warm. When the summer comes, I shall shed the pounds as a horse does a winter coat.'

Laughter rippled in Kate. 'It's to be hoped not so patchily.'

'It isn't my fault that you don't recognize a fine figure of a man when you see him.'

'The best of a poor lot at Kilmaurs anyroads.' It was unintentional, but Sybilla's mention of Kilmaurs brought a chill that cut the chaffing as a scythe would straw.

The door bounced on its hinges.

Maggie was cradling a bird's nest, twigs and feathers and wisps of hay woven together into a perfect cup shape.

Kate frowned. 'Maggie, you shouldn't disturb . . .'

'I didn't.' Maggie's eyes, fixed on the nest, were robin-bright. 'It was Tabs, scraping around under the thorn bushes behind the byre. I thought it was a bird and called her away and then I crawled in and found this and I thought it wouldn't do harm to bring it home. Uncle Archie!' She flung herself across the room and he caught her and birled her round, her skirts lifting to display the petticoats beneath.

'You haven't forgot me then?'

'Robbie will be cross,' Maggie sounded smug. 'He wouldn't come with me, though I tell't him I thought I saw horses, and then we saw Tabs and . . .'

'And I must see this nest.' Archie hunkered down, taking it from her. It was about four inches across and less than an inch thick, the inside soft with down.

'Do you know what kind of bird made this?'

She shook her head.

'A sparrow – to judge by the size and the making. See how tightly it hangs together. And all with her beak.' He tapped his finger against Maggie's mouth. 'Do you think you could do so well with your teeth?'

She shook her head again, her eyes solemn, then grabbed the nest back, hugging it against her.

'Maggie! Don't be rude.' Kate shot an apologetic glance at Archie.

'He can't have it.'

'Maggie!'

Archie shook his head at Kate, then touched Maggie's nose. 'Of course I can't, it's yours. But what will you do with it?'

'Put it back, where Tabs can't get it.' She switched her attention to her father, 'How many eggs will there be?'

Munro hunkered down beside Archie and stroked Maggie's hair. 'I don't think there'll be any eggs, sweet, not in this nest.'

Maggie glared at Archie. 'But you said it was well made.'

'And so it is.' Munro cupped her face in his hands. 'But if you put it back now the bird would smell Tabs and would be feart to lay her eggs.'

Maggie's shoulders drooped.

Munro pulled her towards him, taking care not to squash the nest. 'The sparrow'll build another one, just the same, you'll see, and you may keep watch on Tabs to make sure she can't fright her a second time.' He tweaked a curl that swung in front of her ear. 'I'm sure you can find a use for this one.'

Archie and Sybilla rode out early the next morning, eager to get her father's affairs sorted and have leisure and to spare to plan for a happier occasion.

'We have three days only.'

Kate heard the regret in Archie's voice and was cheered, minding his last visit, when he was less comfortable with their company.

As they dwindled down the valley she leaned against the barmkin wall. Ellie was perched on Munro's shoulder.

'It'll be a fine thing to arrange a wedding,' Kate said, 'While I'm still young enough to enjoy it.'

'You'll hardly be ancient in twelve or thirteen year's time, at least I hope not, or I'll be thinking it's a poor bargain I've made.'

'Maggie'll not marry at sixteen, or not if I have any say in the matter.'

'What makes you think you will? She's got gey enough spirit the now. I can't see her changing.'

'Spirit maybe, but sense too I hope, before she's the age for marrying. And to throw herself away at sixteen . . .'

'Not like her mother then.'

She rose to the bait. 'I was practically seventeen, though . . .', mischief in her eyes, '. . . I concede the lack of sense.' She lifted Ellie to the floor, protesting, and rested her chin on Munro's chest. 'I have few regrets, which is maybe,' she pretended to think, 'an indication that I still lack sense.'

The wind was picking up and fat grey clouds moved across the valley, holding the threat of rain.

Munro assessed the sky and followed them in, responding to Kate's questioning glance with, 'They won't aye be bairns, and what I miss can't be recovered.' He broke off, the words hanging heavy between them, then touched his fingertips to her cheek in mute apology. 'The work will wait.'

He stretched out on the floor of the solar, a doll on either side of him and ate crumbs of cake and drank thimblefulls of milk from a miniature pewter tankard that Maggie replenished at regular intervals, in between the scolding of her dolls for their apparent lack of appetite. Kate sat on the settle, a petticoat spread over her lap. It had been torn on a briar as she over-reached to gather the last of the brambles, so that she sought to make the best of the damage by re-fashioning it for Maggie. Her head was bent, concentrating on cutting and tucking and pinning.

Robbie dragged a stool beside her, his chequer-board under one arm. It was the first time he had touched it since Anna's death and seeing it, Kate found it hard to swallow, as if a fish-bone stuck in her throat.

'Set it up then, and see if you can best me.'

Ellie, though sixteen months and dainty, was still not quite steady on her feet and scooted her wooden walker around the room by bouncing in the cambric sling until the tips of her toes contacted with the floor. She had a fair grasp of the workings of the thing, but it didn't always do exactly as she wanted so that her giggles were punctuated by angry squeals when she found herself propelled in the wrong direction.

They had brought it home with them from the jaunt to Edinburgh, a purchase that had Agnes grumbling over their lack of sense.

'New-fangled nonsense and the likely outcome, disaster.' She had grudgingly admitted the quality of the thing. 'The wood is smooth enough, I grant you. At least she won't snag her clothes.'

'No, indeed.' Kate thought her almost won round. 'We were assured the cloth is also of the best and would carry a child twice Ellie's weight, and the legs are well splayed and prettily turned forbye.'

Agnes, her fears renewed by the fineness of the four spindles to which the balls allowing the walker to slide across the floor were attached, countered, 'And what use prettiness when she coups and they splinter.'

But Ellie hadn't couped, though she had come close on the first day, fetching up against the edge of the rag rug, which Kate hastily rolled up and which was now stowed away until the time for the walker was past. The square frame, running around the outside of the legs a couple of inches from the floor, gave it added stability. It had already proved its value in giving Ellie a measure of the mobility she so clearly wanted. Whether it had also slowed her progress in walking was a debatable point, but the additional freedom it gave Kate, was, in her opinion, worth the risk.

She had played her trump card. 'It's good exercise for the child, and saves the wearing out of stockings.'

And Agnes had let it be, for Ellie, crawling from six months, had already rubbed through more stockings than all the other children put together.

She spun across the floor and reaching Robbie grasped the chequer-board and thrust the edge of it into her mouth, so that the remaining chequers slid onto the floor and rolled in all directions.

'I had you beat,' Robbie leapt up, indignant. He stamped his foot and pulled the board from Ellie's hands, shoving against the walker, sending her shooting towards the other end of the room, so that she ran over Maggie's doll and Munro's tiny tankard *en route*.

Munro was on his knees retrieving the tankard, Kate soothing a wailing Ellie, Maggie scolding Robbie, while he, ignoring her, scrabbled for the chequers, as Archie and Sybilla entered, flushed and damp from the ride.

'Maybe if we go out and come in again it will be a mite more welcoming. I don't know that I'm ready for this.'

Sybilla tugged Archie towards Ellie. 'Time you learnt. Next year . . .'

'Marriage is one thing. And fine. But bairns . . . though ours, of course, won't fight.'

'With you as their father?' Kate patted the cushion beside her. 'Sybilla, come and dry yourself out and I shall tell you, if you don't know already, some of what you're letting yourself in for with Archie. He and Munro aye fought the piece out and Archie was fair feisty, for all that he was the younger by six years. Growing up practically in their backyard, you'd have thought I might have had more sense than to marry onto them.' She was looking at Munro, settled again with Maggie, his tankard re-filled, and her smile was indulgent. 'Serious though, we have been fortunate: nine years and most of them . . .' the shadow of Annock and of Anna flickered for an instant between them, '. . . most of them content.'

Sybilla reached out for Ellie. 'Can I? Practice won't do harm.'

Archie, on the window seat beside Robbie, set the chequer-board up again. 'The contract is for a wife only, at least the now. We have a home to find, before we can fill it with bairns.'

Munro waved away a refill of milk. 'No thank you, sweet, I think I've had enough.' Then, as Maggie began to pout, 'If you feed me now, then I shan't be able for my dinner and Agnes will be put out. It's the turn of the dolls, for they don't have anything else to come.'

Mollified, Maggie began to feed her dolls and Munro turned his attention to Archie.

'Have you thoughts on the matter of where to live?'

'Thoughts yes, but . . .'

'Glencairn isn't any more aware of them than your wedding plans?'

'No, though I suspicion that he might see advantage in them, but as for William . . .'

'Care to share them?'

'There is a broken-down tower on the Solway. It's Cunninghame land, though Glencairn's hold on it is tenuous. A repaired tower would strengthen his hand.'

'I can't see anything to object to in that, even for William, your company isn't so critical that he couldn't spare you?'

'My company, no.' Archie turned to Robbie, his gaze on the chequer-board. 'Are you ready? I'm not easy to beat, mind.'

'No more am I. I had Mama on the run, but that Ellie wrecked the board.'

Munro was thinking aloud. 'I wouldn't hold out much hope that Glencairn would pay for the repairs. That, I imagine, would be your own concern.'

'Hmm.' Archie hesitated and Kate thought again how changed he was, and for the better, from the brash Archie of the previous year.

Robbie was tugging at his arm. 'Can I start?'

Archie winked at him, 'If you won't trounce me too quick.' He looked over his head at Sybilla, then at Munro. 'I did wonder . . .'

'If I could help?'

'Aye. I know I haven't always been the best of brothers, but . . .'

Kate was definite. 'It's what you are now that counts. Of course we can help. As you can see, my husband has little to do with his time and can no doubt spare some to set you up.' She turned to Sybilla, 'I trust you had some say in the choosing of this tower.'

'We found it together, when riding out from Orchardton. It has a view of Dunisle and the ground below runs down to the firth. It was there we settled things between us, and so,' her eyes were bright, 'will be a fine place to settle, though it'll take some time and much silver before any but crows can bide there.'

'That good?'

'Well, there is a small part still roofed, though how much of the weather it would keep out is another matter, but the walls seem sound enough and the chimneys don't look to be a problem. Two of the floors are there and though springing with damp, are, I think, recoverable. The window glass will be the most expense, though, as it is gey old and small forbye, there aren't many windows.' Archie had switched his attention from the chequers. A mistake, for Robbie, hopping backwards and forwards around the board with his crowner, scooped up Archie's remaining pieces and whooped.

'I tell't you I could best you!'

'That you did, and well done too.' He began to pile up the counters.

'Is it the day after tomorrow you head for Kilmaurs?' Munro was running possibilities around in his mind. 'Could you detour on the way back?'

Archie shook his head. 'Safer not. To tell the truth, I was fortunate to come at all. It was Lady Glencairn's doing. William wasn't best pleased, but didn't dare say anything, for he isn't exactly the favourite at the minute.'

Kate intercepted a warning glance from Sybilla that sent a rickle of cold down her back, as if her dress funnelled a draught.

'Well,' Munro rose and stretched, cracking his elbow. 'When it's sanctioned, send word and I'll come and look it over for you and see what needs must be done and what can wait.'

'And I will stay behind and plan for the wedding.' Kate stroked Ellie's head as she lay sound on Sybilla's shoulder. 'We may not be able for matching James but we will make a fine show none the less.'

The following morning a line of light slanting through a gap in the shutter fell across Sybilla's face. In the moment before full consciousness, she turned her head into the warmth of it, her lips curving in a smile for Archie, who was propped up on one elbow on the horse blanket beside her, tickling her nose with a long strand of grass. Her eyelids fluttered. 'Stop it, Archie . . .'

Maggie giggled, snatching the feather out of reach, then leant forwards again to swish it along Sybilla's chin. 'It's Sunday and we are all up and have had our breakfast and Mama said if you didn't stir soon you'd likely miss the kirk and would have to play the invalid.' Bird-like, she tilted her head. 'What's invalid?'

'Someone who can't get up because they're sick.'

'But you're not sick?'

'No. I'm not sick.' Sybilla pulled herself up in the bed. 'But you'll have to move else I won't be able to get up and will have to pretend that I am.' She caught Maggie round the waist and tipped her onto her side rolling her towards the edge of the bed. Maggie squealed and wriggled and Sybilla, rolling with her, misjudged the distance so that they both ended up in a heap on the floor, the bedspread trailed between them.

She disentangled herself and, setting Maggie on her feet, clambered onto her knees.

'It's glad I am to see you start the day so holy,' Kate poked her head around the door. 'But if it's breakfast you're wanting you'll need to hurry. Robbie is already in the stables supervising the saddling of the horses. With the children we can't make the same pace. Maggie rides with her father but Robbie has his own Sheltie and, though game enough, it isn't built for speed.'

'Is it the kirk in town you make for?' Sybilla stepped into her corset and turned her back to Kate, grabbing the bedpost with both hands as Kate pulled on the strings.

'It's been repaired and we have a new minister.' Kate released the cords a fraction; then knotted them securely. 'I'd better not tie you so tight that you can't sing.'

'What like is he?' Sybilla shook out the worsted wool skirt of her riding habit and picked at furring on the left panel, where the cloth had balled with rubbing against the saddle.

'Gey fond of the psalms and with such a fine voice is precentor and preacher both.' Kate was straightening the bedcovers, an odd, uncertain note in her voice. 'He came newly from St Andrews and, whatever else folk may say, he has a way with words. He speaks for an hour or more and it seems but minutes and all without a crib sheet.'

'Some folk don't like him?'

'He isn't always easy listening and times when he looks straight at you, it's as if he sees into your soul. There are those that don't take to the fire in him, or maybe it's that he hits too close to home.' She gave a final tug to the bed curtains, looping them back against the posts. 'I can't help but like him, for all that listening I feel this small inside.' She held up her hand, the finger and thumb an inch apart. 'We have had a naming and a burying and he made a fine job of both and I have no doubt that he'll marry you right. They were halfway down the stair when she said, 'Mary fair took to him; he didn't miss to visit her every week at the end and gave her right comfort. She died well, and I know it was his doing. I have thought since . . . he has such certainty . . . I envy him that.' She broke off, 'If we get a move on, you'll have a chance to hear for yourself.'

It was well past noon, and though strands of cloud like carded wool streaked the sky, there was enough sun to give welcome warmth as they filed out of the church. James Melville stood at the door, nodding to, or perhaps, Sybilla thought, counting his parishioners. She chided herself for such uncharitability. His straight blond hair and pale face, with just the hint of a shadow around his jaw, gave him the appearance of extreme youth. He had indeed spoken well, if well was to make those who listened shuffle their feet and focus their eyes firmly on the floor, the plain-raftered ceiling, the dust motes dancing in the narrow shafts of light arrowing through the window slits; anywhere except on Melville's sharp eyes, their colour the piercing blue of a rain-washed sky. Evidence to Sybilla, if her own feelings were anything to go by, of inward squirming. Forbye Agnes, who had remained at Broomelaw to look to Ellie, the whole household was there and Melville ducked his head to each in turn.

Maggie wriggled her way to tug at the wide sleeve of his gown, her small face creased into a frown. He patted her bonnet.

'Why was Jesus an auntie?'

Robbie choked and Sybilla bent her head, as if to quiet him, stifling her own laugh. Out of the corner of her eye she saw Kate suck on her cheeks as she too struggled for composure.

Melville tilted Maggie's face upwards. 'What do you mean child?'

'You said "Auntie-Christ".'

Sybilla saw that Melville's eyes also twinkled, though his face was grave.

'I'm glad to see that you paid attention.' He kept his grip on Maggie's chin. 'Though sorry I am that I wasn't clearer in my discourse. It isn't "auntie", like "uncle". This kind of "Anti" means opposite. So . . .' He looked at each of the children in turn.

Robbie lifted his head. 'Anti-Christs are gey bad?'

Over the top of his head Melville smiled at Kate. He touched Robbie's head. 'As bad as ever you could imagine.'

Agnes bustled to greet them as they came through the gate and handed a grizzling Ellie over to Kate. 'I have given her broth and a wee bit bread and cheese, but it's milk she's wanting. It's as well the lunch will keep.'

'We were a mite delayed. Maggie . . .'

'Thought Jesus was an Auntie.' Robbie was hopping from foot to foot, pointing at her.

She flew at him, eyes flashing.

'A perfectly reasonable mistake.' Munro swung her up into the air, shooting a warning glance at Robbie. When Agnes continued to look puzzled, he said, 'We have been right through the Epistle of John. And are well-warned not to fall for Anti-Christs.'

Seeing Maggie's deepening frown, Agnes turned her own laugh into a cough.

Munro tightened his grip as Maggie tried to wriggle free. 'We aren't laughing at you, sweetheart.'

Sybilla mouthed to Archie, 'Lying to the bairn and only out of the kirk . . .' so that he too took a fit of coughing.

Munro brought his face close to Maggie's and pretended to nuzzle her neck. 'But I am hungry . . . maybe I'll just have to eat . . .' He slapped his lips together noisily, nibbling on her ear until she squealed, then set her down. 'No? Well then, lunch will have to do instead.'

Had it not been for the children, they would have stayed close to home all afternoon, the adults content to sit behind the barmkin wall, which gave protection from the light easterly wind, allowing them to enjoy the sunshine. As it was, they managed to steal half an hour of idleness, courtesy of Ellie sleeping sound in the chamber above the solar, while Maggie rooted around for worms at the edge of the vegetable patch and Robbie was occupied with whittling the bark from a hazel switch.

'The beauty of the Sabbath . . .' Sybilla slid her feet from her shoes and stretched them into a patch of sunlight, wiggling her toes against her fine wool stockings.

'Besides the hearing of the Word?' Archie opened one eye.

She paid no apparent heed to his interruption, nor to his finger teasing her collarbone, but directed her conversation at Kate. 'The beauty of it is to do nothing at all and yet be virtuous.'

'Enjoy it while you can.' Robbie had disappeared and Kate cocked her head towards the stable, 'With bairns, 'nothing' generally turns into 'something' quicker than you might wish.'

'They're quiet the now.' Sybilla leaned back against the wall, tilting her face up to the sun.

'Aye, well,' Kate yawned. 'That's when you need to worry. It isn't always wise to leave them to their own devices over long.'

'The devil finds mischief . . .' Archie's mimicry of Mary was so accurate that Munro, who had been drowsing, startled upright.

'Don't worry, she hasn't come back to haunt us.'

They were all laughing: harder and longer than the joke warranted; so that Sybilla guessed that though it had been more than a year since Anna's death, laughter was a rare commodity still.

Robbie appeared, leading his Shetland pony, already saddled. He was a shaggy little beast, tufts of mud-brown, winter coat still protruding at random between the smooth patches that Robbie had brushed to a shine.

'Aunt Sybilla hasn't seen the glen.' Robbie tossed the remark like a pebble into a pool, waiting for the ripple of reaction.

'Neither she has,' Munro kept his face straight.

'And you can't work.' Robbie made a caricature of the minister. 'Not on the Sabbath.'

'Neither I can.'

Sybilla thought Munro would be able to outstare Robbie, but wouldn't have bet so much as a bawbee on it. Maggie appeared around the corner of the tower, her fist tightly curled. Unwilling to go round the pony, she curved herself into a ball and squeezed underneath the sagging belly, unrolling in an explosion of petticoats at Sybilla's knee.

'I want to go.'

'Go where?' Munro was clearly enjoying himself.

'With him.' Maggie uncurled her fist to point at Robbie. 'Oh.' Her lip trembled as she looked at the worm that dangled from her palm, squashed and lifeless.

Sybilla put her arm around Maggie and pulled her in close.

'I didn't mean to . . .' Maggie bit down hard on her lip.

'Worms don't feel.' Sybilla hoped she sounded confident. She poked Maggie in the side, pressing on her ribs. 'You need bones to feel.' Peeling the worm from Maggie's hand, she stood up. 'If we put it on the wall, it'll be food for the birds.' She tried to think of a way to make it, if not right, at least better. 'Maybe even for your sparrow, while she builds her new nest.' She stretched the worm out. 'It's gey long and will make a fine meal.'

Maggie was smiling again, 'There were lots.' She tugged at Sybilla, 'We could get more.'

'If you wish to stay . . .' Munro tossed the comment to Maggie as he checked the saddle of Robbie's pony. 'We can leave you with Sybilla while the rest of us have a wee jaunt to the glen.'

Feeling Maggie stiffen and seeing her face begin to crumple, Sybilla gave her another squeeze. 'He doesn't mean it. We are all to go, and you . . .' she swung Maggie up in the air and set her on Archie's shoulder, '. . . must be our look-out, in case of reivers.'

Munro and Archie kept pace with the Sheltie, which was, though Robbie wouldn't have admitted it, somewhat fat and and lazy and therefore as safe as a pony could be.

Sybilla watched them, Maggie squealing as Archie, exaggerating the unevenness of the ground, bounced her up and down; Robbie chattering non-stop, his voice high-pitched and carrying in the clear air. She said, 'You have a fine brood. I can't wait.' And wished her words back.

'We aren't the only folk to lose a child . . . Anna will aye be here . . . aye young . . .' There was a catch in Kate's voice. 'It is hard . . . may always be so, but it is no time since we planned our wedding and now . . . all this.'

She looked back at the tower-house silhouetted against the sky, its jumble of outbuildings about the base. Even from this distance, it had a prosperous, well-tended air, the walls sharp-edged, the slates even, the thatch of the low buildings trimmed and free from moss.

'I should be . . . am . . . grateful for what we still have. There was a time when I thought it all lost.'

Ahead of them the children's voices faded, swallowed by the woods. She took Sybilla's arm. 'If we don't hurry, they will be there and back again and we will have missed the fun.'

They reached the shade of the trees, the Sheltie tethered beside a track that curved away into the dimness. The 'glen' was little more than a gash in the hillside, sheltered from sun and wind, the ground underfoot springy with moss, ankle-deep in last year's matted leaves. Occasional spears of sunlight pierced through gaps in the trees, across the narrow path. They caught glimpses of Robbie flitting in and out of the shadows: now on the path, now disappearing into the undergrowth, now leaping out again with whoops and shouts. Maggie was still on Archie's shoulders and Sybilla smiled at his play of surprise each time Robbie jumped him.

'The bairns love him. Even when . . .' Kate nibbled her lip. 'The first time Archie came home from Kilmaurs he wasn't quite himself, but even then he had time for the bairns. He'll make a good father.'

They were almost on them now, Sybilla watching Munro as he pounced on Robbie, growling triumphantly, and carried him wriggling back to the path.

'As his brother does.'

'Aye. On a day like this it should be easy to feel fortunate. With family and friends and the leisure to enjoy their company.' Kate breathed deeply, 'What right have any of us to ask for more?'

The path was turning and twisting, following the course of a shallow stream, so that although they were perhaps only a hundred yards behind, there were moments when the woods closed in around them, magnifying the rustling and scuffling of small creatures in the undergrowth.

'Where are we headed?'

'There is a clearing . . .' Kate broke off. '. . . I won't spoil it for you.'

The stream trickled and bubbled beside them and Sybilla was aware of odd splashing sounds.

'It isn't deep enough for fish surely?'

'You'll see.'

They rounded a bend in the path and they were in the

clearing, in the centre a still pool surrounded by aconites, the yellow flowers a carpet of bright faces lifting to the sun.

Both children were hunkered down at the edge of the water, Archie holding firmly to Maggie's waist, Munro, one hand on Robbie's shoulder, pointing downwards. For once the children were silent and as Sybilla approached, she became aware of a background chirriping, almost like birds: short bursts of high notes, punctuated by lower croaking sounds.

Archie turned his head, his eyes alight. 'We don't usually catch them spawning.'

Among the twigs and fallen leaves and spikes of water hawthorn, Sybilla saw the toads, their skin brown and leathery, bulbous lumps like warts scattered across their backs and legs. There were dozens of them, half in, half out of the water, hanging in pairs: the females clinging to bits of stick or lying on small stones; the males, straddling them, gripping firmly with all four legs, head resting on head. They seemed to stare into the distance, unblinking, unconcerned by their audience, voicing their pleasure. From the rear of each pair long, gelatinous threads spun out, coiling and twining on the surface of the water, and inside them the spawn, like double strings of black beads.

'Shouldn't it be clumps?' Sybilla reached into the water, but when she lifted her hand, the spawn slithered through her splayed fingers, leaving only the stickiness across her skin.

'Frogs make clumps. Toads make strings.' Robbie spoke in an 'everyone should know that' tone.

'Can I have some for home?' Maggie was stretching

downwards, guddling in the water, trying to wind a string of spawn around her hand.

'Not today, sweetheart.' Munro spread his hands. 'We have nothing to carry it in.'

She twisted in Archie's arms.

Robbie said, 'You're not here to work, are you, Uncle Archie?'

'No, though . . .'

'Well then,' Robbie was triumphant. 'You can bring us tomorrow.'

They had a late supper, the children yawning before it was finished, so that Kate shooed them away to bed, ignoring their protests, before repairing to the solar to light the candles and put a spill to the ready laid fire.

'It has such a good draw,' she said as she watched the flames leap against the chimney back, the kindling sparking like firecrackers.

'It's a poor show to have my wife take her pleasure from the drawing of a fire.' Munro, laughing at her, reached down and pulled her to her feet. 'Approaching elderly you may be, but not that far gone surely?'

She stepped back a fraction. 'Not old enough to take to my bed straight from supper.'

Sybilla, glimpsing a wicked retort in Munro's eyes, avoided looking at Archie, her own breath quickening. She turned the conversation. 'Robbie played you well Archie. You have little choice but to go gathering spawn the morn.'

'Aye, he's not so daft. Of course . . .' Archie stretched himself along the front of the hearthstone, and leaned his back against Sybilla's knees, 'I would rather help with the spring clean that no doubt you ladies have planned.'

She tugged at the hair springing on the back of his neck and he tilted his head so that it rested on her lap. 'I could take the bairns,' she pulled harder, 'and you could redd-out the pantry.'

'Not if you want a decent dinner.' Munro was settling himself at the opposite side of the fire. 'Archie's idea of redding-out would likely be via his stomach.'

'Serious though, could the spawn live? You might end up with a plague of toads in your yard.' There was a wistful note in Sybilla's voice.

Kate said, 'Did you never grow tadpoles?'

'Mother didn't have much truck with foolishness and the breeding of toads would surely have counted as such. Forbye that she didn't like anything that had more than two legs and the smaller they were, the less comfortable she was with them.'

'We tried every spring for years.' Kate's eyes had the far-away look of distant memory.

'With success?'

'Some years aye, some not. One year we had the tad-poles in a wee trickle of water in a pail in the yard and the next morning water and tadpoles both were frozen solid. I had the idea of thawing them out in the kettle in the kitchen, but forgot all about them until Agnes poured the kettle into the stewpot.' Kate's shoulders began to shake. 'I didn't dare say anything, only prayed that they'd disappear in the boiling or come out like shreds of beef and not be noticed in the gravy.'

'And did they?'

'Mostly, though whether they would've if I hadn't

mashed and stirred at the pot every time Agnes wasn't looking, I don't know. It was hard to eat it though, knowing what was there.'

'It was spring when your grand-dame died . . .' Munro said thoughtfully, ducking as Kate rolled her handkerchief into a ball and tossed it at him. He caught it neatly and lobbed it back. 'I dare say it was but coincidence.'

They sat by the fire talking about anything and nothing until the embers burned down to ash. Kate, moving to blow out a candle that had begun to smoke, paused by the window and Munro came to stand behind her. She leaned into him. 'I have a notion to walk – not far, just to the top of the hill. It's such a fine night.'

He was resting his head on top of hers, stroking her hair with his chin. 'Are you not afraid to walk out with me and the moon is full?'

'A risk maybe . . . but worth the taking.' She swivelled round. 'Sybilla? Archie? It isn't often we have the leisure to star-gaze.'

Though there was little wind the air was sharp and clear and Sybilla, feeling the bite of it on her skin, expelled her breath like a puff of smoke. She tucked her arms under her shawl. 'It's nippier than I expected.'

Archie said, 'I can keep you warm . . . for a small consideration.'

'I haven't much silver.' She knotted the shawl.

'Then I'll have to take payment in kind.' He bent his head and she reached up for him, their breath curling together, the taste of him sweet on her tongue.

Ahead of them, the path wound through gorse and bramble, voices floating backwards: snippets of phrases; Munro's low chuckle, Kate's higher, musical laugh.

'It will be a fine thing,' Archie trailed the back of his hand along Sybilla's neck. 'When we have nine years of marriage to our credit and still be sweet.'

She felt a catch in her throat and a stinging behind her eyes. 'It is a fine thing already and will be finer still to be married at all.' She sucked in an involuntary shiver, as if it was a sliver of ice stabbing her chest, 'We should catch up, else they'll be crying us home before ever we make the top.'

'Or we could wait here . . .' Archie gestured to a patch of shadow a few yards from the path, in the shelter of an overhang.

'I have a reputation to think on.'

'Do you not trust me?' His eyes were dark, the pupils distended.

'I don't trust myself.'

They broke through the gorse onto the open hillside, scrambling the last few feet to where Munro and Kate leant against a slab of rock, softened with lichen.

Sybilla sank down beside Kate, pressing her hand to her side. Below them, Broomelaw reared like a standing stone, rugged, secure, the slates slicked silver by the moonlight, the barmkin wall casting a curving shadow towards the loch. Kate cocked her head and raised her finger to her mouth. A soft splash carried to them through the stillness, as a fish broke the surface of the water.

'One of Robbie's fugitives, I presume.' Archie leaned back.

'Aye, he hasn't improved much since last you were here. It's well we don't count on him to feed us.' Kate switched her attention to the sky arched above them, peppered with stars.

'D'you think . . .' Sybilla stared up at the Pleiades. '. . . there are folk up there, seeing us as a pinprick that sparkles in their sky?' She rubbed her cheek against the velvet of Archie's doublet, 'Wouldn't it be fine to go and see?'

'I have enough trouble traipsing about Scotland after William, without wishing for the stars.'

An uncomfortable silence, in which Sybilla was aware of cold seeping through her skirts and settling on her stomach. She heard only half of Archie's next sentence.

'. . . I have wondered about the Americas.'

Munro shot upright. 'The Americas? Yesterday it was the Solway.'

'Aye and so it is. So it will be. Only . . .'

'Only you would wish to have more distance between us and William than Scotland can provide.' It was said. That which Sybilla had vowed never to say; lest speaking the fear breathed life into it. Turning away from Archie's outstretched hand, she fled for the path, Kate close behind.

The mood of the evening broken, Kate re-appeared only briefly, Sybilla not at all. Munro was leaning his head against the lintel of the fireplace as he poked at the ashes. Behind him, Archie ranged the length of the room, his progress punctuated by the intermittent squeaking of the floorboards. Uncovering a remnant of log, its jagged tip still glowing, Munro criss-crossed slivers of kindling over it and blew, his breath steady and slow.

'Don't revive the fire on my behalf.'

'Archie . . .' Munro stood up, turned.

'Leave it.' Archie had stopped pacing and was staring out into the darkness.

Munro waited, as if an inner sense warned him that answers might come the quicker if unforced.

'I did think on the Americas, but we haven't the silver, forbye the stories that suggest it isn't just plain sailing there either.'

Munro was picking at spikes of gorse stuck to his sleeve, 'This thing with William. Has he been more difficult these months past? Kate fell foul of him in Edinburgh at the Queen's entry and I have crossed swords with Maxwell since.'

'Oh, we heard. Of both. In detail and at length, both Maxwell and William took great pains to make sure of that.'

'There was no mention of the Frost Fair?'

'No. Why?'

'We had the misfortune to meet up with him there also . . . it was a close run thing.'

'I take it he had the worst of it? Or we would no doubt have heard the whole. Though how much credence Glencairn gives to anything William says these days . . . he is more often drunk than sober and all not always as he paints it. Not that that stops the rant.'

'I hope you do not bear the brunt of it.'

'No. My quarrel with William is more personal. What I feared at the first . . . it has come. Sybilla can hardly move without William's eyes on her and her refusal to respond to the direct approaches he has made serves only to quicken his desire. She says she can handle him, but the sooner I can take her away . . .'

'Does Glencairn know?'

'Lady Glencairn does. At least we think so, and that the reason she favours our attachment. . . . Once we are betrothed he won't risk rousing his father.'

'Not if he's any wit.'

'The sooner we get sorted with Glencairn. . . . Perhaps it would be best to leave first thing . . .'

Avoiding thought of the children, the promised spawn, Munro said, 'An early night then.'

'Aye . . . You'll not mind looking at the tower for us? It's far enough away from Kilmaurs that William should not trouble us. At least I trust so.'

'I'm happy to help. Though it will have to wait till after lambing, but I don't suppose you'll have it settled so soon?'

'I dare say not.' Archie was picking at the window frame, scattering flakes of paint onto the sill.

'It won't speed matters if I have to make repairs to my own house.' Munro risked a smile, 'I don't wish to be maudlin, but this marriage . . . it gives us pleasure.'

Chapter Eleven

'It isn't the best way.' Sybilla was adamant. She leant back against the warm sandstone of the disused tower where Archie had suggested they stop for a bite of the lunch that Agnes had provided, and clasped her hands about her knees. 'You have sound arguments for Glencairn and they no doubt will pass, but I don't want the work spoiled for want of a wee bit softening first. I will but drop a hint or two to Lady Glencairn, a wife . . .' she smiled up at him, a hint of promise in her eyes, '. . . can oft forward things.'

'Speak to her then, but don't be long about it.' He touched her hair, turned copper by the sun, as if in apology for questioning her judgement, then reached for her hand and raised her to her feet. An unspoken need to dispel the shadow that had fallen on them the previous night lay between them, and though there was nothing to be gained by a look at this tower, it was so similar in plan to the one at Dunisle that it would be easy to imagine themselves there. They wandered hand in hand through the part ruinous tower, busy with their thoughts, each in their own way seeking to re-capture the anticipation of a life together.

Sybilla looked to the barrel-vaulted kitchen, thinking on the draw of the fire, the potential for storage, the need for a cool room; and in the solar, at present open to the sky, dreamed of a beamed ceiling, the wood richly decorated, and a low chamber above, with a truckle bed or two for the bairns. Archie, whose thoughts she imagined ran more on the getting than the having of bairns, was pacing out the bedchamber, clearly comparing it with that of Dunisle and counting the probable cost of newly-glazed casements.

Noting his smile, she questioned, 'What is it? Surely a pleasant thought.'

'Pleasant enough.' He pulled her towards the bulge in the wall, indicating the rise of a chimney. 'If this was Dunisle and we placed the bed here, it would give us a heat to start off, not that we'd stay cold for long.' His fingers bit into her shoulder.

'Archie! I'm not going anywhere.' She reached up and peeled his hand away, but held it lightly. 'Archie?' This time it was a question, concern shining in her grey-blue eyes.

He shook his head and forced a smile. 'We should go. I don't wish for it to be past dark before we get back.'

They arrived at Kilmaurs to a house in turmoil, the youngest bairn taken with a fever. Lady Glencairn had refused to let her be bled, standing her ground against the physician with a ferocity that none of the servants had encountered before. Sybilla and Lady Glencairn took it in spells to sit with the child, swabbing her with cloths wrung out in endless supplies of water ferried from the well in the yard. The sheets and the child's shift they changed daily, morning and evening dribbling tincture of aconite onto her tongue.

For five days they battled, until at three in the morning of the sixth day, the fever broke. Sybilla flew to Lady

Glencairn's bedchamber and without thought of knocking, slipped in to whisper her awake. 'Praise God . . . she sleeps.'

They sat together on either side of the bed, content to watch the even breathing, and to see the colour in her face fade from fever crimson to pale rose.

'I thought us like to lose her.' Lady Glencairn tucked away a stray tendril of hair that lay damp across the child's mouth and reached to touch Sybilla's arm. 'And maybe would have done without you. When you have bairns of your own, I trust that you will have as ready a helper if ill should come.'

Sybilla picked at a loop of loosened thread in the coverlet, considering whether this was the moment to speak of her own plans, when, as if she read her thoughts, Lady Glencairn touched her arm again.

'I would miss you sore, but you must know, especially now, I will not stand in your way.'

'Archie . . . we have talked . . .'

'Well then,' Lady Glencairn's smile was warm. 'You have only Glencairn to pass and that should be little problem now.'

Sunlight was creeping around the edge of the shutters as the child stirred and stretched and puckered her face in a cross between a question and a smile; as if bemused to find that she woke, not in her own cot in the attic, but in the guest chamber, her mother and Sybilla at her side.

Lady Glencairn gathered her up in a fierce hug. 'You've been ill, but will be bravely soon.' She released the child back against the pillows, 'But don't try to rise yet. You have lost a ween of days and are in need of rest and food both.'

The crisis past, Glencairn showed himself uncharacteristically soft, saying, first to his wife, 'Look to yourself, madam. You have saved the bairn – see that it isn't at your own expense', then to Sybilla, 'Nor will your part in this be forgotten.'

William trailed Sybilla to where she rested, at Lady Glencairn's behest, in the small, walled garden on the east side of the castle. He slid onto the bench by her side. 'I hear we owe you thanks.'

She edged away from him. 'I did only what anyone would have done and the bairn so poorly.'

He stretched out his legs, so that one elegant boot held down the hem of her dress. 'That's not what mother says – she cannot speak highly enough of you. In her eyes you are an angel.' He slid closer and, trapped by her skirt, she felt the heat of his breath on her face.

She tried to laugh him off. 'I'm not an angel.'

'No?' William raised his arm, placed his hand behind his head. 'That is good news.'

Her head was bent, her hair rippling from her coif, an escaped curl lying, like a question mark, across her cheek. William liked copper, even if his luck with red-headed lassies hadn't always held. He thought of the wee slip in Stirling, and his hand slid inside the front of his ruff, tracing the fine scar on his neck, his eyes darkening. The little trollop wouldn't have got the better of him if Munro had stayed sober and alert, but instead, humiliation. There had been no denying that the girl had clear, young skin and fire in her hair and a promise of a figure, though that too had proved a cheat . . .

His thoughts slid back to Sybilla. To her smooth skin, unbroken but for the dusting of freckles on the bridge of her nose. As to figure, it was aye difficult to estimate what lurked beneath a corset. But the discovery of it . . . he allowed his gaze to travel over her shoulders, down her neck, her bodice, counting the neat line of buttons, imagining opening them one by one. Oh yes . . . the discovery was half the pleasure. He'd dreamed of that particular voyage since first she came. Archie away on some business for his father and the rest of the household looking to his mother and to the bairn, the opportunity that had thus far eluded him was finally within his grasp. Casually he trailed his hand along the wall, tracing the pointing between the stone, the tips of his fingers reaching her neck. He felt her stiffen. He enjoyed spirit in a girl, it added spice to the proceedings.

He grasped her chin, forcing her head up.

She tried to twist away, to rise. 'Lady Glencairn . . .'

"Is resting, as is the bairn, and you,' William ran his tongue across his upper lip, 'were sent to enjoy the sunshine. And I,' his tongue completed the circle, 'have come to see that you do.'

'Let me go!' She tugged at her skirt but he settled his feet more firmly on it, his grip on her face tightening.

'I do but wish to give you the thanks you deserve.'

'I have been thanked.'

He raised her hand and her sleeve fell back revealing her narrow wrist, the white flesh above. Releasing her chin he bent his head towards her palm, but she clenched it tight. He smiled, his eyes like glass, his tongue teasing at his teeth. Thought, feisty indeed. She stared at him unflinching and he returned her gaze.

'Good, very good, but don't think you'll best me.' He bent his head and drew a spiral on her wrist with his tongue, tasting salt and oil of roses and the faint sheen of sweat, each widening circle bringing him ever closer to the soft hollow of her elbow, his breath quickening. She was holding herself very still. 'Soon,' he said, 'Soon you will be begging me . . .'

She thrust sideways, and down, throwing him momentarily off balance, and ducked away from his grip, dropping to the ground, scrabbling backwards, gathering herself to run; but he was too quick for her.

He hauled her up, seizing her elbows and, kicking aside the bench, pressed her into the angle of the wall, placing his hands flat against the stone on either side of her.

'You cannot think to leave now, when things are getting interesting.' He leaned into her, moulding the folds of her skirt to her legs, feeling the length, the warmth of them. Her shoulders were hunched, a coil of hair hanging like a tassel down the side of her head. He slid one hand from the wall, his fingertips exploring the pale skin of her neck and throat, the line of her shoulder blade. Grasping the length of loosened hair, he stroked it across his face. Felt her tremor as he slid the hair under her chin, jerking it sideways and up as if tightening a knot, pulling her head back. His mouth fastened on hers. She fought to keep her lips closed but he forced his tongue between them, worrying at her clenched teeth, his kiss insistent and bruising, while with his free hand he worked at the bodice of her dress.

In one swift move she opened her teeth to let his tongue slide between them, then bit down hard, at the same time kneeing him in the groin, so that he reeled backwards with the twin pains, blood in his mouth. As he reached for her again, she gathered up her skirts and fled.

She was in the small chamber she shared with two of the other servants when the youngest maid came to cry her to the hall. Her hand at her mouth, she stared at Sybillia's neck, at the skin scrubbed red, the crumpled dress discarded on the bed and the scissors that Sybilla was using to chop at the shank of hair she clutched in her hand.

'Ye're wanted below' Then, in a whisper, 'What are ye doing to yer hair?'

"Who wants me?" Sybilla continued her assault on the hair. With a final clip she swung round, the scissors flashing, the jagged remnant of hair sticking out from the side of her head like frayed rope. The maid was on one foot, as if poised for flight. Sybilla repeated the question more gently, 'Who wants me?'

'Glencairn.' Curiousity replaced the maid's fear. 'What for did ye do that?'

"It's nothing.' Sybilla licked her fingers and plastered down the uneven strands. Replacing her coif, she rummaged in the trunk under the window, emerging with the striped damask dress that Lady Glencairn had given her only this morning. An understanding between them that it would be more than suitable for a wedding. She shook out the copper folds and wriggled into it.

Archie and Glencairn were standing on one side of the hearth as Sybilla entered. William, who was by the window, neither turned nor acknowledged her. Lady Glencairn flashed a look at William's stiff back, then at Sybilla, radiating defiance. Her voice was light, her words deliberately inconsequential.

'I knew it was the colour for you more than me. Is this a dress rehearsal?'

Glencairn was hearty. 'I hear we are to have a wedding and another Cunninghame stronghold. Dunisle, did you say Archie, on the Solway? I have long wished to consolidate our links with the Maxwells in those parts.'

'Aye. It's in a sorry state, but my brother . . .'

Sybilla intercepted the prompting glance that Lady Glencairn shot at her husband.

'You cannot have too many hands for work such as that. When the lambing is over there will be help and to spare here also.'

Lady Glencairn continued to stare.

'And I daresay some materials can be found. It is but small thanks for the life of the bairn.'

Sybilla felt her tension draining as she moved towards Archie.

William had turned, 'Why not Rough? It's closer to Orchardton than Dunisle and though smaller, is a finer tower in better fettle and so will be less effort to right, less expense.'

Sybilla, searching for understanding and finding none, gnawed at her lip. Glencairn narrowed his eyes, stared at the square of window behind William, who continued, yawning as if it was but a passing thought,

'The island it sits on is well placed to guard the firth and is easy reached, on horseback and on foot, though only at low tide.'

'Rough Island . . . hmm . . .' Glencairn nodded to Archie. When the lambing is past, I'd like fine for you to take a look at the tower on Rough.

Chapter Twelve

Munro picked his way through the narrow defile, following the course of a burn, the hills rising steeply on either side. He was thankful, not only that the weather held, but that this chilly section of his journey would soon be past. The ride down the eastern side of Loch Ken had been pleasant enough, the sun turning the water into a mirror, on which the untidy outline of the farther shore rode like a series of ships at anchor, tall pines the masts. Points curved out from the near side also, like hooks, enclosing bays fringed with shingle. He had counted eight islands in the lower loch, though some had been little more than a bare outcrop breaking the surface of the water. On one of those, he saw a heron, statue-still, his grey wings folded back, his white neck and head stretched upwards, the black crest a feathered quill behind him. Munro stopped and drinking deeply from the water bag at his side, looked back. From this angle he saw the yellow dagger-bill and the streaks of black trailing down to the soft underbelly. There was a flash as its head arrowed into the water, emerging with a fish, the scales iridescent. Deftly the heron turned and swallowed it in one swift movement, before freezing once more.

At the foot of the loch he followed the Dee southwards, then struck east towards Carlingwark, where he stopped for a bite to sup, and hay and respite for Sweet Briar also. It was there they gave warning of this narrow valley where the sun never penetrated and the silence oppressed.

'A two-mile stretch, dreich as winter whatever the season, and like to spook you and horse both, but once through, strike directly south and you will need but half an hour to the firth.'

They were now, he guessed, perhaps half-way, caught in the clamp of the hillside, the stream-bed providing the only possible passage. High above him on each side, where the ground met the sky, the remains of ancient forts, far enough apart to be outside arrow range, rendering them safe from each other at least. He thought on Broomelaw, likewise poised against the horizon and also built more for protection than for comfort, and of Archie's revised plans, made at Glencairn's behest, to repair the tower on Rough Island rather than that of Dunisle. He patted Sweet Briar. 'However old these ruins, lass, folk haven't made much progress.'

The valley walls beside him began to recede, to tilt, the bare stone softened by creeping vegetation and then he was in the open, the burn swinging away to his right, the sun full on his face, his tension eased. Ahead of him the ground sprung, moss-green, tufted with spikes of bog cotton, the stream became a river, flowing in wide meandering loops towards the distant sea.

Munro reined in Sweet Briar where the river met the shore. The bay was scooped from the surrounding land, broken in two by a promontory jutting out into the sands. It was, he estimated, perhaps a mile across the sands to where Rough Island stood sentinel. He narrowed his eyes, shading them with his hand against the sun. Beyond the island the expanse of sea was a silver glint on the horizon, the tide far out. And curving from behind the wooded promontory on his left, a single line of posts swung out to touch the island's edge.

On his right, topping a small rise, Orchardton Tower. Wondering in passing what like the hospitality of these Maxwells would be, he looked up at the sun: several hours yet till supper, ample time to reconnoitre. He encouraged Sweet Briar into a trot. As they crossed the rough grass, the ground soft, he remembered the last injunction given him as he left Carlingwark to make for Orchardton and the coast.

'Don't try to make straight for Rough Island without checking the tide poles, for the Solway is gey treacherous and there are aye folk who take a risk and pay the penalty.' And as an afterthought, 'And don't be fool enough to make your own way. The marker posts are there for a reason, for the sands likewise aren't kind.'

He threaded through the trees that hugged the landward end of the point, following a rutted track. Through the mass of foliage a small hill protruded, a bony knuckle on the finger of land. He was half-way along when the trees gave way to open ground: rocky outcrops punctuated by pockets of grass and clumps of stunted gorse, straggled with bramble. From this vantage point Munro again saw the line of posts marching across the sands and beside them two slow-moving specks.

'No doubt it was the linking of arms they wanted, and that can't be done on horseback. But it'll give us a chance to catch up with them.'

Sweet Briar's ears pricked.

The track skirted an area of swamp and dropped down to a sheltered cove that signalled the start of the way-marked crossing. Sweet Briar halted, nickering to the two horses that cropped the tough grass, their reins looped around a stump of gorse.

'No time to be social the now, lass. We have a tower to see.'

A slithering behind him and the rattle of shingle. The man sliding down from the lip of the cove was squat, bow-chested and with the distinctive square face and jutting forehead of a man with less than average capabilities. His agitation was clear in the fluttering of his hands and in the way he choked on a rush of half sounds, his repeated 'Na, na' all that Munro could decipher.

He acknowledged the man and gestured towards the sands. 'My brother and his betrothed. I go to meet them, to visit the island.' As he began to swing Sweet Briar round the man grabbed hold of the bridle, his jabbering more intense, his head shaking.

'Not the horse?'

'Na, na.'

Munro dismounted, tossing Sweet Briar's reins to snag on the overhanging gorse. 'It seems you are to get a rest after all.' And to the man, 'Thank you, I'll have to walk then.' He took a step forward but the man leapt at him again, hanging on his arm, his mouth working, the sounds more strangled than before. He was trying to pull Munro towards a large clump of gorse, his feet scrabbling on the shingle.

With a shrug, Munro allowed himself to be led. 'You have something to show me? All right; then I must go.'

The man dropped to his knees and tugged at the twisted stems, a bundle of dead twigs coming away in his hands. He drew aside the living branches. Munro bent down beside him and stared into the gap. It took him barely a moment to register the significance of the bundle of marker posts, their bottom ten inches or so smeared with sand. They were undamaged, the paint rings which served to indicate tide levels unmistakeable, so that Munro knew of a certainty that their removal had been deliberate, the murderous intention clear – dear God . . . He plunged back down the slope, grabbing Sweet Briar's reins and swinging up into the saddle, shaking off the man who still clung to him.

At his urging Sweet Briar pounded along the way-marked track, damp sand flying with every hoofbeat. Munro's eyes were fixed on Archie and Sybilla and on the line of silver sweeping towards them. They halted, hesitated, began to run.

Munro was pushing Sweet Briar to the limit, screaming at Archie and Sybilla and he saw them turn at his call, as if uncertain which way to go. And in that instant he saw them fall, stumble to their feet, fall again under the weight of water. Twice more he saw their heads rise like seals, then nothing, bar the quiet blue of the tide, swallowing the posts one by one. He pressed Sweet Briar onwards, fixing the point of their disappearance in his mind, until the water swirled around her fetlocks, inched up the cannon bone, reached her knee. She faltered. For a moment he considered keeping going, however futile, but the suck of the tide increased and he felt the sand underneath begin to shift. An image of Kate and the bairns, and then it was his own race back to the shore, Sweet Briar infected with his fear, with the storm gathering in his chest.

They slid to a halt on the shingle. Munro slipped to the ground and for a moment laid his cheek against Sweet

376

Briar's face, running his hand down her neck He had no words. Behind him an uneven shuffle and another hand matching him stroke for stroke. Munro lifted his head, acknowledging the offered sympathy, and though he knew it was fruitless, turned again to scan the surface of the water, unbroken save for the marker posts nearest the shore. The pain of failure, his inability to save Archie and Sybilla, gave way to anger, lending a harshness to his voice.

'You know who did this.' It came out as an accusation, its effect to make the man step back, rocking on his heels, holding his hands out in front of himself as if to ward Munro off.

Munro tried again, more quietly, 'Come with me. To Orchardton.' He placed a hand on the man's arm as an encouragement, but he shook his head, his eyes wide.

His whole body was shaking, matted trails of hair slapping against his cheeks, his repeated 'Na, na,' increasingly desperate. Munro released his grip – whoever had done this would make mincemeat of him, and with an effort managed,

'Thank you; for showing me.' He gestured towards the clump of gorse, his voice hardening afresh, 'I'll find the man responsible.'

He rode Archie's horse to Orchardton, leading the others, and it was gone six when he entered the courtyard. A lass, crossing from the kitchen to the tower, saw the three horses and dropped the board she carried, loaves flying.

'Fetch your master.'

She picked up her skirts and ran, the door banging

behind her. Munro dismounted, busied himself with sorting the reins, soothing the horses.

'Munro?'

It was John Cunninghame.

'I didn't expect . . .'

'I came with them, to see to materials, William also, though,' there was an odd inflexion in John's voice, 'More for the jaunt, I presume, than for any help he has been.' He was picking up and dusting down the loaves the girl had dropped. 'Where are Archie and Sybilla?" The beginnings of a smile curved his lips. 'Don't say they marooned themselves?'

Munro met his eye, killed the smile. He pressed his fingers against his forehead, forced speech. 'I saw them . . . tried to reach them . . . but the tide . . . it had me beat.' An argument hammered in his head, one voice prompting: Go on, say it, tell the whole. Another, more demanding: Wait, wait for proof. He managed, 'I brought back the horses.'

John uncurled Munro's fist, released the reins, called for a stable lad. Retaining his hold on Munro's arm, said, 'Come inside. You need a drink.'

They climbed to the hall, Munro moving like a mechanical toy. A woman rose from the settle, mouse-haired, the welcome in her green eyes become, in a glance, fear. Automatically he took her hand, bowed over it, silent. She drew him to the fireside, pressed him down. John was there, holding out a glass. Munro tossed it back, coughed.

'Steady.' The voice came from far way.

The glass was removed, refilled, and he drank again. A third drink and his head began to clear, to harden into resolve. He stared at the floor, seeing not wood, but sand. 'I intended to reconnoitre. When I came on the cove, they

378

were three-quarters of the way to the island, maybe more.' He thought how to tell only what he had decided. 'I went to follow . . . I didn't think a tide could come so fast . . . I saw them stop, as if to turn back, then run for the island. The water . . .' He shut his eyes against the memory. 'One minute they were there, the next . . . there was only the tide, engulfing them.'

He felt the light pressure of cool fingers on his forehead.

'I don't think I would have made it back but for Sweet Briar. At low tide,' he looked sideways at the woman, 'Will we find the bodies?'

She didn't meet his eye, but he heard her whispered 'Oh dear God.'

'No bodies?' The voice was someone else's entirely, though it inhabited his own mouth.

Dawn crept on Munro as he lay hunched against the rock, sheltered from the landward breeze by the bushes that surrounded him. He flexed his stiffened muscles as his eyes, adjusting to the pale light, roamed the shoreline, the rocky promontory, the gorse with the cache of posts. The clutter of dead wood still sealed the gap. He stood up cautiously, his ears straining for any sound. Nothing. Yet.

Despite that he had shut himself away so soon as a chamber had been prepared for him, it had been gone one o'clock in the morning when he collapsed, fully dressed onto the box bed. He should by rights have shared a chamber, but Mistress Maxwell, her eyes dark and damp, like fresh moss, had displaced her older boys to give him privacy. He had expressed himself grateful, and craving her understanding, had declined either to join the company for supper, or to have food brought to him, insisting that he could not eat. John had made one attempt at persuasion, but mindful of William's presence among the party, refrained from pressing.

When the tower was quiet, save for the scratchings and scufflings of mice and the occasional groan as the fabric of the building re-adjusted to the cool night air, Munro had eased himself from the straw mattress, pausing at every creak of the planks beneath. As he set his feet on the floor, the cold from the bare flags seeped up through his woollen hose. He carried his boots down the stair to the main door, careful not to slip on the polished hollow of the steps, and across the courtyard to the stall where Sweet Briar drowsed. She blew a puff of warm breath into the hand that he placed over her nose and dipped her head to nudge his chest, lifting her hooves at his touch while he swathed them in sacking. Danger lay in the crossing of the barmkin, but no lights flickered in the tower above and Munro exhaled softly. He kept Sweet Briar to a walk until they made the foot of the rise, then removed the sacking and bundled it into his saddlebag, before mounting and making for the woods.

The slip-slap of the waves as they washed the cove had drifted him into an uneasy sleep, in which a swirling tide flowed, sucking and surging around his ankles, his waist, his neck. He woke, gagging on saliva, the tang of salt sharp in his mouth and nose, but when he looked towards Rough, the sea was a broken line of white receding beyond the outline of the island. The flats stretched undisturbed, so that he could have thought he imagined the events of the previous day, were it not for the knowledge of the two rider-less horses in the stable at Orchardton and the anger that hardened in a lump below his breastbone.

There was a jingle of harness and a muffled oath. Munro slid back into the shadow of the rock. For this he had crouched, uncomfortable, in the cold hours before dawn, sure of who he would see, less clear what he would do. He fingered the pistols, ready-loaded at his side. A shot to the belly was too easy. He wanted William to crawl on his hands and knees at his feet, to taste the wet sand in his mouth, as perhaps Archie and Sybilla had as they were overturned by the tide. He wanted William to beg for his life before he killed him. For it would be William who came to replace the posts – of that he had no doubt.

He could hear the soft sound of the horse's hooves brushing the marram grass, and traced the movement towards him so that he gauged almost to the second the moment when the horse halted on the other side of the gorse. There was a thump and a fissling and the scrape of thorn on leather, followed by the light footfall of someone who walked with a spring in his step. A low whistling as Munro waited deep in the shadows. Waited until the man parted the gorse, bent down to retrieve the posts, re-emerged still whistling, cradling the bundle in his arms.

'So it was you.' Munro severed the silence.

William swung around, fear flickering in his eyes as he stared at the pistols Munro held in each hand.

'You wouldn't be so foolish.'

'No?' Munro held both guns steady.

William's left hand strayed.

Munro shifted his aim downwards and fired, the ball raising a puff of sand no more than an inch from William's boot. 'No?' he said again, the second gun once more trained on William's face.

'What do you want?'

'Apart from killing you? – The truth.'

The fear in William's eyes was joined by calculation.

'To know what it is you gain by the death of my brother, of Sybilla.'

'She slighted me.' William was dismissive. 'And Archie had more of you in him than I cared for. They were of little importance.' Then, as if seeking the advantage, 'What would you gain by killing me? My father . . .'

'Has another son, and he, though young yet, will grow. If . . .' Munro's voice was deceptively calm, '. . . When I kill you, it will be no great loss.'

William allowed the posts to drop, 'Would you risk your own life for that trollop of your brother's?'

Munro cast aside the pistols and drew sword and dirk both, advancing on William, driving him towards the gorse. Then he too had drawn and they circled, feinting and parrying, clashing the blades, each taking the measure of the other, watching for the fractional flinch that would indicate a weakness. Munro thought of nothing save cut and thrust, movement and balance, distance and speed. Seizing the initiative he swung his sword in a full arm upward cut. William parried with the flat of his sword and Munro allowed his own blade to slide downwards, then back and left, in a wide, horizontal slice. William raised his dirk as guard, and Munro stepped back, then attacked with a series of rapid slashes, the momentum carrying him forwards; his breathing short, in time with his swordplay. Attack . . . attack . . . redouble . . . redoublement . . . closing in.

He stumbled on an exposed root, dropping to one knee and William, pressing the advantage, jabbed at his neck, puncturing the skin below the jaw. Recovering, Munro sidestepped and twisted behind William, who spun, his sword raised. He drove downward in a high backhand strike, but Munro intercepted the cut with the flat of his own sword, knocking away the blade. One moment Munro's back was to the shore, the next he faced it, each glimpse of the marker posts renewing his energy. Sweat trickled into the corner of his eye, soaked his shirt, threatened his grip. William too was glistening, his hair plastered to his forehead, his breathing shallow. Munro shook his head, blinked, moisture flying from him. Over William's shoulder he could see a tunnel of gorse, leading to an outcrop of rock that jutted knee-high over the rim of the cove.

He pressed forward again with three sharp thrusts, forcing William back into the narrow gap between the gorse. The bushes pressed in on them, reducing their swing, giving Munro, shorter than William and therefore with the shorter sword, an edge. Tired though his muscles were, he increased the pace, changing from deep slicing swings to sharp diagonal strikes, gaining ground with every step. He gauged the distance to the rock: five, perhaps six steps. He took advantage of a gap in the gorse on his right, the extra space enabling him to increase his swing, slashing downwards, catching William on the side of the knee, but leaving his own left exposed. William lunged at him, his blade slicing down Munro's arm, peeling back his doublet and shirt, opening a gash from elbow to wrist. Munro felt the hot sting of blood and flung himself forward, his sword arm straight and taut, the blade slightly elevated, so that the tip caught William's face, raking across his cheekbone.

Forced backwards, William was funneled towards the outcrop of rock, and as Munro continued to press, he stumbled against it, his legs buckling. Off-balance their blades met and held, but Munro, with the advantage of solid footing, used his body weight to topple William over the rock. As he sprawled on the ground, his dirk spinning away, Munro leapt the rock and stamped on his wrist, releasing the sword, which catapulted over the lip of the cove onto the sands below. Beyond William the bay stretched to the horizon, the dark outline of the island and the tower that crested it rising from the sand. Munro had a vision of he tide sweeping in, enclosing the island, engulfing the sand . . . the posts . . . Archie and Sybilla. He raised his sword, the point poised above William's throat – an eye for an eye. As he thrust, enjoying the terror in William's face, at the last second he flicked his wrist, to plunge the sword deep into the soft ground inches from William's ear.

A movement at the periphery of his vision, a voice, stirring the silence.

'A wise choice, if unpalatable.'

'John. How long have you been here?'

'Long enough.'

'He murdered them.'

'I know. I saw the posts.'

'He deserved to die. While we fought . . . one good strike . . . I would have done it gladly . . .' Munro took a deep breath. 'But standing over him, unarmed . . . I thought of Kate . . .'

John's voice was deliberately harsh, 'Two dead for spite, or ten in reprisal. Our hands aren't exactly clean.'

Behind Munro William was on his feet, Munro's sword in his hand, swinging it waist high. John shouted a warning and leapt at him, his hands clenched together, smashing his wrists against the flat of the blade below the hilt, knocking it upwards and to the right, so that instead of taking Munro in the chest it clipped his shoulder. Before William had time to recover, John rushed him again, this time swinging linked arms at his throat, jerking him backwards, following through by flinging himself against him. The momentum brought them both crashing to the ground, William's head cracking against a boulder as he fell.

John pressed two fingers against William's neck then stood up. 'You nearly got your wish, but not quite.'

Munro had his hand clamped on his shoulder, blood oozing between the fingers.

'Let me have a look.' John jerked his head at William. 'I imagine we'll have a moment or five before he troubles us again. That was a gey hard crack.' There was satisfaction in his voice. He helped Munro out of his doublet, pulled aside the shirt. 'You'll live. A superficial cut only.' Bending over William, he tore strips from the tail of his shirt. 'Once I have it bound, make for home.'

'The posts?'

'I'll see to them. The less who know the whole of it . . .' John waved down Munro's protest, '. . . it will be safer for all.'

'And the Maxwells?'

'They may guess, but they won't ask what I don't volunteer.' He gave a final tug to the knot in the binding on Munro's shoulder. 'It may not be the easiest ride home, but if I were you, I wouldn't linger.'

'Glencairn?' Munro was still calculating the dangers.

'He'll know, likely without the telling. If not . . . whatever I say abroad, it will be the truth I tell at home.'

'You know this is the end of the road.' Munro's voice

was devoid of intonation. 'Glencairn's follower I was born, but I won't die William's.'

John looked down at William, still out cold at his feet. 'It is a dangerous road you choose. You have a wife and bairns to think on. William isn't worth their loss.'

'Do you think I don't know that? But if I let this pass I have lost them anyway, for that Kate would not look me in the face again. I will go home and take my chance.'

John glanced around. 'Where's your horse?'

'In the woods.'

'I'll see you to her then, you'll need help to mount.'

Having reclaimed Sweet Briar, Munro followed the Urr Water northwards, stopping only briefly to refill his water skin and to buy a couple of bannocks and a draught of ewe's milk from a shepherd, whose eyes slid to Munro's left arm, held stiffly by his side, then as quickly away again. Occupied with churning the possible routes home, weighing them up, arguing his way through to a decision, he didn't hear the approaching hoofbeats until the rider was almost on him. Too late to avoid the potential danger, he instinctively wheeled Sweet Briar sideways.

'You didn't linger.' John's horse was lathered with sweat. 'I was hard pressed to catch up with you, and indeed thought I'd called the route wrong, until I squeezed word of your passing from the shepherd a while back.'

For a moment the thought swelled in Munro that William hadn't regained consciousness after all.

As if he read his mind, John said, 'I saw to William and to the posts and am come now to give you warning.'

Munro felt an increased throbbing in his arm, matched by a pulsing pain across his forehead.

'Humiliation is a bitter draught and William won't let it lie.' There was a weariness in John's voice. 'We rest tonight at Orchardton, but tomorrow we ride for Kilmaurs and from his talk, Broomelaw won't be far behind. I can hold him a day or two, no more. It will be best if we don't find you or yours when we are come.' He chewed his lip, 'It is the season for reiving . . . and William has never been one to object if others do his dirty work.'

A long look passed between them, then Munro reached out to clasp John's hand.

'You'd best go back before your absence is noted, but I won't forget who and what I owe.'

Chapter Thirteen

It was gone midnight on the second day when Munro reached the loch below Broomelaw. Above him, the tower was silhouetted against the skyline, the angle of gable and roof clearly defined. He picked his way up the slope in the moonlight, thinking of Kate and the bairns, of what he must and mustn't say. A few sheep, their lambs curled into their sides, stirred as he passed, their lifted faces expressionless. From the byre came the soft shuffle of cattle and far up on the hill an owl called.

He went first to the stable to rouse the boy, then to Agnes, who, as neat asleep as awake, lay stiff as an effigy. Munro shook her, one hand over her mouth, stifling her protests.

'There is no time for explanation. Gather anything of value and what clothes you may, but only what one horse can carry.'

Kate turned over as he entered their chamber, pulled herself up against the pillows, her hair tumbling over her shift, her eyes only partly open. She said, 'I didn't expect you so soon.' There was a welcoming lilt in her voice and a smile spreading across her face that faded as he sat on the edge of the bed and gripped her arms. She tensed as if she knew what was to come.

'You have to leave. Now. Archie and Sybilla . . .'

'No!'

'Yes' He forced himself to keep looking at her, his voice

cracking. 'They drowned, Kate, with me watching and not able to save them, and all William's doing.'

'And we are threatened?'

'Yes.' One-handed, he pulled her against him, felt her stiffness melt while he told her the whole, talking into her hair, the taste of rosewater catching at the back of his throat. And when he had done, he caught hold of her hand and brought it up to his mouth, kissing each finger in turn, as if he could imprint the touch of her on his lips. 'Go with Agnes and the bairns to Braidstane, but by the south road, not by Kilmaurs. You won't be looked for there. Elizabeth will see you right.'

She stretched back to look at him, her hand straying to his cheek. 'And you?'

'I have something I must do.'

Her eyes were luminous, glossed with unshed tears.

He trailed his hand along her collarbone towards the hollow at the base of her throat. 'I made you a promise, Kate. But this . . .'

She reached up to twist her fingers in the hair that clung on his collar, damp with sweat. 'You have kept it.' Then she took his face in both hands and pulled it down to hers. As their lips touched, he fastened on her hungrily, all thought of time spiralling away. Kate broke first, swinging her legs over the edge of the bed, scrambling for clothes.

A different urgency returned, he ran for the stair. 'I'll rouse the bairns.'

Fifteen minutes later they clustered in the barmkin: Agnes with Ellie strapped in a basket in front of her, Maggie behind Kate. Robbie, puffed with pride, was mounted, not on his own Sheltie but on a larger pony, the leading rein of the packhorse held tight in his left hand.

Munro took hold of Robbie's saddle, noting how he held his back as if attached to a pole, though his hands gripped the reins as if a lifeline. 'You are the man of the party, Robbie, I depend on you.'

He ducked his head in a semblance of a bow then spoilt the effect somewhat by grabbing Munro's hand. 'You won't be long behind us?'

Munro nodded his head – it isn't as much a lie as if I said it out. He touched each of the other children in turn, first twisting a wisp of Ellie's hair around his finger, then tilting Maggie's head upwards, forcing a wink. 'Pay heed to your mother now.' He had reached Kate, capturing her hand, intertwining her fingers one last time. Their eyes met and held, and his pressure increased. 'Promise me, Kate,' he chose his words carefully, mindful of Agnes, of the bairns, 'That you won't believe all that you hear.'

She looked down at him as if she saw into his soul. 'You know where to find us. I'll be waiting.'

And then they were gone, cantering down the valley in the moonlight, the jingle of tackle and the rhythm of hoofbeats loud in the darkness.

Munro turned to the boy. 'We may not have much time. Once we are done here, drive the stock to Glasgow and get for it what you can. The money . . .' he considered, '. . . take it to Leith. Look for a Norwegian ship: the master Sigurd Ivarsen; he will know what to do with it, and with you.'

The boy opened his mouth as if to question, his brow puckered.

'Reivers, lad, that is what this must look like, or we are none of us safe. Fetch yourself a spade, we have work to do.'

Munro ran down the hill to the boggy hollow below

the sheep pen, the boy trailing behind him. He started on the first mound but, as his spade began to bite, hesitated, Anna's face floating before him, mischievous, smiling. The boy was hanging back, his eyes wide. Munro leant his forehead against the spade – I can't touch Anna. He turned to hack at the turf of the second mound and as the boy still didn't move said, for himself also, 'The dead can't harm us; the living will.'

They worked fast, methodically stripping back the turfs, lifting the soil, revealing the oak kist. A moment's hesitation, then, forcing the corner of the spade into the narrow gap between side and lid, Munro pressed his weight downwards on the handle, straining against the nails until the lid lifted, exposing three swaddled bodies, differing only in length. His touch gentle, he peeled back the waxed cloth wound about the head of the smallest corpse. Skin, dark as newly tanned leather, stretched taut over the skull, remnants of hair still clinging to the scalp. The boy retched.

Munro kept his voice controlled, matter of fact. 'They are but dressed bones. My three sisters, taken with the same infection in a ween of days.' He strove for conviction. 'They can hardly mind.' He gestured to the largest of the mounds. 'You take that one: my father is long dead and likewise won't have reason to care. But don't lift him by yourself,' Munro's mouth contorted into a travesty of a smile. 'He won't be of use if he falls apart.'

The newest mound lay at the bottom of the slope, covered in moss, the spade cutting easily into the damp soil. At five feet, Munro altered the angle, afraid to dig too deeply, a tightness in his chest. He felt the resistance of the wood before he saw it and dropped down into the hole scraping the remaining soil away, using his dirk to prise up the lid.

The boy was standing by the edge of the grave, looking everywhere but at the shrouded body.

Munro glanced up at him. He cleared his throat. 'Fetch the cart. We don't want more than one journey.'

Munro carried his mother's body in first, unwrapping her gently and laying her in the bed that Kate had so lately vacated, spreading out the nightgown she had been buried in. He stretched his father out beside her, draping one of his own gowns across him, pulling up the sheet to cover them both. He left the candle flickering in the sconce, a kind of recompense for the sacrilege of what he did. The bairns' bodies he placed, likewise covered, in the three cots in the chamber above the solar, opening the casement behind them to create a draw.

The boy was huddled tight on Munro's tail as if he feared to be left alone in this company.

Munro, noting his tremor and hoping that he would be equal to the job said, 'I'll finish off here. You away and round up the stock; it's as well that you aren't near when the fires are lit. There will be enough of a job to drive them without spooking them first. And take Sweet Briar and tether her by the sheep pen.' He shook the boy. 'You carry dangerous knowledge lad. See that you keep it to yourself.' And as an afterthought, the words unfamiliar on his tongue, 'God be with you.'

Alone, Munro worked fast despite his useless hand, raiding the storeroom for fish oil to pour over the rugs and the bed in his chamber, repeating the process in the bairns' room also. The rushes from the kitchen he spread on the floor of the hall, distributing lumps of lard evenly among them. The remaining oil he poured on the furniture and the window seats, taking especial care to saturate the cushions – if the ruse is to have any chance of success the fire must needs be fierce. He cast a final glance around the room, blood pounding behind his eyes as they came to rest on Ellie's walker, half-hidden in the corner.

Mentally he checked and re-checked: the stabling and the byre, they would likely burn merrily without help, but lard scattered wouldn't harm. A thought, ice-cold – the main door. He plunged down the stairwell and took an axe to it, splintering the sturdy planking as if it was tinder, trying not to think of the care he had taken in the making of it. All the years, the work, to come to this.

For a moment only, he reached up to rest his hand against the stone lintel feeling the impress of the carved initials under his palm. There was no other way. He returned to the hall to toss lighted rags dipped in oil through the doorway, retreating from the heat and the flames that flared behind him, and from the smoke that spiralled down the stair in his wake, stinging his nostrils, acrid on his tongue.

At the entrance he pulled the heavy yett into place, jamming it shut with an iron bar. The straw heaped in the passageway behind it ignited with a roar, the flames fanned by the wind, tongues of fire licking at the doorframe. He lit the last of the rags as he ran towards the jumble of out-buildings, lobbing one onto the thatch, one through each open door, retreating as the flames took.

On the horizon, dawn was seeping into the sky, crimson and white.

One job remained.

He plunged down to the hollow to back-fill the graves, smooth the mounds, trample down the turfs. He raced to Sweet Briar, who pawed at the ground, her head up and back, eyes rolling, straining to break free of her tether. He caught at the bridle and pulled her face into his chest, stroking her neck, mumuring into her ear, taking the time to calm her before swinging into the saddle.

Behind him a crash, as part of the chimney toppled inwards, the flames reaching for the sky. Another explosion, sparks flying. Curls of smoke rising from the gorse, first one, then another and another, then a wall of fire sweeping across the hillside, leaving in its wake a tangle of blackened stems, like wraiths, etched against the dawn sky. He turned to take one last look at Broomelaw as the flakes of ash sifted downwards, settling on him like rain. In the flicker of the flames, faces: Anna, Archie, Sybilla . . . the Montgomerie lad.

Voices on the wind: John, by the shore at Rough, 'Our hands aren't exactly clean.' Lady Margaret Langshaw, 'I am a Cunninghame, God help me.'

He drew a deep breath – a Cunninghame no longer, one thing remained: that Kate and the bairns be safe. Today or tomorrow, William would come . . . and John. He could trust John. And Kate had said that she would wait. He wondered what like it would be in Norway and if Sigurd was indeed docked at Leith, as his normal pattern would suppose.

Gathering the reins, he turned towards the east. The sun, gaining in intensity, warmed his face as the blazing tower scorched his back. Another roar, another rumble of falling masonry, Sweet Briar startling afresh. Munro leant forwards, rested his good hand for a moment on her neck, promised himself, 'I won't stay long away.'

Afterword

Throughout its hundred and fifty year duration the feud between the Cunninghames and Montgomeries was characterized by repeated acts of brutality and murder on both sides, evidence of the reality that, as *Ayrshire, Its History* puts it, 'blood feud was the custom of the times'.

However it was my choice rather than a reflection of documented history to cast William Cunninghame and the Earl of Glencairn as the primary villains of this story. The Massacre of Annock is well documented, though sources differ in regard to the numbers involved on each side. I have used the account in the Montgomerie family manuscripts as my primary source. The fate of key members of the Cunninghame faction in the aftermath of Annock as written here, is generally accepted. An enduring animosity between Hugh Montgomerie and William Cunninghame and the quarrel Hugh has with Patrick Maxwell are also on record, though without detail as to the timing, the cause of the quarrel, or who prevented them killing each other. In the interests of the story I have taken some liberites with the timing of events and with William Cunninghame's age. In casting Maxwell as a villain I have done him no disservice as the real Patrick Maxwell was a much more unpleasant character than depicted here: gaining notoriety for physically abusing his wife.

Glossary

aught (n): anything
bailie (n): magistrate
bailieship (n): office of magistrate
bailiewick (n): district under magistrate's control
barmkin (n): enclosed area within the outer fortification of a castle or tower house
bawbee (n): small value coin
baxter (n): baker
birl (v): to whirl around
bliant (n): expensive fabric probably made of silk
bonnet-laird (n): minor laird
butterbur (n): plant, rhubarb-like in appearance
cap-house (n): guard chamber at roof level in a castle or tower house
cap-stone (n): coping stones topping a wall
caul (n): cap
champ (v): to be eager
clack (n): talk, gossip
clatching (v): to transport mud on the soles of shoes (from clatch, noun: mire)
clegg (n): gad-fly
cludgie (n): earth closet
coney (n): rabbit
coup (v): to overturn
craw (n): gullet
curtain-wall (n): outer fortification, rampart

deeve (v): to weary by constant talking
dour (adj): humourless, sullen
dreich (adj): damp, miserable
dunt (v): to bump into
dwam (n): stupor, trance
farl (n): a flat bread formed by cutting a circle of dough into quarters before cooking
feart (adj): afraid
feisty (adj): spirited
fissling (adj): muted rustling sound
fitty (adj): fitting, appropriate
flesher (n): butcher
forbye (n): besides, in addition to
foundered (adj): extremely cold
ganch (n): dull-witted person
gey (adv): very
glaur (n): slime, soft mud
grizzle (v): to whimper
hackbut (n): early form of firearm
hall (n): main public apartment in a castle or tower house
heft (v): to lift (esp. onto shoulders)
hirsel (n): wheeze, catarrhal sound in chest
ingle-nook (n): corner by a

fireplace, usually with seating

looby (n): ill-educated person

lucken-booth (n): covered stall which could be locked up

midden (n): refuse heap

neep (n): turnip

nicker (v): to whinny softly

pauchled (adj): exhausted

pawky (adj): vivacious

peched (adj): gasping for breath

plackard (n): piece made to fill in a U or V-shaped opening in a bodice

pommel (n): knob on the hilt of a sword

posset (n): a drink of hot milk, curdled with ale or wine, sometimes flavoured

pruch (n): goods

put to the horn (figure of speech): banished

ram-stam (adj): reckless or precipitate manner

redd-out (v): to spring-clean

reek (n): stench

scunner (v): to annoy, irritate, disgust

simple (n): herbal remedy made from a single ingredient

sit (v): to maintain (spec. Scots)

skitters (n): thin execrement

slub (n): raised imperfection in the weave of cloth

smoult (n): young salmon, trout

sneck (n): latch

snood (n): close fitting outer cap (esp. of fur)

solar (n): private, family apartment in a castle or tower house

sonsy (adj): comely, attractive

souter (n): shoemaker

speir (n): talk, gossip

stook (n): bundle of cut sheaves of grain, set up to dry

thole (v): to suffer, endure

turnpike stair (n): spiral staircase, usually stone

wabbit (adj): weak

wall-walk (n): an external walk-way at roof level where a watch can be kept, often leading to a cap-house

wandered (adj): mentally incompetent

ween (adj): small amount

wheest (imp): be quiet

whiffler (n): person at the front of a procession, clearing the way

wynd (n): narrow alley or lane leading off a main thoroughfare

yett (n): defensive metal grid door, in addition to external main (wooden) door of a castle or tower house

A House Divided

'When you must face Maxwell, give evidence
before the King. Have you thought on that?'
'If I do not face Maxwell, I will not
be able to face myself.'

Scotland 1597. The truce between the Cunninghame and Montgomerie clans is fragile. And for the Munro family, living in hiding under assumed names, these are dangerous times.

While Munro risks his life daily in the army of the French King, the spectre of discovery by William Cunninghame haunts his wife Kate. Her fears for their children and her absent husband realised as William's desire for revenge tears their world apart.

A sweeping tale of compassion and cruelty, treachery and sacrifice, set against the backdrop of a religious war, feuding clans, and the Great Scottish Witch Hunt of 1597.